a
theory
of small
earthquakes

ALSO BY
meredith maran

My Lie

50 Ways to Support Lesbian & Gay Equality

Dirty

Enough About You

Class Dismissed

Ben & Jerry's Double-Dip (with Ben Cohen & Jerry Greenfield)

Notes from an Incomplete Revolution

What It's Like to Live Now

Chamisa Road (with Paul Steiner)

a
theory
of small
earthquakes

A NOVEL

meredith maran

SOFT SKULL PRESS
AN IMPRINT OF COUNTERPOINT

Library of Congress Cataloging-in-Publication Data is available.
ISBN 978-1-59376-430-2
Cover design by Kimberly Glyder
Interior design by Neuwirth and Associates, Inc.

Soft Skull Press
www.softskull.com
An imprint of COUNTERPOINT
1919 Fifth Street
Berkeley, CA 94710

Printed in the United States of America
Distributed by Publishers Group West

10 9 8 7 6 5 4 3 2 1

For Dan

And for Axel:

May this story be outdated by the time you fall in love

· part one ·

1.

Alison stood in the doorway of Room 113, peering into the classroom through the window in the door, eyeing her new professor, who was exactly as Alison had imagined she would be.

Square, stocky body. Doc Marten boots with replacement lavender laces. Purple oberlin WOMEN TAKE BACK THE NIGHT T-shirt. Wide leather belt cinched mid-torso. Overloaded metal key ring clipped to terrible jeans. *Why do lesbians have so many keys,* Alison wondered, not for the first time.

And the hair. Oh, the hair. The "wimmin-loving wimmin" of Oberlin wore their Bobby Kennedy haircuts as if their heads were tourism billboards for Lesbian Nation—just in case their T-shirt slogans, ill-fitting jeans, and janitorial key chains didn't make their shared, superior sexual orientation clear.

Two weeks into her senior year, Alison had decided that her

Deconstructing the Postmodernists class was a little too decon-structing for her. Hoping to pick up a few writing tips at least, she'd put in for a transfer to Professor Pierce's women's studies seminar, Feminist Transformations: Retelling of Myth and Metaphor.

Hand on door handle, Alison hesitated. Her least favorite moment of every class was this one, subjecting herself to a new set of classmates and, worse yet, to her own foolish hope that she'd make a friend out of them. She reminded herself that she'd quit the last class; she could always quit this one. Escape plan in place, she pulled the door open and stepped inside.

Twenty-five heads swiveled in Alison's direction. Twenty-five sets of eyes looked her up and down.

"Who's the Barbie doll?" one combat-booted girl whispered loudly to another, scowling at Alison's bra-bound breasts in her slogan-free T-shirt, her narrow waist and long legs making the most of her knife-creased khakis, and, the greatest travesty of all, her long, wavy auburn hair.

Alison was used to it, the envy and the scorn. She'd been a pretty child. But when she turned fourteen her body bloomed into beauty. Her breasts swelled, her hips flared, her olive skin shone. Suddenly every boy wanted her, or wanted something from her. Girls loathed her from a distance, which was as close as Alison wanted them to be.

She'd come to Oberlin hoping for a miracle. The school was known for its emphasis on "human potential," and she needed help fulfilling hers. Her goal was to graduate Oberlin a different person, not the difficult girl her mother had always said she was. Not the lonely girl she'd been since her father died in a pileup on the Long Island Expressway when she was nine. Alison prided herself on setting challenging goals and meeting them. But this was her last year at Oberlin, and it wasn't looking good.

"Professor Pierce?" Alison offered up the canary copy of her transfer form. The professor squinted at it and then at Alison. "Are you the one who wrote the article in the paper?"

Here we go, Alison thought. "That's me." Her first published essay, "Only Your Body Can Make Up Your Mind: An Open Letter to Oberlin's Lesbians-for-a-Day," had just appeared in that week's *Oberlin Review.*

The piece was Alison's critique of what she called "Obie's Quixotic, Quickie Queens of Queer": the girls who could be seen making out with their boyfriends in the Student Union one day and declaring themselves lesbians at gay rights rallies the next, never to be seen again without their entourage of "sisters" and their DYKE POWER buttons and regulation haircuts.

"Sexuality is personal, not political," she wrote. "It's not a social construct. It's not a club you can decide to join. Even if your boyfriend leaves the seat up or talks about himself too much, even if you like your female friends more than you like him, you can't just decide to be gay."

Oberlin was a circus of costumed cliques. None rankled Alison the way the fake lesbians did. Not the punks with their black lipstick and safety-pinned ears. Not the Jews Against Zionism, who embarrassed her and drove her Jewishness even deeper undercover than it was. Not the dashiki-draped black nationalists or the serape-swaddled La Razistas. Not the buttoned-down, bespectacled nerds, or the conservatory prodigies strapped into their guitars, or the WASPy trust fund kids who shuffled around campus barefoot in thrift-store clothes, pretending not to have the money they'd always had and would always have.

Alison had a nose for rich kids pretending to be poor, and she had a nose for coddled straight girls pretending to be tough dykes. She could smell it on them: the adoration of their parents, who'd poured self-esteem into their daughters like gardeners watering potted violets lined up on a sunny sill.

The Queens of Queer wore buttons that said "One nuclear family can ruin your whole life." Alison's life had been ruined by not having one. She would have killed for parents like theirs, who paid their daughters' tuition, sent them homemade brownies, and leapt out of their Volvos on Parents' Weekend, bent double with eagerness to get their hands on their ungrateful girls.

Their families' love had made those girls so safe in the world, so certain that they could have anything they wanted, whenever they wanted it, that they could scorn the thing Alison wanted most, the dream that sustained her after her dad died: kids of her own, a family of her own.

As a teenager she hired herself out as a babysitter. She had a passion and an aptitude for the job. Unlike her mother, unlike other kids her age, unlike Alison herself, the children she took care of liked her just the way she was. She craved their innocent adoration the way a sunflower twists toward sun.

"I don't agree with what you wrote," Professor Pierce said. "But I admire the guts it took to write it."

"Thanks." Alison pulled herself up to her full five feet ten inches, which put her a head above her professor.

"Sit anywhere. Oh, and call me Mariandaughter. 'Professor' just reinforces the male hierarchical power imbalance. And Pierce is my father's name."

Alison looked around the room. The chairs were arranged in a nonhierarchical circle. Twenty-five sets of feet were planted on the floor. Alison took a seat near the window and crossed her legs.

"Did everyone make it to *The Big Chill?*" Mariandaughter asked.

All the students nodded, except Alison.

"Good. Let's discuss the patriarchal subtext of the film."

Hands waved. "Zoe," Mariandaughter said. Alison followed her gaze to a girl with the lean physique of a handsome boy, the sculpted cheekbones and sultry lips of an old-time movie star. Her face was striking; her haircut was short but stylish, streaked with gold and platinum and white. Her outfit was a complicated, clashing collage of colors and textures—orange and lime green, polka dots and stripes, crumpled linen and corduroy and velour.

Alison attempted to sort this Zoe person into one of her tidy boxes. Zoe wouldn't go. She was too chic to be a lesbian, too animated to be a punk, too flamboyant to be a nerd. Who was she?

"The screenplay was a collaboration between a man and a woman. But it's obvious the film was directed by a man," Zoe said. Her voice was hoarse and lilting, tinged with a faint accent Alison didn't recognize. Her fingers, blunt and splattered with several colors of paint, drew pictures in the air as she spoke.

"Kasdan let the women decide whether Meg gets pregnant by artificial insemination or by having sex with Sarah's husband," Zoe continued. "But that was just a feminist façade slapped onto a sexist film. The men were the ones with the real power in the group."

Mariandaughter nodded approvingly. Several women signaled their agreement by snapping their fingers in the air.

"Excellent analysis, Zoe." Mariandaughter addressed the class: "This is why I don't hold to arbitrary grade distinctions. If I did, we wouldn't have a bright freshwoman like Zoe in a senior seminar."

Again, fingers snapped.

"Senior *ovular*, you mean," Zoe said, deadpan.

Alison stared at Zoe, measuring the distance between them. How could anyone be so self-assured, so firmly grounded where she was? Zoe caught her looking and smiled, as if she caught people staring at her all the time. Alison flushed and looked away.

"I've never considered the etymology of the word *seminar*," Mariandaughter said, frowning. "Thank you, Zoe. I won't use it again."

Alison recalled a joke she'd overheard one guy telling another in the Student Union: "How many feminists does it take to change a lightbulb? One. And it's not funny."

"Any thoughts on how we can apply Dworkin's gender analysis to the film?" As the conversation continued, Mariandaughter passed out mimeographed copies of their homework assignment. Alison glanced at hers. It was an open-book quiz about the course text, *Pornography—Men Possessing Women,* by Andrea Dworkin, an author Alison had never read. She reminded herself that she'd joined this class to be exposed to books and writers she might not otherwise discover. She'd pick up a copy of *Pornography* at the school bookstore.

After the bell rang, Zoe intercepted Alison in the hall. "I read your article in the *Review*," she said. "You've got balls to put yourself out there like that." Zoe smiled. "*Ovaries,* I mean. Seriously, you're an amazing writer."

Was she being sarcastic? It didn't feel like it. "Thanks," Alison said. "That was my first published piece."

"You're kidding!" Zoe said. "Well, write on, sister. You've definitely got some skills."

As their classmates filed by them, the girl who'd called Alison a Barbie doll shot a hostile look in their direction. Zoe glared back.

"I've been kind of worried about the reaction I'll get," Alison admitted.

"I hear you. I'm a painter, and I freak every time someone even *threatens* to give me an opinion of my work." Zoe glanced at her watch. Alison was startled to see it was the same one she'd admired at the school bookstore, a clear plastic Swatch that revealed its inner workings as it ticked.

"Gotta run." Zoe gave Alison's shoulder a light squeeze. "Don't let the turkeys get you down," she said. She sauntered off down the hall. Alison stood there, watching her disappear.

Sitting at a table in the back of the Oberlin cafeteria, sipping milky lukewarm coffee from a chipped white mug, Alison sighed and went back to pretending to write about the Dworkin book she'd been pretending to read.

Despite Mariandaughter's apparent conviction that analyzing Dworkin was second only to godliness—*goddess*-liness—Alison was more engaged by a mission of her own. Fortified by Zoe's praise, she'd parked herself in the cafeteria to monitor the student body's reaction to her op-ed. For the past hour she'd been nervously watching the Obies pouring into the cafeteria, the girls with spiked Mohawks and smoky kohl eyes; the boys with shaved heads and graffitied Converse high-tops, some of them plucking copies of the *Review* off the pile on the floor, some not. Not one of them, as far as she could tell, was reading her piece.

Alison ached, suddenly, with missing her dad. He'd loved the stories she wrote, so she wrote one for him nearly every day. As soon as he came through the door at night, one he'd ask her to read to him. "Whatever happens, Beautiful, don't stop writing," he always said. Later she wondered if he'd known somehow that he wouldn't be around to give her the daily doses of encouragement she only got from him.

When he died, Alison lost her hero, her best friend, her shelter from her mother's storms. She lost the girl she'd been with him too. She wasn't anyone's smart, funny, beautiful girl anymore. The less she remembered that girl, the more she became the "difficult girl" her mother said she was. When her mother wanted to go out for Italian food, something inside Alison made her ask for Chinese. When her mother ordered Chinese, Alison wanted pizza. The fragile peace Alison's dad had brokered between Alison and her mother died when he did.

One day when Alison was in sixth grade, her teacher held two magnets wrong end to wrong end to demonstrate magnetic repulsion. In that moment, Alison found a name for the feeling she had when she and her mother were together. Even when her mother hugged her, Alison felt shoved away. Repulsed.

"Why must you be such a difficult child?" her mother would ask, ice cubes clinking in the squat glass of vodka she sipped from all day every day. *I wasn't difficult with Daddy*, Alison wanted to say. But her mother had a hot temper and a fast hand. Alison worried that one day she'd slap her mother back. And *then* what might happen?

Was Alison difficult because her mother didn't like her? Or did her mother dislike her because she was difficult? When her dad was alive, it didn't matter. He'd loved Alison enough for two.

Every night Alison prayed that her mother would wake up happy in the morning. But on the rare occasions when her mother was pleased—by a pair of shoes she'd found on sale, by a TV show that didn't disappoint her, by an upcoming date with a man—Alison got mad at her mother for reasons she didn't understand and mad at herself for being so difficult.

Alison knew what she wanted only by its absence. She knew that if she stayed the way she was, she'd never have the future she wanted. Wasn't that what college was for, to try new things? To become someone new?

After three years at Oberlin, Alison wasn't anyone new. She

hadn't made a single lasting friendship, let alone a best friend. One friendship after another had started promisingly, then ended for reasons Alison couldn't understand. The clock was running out on her self-improvement project. Adulthood waited, tapping its impatient foot. Which was why she figured she might as well publish an article that could give her writing résumé a boost, even if it earned her more enemies than friends.

Alison gave up waiting for something better to happen. She stood up, stuffed the Dworkin book into her backpack, wove her way through the labyrinth of chairs and tables, and left the cafeteria, alone.

A few days later, Alison found a fat manila envelope from the *Oberlin Review* in her dorm mailbox. She dropped her backpack onto the mailroom floor and tore the envelope open. It was stuffed with letters to the editor in response to her piece.

Skimming them, Alison counted nine protesting her homophobia, two defending her right to free speech *despite* her homophobia, and one anti-lesbian rant. *At least someone read the damn thing,* she thought.

"Great response," her editor had written on a sheet of Oberlin letterhead. "I hope you'll write for us again."

Alison allowed herself a fantasy. For the rest of the school year, she'd keep writing for the *Review.* She'd send her best clips to a bunch of real newspapers and magazines, see if she could land an assignment or a job offer, maybe even before graduation. If Oberlin couldn't improve her, at least it could improve her future.

Alison's daydream spun on. She'd bring the letters to Marian-daughter's class and show them to Zoe. Zoe would be outraged on Alison's behalf.

"Whatever happens," Zoe would say, "don't stop writing."

One of Alison's dorm-mates walked in, snapping her out of her reverie. She slung her backpack over her shoulder and pushed through the mailroom's swinging door.

2.

oberlin college
September 1983

Mariandaughter's students were buzzing as they filed into the classroom. "I'm canceling the quiz," Mariandaughter announced. "We're going to deconstruct what happened in Atlantic City over the weekend. This is big news, wimmin."

Snap, snap went the fingers. Alison had no idea what had happened in Atlantic City or anywhere else. She'd spent the weekend in her room pounding on her IBM Selectric as if she could beat an op-ed out of it. Three seats away, Zoe wasn't snapping either. She had a bemused look on her face and the body language of a theatergoer waiting for the show to begin.

"Everyone knows what I'm talking about, right?" Mariandaughter asked. Alison and a couple of other students shook their heads.

"On Saturday, Vanessa Williams became the first black woman in herstory to be named Miss America," Mariandaughter said.

"So. Which gender does this benefit? Which class? Which race?"

The room was silent. "Come on, sisters," she snapped. "What's the point of reading Dworkin if you can't apply her analysis to real-world events?"

Zoe reached around the women between them and handed Alison a tiny square of paper. "For me?" Alison mouthed. Zoe nodded impatiently. Alison unfolded it and saw a caricature of Mariandaughter with her eyebrows knitted and smoke billowing from her ears. Below the sketch Zoe had scribbled, "She's cute when she's mad."

"Even cuter when she's deconstructing," Alison wrote back. Zoe grinned.

"This is good for black people," a skinny, boyish girl said. "A black woman being crowned as a beauty queen challenges the racist traditional standards of beauty."

"I disagree," another girl said. "The Miss America contest itself reinforces standards of beauty that are life threatening to women of all races, no matter who wins it. Karen Carpenter just *died* from anorexia, remember?"

The only black girl in the class, sporting a huge Afro, gold hoop earrings, and a mud cloth tunic, raised the index finger of her right hand as if she were at an auction, bidding bored.

"Nia." Mariandaughter's face assumed the obsequious gaze she reserved for Nia and Carmen, the only two nonwhite students in the class.

"Vanessa Williams is a Tom," Nia said. "You think she'd even be in the running if she didn't have Caucasian features and conk her hair and kiss white ass?"

"Excellent point," Mariandaughter said adoringly.

Nia ignored her. "This didn't happen because the Jim-Crow-Miss-America committee was out to change racist beauty standards. It happened because rewarding a house nigger co-opts the liberation movement and keeps the white power structure in place."

Alison had never seen her classmates in such a state of rapt attention. Nia ran with it. "That's the reason Reagan just got himself a black astronaut. Same reason they gave Alice Walker the Pulitzer for *The Color Purple*. To set good Negroes against bad Negroes and black women against black men."

The room went silent. Mariandaughter looked stricken, standing in front of the posters of Audre Lorde, Adrienne Rich, Zora Neale Hurston, Grace Paley, and Alice Walker she'd tacked to the wall. "You can see how many valid womanist perspec tives there are on this issue," she managed. "Which is why, to promote the diversity of our discourse, I've designed a special collaborative project in line with the 'feminist transformations' theme of our class."

Mariandaughter handed a stack of mimeographed sheets to the student next to her, who took one and passed the stack on. "We're going to break up into six groups of four. For the midterm final, each group will create a representation of your collective analysis of the crowning of the first black Miss America."

The students counted off. Alison could hardly believe her good fortune: she and Zoe were both "threes." The two of them moved their chairs together. They were joined by their team-mates, Chelsea and Renate.

"We have to do this by *November*?" Renate complained.

"So much for a mellow senior year," Chelsea shook her head. Her Mohawk, dyed purple and gelled to resemble a rooster's comb, didn't budge.

"Don't freak, you guys," Zoe said. "If we get together once or twice a week, we'll get it done."

"Wimmin," Renate corrected her.

Zoe winked at Alison. Alison rolled her eyes, imitating a normal person making a friend.

"Can everyone meet on Saturday afternoons?" Alison asked.

A few days later the four of them settled into a booth in the Student Union, Chelsea and Renate on one side, Zoe and Alison on the other.

Zoe exuded a subtle, spicy scent that made Alison dizzy. She unstuck her thighs from the sticky Naugahyde seat and put a few more inches between herself and Zoe.

"Ideas?" Zoe asked.

"We could do a diorama of the Miss America Pageant, with the contestants made out of sausages and the judges made to look like pigs," Renate suggested.

How original, Alison thought sarcastically. She'd seen that scenario on TV years before, when feminists had stormed the pageant wearing dresses made of sliced lunch meats.

"I'm pretty sure I saw something like that somewhere." Chelsea lit a Gauloise and twisted her head, exhaling a thick plume of blue smoke. "Maybe we could do something far out with embroidery or quilting or something. Make fun of the traditional female homemaker thing."

"Uh-huh," Zoe said. She nudged Alison with her elbow. "You're quiet over there."

Alison flushed. "Let's hear your idea first," she said.

Zoe shoved Chelsea's ashtray aside, pulled a sketchbook out of her book bag, and flipped through the pages.

"I say we go after the connection between slavery and the pageant." Zoe laid the sketchbook open on the table. "We build a Miss America stage set that's actually a slave auction block."

"Your sketches are amazing," Chelsea said what Alison was thinking.

Zoe turned to the next page. She'd drawn four figures, barefoot, wearing tattered dresses, their faces black.

"Instead of ball gowns or bikinis, we'll wear slave clothes and blackface. Where the emcee would stand, we'll have a guy dressed as a slave auctioneer instead. So the four of us are standing on the riser as if we're waiting to hear if we won Miss America, but—"

"But we're actually slaves, waiting to be auctioned off," Alison interjected.

"Exactly!" Zoe smiled at Alison.

Renate frowned. "I've never built anything in my life," she said. "I don't know where we'd get the supplies. Or where we'd make all this stuff."

"I'm pretty handy with a hammer," Alison lied.

Zoe shot her a surprised look. "Me too," she said. "I make all the frames for my paintings." She turned to Renate. "I already talked to the guy who runs the woodshop. He's totally into helping us."

"Zoe and I could do the construction part," Alison said to Renate. "You and Chelsea could do the costumes and props."

"Sounds good to me," Chelsea said, reaching for the ashtray, stubbing out her cigarette.

"I guess," Renate said, still sulking.

"Sisterhood is powerful," Alison said, thrusting a clenched fist over her head.

"Right on, sistah," Zoe raised her own fist and knocked it against Alison's. The four of them slid out of the booth. Renate and Chelsea went off together, headed for the thrift store in town.

"Going my way?" Zoe asked Alison.

"Which way is that?"

"Wherever you're going."

How can this be happening, Alison asked herself. "I have a hot date with my typewriter," she said. "I need to come up with another op-ed ASAP."

"You're gonna *work?* In your *room?* On a gorgeous Saturday like *this?*" Zoe faced Alison, blue eyes flashing, hands on hips. "Rapunzel, Rapunzel, let down your hair."

"Let down my editor, you mean," Alison stalled.

"Your editor's probably kicking back right now, smoking a doobie," Zoe said. "C'mon. Hang out with me. I'll have you home before you turn into a pumpkin." She drew an X over her heart with two fingers. "Scout's honor."

"That's a whole lot of mixed fairy-tale metaphors."

"Just give me a half hour." Zoe linked her arm through Alison's, pulling her along. Alison's knees went rubbery. *This girl makes me nervous,* she thought. But nervous wasn't exactly what she felt.

They left the building and took the paved path to Tappan Square, the park that joined Oberlin the college to Oberlin the town. The school brochure described Tappan as "the meeting place for students and townspeople;" as "Oberlin's Times Square." The comparison didn't hold up for Alison, who'd spent her adolescent weekends wandering the teeming streets of the real thing. Despite or because of her mother's ban on travel below the sanitized Upper East Side, Times Square was Alison's favorite forbidden destination, a place to peer into discount camera shops and peep shows and tattoo parlors, gathering ideas for characters and stories that the boutiques of Madison Avenue and the sarcophagi of the Metropolitan Museum of Art didn't provide.

The warm weekend day had brought out the Obies in all their iconoclastic glory. On the tree-studded lawn, scruffy kids tossed Frisbees, munched on sprouty sandwiches, necked on wooden swings hanging from hundred-year-old elephantine elms. Above their heads, Oberlin's famous albino squirrels chased each other frenetically, leaping from branch to branch as if suspended by wires. In the shadow of Memorial Arch, students and local hippies sat at card tables selling homemade duct tape wallets, hand-thrown mugs, and seashell hash pipes. Some offered petitions instead:

INCREASE AID TO THE VICTIMS OF HURRICANE ALICIA!
INVESTIGATE THE ASSASSINATION OF BENIGNO AQUINO!
INVESTIGATE THE TIES BETWEEN OBERLIN AND DOW CHEMICAL!

As they browsed the bizarre bazaar, Zoe's arm crooked through Alison's, Zoe's body close to hers, Alison grew more and more nervous. She used the excuse of signing a petition—"Increase scholarships for minority students!"—to extricate herself. When she straightened up, Zoe took her arm again.

Alison made a show of checking her new transparent Swatch. "Uh-oh," she said. "Rapunzel's about to turn into a pumpkin."

Zoe caught Alison's gaze in hers. That funny, rubbery feeling radiated upward from Alison's knees.

"Right," Zoe said. "Well. Good luck with the writing." She jammed her hands into her harem pants pockets and sauntered over to the next table.

Alison stepped around the knots of people having fun, wondering why she was depriving herself of a sunny afternoon with Zoe, disappointed that Zoe hadn't offered to walk her home.

3.

A lison stood outside the Oberlin woodshop, inhaling
the loamy scent of fresh sawdust, remembering.

Her dad had been an ad exec by vocation, a wood carver by
avocation—an unusual hobby, to say the least, among Upper
East Side Jewish men. Alison's grandfather had taught his son
to carve, and her dad had taken great pleasure in teaching the
craft to her.

On Saturday mornings, while her mother slept late, her dad
would cover their kitchen table with the past week's issues of
the *Times*. Then he'd open his father's buttery leather satchel and
arrange the wood-handled tools on the table like a surgeon preparing his instrument tray. When Alison begged to carve a piece
of her own, he told her she was too young to handle the gouges
and carving knives. "When you're ten," he promised. By her tenth
birthday, he was dead.

Her dad began each sculpture by turning the raw chunk of wood in his big, hairy hands. Then he'd hand it to Alison and ask her the same question: "What does it want to be?"

She learned to match her answer to the shape of the wood. If it was rounded, she'd suggest a face or a globe. If it was squarish, she'd ask him to make her a magic treasure chest, a wagon, or a book. If it was oblong, she'd ask for a dragon or a bird. As her dad began to carve and the pile of brown, red, or blond shavings grew, Alison would throw out guesses. "It's a dragon!" "Is it *me*?"

In every room she'd slept in after her father died, she'd made a shrine of his carvings. The shrine lived in her dorm room now, on the bookshelf above her desk: a rough-hewn oak squirrel clutching an acorn, a mahogany mama bear holding her baby, and a book carved from redwood, with "*Stories Yet to Be* by Alison Rose" whittled into the whorled grain.

Alison took a breath, let it go, and pulled open the shop's metal door. Zoe was perched on a tall metal stool at a workbench. "Hey, Al!" she called. "Come meet Tom."

A man in plastic goggles and denim overalls was guiding a plank through the table saw in the middle of the room. As Alison and Zoe approached, he flicked off the saw and pushed his goggles up onto his forehead, staring at Alison. She stared back. He looked like the Marlboro Man minus the chaps and cigarette.

"Tom, this is Alison." Pointedly, Zoe cleared her throat, "As you seem to have noticed."

Tom broke their gaze, pulled his goggles down, flipped the switch, and went back to work. "You're staring," Zoe whispered into Alison's ear. She laughed. "I don't blame you. He's a hunk."

She led Alison to the tool bench, where she laid out two boards and handed Alison a hammer and a box of nails.

"I'm putting you in charge of the supports." Zoe showed Alison the pencil marks she'd made on the boards, indicating where each nail should go.

"Yes, boss."

Zoe looked contrite. "Am I being too bossy?"

"You?" Alison said sarcastically.

Zoe winked and walked away. Alison started nailing the first set of two-by-fours together. The nails slid easily through the soft fir, and it was nice having Zoe's marks to follow. She glanced over at Zoe—and smashed the hammer down on her thumb.

"Ow!" she yelped. Zoe rushed over, took Alison's hand in hers, and examined her thumb.

"Poor baby. You're going to lose that fingernail." Zoe took the hammer out of Alison's other hand. "Good thing you have that writing thing to fall back on," she said. "I'm not sure you've got a future in carpentry."

Alison burst into tears. Zoe's grin disappeared.

"What's wrong?" she asked gently.

"My dad—" Alison swallowed hard.

"Your dad," Zoe repeated, her voice low and soft.

Alison shook her head.

Zoe hung her hammer and Alison's on the pegboard above the workbench. "I'm starving," she said. "Let's go get some dinner." She put her hand on the small of Alison's back and guided her toward the shop doors.

The path through Tappan Square was bathed in golden light, sunset shadows dancing through the leafy arms of the trees. The evening air was hot and soupy. Alison's limbs felt limp.

"I wonder why they call it Indian summer," Zoe mused.

"Native American summer. Have you learned nothing from Mariandaughter?"

"I appreciate the constructive criticism, sister."

"*Deconstructive* criticism."

Zoe laughed. "It gets hot in the fall where I come from," she said. "But not as sticky as this."

One squirrel chased another across the asphalt in front of them, white blurs against gray. "Where's that?" Alison asked.

"Hilton Head, North Carolina. It's—"

"I know what it is," Alison said. *A resort town for really rich people*, she didn't say. Under the guise of scratching her nose, she swiped sweat off her upper lip. "One of my favorite historical fiction writers lives there."

"John Jakes?"

"I can't believe you've heard of him!"

"That was the best part of growing up on the island. Lots of writers and artists and musicians. Theaters. Museums. Galleries. *And* gorgeous beaches."

"Sounds great," Alison said, choking down envy.

"It was. But it's not what I want for *my* kids. I'm not going to raise them on an island, literally or figuratively."

"I grew up on an island too," Alison said. "Literally *and* figuratively."

Zoe looked at her quizzically.

"Manhattan," Alison explained. "And my family was really . . . isolated."

"My mom always talked about moving us to Berkeley," Zoe said. "She made it sound like the best place on earth to raise kids."

Two young boys on skateboards zoomed past them. Zoe picked up a bubblegum wrapper they'd dropped in their wake, balling it in her fist.

"Are you Jewish?" Zoe asked, as if she were asking if Alison was hungry.

"Ethnically, yes," Alison answered. "Religiously, no."

"So you didn't get bat mitzvah'ed?"

"No Hebrew school. No Jewish holidays. None of it. My parents were both raised as religious Jews, and they hated it."

"Too bad. I think the Jewish religion is super-cool. Except for the patriarchal stuff."

Spoken like a true non-Jew, Alison thought. "You don't sound like you're from the South," she said.

"I went to boarding school in New Hampshire. They scrubbed the South right off me."

Alison thought, *She's smart, she's funny, she's rich. Why would she want to be friends with me?*

"What's going on, Alison?" Zoe asked. "Your vibe changed just now."

Alison didn't answer.

"You think I'm one of those spoiled Oberlin trust fund brats."

"I don't—"

"Well, I *was* spoiled. And I did inherit a bunch of money when my grandfather died. And I've had a hell of a time making friends here because of it." Zoe shook her head. "Obies love to hate kids from families like mine. The rich kids come here to get away from their 'white privilege.'" Her fingers made quote marks in the air. "And the kids who don't come from money judge me for having some."

Alison was stunned. How could she and Zoe be so different and see things so much the same way?

Zoe put her hand on Alison's arm. "If that's an issue for you, I really wish you'd say so now. I'd hate to get to know you, and then . . . "

"It's not," Alison lied. *I won't let it be,* she promised herself. *Even if I'm here on a full scholarship, and even if I'm barely going to make it to graduation on what's left of my inheritance.*

They walked past a historic marker commemorating Oberlin's part in the Underground Railroad. One of the boulders surrounding it had been painted white with black lettering. Zoe read the message out loud: THIS ROCK IS SO BORING.

Zoe laughed. "A little less boring now," she said. "Don't you love street art?"

What's street art, Alison wondered. "Love it," she said.

They walked on toward Oberlin's tiny downtown, stepping over a granite plaque set into the ground, blanketed by a scattering of fiery fall leaves:

TIME CAPSULE
sealed July 4, 1976
open July 4, 2076

"Every time I pass that thing, I wonder what's in it," Alison said.

"Let's see. Seventy-six," Zoe said. "A Ramones album?"

"A copy of *Roots?* A FREE PATTY HEARST button?"

"Can you even *imagine* 2076?" Zoe asked.

"I can't imagine 1984," Alison answered. "And that's next year."

They strolled along Main Street, past the brick façades of antiques stores and quilting shops, beneath the flying buttresses that flanked the Ohio State Bank. The red neon letters of Oberlin's Apollo Theater always made Alison wonder if some transplanted New Yorker had named it as an ironic homage to Oberlin's urban opposite, Harlem, home of the *real* Apollo. *Mr. Mom* was on the marquee.

Zoe stopped to check out the art supplies displayed in the window of the Ben Franklin store. Alison waited for her in the doorway of the bakery next door, wondering why no bakery anywhere smelled as good as every bakery in Manhattan.

Zoe came up beside her, wrinkling her nose. "Yuck. Smells like Crisco. I'd kill for some Zabar's rugelach right about now."

Alison did a double take. "What do *you* know about Zabar's?"

"My mom and I spent every Christmas with my grandparents in New York."

Alison had a vision of Zoe as Eloise at the Plaza Hotel, red bow topsy-turvy in stick-straight blond hair, straggly skirt barely held up by red suspenders, white kneesocks bunched around her ankles.

"At the Plaza?" Alison asked.

Zoe stared at her. "How'd you know?"

"Just a guess."

A young woman pushed an umbrella stroller through the bakery's open door. As she passed Alison and Zoe, a pacifier hurtled out of the stroller and bounced off Alison's leg.

"Nice throw, Rainbow," the mom gushed in a syrupy voice.

Alison picked up the pacifier, handed it to the mom, and knelt in front of the stroller. She smiled at the baby, who was wearing a tiny tie-dyed T-shirt and bright orange snap-up pants.

"She's adorable," Alison said. "Or is it a boy?"

"We're raising Rainbow to be gender free," the mom whispered. She put the pacifier in her calico diaper bag and her nose in the air and pushed on.

When she was barely out of earshot, Zoe and Alison burst into laughter.

"I'm going to raise *my* kids tie-dye free," Alison said.

"I'm going to raise my kids stupid-name free." Zoe looked at Alison. "You were sweet with that baby," she said.

They stopped to smell the pink sweetheart roses spilling over the fence of the Oberlin Inn. "Do your parents stay here when they visit?" Alison asked.

"My mom died a year and a half ago," Zoe said. "I never knew my dad."

"I'm so sorry." Alison's hand floated toward Zoe, hung in space, fell back to her side.

"Mom was a wild thing. She had me when she was nineteen. We were best friends. I miss her every minute of every day."

"How did she—?"

"A stroke. In her sleep." Zoe's eyes filled with tears, but her gaze didn't waver from Alison's. "She had a little too much fun before she had me. It caught up with her."

Put your arms around her, Alison told herself. *That's what Zoe would do for you.* But she just couldn't. "I'm sorry," she said again.

Zoe smiled through her tears. "I still talk to her. And I swear she talks back. We knew each other so well. It's easy to imagine what she'd say. You know what I mean?"

"I do," Alison said. "My dad—my parents are dead too."

"I had a feeling," Zoe said. "Don't take this the wrong way. But you seem really . . . alone."

I was, Alison thought. "I am," she said.

"Two for dinner," Zoe told the hostess at Presti's, Oberlin's old-time Italian joint. The restaurant smelled of scotch and disinfectant, tomato sauce and stewing meat.

As Alison's eyes adjusted to the murkiness, she saw that the decor had been upgraded since the last time she'd been here, junior year, on a date with an octopus-armed senior who'd never made it to date two. Chianti bottles in straw baskets hung from the ceiling. A red, white, and green map of Italy was painted onto the wall behind the long mahogany bar.

"Welcome to the fifties," Zoe whispered as they followed their waitress, her beehive hairdo wobbling, her stocking-clad legs swishing, her orthopedic shoes squeaking on the black-and-white-checkered floor. She waved them into a red leather booth in the back, tossed two menus onto the table, and said she'd be right back.

"Is there a single vegetable on this menu?" Zoe asked, turning pages.

"Ketchup," Alison said.

Zoe rolled her eyes. "Or so President Hollywood says."

The waitress set two red plastic glasses of water on the table, flipped her pad open, cocked her hip, and waited. Zoe ordered eggplant Parmesan. Alison ordered a chef's salad and coffee.

"*Coffee?*" Zoe said when the waitress was gone. "For *dinner?* Have I worn you out already?"

"Of course not," Alison said. In fact, she felt exhausted. Her eyelids were heavy. And she was fighting the strangest urge to *just lie down.*

The waitress brought Alison's coffee and their food. Alison emptied the cup in two long swallows and waved at the busboy for more.

"Tell me about your parents," Zoe said.

"My mother died of colon cancer," Alison said. "My senior year of high school."

"That must have been *awful.*" Zoe gave Alison a tender look. Alison felt guilty. She didn't deserve that much sympathy.

"Even before the cancer, she was miserable," Alison said. "It's better for both of us that she's gone."

Zoe looked shocked. "How can you *say* that? She was your *mom!*"

Two cups of coffee hadn't lifted Alison out of her fog. How could she tell the truth without sounding like a monster? "She wasn't what you'd call a *mom*. She never liked me."

"What kind of mother doesn't like her own daughter?"

"Mine."

Zoe shook her head, incredulous. "What about your dad?"

Alison lifted her cup to her mouth, then realized it was empty and put it down. "We were close."

"At least you had *one* good parent."

"I did. But—"

"But having a good dad just isn't the same as having a good mom," Zoe interjected. "I understand."

Alison was infuriated, suddenly, by Zoe's arrogance. "My dad died when I was nine," she snapped.

"Oh, man. I'm such an idiot," Zoe put her hand on top of Alison's. "Sorry," she said.

"No. I'm sorry." Alison reached for her water, pulling her hand out from under Zoe's. "I'm being much too touchy. I guess I *am* tired."

"Maybe you're getting sick." Zoe touched the back of her hand to Alison's forehead. "You are a little warm." She pulled bills from various pockets and tossed them onto the table. "Let's get you home."

"Thanks for understanding," Alison said, although she herself didn't understand.

As they walked back to campus in the dark, Alison let Zoe choose the route, watch out for cars, walk her to her dorm. They stood together on Baldwin's wide veranda, the porch lamp holding them in a circle of yellow light.

"Sorry I'm such a mess," Alison said.

Zoe reached out and tucked a strand of Alison's hair behind

her ear. Her hand lingered on Alison's cheek. Alison swayed on her feet.

"Would you come to my studio sometime?" Zoe sounded almost shy. "I want to show you the paintings I'm working on."

Alison braved a look into Zoe's eyes. She saw a smooth sea of blue. She imagined sailboats skipping across those eyes, schools of silvery fish swimming through them.

"I'd love to."

"Cool. Now get some sleep." Zoe squeezed Alison's hand, let it go, and disappeared into the dark.

Slowly, heavily, Alison climbed the stairs to her room. She dropped onto her bed and stared across the room at her dad's wood carvings.

She'd wanted so badly to be friends with Zoe. It felt like she'd gotten what she'd wanted. And it felt like something else.

4.

oberlin college
October–December 1983

"Close your eyes," Zoe said. They were standing in front of a corregated metal door in Oberlin's arts building. "Don't open till I tell you to."

Alison heard Zoe fumbling with keys, heard the door clattering open, smelled turpentine fumes.

"You can look now."

Zoe sounded nervous. Alison was gratified to know Zoe was capable of insecurity.

"I said *look*," Zoe repeated.

Alison opened her eyes. Leaning against the wall of Zoe's studio were eight floor-to-ceiling canvases saturated with dense, dizzying red and orange swirls. The paintings' energy pulled her across the room.

"Wow," she said, moving from one canvas to the next.

"Wow good?" Zoe asked in a strangely high-pitched voice. "Or wow bad?"

"Wow *amazing*."

Alison took a few steps back and saw that each swirl was a breast. In the red paintings the nipples were orange, the size of dinner plates. In the orange ones the nipples were red, beckoning, erect.

"You like?" Zoe asked.

"I *love*." Alison stepped closer to the paintings again, resisting the urge to touch a finger to the glistening paint. "I love the texture. And the colors. And the scale."

"They're totally impractical," Zoe said. "Only a Rockefeller would have the wall space to hang them."

"They're great." Alison was startled to realize that she was doing for Zoe—encouraging, supporting, mothering—what Zoe usually did for her. She wondered if this was what best friends did for each other: play whatever role was needed; slip into each other's shoes.

"They'll never sell." Zoe stood beside Alison, squinting at the canvases.

"You don't *need* them to sell. You just need to love them."

"And store them."

"You're doing that thing girls do," Alison said.

"What?"

"Fishing for compliments by deflecting one."

Zoe looked at her, surprised. "You're right," she said.

"You get a do-over," Alison said. "Let's take it from the top. Your paintings are amazing." She liked playing Zoe's part. It made her feel competent and generous and kind.

"Thank you. You're sweet." Zoe sounded like Zoe again.

And Alison felt like Alison again, flustered and insecure. "What are you calling the series?" she asked.

"Look who's deflecting a compliment," Zoe teased.

Alison flushed. "Okay, okay. Thank you for the compliment."

"I'm calling it Mammary Lane."

They looked at each other and started laughing. Then they were laughing so hard they couldn't stand up. They collapsed onto the paint-splotched floor.

Alison sat up, shaking her head.

"What's wrong?" Zoe put her hand on Alison's back.

That's not helping, Alison almost said. "I'm dizzy. Must be the fumes."

Zoe scrambled to her feet and pulled Alison upright.

"I need some air," Alison said. "I'm gonna go."

"Good idea. I could use a walk myself."

Since the day they'd met, Alison hadn't stopped worrying about Zoe rejecting her. Now she was trying to get away from Zoe, just for a little while, and Zoe wasn't taking the hint. *Would I be as confident, as unshakable,* Alison wondered, *if I'd had a mom like hers?*

"I'll be ready in a minute," Zoe said, frowning at the row of canvases, switching their positions around.

"No hurry," Alison said. *I'll just stand here and watch you be you,* she thought, *and hope that a little of you rubs off on me.*

They were friends. There was no denying it, although Alison reminded herself daily that Zoe didn't know her well; that even if it lasted until June, they'd be going their separate ways then.

But for now, Alison felt altered by their friendship in the best possible way. Having someone to tell when exciting things happened—when she finished a story, got feedback on a story, overheard a particularly wacky conversation in the hall—actually seemed to make more interesting things happen.

She and Zoe talked about everything. Their classes and classmates, their childhoods, the books they were reading, the Miss America project they were working on together, the projects they worked on when they were apart. The only subject they avoided was their love lives, which was fine with Alison. She didn't have one. And if Zoe cared about someone else—male or female, friend or lover—Alison didn't want to know.

Most weekdays they ate lunch in the cafeteria together. On weekends they walked into town, poked around the thrift shops, smuggled warm bags of microwave popcorn into second-run movies at the Apollo: *Tootsie, E.T., An Officer and a Gentleman*.

Zoe had a roommate, so they made Alison's "senior single" room their home base. They stayed up late sharing Top Ramen dinners, Zoe on Alison's vinyl beanbag chair with a bowl balanced on her lap and Alison on the floor, or vice versa, talking voraciously as they slurped their MSG noodles.

They had the most profound thing in common: they were both orphans. But Alison was amazed by how many of the same things, personal *and* political, they were passionate about. They were both opposed the invasion of Grenada but disagreed about the bombing of the U.S. embassy in Beirut. Zoe said the United States had it coming; Alison found that a heartless response. Alison said *The Color Purple* deserved a Pulitzer for its cultural impact if not for the quality of the writing. Zoe argued that a book should be judged for its art, not its politics. They agreed that artistically, the novel didn't make the grade.

Alison was far more cynical about the quirks of the queer movement, but they agreed that *Torch Song Trilogy* winning a Tony was a great advance for civil rights. They disagreed about whether Zoe should shave her head—she didn't—or dye her thick shock of platinum-white hair jet black, which she did.

Zoe's commitment to her art inspired Alison to take her own more seriously. Their friendship dulled the sharp edge of Alison's loneliness, which made her less inclined to issue caustic commentary. She was relieved to return to quieter forms, the short stories and poems she used to read to her dad. Like her dad, Zoe was always asking about Alison's writing. She read every word Alison wrote, and her critiques were surprisingly astute. "You don't need all those flowery adjectives." "Cut the hyperbole. Your writing is powerful enough without it." "Trust your talent—forget the tricks."

"For a painter, you're a pretty good editor," Alison said. Zoe's attention made Alison believe there *was* hope for her as a writer, a wife and mother, a human being. Zoe tended to Alison the way Zoe's mom had tended to her, tracking the details of her life, asking about her thoughts and feelings, caring about Zoe's art projects as if they were her own. Alison had never felt so *not alone*.

Zoe helped Alison pick her two best stories to send to Oberlin's literary journal. The *Field* published both of them. Marian daughter assigned them as readings for their class. She gave Alison an A+ on her essay about Catharine MacKinnon and wrote on the back, "I'm gratified to help you come into the full flower of your womynhood. In sisterhood, M." A reporter for the *Review*, eyes fastened on Alison's breasts, interviewed her about writing fiction versus commentary. He hadn't read her op-ed, he said, but he'd skimmed her stories. He said her sex scenes were hot. He wondered if she'd like to see a movie sometime.

Alison bought Zoe a set of mink paintbrushes to thank her for her support. Zoe bought Alison an antique fountain pen and a tiny, cut-glass bottle of red ink to celebrate her success.

O n a Friday night in November, Alison and Zoe decided to go see *Sophie's Choice* at the Apollo. A bitter wind came up as they were crossing the campus, so they stopped by Zoe's dorm to get some warmer clothes.

While Zoe ransacked the antique steamer trunk she used as a dresser, Alison scanned Zoe's half of the room. The scarred walls were covered with Georgia O'Keeffe prints that looked like Technicolor female genitalia. Political buttons in various sizes, colors, and convictions marched up and down the Indian-print bedspread that hung from the ceiling, dividing the room. FEMINISM IS THE RADICAL NOTION THAT WOMEN ARE PEOPLE. CREATIVITY TAKES COURAGE. U.S. OUT OF MY UTERUS. MAKE ART, NOT WAR.

Books, paintbrushes, belts, beads, costume jewelry spilled from the fruit crate, turned on its end, that served as Zoe's nightstand. Alison couldn't stop looking at the tousled narrow mattress on the floor.

Zoe handed Alison a woven orange and turquoise poncho. Alison grimaced. "Is it deer season in downtown Oberlin? Are you trying to keep me from getting shot?"

"Come on, preppie. You know you love it."

"*Love* is a little strong. I'd say . . . I hate it."

Zoe grinned and pulled the serape over Alison's head, clucking like a mother stuffing a fidgety child into a snowsuit.

"See? It looks great on you!" Zoe took Alison by the shoulders and turned her, framing the two of them in the mirror on the back of the dorm room door.

They stood there looking at themselves together. Alison's dark hair, dark eyes, dark skin; Zoe's jet-black buzz cut, blue eyes, porcelain face. Alison's lean length; Zoe's broad torso and narrow hips. The crevice of Alison's cleavage in the deep V of the serape; the poke of Zoe's nipples through her yellow thrift-store cashmere cardigan.

"We fit," Zoe said. Her voice was low and hoarse.

Alison wriggled out of the serape and tossed it into the open trunk.

"Where'd you go?" Zoe asked.

"I was hot," Alison mumbled. How could everything feel so natural between them one minute and so strained the next? "I mean, it's hot in here."

"I've been meaning to tell you," Zoe blurted. "I'm going away."

Alison's heart lurched.

"Remember I told you about Corrine, my friend from boarding school? She invited me to her parents' winter place in Aspen for Christmas break."

Alison imagined herself on the deserted campus for three weeks, alone. Eating Top Ramen for Christmas dinner, alone. Seeing movies at the Apollo, alone. She saw Zoe on a ski lift, red cheeked and laughing, cuddled cozily on a fireside ski lodge couch. "Sounds fun," Alison said, fighting to keep her feelings off her face.

"I'm going to ask Corrine if I can bring you along," Zoe said. "Her parents' house is *huge*. They won't even know you're there."

Alison felt like she'd been slapped. "The invisible Jew," she said. "The perfect accessory for the Christmas table."

"You know that's not what I meant."

"Whatever you meant, thanks but no thanks." Zoe seemed to have forgotten everything she knew about Alison—that she couldn't afford to fly to Aspen, that she was nervous around strangers, especially rich WASP strangers, that she'd never skied.

"Are you worried about the money?" Zoe asked. "I'll buy the tickets."

"I'm not *worried* about the money. I don't *have* the money. And I'm not your Christmas charity."

"No, you're not," Zoe said quietly. "You're my friend."

She closed the trunk lid, sat down on it, and pulled Alison down next to her. "I'm sorry," Zoe said. "I told you about the trip in the worst possible way. I don't blame you for being upset."

Alison felt like a punctured balloon, the anger hissing out of her. "I'm an idiot," she said.

"Come to Aspen. It'll be our Christmas presents to each other."

Alison adjusted her weight so her hip was no longer touching Zoe's. "You should be glad I'm not coming," she said. "I'm saving you eight nights of Hanukkah gifts."

"Such a deal," Zoe said dryly. "But I thought you don't celebrate Jewish holidays."

Alison looked at her Swatch and jumped to her feet. "If we don't leave this minute, we'll be late. You know I hate to miss the coming attractions."

A fter the movie they went to the Tap House, split a bottle of Mateus rosé, and argued about the film. Alison said the book had been a hundred times better. Zoe hadn't read it, but that didn't keep her from swearing that no book could beat Meryl Streep's performance. Alison thought, but didn't say, that Zoe looked a bit like Meryl Streep.

Instead she told Zoe that her mother had hated Germans, whether they'd been born before, during, or after the Holocaust.

Zoe confessed that her great-uncle had been a fanatical fan of Hitler. Alison confessed that every time she saw a movie or read a book about the Nazis, she promised herself she'd never do it again, but then the next one came along and she just had to.

They stumbled out of the bar into bone-chilling air. Alison's fingers tingled inside her wool gloves. "Maybe we should call a cab," she said, her breath billowing from her mouth.

Zoe whipped the orange cashmere scarf off her neck and wrapped it around Alison's. "C'mon, wimpy wimp," she said. "We'll walk fast."

Alison couldn't walk fast. She was too cold, too buzzed, too upset by the film and by the argument she and Zoe had had before the film, and by the thought of being alone on campus for three whole weeks over Christmas, the time of year she always felt loneliest.

"You're such a cheap date," Zoe said. "Half a bottle of wine and look at you. Wino!" She started walking backward, her laughing eyes on Alison's.

"Look who's talking." Alison's tongue was thick. "I'm not the one who's walking backward."

It seemed too cold for snow, but fat flakes started falling, a thick white blanket flung across the night. "God, it's gorgeous." Zoe threw her head back and stuck out her tongue. Alison watched snowflakes melting in Zoe's mouth. Her own teeth were chattering.

"You're freezing, poor thing." Zoe pointed to an old stone church across the street. "Let's go warm up in there."

"Is it open this late?" Alison asked.

"God's house is always open." Grinning, Zoe wrapped her arm around Alison's shoulders and pulled her along. Through her woozy wine haze, Alison felt the swell of Zoe's breast against her arm.

She let Zoe lead her up the snowy stone steps and she let Zoe pull the heavy wooden church door open and she let Zoe lead her inside. The door thumped shut behind them. They stood in the vestibule, nearly nose to nose, staring at each other. Snow glittered like bits of broken glass in Zoe's spiky black hair.

Were there people in the pews, praying, or waiting for a break in the storm? Was a priest watching from the altar, waiting to see what might happen next? Alison had time to wonder but no time to find out.

Zoe pulled Alison's glove off her right hand and stuffed it into her own jacket pocket. She took Alison's hand and rubbed her fingers, slowly, one finger and then the next. Alison wished she had twenty more fingers. *Don't stop.* A hundred fingers. *Please.*

Zoe took Alison's other hand. Alison was sweating and shivering, her vision blurring or votive candles flickering, or maybe she was having a dream. She panted shallowly, paralyzed in place.

Alison rocked on her feet. Zoe caught her. She unzipped Alison's jacket and slipped her hands under Alison's sweater and found the flesh beneath her thin silk chemise.

Zoe pressed the hot palms of her hands against the cold curve of Alison's waist. Her hands were moist and rough, a cat's sandpaper tongue.

"I want to kiss you," she said. "Can I kiss you, Alison?"

No, Alison meant to say.

5.

A lison awoke alone in her bed for the first time in weeks. She stretched her legs across the expanse of icy sheet and pulled Zoe's pillow to her face, inhaling her patchouli scent.

Zoe was away for five days, on a road trip with her painting class, taking a tour of Midwest art museums. Alison was grateful for the break in the action, for a chance to touch her own fingers to her own toes, to take stock of who she was three months into the first love of her life. She hadn't felt this raw, this smitten, this terrified since her dad's death.

She got dressed, stripped the bed, and carried a pillowcase bulging with linens down to the laundry room. Taking one last whiff of patchouli-scented pillowcase, she shoved a quarter into the machine to start the load.

Alison didn't want to go back to her cold, empty room. She

plucked the remote from its holster on the wall, clicked on the small TV that hung from the ceiling, tuned in to CBS Morning, and sank into the sagging easy chair.

"A healthy baby was born today at the UCLA Medical Center," Charles Kuralt was saying. "But this was no ordinary baby. This was the first live birth in history to result from transferring a developing embryo from one woman to another."

An animated graphic illustrated the process as Kuralt described it: "An embryo was conceived in Woman A by artificial insemination. That developing embryo was then implanted in the uterus of Woman B, who gave birth thirty-eight weeks later. The sperm used in the artificial insemination came from the husband of Woman B, the woman who bore the baby." Kuralt shook his head. "If you could follow all that," he said, looking directly into the camera, "you're doing better than I am. Now, a word from our sponsor."

The commercial rolled. White men with shaved heads marched in lockstep, Nazi style. A muscular woman in a tank top and running shorts hurled a sledgehammer at the projected image of a Hitlerian leader as he boomed, "We. Shall. Prevail." And then a calm voice announced, "On January 24, Apple Computer will introduce Macintosh. And you'll see why 1984 won't be like 1984."

Alison sighed. Zoe had been trying to talk her into giving up her typewriter for a word processor. Luckily, Alison couldn't afford one, let alone a $1,500 computer. But she saw that train speeding down the tracks at her, whether she wanted the change or not, whether she could afford it or not. Three months ago she would have said the same things about being lovers with Zoe. And now she was waiting for Zoe to come back to her bed.

Alison flicked the channel to the local news, not quite

admitting to herself what she was watching for: an accident on a local highway, a van full of Oberlin students dead.

Please come home, she begged Zoe silently. Then the movie in her head began to play—not *1984,* but 1971.

"Y ou know, your father adored me until you came along," Alison's mother was telling her. They were in the backseat of a black limousine, being driven home from her father's funeral.

Her mother was sitting as far from Alison as she could. But still, every time Alison took a breath, she inhaled her mother's sour sweet perfume, her Aqua Net hair spray, the mothballs from the closet where she hung her fur coat.

"I was thin then. Thin and beautiful," her mother went on. "That's what he called me, you know. 'Beautiful.'"

He called me that too, Alison thought. Her mother pulled her fur coat tight across her enormous chest. "He worshipped me. Couldn't do enough for me. Until you came along." She smoothed her black skirt over her black-stockinged knees. "After that, all I ever heard was Alison this, Alison that. My beautiful little Alison."

Alison's eyes, inflamed from days of crying, filled with fresh tears. *If I were a good girl,* she thought, *I'd lie and tell her that Daddy loved her more than he loved me.*

Alison inched across the spongy leather seat until her skinny leg, swaddled in two pairs of black tights, touched the soft fur of her mother's coat. Her mother didn't seem to notice. *Now that Daddy's gone,* Alison thought, *maybe we can be sad together.*

She opened her mouth to comfort her mother. What came out wasn't what she meant to say. "It wasn't my fault," she said— truthfully, hurtfully, two things that often seemed to go together when Alison spoke.

Her mother's swollen eyes narrowed. Her nostrils flared. "Whose fault was it, then?" she hissed at Alison. "Whose stupid little *stories* did he rush home to read every night? You think he was driving fast the night he died to get home to *me?*"

Alison stared at her mother in horror, hoping she'd take it back. But she turned away, staring out the tinted window.

When her mother told her that her dad had died in a car wreck, Alison's first thought was, *It was my fault.* Now she knew it was true.

Who would love her now that her dad was gone? Who would she love? If her father's death was really her fault, did she even deserve to be loved?

"He cared about you, too," Alison said to her mother's back. Over her mother's shoulder, the trees' bare, black branches rolled slowly backward. "He told me that all the time."

Her mother whipped her head around. "How dare you?" she spat. "You selfish bitch."

A ball of fire burned in Alison's belly. As quickly as it erupted, her rage dissolved. She felt empty, suddenly, a cracked glass of water. She felt she was a meteor, tethered to nothing and no one, lost in space.

Over the next few months, her mother seemed to double in size. When Alison came home from school, she'd find half-empty Entenmann's cake boxes on the kitchen counter, empty ice cream tubs stuffed into the trash. She'd rummage through the fridge, looking for something to eat among the loaves of Roman Meal diet bread, square packages of low-cal, sliced Kraft American cheese, moldering grapefruits, pink cans of Tab.

"Don't eat my diet stuff. You're too skinny as it is," her mother would say from her spot at the kitchen table, where she sat each day in a shapeless silk caftan, sipping daintily from a square glass of vodka and ice. "Go get a milkshake or something. Put some meat on your bones."

Alison wondered why her mother didn't know what she knew. Food couldn't fill the hole her father's death had left. Alison had filled her emptiness with steely resolve. She was alone in the world and she knew it. She didn't have her dad to protect her anymore. She had to learn to protect herself, and she did. She promised herself she'd never count on anyone else the way she'd counted on him.

As she got older, Alison realized that the wall she'd built around herself didn't just protect her. It imprisoned her too. It made her distrust people who were kind to her and scorn anyone who wasn't. It made her schoolmates dislike her, her teachers punish her, and the boys she dated stop dating her. It made her desperate to be a mother, and it made her despair that she'd never find a husband so she could be one.

Soon after they met, Alison told Zoe that she'd always been difficult. Zoe laughed and said, "You're not difficult for me." Alison had argued with her, but now she saw that it was true. When Zoe suggested a play to see, a walk to take, a sexier outfit to wear, Alison always found herself saying yes.

Which movie should they see? They were both orphans, so no to the sobbing Shirley MacLaine in *Terms of Endearment*; yes to *Flashdance* with sexy Jennifer Beals. Which records should they buy? Yes to Cyndi Lauper and David Bowie; no to Boy George.

When Alison wanted pizza, Zoe said she was drooling for mushrooms and peppers. When Alison wanted Chinese, Zoe had an instant longing for mu shu tofu. And when Zoe had one of her weird cravings—frozen microwave burritos from the corner liquor store, bananas slathered with Marshmallow Fluff, "dinners" in bed of Cheese Nips and Moët & Chandon—Alison gamely burned her mouth on molten cheese and gummed down sticky bananas, reveling in her own unexpected acquiescence and in Zoe's delight.

Zoe didn't make fun of people the way Alison did, but she didn't judge Alison for her judgments. She said she was "entertained" by Alison's rants. Most of the time, Zoe's unconditional adoration made Alison calmer and happier than she'd ever been. Sometimes it made her feel like an imposter, imitating a less difficult, more compliant version of herself. How could it be? And yet it seemed true: unlike Alison herself, Zoe wasn't waiting for Alison to change.

Alison heard familiar footsteps, pounding down the hall toward her room. Before the thought—*she really did come back*—had quite registered, the door flew open and she was safe again, her good self again, in Zoe's arms. "I missed you so much," Zoe crooned into her ear.

"I missed you too."

"Baby." Zoe pulled Alison close, stroked her back, worked one hand between her legs. "I love you."

"I love you too."

Zoe backed them up the few steps to the bed and kneeled over Alison, pulling Alison's sweater over her head, unbuttoning her 501s. "I missed *this* so much." Zoe feathered kisses over Alison's belly, licked her thighs apart. "Keep your eyes open, Al," she whispered. "Be with me."

Alison moaned, masking a flash of irritation. Why was Zoe asking for more when Alison was turned on, wanting, ready? "I'm with you," she murmured, stroking the back of Zoe's head. *Now*, she willed Zoe, *please make me come*.

When they were finished, Zoe drew the sheet over them and

held Alison close. "How are you, babe?" she asked in the probing voice that meant "Fine" would not do. *Men are so much easier,* Alison thought in a wild moment of regret. *When I had sex with men, I could just have sex.*

"You don't have to protect yourself from me." Zoe stroked her hair. "Are you scared, Al?" she asked.

What would I be afraid of, Alison started to say. But a big yes rose from deep in her belly. It washed away the anger she was trying to hang onto, the wall she was trying to erect. "I am," Alison whispered. "I am scared." She started to cry.

Zoe held Alison as if she could never cry too hard or too long, as if she thought Alison deserved to be held forever.

I t s u r p r i s e d Alison how easily she'd taken to lovemaking with Zoe, how hungrily she craved it, how *not that different yet somehow better* it was than the occasional sex she'd had with men. But Zoe wanted one yes in bed that Alison couldn't give her. *Wouldn't,* Zoe insisted.

Before Zoe, Alison had never really made love. Sex had been a solo trip for her, her lovers there to send her off at the begin-ning and greet her at the end. The men she'd slept with hadn't cared how she got her orgasms, or even if she had them. But Zoe wanted to be with Alison, inside Alison, all over Alison during every breath, moan, and shudder along the way.

Alison promised Zoe she'd work on her "intimacy issues." She started by trying to keep her eyes open when they made love. When Zoe wanted to snuggle afterward, Alison focused on how good it felt to be held instead of how bad it felt to be trapped. She taught herself to say no to her fear when it wrapped its tentacles around her and pulled tight, when her heart creaked open and threatened to slam shut. When she started obsessing about Zoe dying or leaving or lying to her.

"I'm scared," Alison learned to say, instead of disappearing or starting a fight. Sometimes she didn't even have to speak. Zoe could read the signs from across a room. She'd go to Alison and rub her neck and talk her back from the edge.

"You're safe with me. I love you," Zoe said over and over, while Alison took deep breaths, trying to believe her.

Zoe's love felt like a prize Alison had won without knowing exactly how or why. Alison wanted to deserve it. She wanted to give Zoe everything she had in her to give. No. She wanted to give Zoe more.

"Sisters!" Mariandaughter stood in the center of the circle. "It's eight months till the presidential election. Let's discuss feminist strategy. Which campaign should we support? Or do we ignore the whole electoral process and vote with our feet?"

"The Black Student Union is supporting Brother Jesse Jackson," Nia said.

"La Raza Unida *también*," said Carmen.

"Right on," Mariandaughter said.

A frizzy-haired girl named Wendy raised her hand. "I'm not voting for an anti-Semite, even if he *is* black," she said in a thick Long Island accent. "Jesse Jackson referred to New York as Hymietown." She shot Alison a meaningful, Hymies-should-stick-together glance. Alison looked away, wondering how Wendy knew she was Jewish.

"That's just slang," Nia said. "He didn't mean anything by it."

"*Slang?*" Wendy stared at Nia. "You of all people should—"

"There's no way Jesse Jackson is anti-Semitic," a short blond girl wearing an ERACISM button interjected. "Anyway, he apologized."

"He'll never win," said Root, a stocky girl who "self-identified" as a "born-again pagan" and had once invited Alison to join her coven. "Nominating him would be like handing the election to Reagan."

Mariandaughter's eyes darted around the circle. "Has anyone heard the rumors about Mondale's running mate?"

"He said he'd ask Geraldine Ferraro if he gets the nomination," Root said. "I think we should all visualize a woman vice president."

Mariandaughter glowed with the euphoria that a dicey conundrum always lent her. "Mondale also promised to support the Equal Rights Amendment. So, given historic campaigns by two liberal candidates, how do we vote our values?"

"This is so confusing. My head's on fire," Wendy said.

"You and Michael Jackson," Zoe said.

"That is *not funny!*" Nia barked at her. "Michael Jackson is an important role model for black children. He could have died for Pepsi-Cola's profits."

"Just to clarify," Alison asked Nia, "would dying for *Coke's* profits be funny?"

"I can't believe you two are joking about this," Nia fumed.

You two, Alison thought. *I like the sound of that.*

Oberlin was nearly deserted over spring break. It happened every April, and every April Alison imagined all those poor little rich kids skiing in Aspen, shopping in Paris, being Sherpa'ed up some mountain somewhere. But this year she was in love with one of those poor little rich kids, who'd skipped Aspen to stay on campus with her.

She and Zoe soaked up the quiet, lying around reading, lying in bed talking late at night, making love noisily in the empty dorm. On the last night of break they were snuggled up on Alison's floor, eating their way through a Whitman's Sampler.

Zoe sat up and faced Alison. "I have an idea," she said around a mouthful of caramel.

Alison knew that voice. It meant Zoe's mind was made up. And it meant that in some way, big or small, Alison's life was about to change. Alison said the small prayer she reserved for these occasions: whatever it is, please don't let it end us.

"Let me guess," Alison said, keeping it light. "You want to paint the student union orange. Join Earth First. Make me wear your clothes."

"None of the above." Zoe was bouncing with excitement. "I want us to move to Berkeley when you graduate."

"Us?"

"Well, yeah." Zoe looked at Alison, puzzled. "What did you think would happen in June?"

Zoe's certainty settled over Alison like a feather quilt.

"You've been *saying* you don't know where to go after graduation," Zoe cajoled her. "You haven't even wanted to *talk* about it."

Alison hadn't wanted to think about it, either. When she did, all she could see was Zoe at Oberlin, staying up all night with someone else, and Alison somewhere—New York, probably—in her meteorite drift through space.

"What about your last three years of school?" Alison asked.

"College is useless for a painter. And if I decide I want to finish for some weird reason, I've heard they have colleges in California."

"I've never even been to Berkeley. Have you?"

"I've seen pictures. Blue sky. Cute houses. Sit-ins at Sproul Plaza. An artist in every garret. What more do we need to know?"

Alison remembered Zoe telling her, on the night they now referred to as their first date, that her mom had always wanted to move to Berkeley, that Zoe wanted to raise her kids there. *This is about Zoe's mom*, Alison realized. *And if I say no, that'll be about my mother. And it'll be the end of us. And my mother will win.*

Alison pictured the two of them holding hands on a cable car clanging up Nob Hill. The two of them walking the Golden Gate Bridge, strolling arm-in-arm through drifts of fog, San Franciscans smiling at them approvingly. Where else besides the Bay Area could they find the safety and the freedom of that?

They'd buy a motorcycle, follow the Pacific down Highway 1. Grow their own oranges. Learn to surf. Alison would be a reporter at the *San Francisco Chronicle* or a freelancer based in Berkeley. Zoe would go to art school. There had to be an art school, or a dozen art schools, in San Francisco.

"Do you have any idea what the *weather's* like in Berkeley?" Zoe asked. "It never snows. Ever! It's sunny all year round."

"Okay," Alison said.

"What do you mean, okay?"

No wonder she doesn't believe me, Alison thought. *I never do this.* "Okay, let's move to Berkeley," she said.

"Really?" Zoe jumped up, pulled Alison to her feet, held her close. "Oh, Al. You're the best. The *best*, you hear me?"

"I hear you," Alison said. But was this the real Alison speaking? Or was she imitating the Alison she hoped to become?

She suspected it was the latter. And she wondered how long she could keep up the act.

6.

A lison sprinted up the BART station escalator, hurrying home to tell Zoe the big news.

She pushed through the turnstile, peeling off her linen blazer as she burst into the sweltering autumn afternoon. Three months after their move to Berkeley, she'd finally gotten used to the foggy, fifty-degree northern California summer just in time for the relentlessly sunny, ninety-degree fall.

Loping north on Sacramento Street, she ran into a display of wooden birdhouses spilling out of a stucco garage. She laughed out loud, reading the sidewalk sandwich sign:

BERKELEY BIRDHOUSE COLLECTIVE
PROVIDING HOUSING FOR HOMELESS BIRDS SINCE 1964

We are an alliance of proactive grassroots militant radical birdhouse builders who are committed to bringing affordable housing to birds of all stripes, nationalities, genders, and sexual persuasions. Viva la Che! Viva la revolucion! Viva la CASA DE PAJARO RUSTICA.

Alison stepped around the "Low-Income Subsidized Birdhouse" and the "Love Triangle A-frame Birdhouse," surrendering to a moment of delight. Berkeley had charmed her, even if she thought of it as Oberlin for adults who refused to grow up. The town was a living museum of the sixties, populated by idealists frozen in time. Unlike her hometown New Yorkers, who dressed and spoke and lived as if the present was already passé, Berkeleyites still dressed and spoke and lived as if the youth revolution was just a shot away.

She turned right on Lincoln, one of her favorite Berkeley streets. The front yards she passed were unfenced, unfettered by design; they looked like they'd been planted by Dr. Seuss. Purple-blossomed princess trees, shocking pink impatiens, Day-Glo orange nasturtiums bloomed in madcap profusion amid rusty metal sculptures, toilets sprouting red geraniums, towering papier-mâché peace signs. Strings of tattered Buddhist prayer flags danced to breezes blowing east from the bay.

Rounding the corner onto Grant, Alison saw their '72 Volvo wagon parked in front of the cottage she and Zoe shared: the smallest, funkiest house on the block. The others were classic Berkeley brown-shingles, windows trimmed in riotous rainbow hues, crouched on earthquake-reinforced haunches like friendly, disheveled dogs. Alison unlatched their rickety knee-high wooden gate, righted the peeling picket fence which tended to swoon to the touch, and made her way through the tumble of blackberry vines and sweetheart roses competing for domination of the mossy brick path.

Zoe flung the door open.

"I got the job!" Telling Zoe made it seem real, suddenly, the way telling Zoe always did.

"I told you! I knew it!"

"I showed them my clips from the *Field*," Alison pushed on. "They loved my writing."

"What's not to love?"

"Here's the best part." Alison took Zoe by the shoulders, backed her five steps into the kitchen, sat her down in one of their flea market oak chairs. "Drum roll, please."

Zoe thumped her palms on the edge of the yellow Formica table they'd scored in the affluent Berkeley Hills on Bulky Trash Day.

"They made me a copywriter! I'm going to write ads for Planned Parenthood and Friends of the Earth. And my starting salary is thirty thousand dollars a year."

"Wow." Zoe's lips twisted into something resembling a smile.

"What's wrong?" Alison asked.

"What could be wrong?" Zoe put on her mock-Yiddish accent. "Why does something always have to be wrong, already? That's great, dollink. Mazel tov."

Alison's heart sank. How could she have been so insensitive? Poor Zoe had spent weeks driving around San Francisco with a dozen of her paintings in the trunk, trying to get a gallery to represent her. She'd been turned down by every one.

"God, Zoe. I'm sorry."

"For what?"

"For going on about my new job when you've been having such a hard time with your career."

Zoe's laugh sounded hollow. "You think if you don't talk about your great job, I'll get a gallery?"

Alison couldn't argue the point. But she'd seen the unhappiness on Zoe's face. And she was the one who'd caused it.

"I'm happy for you, baby. Can you get that through your beautiful head?"

"Let me buy you dinner at Chez Panisse," Alison said.

"Downstairs or upstairs?"

"We're going whole hog. Downstairs."

"Whole artichoke, you mean." Zoe's eyes gleamed. "Wait. There *is* something you can do for me." She pulled Alison out of her chair and danced her down the short, dark hallway where they'd hung Zoe's Mammary Lane series.

In the bedroom doorway, Zoe pulled Alison close and kissed her hard. She ran her lips over Alison's nose, her eyebrows, one earlobe, the other. Alison's breath quickened. Zoe still made her dizzy, still made her want to *just lie down.* It was delicious, not torturous, now that Alison wasn't trying not to feel it.

They lurched across the glistening oak floor they'd unearthed under layers of linoleum. They sank to the bed, tossing shirts, pants, socks, and panties over their heads.

"Wait." Alison wiggled out from under Zoe, went to the window, and pulled out the hairbrush they used to prop it open. Then she closed the curtains and went back to bed, back to her favorite part of sex with Zoe: blissfully surrendering, for once, to mindless desire.

Zoe's head drifted down the length of Alison's body. Her tongue, her fingers were everywhere. Their breathing grew faster, shallow, rasping.

"I love you," Alison whispered into Zoe's sweaty neck. It felt like an apology.

* * *

I t was shocking to Alison: the cozy, white-lace-curtains, home-made-chocolate-pudding life she shared with Zoe.

Since she was home all day, Zoe planned the meals and bought the groceries, but she and Alison cooked together nearly every night. Bumping hips in their daffodil-yellow kitchen, boom box blasting, they sang along to "Borderline" and "What's Love Got to Do With It" while Alison whipped up a stir-fry in the wok or Zoe chopped onions for lentil soup. Then they sat and ate at their table for two, telling each other about the time they'd spent apart, planning the things they wanted to do together. Paint the bathroom teal. Take a day trip to Point Reyes. Beat back the black-berries and roses, reclaim the front yard. Plant Dutch iris. Grow zucchini, lettuce, red and yellow chard.

This was the passionate, peaceful domesticity, the loving and being loved that Alison had always dreamed of. The late-night pillow talk, the bone-melting sex, the best-friendship she had with Zoe were so good, they pushed her to the edge of belief. But Alison wanted more than a lover. She wanted a family.

Zoe had started talking about having kids someday. She wanted at least two, and she was full of ideas about how they could have them. She knew lesbians who'd had kids—boys, every one of them, for reasons no one understood—using donated sperm and artificial insemination. It was easy to do, she said, and getting easier all the time. "You'll have the first kid, since you're older," Zoe told Alison. "I'll have the second one. We'll use the same donor. Our kids will be siblings for real."

Alison found these conversations disturbingly clinical. She always changed the subject, and Zoe seemed to have taken the hint. They hadn't discussed it for a while.

But now all the gay papers and magazines were running sto-ries about "the lesbian baby boom." Mama Bear's, the women's bookstore in South Berkeley, had hung an exhibit of photos of two women and their son. The little boy was adorable. But his mothers were big and butch, both decked out in full "wimmin-loving-wimmin" regalia. They were *dykes*, nothing like her and Zoe.

The exhibit was titled "Love Makes a Family, Nothing More, Nothing Less." Alison knew better. She'd been stuck in a family without love after her father died. Now she had love with Zoe, but they weren't a family.

Leaflets stapled to telephone poles all over Berkeley offered three words of advice: be here now. Alison took the reminder personally. Being where she was now, she was happier than she'd ever been, happier than she'd ever thought she would be. But sometimes late at night, with Zoe sleeping beside her, Alison's maternal longings bubbled up and she couldn't swallow them down. She'd lie awake, twisting the Rubik's Cube of her future into scenarios, none conceivable. Staying with Zoe but not having children. Having children with a man but not being with Zoe. Conceiving a test-tube baby with some stranger's sperm and raising it with Zoe. Medical science had figured out how to turn lesbians into mothers and lesbian couples into "alternative families," but Alison was too wounded by her own childhood to force any kind of freakish childhood on her kids.

Alison's search for a happy ending always brought her to the same unhappy conclusion. To have what she wanted most, eventually she'd need to give up what she had.

A lison's job at San Francisco's most progressive ad agency, Public Media Center, was much more than a paycheck to her. She liked the grown-up life she was living, the parentheses of a structured workday, the built-in camaraderie with her smart, committed coworkers and clients, the views of Union Square from PMC's glass-brick and steel-beamed office. The steady build of regular income eased Alison's nervousness about depending so much on Zoe. Paying her half, having her own savings account, made Alison less afraid of ending up as poor and bitter as her mother had.

"My biggest mistake was putting all my eggs in one basket," her mother had told her often. "When I got married, I thought I was set for life. And what did I end up with besides a little insurance money? Nothing."

It was satisfying to help the firm's nonprofit clients get their messages out, thrilling to see her words in print in full page *San Francisco Chronicle* ads and the fund raising packets that came in the mail. Learning to write to the pica, to say the most with the least number of words, was bleeding into her poems and short stories, making them more incisive and concise.

Alison was away from home ten hours each weekday, but she and Zoe kept their art at the center of their lives. Zoe turned the falling-down shed in the backyard into her studio. Alison used their second bedroom as hers. She painted the walls a soothing gray-green, assembled a plywood-and-file-cabinet desk, threw a Cost Plus Indian print bedspread over the easy chair she'd scavenged on trash day in the hills. Above her desk she hung a broadsheet that Black Oak Books had printed as a New Year's gift to its customers, her favorite Raymond Carver poem, "Late Fragment":

> And did you get what you wanted from this life, even so?
> I did.
> And what did you want?
> To call myself beloved, to feel myself beloved on the earth.

* * *

After dinner most nights, Zoe went back to her studio to paint and Alison carried a mug of peppermint tea to her desk. No matter what had happened at work that day, once she started scribbling, she slipped into a mellow, meditative trance: deeply happy, deeply alone.

Writing cracked Alison open, and she let it because no one and nothing could take her writing away. All those letters and commas and paragraphs were hers for the borrowing, hers to rearrange. In a world of her own creation, her fears and defenses fell away. She never even felt them go.

Alison had always been a stumbling, halting, demon-driven writer. Now she wrote with an ease, a confidence, an effortlessness that she felt only one other time: when she and Zoe made love. Now that Zoe made her "beloved on this earth," Alison had the courage to start a poem or a story and keep going, even when she had no idea where it might take her or how it might end.

Most of their evenings ended the same way. At ten or eleven or midnight, one of them would glance at her watch, pull herself up and out of her trance, and go fetch the other out of hers. There was no sweeter moment in any day than when Alison heard Zoe say, "It's midnight, sweetie," and she put her pen down, spun her chair around, and saw Zoe right there, smiling at her, waiting for her to come to bed.

It costs twenty-two cents to send your poems to some obscure literary journal no one will ever read," Zoe said, flipping through the envelopes Alison had left for the mailman. "And it costs twenty-two cents to send them to *The New Yorker*." She waved the envelopes at Alison. "Why isn't *The New Yorker* in here?"

Alison bit her tongue to keep from mentioning the obvious. Zoe was still painting, but after two years, she'd given up trying to get her paintings into prestigious San Francisco galleries. When stacks of finished canvases threatened to squeeze her out of her studio, she'd load a few into the Volvo and drive to one of the Berkeley cafés, pizza joints, hair salons, and Laundromats that displayed rotating shows of their customers' artwork. When she had an "opening," she mailed out the postcards and paid for the wine and cheese herself.

Alison's real writing career wasn't going any better. Zoe's relentless encouragement, which often made Alison feel more harassed than encouraged, did keep her sending out submissions. But she was collecting rejection letters, not readers.

"I love writing," she told Zoe one Friday night over beers and oozing slices of Zachary's stuffed pizza. "But I think I'd love it even more if anyone ever read what I wrote." Alison sprinkled red peppers on her slice. "Besides you, I mean," she added before Zoe did.

"Why don't you try journalism?" Zoe asked. "You're so good at those profiles you write for work. And you're always saying poetry and fiction aren't political enough."

Alison swallowed a mouthful of mozzarella and wondered why she hadn't thought of that herself. She'd been writing for the company newsletter, mostly stories about the activists who ran PMC's client organizations. She liked doing the interviews, and her boss and clients were always happy with the results. Maybe she could use her PMC clips to get assignments from newspapers and magazines the way she'd used her *Oberlin Review* clips to land the job at PMC.

"I'll try it," Alison said. She waggled a finger at Zoe. "But don't start bugging me about pitching the damn *New Yorker*. I'm going to start small."

"Promise." Zoe lifted her beer, Alison lifted hers, and they clinked glasses. "But you *will* try *The New York Times*, right?" Alison started sputtering. Zoe laughed. "Kidding," she said.

Suddenly the table shuddered. Plates rattled. Their beer glasses tilted, sloshed, and righted themselves. The walls creaked. The chatter stopped. At the next table, a man grabbed a toddler out of the high chair beside him, hugging her to his chest. "Earthquake," several people said into the silence.

And then it ended. There was a hushed pause, a waiting, a breath held.

Gradually the din resumed. The pizza makers went back to slamming oven doors. The greeter called out the next name on the list.

"Hey, that was our first earthquake," Alison said. "Shouldn't we have a kiss to celebrate?"

Zoe didn't look like a person who wanted a kiss. She looked like a person who wanted to disappear. Her face was pale. Her eyes were big and round.

In their three years together, Alison had never seen Zoe so scared. Alison didn't know what to do for her, what to say. In an instant, the earthquake had shaken them into each other's roles.

"Do you know the theory of small earthquakes?" Alison asked, hoping to distract Zoe from her panic.

Zoe didn't seem to have heard her.

"They say each little earthquake releases pressure from the fault line," Alison said, "which makes a big one less likely. So that was actually a good thing."

"Not to me," Zoe said through clenched teeth.

"I'm taking you home." Alison threw a twenty-dollar bill on the table, walked around the booth, and pulled Zoe to her feet.

Alison remembered lying in her narrow dorm room bed with

Zoe, talking about the move to California. Alison kept coming up with what-ifs; Zoe kept shooting them down. There *were* good jobs for writers in the Bay Area, Zoe reassured her. They *would* find a great place to live. They were *moving* to Berkeley, not *marrying* Berkeley. And then Zoe hoisted herself up onto one elbow and looked down at Alison. "You're safe with me," she said. "I'm the one you want to be with in a crisis."

Alison had let Zoe swaddle her in that blanket. And now Zoe was the one who needed swaddling.

A lison came up with a list of story ideas that overlapped with the research she did for her job. She went to the library and gave herself an immersion course on writing and selling magazine pitches, tearing through stacks of books and trade magazines.

She mailed her pitches with copies of her PMC clips to every alternative newspaper in the Bay Area: the *Berkeley Express,* the *San Francisco Bay Guardian,* the *Pacific Sun,* the *Berkeley Monthly,* *SF Weekly,* even the *Point Reyes Light.* When the editors didn't call her, she called them. When they dodged her calls, she wrote to them again. Finally, the *Berkeley Monthly* paid her $100 for an essay about the spiritual aspect of recycling. Two weeks later, the *San Francisco Bay Guardian* assigned her a $250 update piece on Bay Area abortion clinics. New clips in hand, she sent bigger, broader pitches to national magazines.

Six months later, Alison had an impressive collection of new rejection letters. She was convinced that the problem was her lack of time, that she could get the assignments she wanted if she weren't squeezing writing in around her job, around the time she wanted to spend with Zoe—and, more problematically, the time

Zoe wanted to spend with her. Although she often stayed up half the night painting, Zoe fussed and tugged at Alison when she tried to write on weekends. She had to choose between keeping Zoe happy and putting more energy into getting published. Freelance writing practically guaranteed disappointment. Zoe guaranteed joy.

Alison decided to stop working on weekends. She had a lifetime of writing ahead of her. But she didn't know how long this good life with Zoe would last.

7.

A lison came home from work and plucked the mail out of the wicker basket beneath the slot in the front door. She sifted through the thick pile of junk mail, some of which she'd produced.

Campaign packets from Jesse Jackson and Michael Dukakis: hers. Fund-raising letters from the Sierra Club (hers) and the Pacific Center for Sexual Minorities (a rival agency's). Bills from PG&E, Waste Management, Pacific Bell. And a letter for Zoe from Anthony Meier Fine Arts in San Francisco.

Zoe's key turned in the lock. Alison handed her the envelope. Zoe ripped it open. "I got a gallery." She grabbed Alison. "I got a gallery!"

"Congrats, babe. But how'd that happen? You told me you'd given up."

Zoe dragged her into the kitchen. They sank into their chairs.

Zoe's cheeks were shiny and pink. "I didn't want to tell you I was still trying. I felt like such a loser. All those rejections. My paintings getting splattered with grease in pizza parlors . . . "

"So when you said you were home, painting," Alison said slowly, "you were really in San Francisco, meeting with gallery owners?"

"It only happened a few times." Zoe laughed. "Listen to us! I was just trying to surprise you. We're acting like I was having an *affair!*"

If she could lie to me about this, Alison thought, *she could lie to me about anything.*

"Aren't you happy for me?" Zoe asked plaintively. "It's a new gallery, really avant-garde. They want my whole Chernobyl series."

"Of course. It's great news." Alison forced a smile.

"Champagne!" Zoe cried. "We must have Champagne." She grabbed the car keys. "Back in a flash," she said, flying out the door.

She wasn't really lying, Alison told herself. *She was just trying to surprise me.*

Selfish bitch, Alison heard her mother saying. *This is Zoe's big moment, and you can't let her have it. All you care about is yourself.*

Alison went to the leaded-glass built-in that flanked the fireplace and pulled out their special thrift store cut-glass flutes. She carried them to the freezer, shoved aside the iced-over packages of ham hocks and phyllo dough, and made a bed for them on a pair of Nancy's Yogurt containers full of Zoe's lentil soup.

Zoe burst through the front door, brandishing a sweating bottle of Veuve Clicquot. She popped the cork and filled the flutes.

"To the best thing that's ever happened to me," she said, lifting her glass.

"To your gallery."

Zoe shook her head, rolling her eyes. "Not the gallery, goof-ball. *You*."

Alison stared into her flute, mesmerized by the perpetual font of perfect, tiny bubbles.

"To the best thing," Zoe said again.

"The best thing," Alison repeated. Bumping against each other, their glasses made a sweet tinkling sound.

Flush with extra cash, Zoe made an appointment with a socially responsible investment adviser at Working Assets in San Francisco. She asked Alison to come along.

The adviser told Zoe to buy a house and invest the rest. Bay Area real estate prices, he said with no apparent sense of irony, were going through the roof.

"Let's buy the cottage," Zoe said as she drove them home across the Bay Bridge.

"The cottage is falling apart," Alison said. "And I don't have money for a down payment."

Alison heard herself and shuddered. When had she started sounding like her mother, negative about everything, fearful of anything new? When had she stopped saying yes to Zoe?

"The money doesn't matter," Zoe said. "I've told you a million times. What's mine is yours."

Outside the passenger window, Alison saw a freighter gliding slowly along the gray surface of the bay. Stacked with bright squares of red, green, yellow, and blue shipping containers, the ship looked like it was made of Legos.

"It matters to me," she said.

"You're impossible, you know that?"

Alison heard the wheels turning in Zoe's brain. "Here's what we'll do," Zoe said as they passed the turnoff for Treasure Island. "I'll cover the down payment and the renovations. You can make the mortgage payments. After a few years, we'll be even. We can split everything after that."

"You're impossible, you know that?" Alison teased, stalling.

"Poor you. It's rough, isn't it, letting me take care of you?"

Yes, Alison thought. *It is.*

"Think about it," Zoe said. "We'll buy a lawn mower. Fight about sink fixtures. Just like real married people."

But we're not real married people, Alison thought. *And we never will be.* "Look! A heron." She pointed to a gangly snow-white bird poised on one matchstick leg in the marshy mud flats alongside the freeway.

"That's an egret, Alison." Zoe only called her Alison when she was angry. It didn't happen often. "And don't change the subject. Why wouldn't you want to buy a house with me?"

"I don't know," Alison said.

They fell into an uneasy silence driving east on University toward the hills, past the Leaning Tower of Pizza, past Berkeley Indoor Garden, where the pot growers bought their supplies, past the Santa Fe Bar and Grill, the new Jeremiah Tower restaurant in the old railroad station.

As the Volvo idled at a red light, Alison watched parents and kids spilling down the steps of the Berkeley Montessori School. The moms clutched their children's hands and their dimpled finger paintings and lunchboxes and jackets, calling to each other over their kids' heads, planting kisses on their children's cheeks.

I want that, Alison thought. She felt a stab in the region of her heart.

She wanted the pain to stop. She wanted her dread of the

future to stop. She wanted to stop living in two realities, the yes
now and the looming no.

Maybe if she loved Zoe the way Zoe loved her, without hesi-
tation or reservation, she'd feel the certainty, the lightness, the
happiness that Zoe felt.

"Okay. Let's do it," Alison said.

Their landlady was delighted to sell to them, and no
wonder. The inspector they hired found dry rot, termite
damage, a leaking roof, clogged galvanized pipes, and an eighty-
year-old electrical system in dire need of repair. Then there was
the mess of the garden. Armed with the inspection report, their
Realtor haggled the price down from $220,000 to $169,000.

On July 4, 1988, exactly four years after their move to Berkeley,
Zoe wrote a check for the down payment. Just like real married
people, they listed themselves on the deed as equal owners.

Alison's instinct proved right. Saying yes to Zoe, buying
the cottage with Zoe, made her feel more secure, more in
love, happier with Zoe than ever.

They took a celebratory shopping trip to the Ashby Flea
Market, needing nothing, wanting a souvenir of this magic time.
They found it leaning against the wheel of a vendor's pickup
truck: a gilt-edged, etched antique mirror.

"It's gorgeous, babe!" Zoe exclaimed.

They stood hip to hip, looking at themselves in the hazy, age-
blotched glass. Was it the mirror's distortion, Alison wondered,
or was she starting to look like her mother?

"It's kind of blurry, actually," Alison said.

"Wait till we're old and wrinkled. We'll be glad to miss the details." She ran her hand up Alison's back, drizzled her fingers through Alison's hair. Alison pulled away. Zoe never seemed to notice or care if people knew they were gay.

"How much?" Zoe asked the old black man who was selling the mirror.

"Twenty dollars," he said.

"Ten. The glass is all messed up."

"If you were as old as that mirror, young lady, you'd be all messed up too."

Zoe smiled at him flirtatiously. "Fifteen."

"Deal." The man squinted at them. "This thing's heavy. You ladies got a man to help you lift it?"

Zoe threw her arm around Alison's shoulders. "What on earth would we need a man for?"

Alison winced. She and Zoe carried the mirror to their car.

Zoe's gallery sold one of her Chernobyl paintings. The owner asked to see more of her work.

Elated, Zoe decided she finally deserved a real studio. She combed the *Oakland Tribune* classifieds and found a warehouse space she liked. Before she signed the lease, she wanted Alison to like it, too.

As they drove south on Martin Luther King Jr. Way, the Victorians got more decrepit, the liquor stores and storefront churches more prevalent, the cars older and rustier, the bass beats booming from their open windows more explosive.

Their cottage was only a mile and a half north of the Berkeley–Oakland border, but Zoe and Alison rarely crossed the Oakland line. Mostly poor, black, and residential with a wasteland of a downtown, the city didn't have much to draw people like them.

Zoe parked in front of a graffiti-splattered, three-story brick building. "It's not much on the outside," she said, "but wait till you see the space."

"Can't wait," Alison sat in the passenger seat looking around, in no hurry to leave the car.

A person of indeterminate gender slept in a nest of rags in the doorway. Butting up to the warehouse was a weedy vacant lot full of rusted car axles, shredded tires, and jagged chunks of cement. On the corner, a group of men leaned against the liquor store wall, tipping brown paper bags to their mouths. The row of hundred-year-old Victorians across the street with boarded-up windows looked like a lineup of old people, closing their eyes to whatever might happen next.

"You think it's safe to leave the car here?" Alison asked.

Zoe frowned, opened the passenger door, and ushered Alison past the mound in the doorway. The gloomy lobby smelled even worse than it looked.

"The elevator's huge," Zoe said. "And so's the space. I'll be able to make big paintings again." She punched a big red button. Above their heads, gears and pulleys creaked and groaned.

"Couldn't you have found a studio in Berkeley?" Alison asked.

Zoe pinched Alison's cheek. "What's wrong, Miss Politically Correct Ad Exec? You scared to hang out in the 'hood?"

The freight elevator announced itself with a crash of metal against metal. Zoe rolled up the door. "Next stop, women's lingerie, women's shoes, woman's studio."

Two stories up, the elevator wheezed to a stop. Zoe pulled

Alison into a football field–sized room. Dust motes danced in shafts of muted light. Bare redwood rafters and dangling metal warehouse lights trailed necklaces of gray dust.

Alison followed Zoe to a wall of floor-to-ceiling industrial windows blanketed in grime. "The light will be great in here as soon as I get these windows washed." Zoe rubbed a small patch clean. "I'm pretty sure you can see the Bay Bridge from here."

Zoe whirled around the room, her parachute pants billowing, her Chinese silk slippers skipping across the filthy floor. "I'd be crazy not to take it, right?"

"Crazy," Alison said.

At first the change was subtle, predictable. Of course the kitchen didn't smell of Zoe's cooking anymore when Alison came home from work. Of course their bed wasn't made, the feather pillows un-fluffed, the sweetheart roses on their nightstand shedding petals, the hearth a dark, empty hole. Zoe wasn't home all day anymore. Sometimes she didn't get home until eight or nine. When she did, she was quieter than she used to be, less effusive. She went to bed early. Often, she went to bed alone.

Alison reminded herself what Woody Allen had said in *Annie Hall*, her favorite movie: relationships are like sharks; they move forward or they die. She reminded herself that change was good or at least inevitable. She fought her fear that buying the house with Zoe had been a mistake, that Zoe *had her* now and didn't need to court her. She reminded herself that she used to crave time alone. She told herself to use the time well. She struggled to silence her mother's voice scolding, *Why would she buy the cow when she can get the milk for free?* (*Was there still milk involved,* she wondered, *when there were two cows in the relationship and no bull?*)

If Zoe wasn't home by seven or eight, Alison would defrost a container of her soup from their freezer, take a bowlful to her office, and work on a query letter, or research a story idea, or play with a poem. Sometimes Alison sank deliciously into the solitude. Sometimes she was listening hard for Zoe's key in the front door.

Fighting loneliness, beating back the beginnings of panic, one night when Zoe went to bed early, Alison went with her.

"Are you okay?" Alison asked, pressed against Zoe's velvet back, her hands cupping Zoe's velvet breasts. "Are we okay?"

Zoe rolled over, smoothed Alison's hair back from her forehead, stroked the curve of her hip. "We're fine," she said. "And I'm more than fine. I'm happier than I've ever been, babe. I'm *painting*. I'm hanging out with other artists in my building. I have you. I'm living my dream life."

"I'm happy for you," Alison said, wishing that was all there was to it.

Looking into her eyes, Alison saw that this was true. Zoe still loved her. The difference was that she wasn't living for Alison anymore. Zoe was doing exactly what Alison wished she herself could do: making art full-time, making friends, finding an audience for her work. Zoe was sated, and Alison wasn't her only source of satisfaction anymore.

"Poor baby," Zoe said. "Coming home to a cold, empty house. Eating leftovers alone. You miss your little Maxwell Housewife."

"I miss *you*."

Zoe wrapped her hand in a hank of Alison's hair. "You're right," she said thoughtfully. "Our lives are getting too separate. We need to find something to do together. Something that means a lot to both of us."

Her face brightened. "We can volunteer for the Dukakis campaign!"

"Dukakis?" Alison was thinking candlelit, home-cooked meals that came from the stove instead of the freezer. And Zoe was thinking a presidential campaign for a dork known as Zorba the Clerk?

"I know, I know," Zoe said. "The guy's a robot. But remember how bad we felt when he got the nomination and we hadn't done squat for Jesse Jackson? We'll feel worse if that asshole Bush wins and we didn't do anything to stop it."

Zoe untangled her fingers from Alison's hair. "I'll call Dukakis headquarters tomorrow. See what they need."

"How romantic," Alison said.

Zoe laughed. She pulled Alison on top of her, feathered kisses up and down her neck. "What do you need, my love?" she asked.

Her kisses grew more urgent. She slid a hand between Alison's legs. "Do you need this?" She put her knees between Alison's, spread them open. "Do you need *this?*"

"I need you," Alison whispered. "Stay with me. Please."

"I'll never leave you," Zoe promised.

Alison remembered when Zoe used to beg *her* to stay.

8.

berkeley
1988–1989

They gave it a try. They showed up for training at Dukakis headquarters in Oakland. They memorized the canvassing script. They spent a few Saturdays knocking on doors and an agonizing afternoon attempting to register shoppers in the parking lot of an East Oakland Safeway store.

The outcome of every front porch and telephone conversation was utterly predictable. The Democrats they spoke to promised, dispiritedly, to vote for "the lesser of two evils." The Republicans sneered.

The script instructed them to win people over based on Dukakis's positions on capital punishment (he opposed it), the defense budget (he'd shrink it), and mandating school kids to recite the Pledge of Allegiance (he said it was unconstitutional). Instead they ended up defending Dukakis against his own reputation—for freeing repeat rapist Willie Horton; for saying he wouldn't execute his own wife's hypothetical murderer; for dressing up in full combat gear and posing on a tank, machine gun pointed at the camera like some kind of military clown.

"We're wasting our time," Alison said a month before the election.

"We'll find something else to do together," Zoe said.

But they didn't. Zoe went back to spending long days at her studio. When she talked about her days, her reports were sprinkled with names of people Alison had never met. Alison started buying takeout food on her way home for her solitary dinners. When Dukakis/Bentsen lost to Bush/Quayle by a landslide, she took it as a bad omen. Why had she and Zoe wasted their time bucking the inevitable?

Zoe brought home flyers for ACT UP die-ins, demonstrations against nuclear testing in Nevada, teach-ins about the Iran-Contra scandal. She complained that her activism was taking too much time from her painting. But then she found time to join the planning committee for the annual Dyke March.

"If you want to see dykes on parade," Alison said, "can't you hang out in the cat food aisle at Safeway instead?"

Zoe didn't laugh. "Dyke visibility is really important right now. We're always there when gay men need us to help fight AIDS, but who's fighting breast cancer with *us*?"

Dyke visibility? Zoe sounded like the lesbians she and Alison used to make fun of at Oberlin.

"I really want to go to this meeting," Zoe said. "And I really want you to come."

Alison heard the warning in her words. "Should I wear my flannel shirt and work boots," she said, "or is it casual dress?"

Again she waited for Zoe to laugh, to tease her back. Zoe rolled her eyes.

They took BART to Sixteenth Street, rode the long escalator up to the street, and emerged into the uproar of the Mission. Alison had spent years training Zoe not to make public displays of affection, especially in neighborhoods like this one where openly gay people were routinely harassed or worse. But now, desperate for connection, she took Zoe's hand.

They walked to the Women's Building on Eighteenth Street and stood on the sidewalk, gazing up at the mural that climbed the walls. A couple of heavily tattooed women in men's work clothes walked by, glanced at Alison blankly, cruised Zoe blatantly, and swaggered inside.

"Gosh," Alison said, "you think they're gay?"

Zoe dropped Alison's hand and gave her a chilling look. "What a wonderful world it would be, Alison," she said coldly, "if only everyone were as femmy as you."

Zoe turned on her heel and walked into the building. Alison stood there, stunned. Through the glass door, Zoe gestured angrily for Alison to follow her. Alison walked into the lobby, expecting an apology, a hug. "Come on," Zoe said.

They took the stairs to a conference room on the second floor. A note on the door read, "This meeting is smoke-free, scent-free, and testosterone-free." The walls were lined with posters of Rosa Parks, Amelia Earhart, Emma Goldman, and young Sandinistas brandishing AK-47s. Zoe nodded to a few women, all of whom ducked their heads back at her. Alison wondered how Zoe knew them. What else didn't she know about Zoe's life?

For the next two hours, Alison sat on a folding chair, listening to twenty-five lesbians arguing loudly about whether male-to-female transsexuals were real women and therefore eligible to participate in the Dyke March. To signal their agreement with a comment, they snapped their fingers in the air like the women in Mariandaughter's class. Like the women in Mariandaughter's class, they either glared at Alison or ignored her. She kept glancing at Zoe, trying to initiate a little conciliatory eye rolling. But Zoe seemed engrossed in the debate.

For the first time in years, she felt like the old Alison, the odd woman out she'd been until she met Zoe. Zoe was changing, just as Alison had feared she would. Maybe she'd finally seen Alison for who she really was. Or maybe they were both reverting to their true selves: Zoe, Miss Outgoing; Alison, Misanthrope.

When the meeting ended, Alison waited around awkwardly while Zoe hugged one woman after another. Watching Zoe talking intently to a short, heavy woman with a huge ring of keys dangling from her Ben Davis jeans, Alison thought, *Maybe Zoe would be happier with her. Or her,* Alison thought, hearing Zoe's laughter merge with the giggles of a red-haired, punked-out girl who looked all of seventeen.

"What did you think?" Zoe asked as they left the building, headed toward Mission Street.

"If that's what it means to be a real lesbian, I'd rather be a fake bisexual." Alison answered as she would have *before,* when she and Zoe lived inside their bubble built for two, peering out together at a highly imperfect world, finding it all ridiculous.

Zoe laughed, but humorlessly. "My little homophobe. I guess queer activism is a little too queer for you."

Alison was stung. Again. "But not for you, apparently," she said.

"It's a big world, Alison. There's room in it for everyone."

I liked our little world better, Alison thought.

They turned left on Mission, their silence roaring against the clamor on the street. Women rummaged through deep plywood bins that spilled from bustling open-air markets, hefting jicamas, avocados, tomatillos. Dealers on every corner offered heroin, crack, weed. In the doorways of photo shops and copy stores, Latino teenagers hawked fake California IDs. The window of a stripper supply store called Foxy Lady was a leather-and-lace landscape of peekaboo negligees, black lace-up corsets, shocking-pink feathered mules.

As they approached Sixteenth Street, a late-model BMW pulled to the curb. The driver rolled down the passenger-side window and beckoned to a woman in spiked heels, a skin-tight cherry-red vinyl miniskirt, a skimpy white tube top, and a massive platinum wig. The woman leaned into the car, her red vinyl ass in the air. After a brief exchange with the driver, she got into his car.

Alison glanced at Zoe, hoping for a bonding moment. But Zoe was walking five steps ahead of her. She'd missed the whole thing.

"*Perdón*," said a voice behind Alison. She turned to see a woman in a brightly striped serape cradling a baby-size bag of oranges under one arm and a squealing toddler under the other, trying to squeeze through the crush. Alison pressed herself against the window of a check-cashing store to let the woman by.

"*Gracias*." As the woman paused, her baby reached out a chubby fist and grabbed Alison's shirt.

"*No, mijo*," the woman scolded.

"It's okay." Alison offered the baby her index finger. He grabbed it, his round brown eyes fixated on her face. Alison felt an easing of the tension in her belly. The baby stuffed her finger into his mouth and started sucking, pulling on something deep inside her.

His mother laughed, put the bag of oranges down, and gently pried Alison's finger out of her son's mouth. She kissed his thick thatch of black hair, smiling at Alison over his head. Then she rearranged the bag of oranges under her arm and walked on.

Wait for me, Alison wanted to say.

As the mother and child passed her, Zoe turned back to Alison. "You coming?" she called, annoyed.

Alison barely heard Zoe over the voice in her head.

I want a baby, it said. *I want a baby now*.

The next morning, Alison was toweling off after her shower. She glanced at herself in the blurry gilt-framed mirror and dropped the towel.

She cupped her breasts in her hands, wondering what they'd look like, feel like, swollen with milk.

With the palms of her hands, she traced the contours of her body: her blessing, her curse. She looked at herself sideways, imagining her belly nine months pregnant. What would it be like to feel a baby kick from inside her, to be the first home of a child?

"You want toast, babe?" Zoe shouted from the kitchen.

"Sure," Alison called back. She shrugged into her fuzzy chenille robe, knotted the belt around her narrow waist, and summoned her inner Scarlett O'Hara. *I'm only twenty-six*, she told herself. *I don't have to worry about this today*.

But on BART an hour later, she was too distracted to read the paper. All her life she'd dreamed of having children, of doing right what her mother had done so wrong. A sperm bank hadn't figured into her plans. But she hadn't imagined loving Zoe either, and now she did. She hadn't imagined herself a lesbian, and now, apparently, she was one.

Alison closed her eyes and saw herself heavily pregnant, ripe and bursting, filled with warmth and light. She'd look like a regular pregnant woman. No one would be able to tell that she hadn't had sex with her baby's father, that a doctor had inseminated her with a child who would be hers and Zoe's. Pregnant is pregnant. She'd be a real mother. A *good* mother—so much better than her own.

She winced, imagining what her mother would say: *A good mother gives her children a father. That's the best thing I gave you.*

Alison told herself that she wouldn't ask for her mother's advice if she were alive. Why should she take it when her mother was dead?

You always do what you want to do, even when it hurts other people—even when it hurts your child.

Just this once, her mother's voice was right. Life would be hard for a kid with two mothers and no father. It *would* be selfish for a mother to impose that on her child.

Alison imagined taking her baby to the pediatrician—with Zoe. She imagined going to parent teacher meetings at her child's school—with Zoe. She imagined her child's second-grade classmates making Father's Day cards while her kid made a card for Zoe. Walking down the aisle—with Zoe?

Having a baby with Zoe was irrevocable. Whatever happened between them after that, their son or daughter would be forever branded the child of lesbian moms. And whatever happened to Alison in the future, whatever turn her love took, whatever sexual label she adopted or shed, that child would forever be a vestige of her love for Zoe.

I want to have a baby the normal way. It was a certainty, more than a thought. *For once in my life, I want to do what other women do, the way they do it.*

The problem was, despite the distance that kept widening between them, Alison wanted Zoe too.

* * *

Without discussing it, they started working at having the kind of good times they used to have effortlessly, straining for a spark of the electric connection they used to feel.

They'd planned a walk in Tilden Park for the first Saturday in June. When the day dawned foggy, it seemed too risky to cancel. They locked the car near the trailhead, and Zoe pulled Alison into the playground next to the parking lot. Her seemingly light-hearted laughter sounded forced to Alison's ear.

The playground was empty except for a woman pushing a giggling blond toddler on a swing. "She's adorable," Zoe told the woman. "How old is she?"

"I'm free," the little girl piped up. Her mother stopped pushing and beamed at her daughter.

Zoe crouched in front of the girl. "Only three. And you can talk so well already. What's your name?"

"Molly." She looked at Zoe curiously. "What's yours?"

"I'm Zoe." She looked up, grinning her old ear-to-ear grin. "And this is Alison."

Alison smiled at Molly, trying to look at her without really seeing her, willing herself not to melt into the little girl's round brown eyes. Since that afternoon on Mission Street, Alison had been wrestling with her baby lust, beating it down one day, struggling to fit it into her life with Zoe the next. Wanting a baby would lead to harder stuff: breaking up with Zoe or committing to her forever. Alison hadn't been able to make either decision.

"Can Zoe push me, Mommy?" Molly asked.

"If she doesn't mind."

Zoe turned her thousand-watt smile on Molly's mom. "We love kids." She turned to Alison. "Don't we?"

Alison nodded and sank onto the swing next to Molly's. Zoe pushed the little girl from behind.

"Higher!" Molly demanded.

"I don't want to scare you," Zoe said in a sweet, lilting voice.

Alison scuffled her hiking boots in the dirt, watching her beautiful lover playing with beautiful Molly. Zoe's face was as open, as innocent, as radiant as the little girl's.

"You're flying!" Zoe trilled.

"Mommy, look!" Molly scissored her short, plump legs in the air.

Alison's chest felt full to bursting with love for Zoe. *She's my one*, Alison thought. *My person on earth. Who else could I ever love as much as I love Zoe? Who else could I raise a child with? Only Zoe.*

For six years Zoe's happiness had buoyed Alison, grounded her, shown her a better way to be. Zoe's confidence, her optimism, had given Alison a shot at her own. *We've hit a rough patch*, Alison told herself. *Every relationship goes through hard times.*

During their six years together, the world had changed, too— the Bay Area world, at least. It wasn't as strange or as difficult for lesbians to have kids. The little boy Alison had seen five years ago in the photo exhibit at Mama Bear's would be in kindergarten by now, and he might not be the only kid in his class with two moms. Private schools had started advertising themselves as "gay family friendly." The Berkeley public schools had instituted a "gay-affirmative curriculum." Berkeley High freshman were required to take a Social Living class that treated gay and straight sexuality as equally viable choices.

It was happening slowly, but it was happening. Being gay, and being the kid of gay parents, was becoming less stigmatized. Who knew what would be considered normal by the time a child of hers and Zoe's was making a Father's Day card in school, or graduating high school, or getting married? As long as Alison and Zoe raised their child in the Bay Area, would they really be imposing a hardship on him or her?

"Mommy!" Molly chirped. "Can Zoe come over to our house?"

"Maybe sometime," her mother said, exchanging a smile with Zoe.

No one knew better than Alison what a great mom Zoe would be. Until their trouble started, Zoe had been a great mom to her.

Just like that, Alison's yearning for a baby and her yearning to be happy with Zoe became one. All she had to do was say the biggest yes she'd ever said to Zoe. And saying yes to Zoe had always been the right thing to do.

9.

berkeley
August–September 1989

Alison and Zoe were perched on an earth-toned Herculon couch in the waiting room of the East Bay Sperm Bank. Alison was flipping through the current issue of *Newsweek*, surreptitiously checking out the two straight couples in the room.

One of the wives caught Alison's eye, her lipsticked mouth quivering into a small, self-conscious smile. Alison turned back to the cover story, "The Summer of '69 and How It Still Plagues Us in '89."

She glanced at Zoe in her lavender Michigan Womyn's Music Festival T-shirt, pin-striped men's vest, orange harem pants, and black Doc Martens boots with rainbow laces. She remembered when Zoe's clothes used to amaze and attract her. *Used to* had been Alison's operative phrase lately. But she couldn't let herself think that way. Not here. Not now.

She forced her attention back to her magazine. Would it ever stop irking her to see the word *president* in front of the words *George H. W. Bush?* Although for once, he seemed to be doing something halfway decent: banning imported assault rifles. *He must have a hidden agenda,* Alison thought. *An excuse to bust black people. A kickback from a gun company. Something.*

She came to a series of pictures of oil-drenched birds in Prince William Sound, Alaska. "Thank you, *Exxon Valdez*," she muttered.

Zoe peered at the pictures over Alison's shoulder. "Jesus," she said. "Eleven million gallons. Fucking oil corporations run the fucking *world*."

"Shhh!" Alison glanced around the room. Of course, everyone else in it was frowning at Zoe.

"It's a crappy world to bring a child into." Zoe took Alison's hand. "But I'm so glad we're doing this." Alison was always begging Zoe not to draw attention to them in public. But Zoe just went on living as if the world were already the way they wanted it to be.

"Zoe Fairbanks. Alison Rose?"

A cute twentysomething woman with short, stylish hair, white button-down shirt, and rolled-up jeans stood in the waiting room doorway. "Hi," she said, extending a hand to Zoe, then Alison. "I'm Sarah. You two ready to choose your baby's donor?"

"Totally," Zoe said. They followed Sarah down the hall and into a small conference room. Zoe whispered "dyke" into Alison's ear. Alison flushed, hoping Sarah hadn't heard.

The three of them sat around a conference table. Zoe handed over the folder full of health questionnaires, disclaimers, and consent forms they'd filled out after their intake appointment a few weeks earlier.

Sarah tapped the loose-leaf binder on the table. "Each of these men has given us multiple samples. We'll put several vials aside for you as soon as you make your choice. That way, if we need to do more than one round, or if you want your next child to have the same father, we'll have a reserve on hand."

"We won't need more than one round." Zoe gave Sarah her confident smile.

Sarah nodded noncommittally. "Take your time with the profiles. I'll check on you in a bit."

As the door closed behind her, Zoe laid her hand on top of Alison's and looked her in the eye.

"I want you to know how much this means to me," Zoe said. "How much *you* mean to me. I love you, babe."

"I love you too."

"Okay then." Zoe opened the binder. "Let's find us a man."

They studied the profiles, each sheathed in a plastic sheet protector. They'd agreed that they wanted their baby to look like both of them, which meant finding a donor who looked like Zoe, but without the crew cut and Doc Martens.

"Every one of these guys says his hobby is music," Alison observed. "Don't men like *fishing* anymore?"

"Babe, look!" Zoe said, pointing to the page in front of them, bouncing in her seat. "He's perfect!"

Alison read the description of number 1893. He had fair skin and blue eyes like Zoe's. He was tall, six foot one, and lean, 175 pounds, with wavy brown hair like Alison's.

He was a UC Berkeley sociology major with no family history of cancer, mental illness, or alcoholism. He described his personality as "balanced, patient, happy, good natured." His hobbies were "writing, meditation, tennis, basketball, and music." He'd checked the box that said "wishes to remain anonymous."

"Who ever heard of a happy, good-natured writer?" Alison stalled, waiting to be struck by the lightning bolt of certainty she thought she should feel.

"This guy's the one!" Zoe said.

Alison summoned the clarity she'd felt that day on Mission Street with that baby's finger in her mouth, the certainty she'd felt watching Zoe push Molly on the Tilden playground swing.

Zoe looked now the way she'd looked then: like an excited little girl about to blow out the candles on her birthday cake.

If I want a baby, which I do, Alison thought, *and if I want Zoe, which I do, this is how it's going to happen.*

"Number 1893, I think I love you," Alison said.

T hree weeks later Alison and Zoe were greeted at the East Bay Sperm Bank by a short-haired, stocky woman in a flowered smock, turquoise polyester pants, lavender socks, and purple Birkenstocks.

"I'm Naomi, your nurse practitioner. C'mon in."

She led them into a no-frills exam room and glanced down at the forms. "Alison. You're the one we'll be inseminating?"

"It'll be me for our next kid," Zoe said.

Naomi nodded. "Alison, hop onto the table while we talk. I see that you've chosen to start with intrauterine insemination."

"We don't want to waste any time," Zoe interjected.

"IUI *is* more effective," Naomi said. "I just need to make sure you understand that inserting the sperm into the uterus carries a slightly higher risk of infection and more discomfort."

"We know all that," Zoe said impatiently.

"Since Alison's the one who's being inseminated, I'd like to make sure it's okay with *her*," Naomi said.

Embarrassed, Alison nodded.

"You've been taking your temperature at the same time every morning?" Naomi asked Alison.

"Like clockwork," Zoe answered. "Her temperature was up to 99.6 this morning. That means she's ovulating, right?"

"We'll do an ovulation test before we inseminate, just to be sure."

Naomi looked from one of them to the other. "Any questions? Concerns?"

Am I doing the right thing, Alison wanted to ask Naomi. *For me? For my child? Will I regret that I didn't make a baby the way normal people do?*

"Let's get started," she said.

"You're going to feel some pressure here," Naomi said, as the cold metal speculum slid into Alison. Naomi snapped its jaws open and Alison's abdomen spasmed. Her feet tensed against the stirrups clothed in flowered oven mitts. Zoe stroked her forehead, looking concerned.

"Try to relax," Naomi said.

Alison stared at the water-stained, cottage-cheese ceiling, forcing herself to take deep breaths.

"I'm threading the catheter through your cervix now. You'll feel a pinch."

"Ouch!" Alison cried.

"Oh, sweetheart," Zoe groaned.

"Catheter's in. I'm ready to inseminate," Naomi said. She sat back on her metal stool. "You two say when."

Zoe brought her face close to Alison's. Alison saw the tide rising and falling in her blue eyes. She remembered the first time Zoe had carried her out to sea.

Alison felt she'd lived a lifetime since she'd fallen in love with Zoe. She'd been happy for most of that time. A baby would make her—*them*—happier still.

I think I'm ready, she thought. "I'm ready," she said.

Zoe and her hourly interrogations were a swarm of mosquitoes that Alison couldn't swat away. Zoe woke up every morning with questions on her lips: "Any morning sickness? Can I get you anything?" She called Alison at work every day. "You're not cramping, are you? Are your breasts sore?" She went to bed with her hands on Alison's breasts. "I swear they're bigger. They are!"

Alison was sure she wasn't pregnant. Still, on the tenth day after the insemination, when she was at her desk at work and her belly started cramping, her throat hurt too. She tried to ignore the familiar aching. She wrote a headline. She called a client to set up a lunch. She threw away the headline and wrote another. Finally the need to pee overtook her. She took a breath, gathering herself. She stood up. And then she knew.

She duckwalked to the PMC bathroom, closed herself into a stall, confirmed the news her body had delivered. She felt punched in the stomach. And she felt relieved.

"I got my period," Alison told Zoe at dinner that night. As if she'd flicked a switch, the light went out in Zoe's eyes.

"Are you sure it's not just spotting?" Zoe asked, her voice

pinched with desperation. "That happens in the first trimester sometimes."

Alison took Zoe's hand. "I'm sure."

Zoe got up, pulled Alison out of her chair, and held her tight. "Don't worry, sweetheart," she said. "We'll try again in two weeks."

N aomi spread lubricant on the speculum. "Scoot toward me, Alison," she said. Alison clutched the thin blue paper gown to her chest and shimmied her hips to the end of the table.

"I really thought we'd get it on the first try," Zoe said, her hand on Alison's shoulder. "Is there anything she should be eating? Some kind of exercise she could do? Yoga, maybe? Meditation?"

Alison felt the cold, hard wetness of the speculum enter her, feeling more like a lab rat than a mother-to-be. "We're starting fresh today," Naomi said. "So let's think positive, okay?"

She switched her head lamp on. "Take a deep breath, Alison, and let it out slowly."

The catheter poked at Alison's cervix. She felt her cervix fight to refuse it and lose.

"Keep taking deep breaths," Naomi said. "Almost done."

She pulled the catheter out. Alison winced. It hurt as much coming out as it did going in. "I'm going to have you keep your legs up for a while, hon," Naomi said. "Get gravity working for us." She lifted Alison's legs and leaned her feet against the wall. Then she patted Alison's shoulder and left the room.

"Sexy," Zoe said.

"Maybe from where you're sitting. From my end, this is about as far from sexy as it gets."

Zoe kissed Alison's inner thigh. "How 'bout a little girl-on-girl action to help that boy stuff do the job?"

Alison's sadness rushed up from where she'd stuffed it. She was supposed to be making love to make a baby, not lying on a sticky vinyl table with a stranger's sperm inside her and her legs in the air.

"What's wrong, babe?" Zoe asked. "Not in the mood?"

She's oblivious, Alison thought. "Gosh," she said, "I can't imagine why I wouldn't be."

Alison was in a meeting at work two weeks later when she felt the bleeding start. This time she didn't feel relief or sorrow. She didn't feel a thing.

She excused herself from the meeting, went to the bathroom, and cleaned herself up. She washed her hands, looking at herself in the mirror over the sink, and saw her mother's scowling face. *There's a right way to do things*, she was saying, *and the wrong way never works.*

Alison dried her hands and turned her back on the mirror, afraid that her mother was right.

The third insemination didn't take either. Alison wondered if her ambivalence could have taken root where the baby should be, the symbiotic twin of her grief.

"Maybe there's something wrong with me." She and Zoe were lying in bed the night she got her period again—not entwined and naked the way they used to be, but inches apart, not touching, in the pajamas they never used to wear.

"There's nothing wrong with you." Zoe turned onto her side. "My perfect girl," she said tenderly.

The clouds parted. For the first time in months, Alison felt

Zoe's uncomplicated, unconditional love. "Then why isn't it working?" Alison started to cry.

Zoe gathered her up, whispering, "Baby, my baby" in her ear. Alison had almost forgotten how good it felt, letting Zoe in. It felt so good to stop fighting—with Zoe, with herself, with her mother's ghost.

"It hurts," Alison said, meaning the inseminations. Meaning their fighting. Meaning her uncertainty. Meaning her heart.

Zoe's body went rigid. "I can't stand to see you go through all that pain for nothing. The clinic must be doing something wrong." She kicked the covers off and jumped out of bed. "We need to meet with Naomi. I'm gonna go leave her a message."

"Wait," Alison said. "Please. Can you just be with me right now?"

But Zoe was already in the living room, talking angrily into the phone.

10.

"So, ladies. What's the emergency?" Alison and Zoe were sitting shoulder-to-shoulder on the examining table; Naomi sat on a metal stool, looking up at them.

"Alison got her period," Zoe said. "Again."

Naomi frowned. "That's the emergency? I told you, this process takes patience. IUI can take a year or more."

Alison was mortified. Why had she let Zoe drag her into this meeting?

"But you said we had everything going for us," Zoe said. "And it's been three months. Aren't there some tests you can run? Is there some other procedure we can try? I don't care what it costs."

"I know it's hard to be patient," Naomi said, "but it's much too early for more tests."

"The thing is," Zoe said quietly, leaning toward Naomi, "Alison and I, we're special. *Magic.* Our whole relationship has been about crazy dreams coming true. So this just *has* to happen for us."

Alison wondered whether Naomi heard the desperation in Zoe's voice. And whether Zoe heard it in her own.

Naomi flipped through the pages in their file. "I see that you dated men in the past," she said to Alison. "What kind of birth control did you use?"

"A diaphragm." Alison flushed. "Most of the time."

"Any pregnancies?"

"No."

"Why do you ask?" Zoe asked.

"Just looking for indicators of fertility. Nothing conclusive there." She glanced at her watch. "Sorry, ladies. I'm late for my next patient."

She tucked their chart under her arm and stood up to go. "If this is getting too stressful, you could always take a few months off. You're young. You have plenty of time."

As soon as the door closed, Zoe said, "We should try another sperm bank. I don't like her attitude."

Fighting annoyance, Alison reminded herself that Zoe's determination was one of the things Alison loved about her. She reminded herself that there would *be* no Alison and Zoe if Zoe were any other way. She told herself how lucky she was that Zoe wanted a baby with her. How many women would kill for a partner like that?

"Good idea," Alison said as lightly as she could. "We'll just move to LA, where the nearest sperm bank is."

"There's one in Oakland, remember?"

"It only serves *married couples*, remember?"

They emerged from the clinic into a typical September Berkeley morning: cloudless blue sky, no breeze, ninety degrees.

As they walked to Shattuck, Alison counted four panhandlers squatting on the sidewalk. One was a punked-out teenage girl on a blanket with a puppy in her lap and a scribbled sign that said WILL PANHANDLE FOR KIBBLE.

Zoe dropped a quarter onto the girl's blanket. "Normally I only support panhandling for cat food," she said. "But I'll make an exception for you."

Is there anyone she won't flirt with, Alison wondered.

"Come back tomorrow." The girl smiled, black lipstick against white teeth. "I might have a kitten by then."

They walked on past a construction site where Hink's Department Store, Berkeley's oldest family-run business, was being converted to a ten-screen movie theater. "Who needs ten theaters?" Zoe shouted over the jack hammering. "Hollywood doesn't make enough good movies for one."

They crossed Shattuck to avoid the noise. "I like Naomi's idea," Alison said. She paused in the doorway of the EZ Stop deli. "I want to take a break from inseminating."

"We *are* taking a break." Zoe stopped walking, too. "We don't get to try again for two weeks."

Alison sighed. "Trying to get pregnant is taking over my life. I can barely concentrate on anything else. It took me a year to get my first assignment from *Mother Jones,* and it's due in a month. I need more than two weeks off."

"God, Al. You make it sound like it's a job," Zoe said. "A job you *hate.*"

A small herd of Berkeley High girls with tiny tank tops and large breasts pushed past them into the deli. Alison and Zoe started walking again, silently, separately. In front of the Other Change of Hobbit bookstore, five or six scraggly old white guys walked in a circle with Industrial Workers of the World signs, chanting, "Union, yes! Scab labor, no!" Alison squeezed past their left side; Zoe went around them on the right.

As they passed Edy's Soda Shop, Alison looked into the plateglass window and saw a woman feeding oatmeal to a toddler in a high chair. Alison imagined herself smiling at her baby over breakfast. She saw Zoe laughing, spooning oatmeal into their baby's rose-petal mouth.

Alison thought back to a few nights before, the first time in months she'd cried in Zoe's arms, how safe Zoe had made her feel.

Zoe's eyes were facing straight ahead as she stomped down the street, a soldier on a death march.

Alison caught up. "I love you, Zoe. I do want to have a baby with you. It's just that this is so hard. In so many ways."

She waited for Zoe to melt, take Alison in her arms, say she was sorry. Sweat darkened the fringe of Zoe's short platinum bangs, but her face was cold. Alison had to speed-walk to keep up with her, the way she used to run after her mother, trying not to lose her on crowded Manhattan streets.

Zoe ducked into the doorway of Huston's Shoes. "You've never wanted to have a baby with a woman," she spat at Alison. "You're looking for a way out."

She's right, Alison thought. "That's not true," she said. "If it was *your* body going through this, you'd understand."

A scene from her childhood flashed through Alison's head. A few weeks after her father's funeral, she and her mother were in the elevator in their building with the two women who shared the apartment right below theirs. Alison smiled at the women. Her mother stared straight ahead.

"Dried-up old spinsters," her mother sneered when the women got out.

"What's a spinster?" Alison asked.

"A woman who isn't married."

"You're a woman who isn't married. What's so bad about that?"

Her mother yanked Alison by the arm, pulling her into the hallway, her mouth stretched into a thin, angry line. "I lost my husband. I'm not a bull dyke like them."

"Now *there's* a thought." Zoe's angry voice brought Alison back. "You're the one who insisted on carrying our first kid. But since you *need a break,* maybe I should go first."

"That's so unfair. I can't believe you're doing this." Alison was fighting tears.

"Doing what? Trying to have a baby with you?"

"Bullying me. Manipulating me. You're acting like a *man.*"

"Well, you're acting like a homophobe." Zoe's face was red. "You wouldn't say that if I were straight."

"If you were straight, we wouldn't be having this problem."

A bearded, scabby-faced homeless man stumbled into the doorway.

"Spare change?" he mumbled. Zoe scrounged in the pocket of her plaid Bermuda shorts, dug out a dime, and handed it to him.

The man held the coin up to his face, shook his head, and handed it back. "Got anything bigger?" he asked. "I'm trying to get an iced mocha at Peet's."

Zoe pulled out her wallet and handed the man a dollar bill. Without a word, he stumbled away.

"No way," Alison said. "Did that homeless guy just say—"

"You gotta love Berkeley," Zoe said. And then her furious face collapsed and she was laughing. Alison started laughing and couldn't stop. They stood in the shoe store doorway, laughing harder and harder, dizzied by heat and hysterics, holding onto each other to keep themselves upright.

"I'm going to pee in my pants," Zoe gasped.

Alison laughed until she cried.

They did what people do when they're in love and they're having trouble and they want to stay together and it's not as easy as it used to be. They lowered the volume on their righteous indignation. Swallowed the small stuff. Spent stupid money wooing each other with extravagant restaurant meals, exotic bouquets. Raised the volume on fun and sex and compromise.

Softened by Zoe's renewed attention, scared by her own warring emotions, Alison agreed to be inseminated in October. Zoe agreed that if their fourth effort didn't take, they'd take a one-month break before the fifth.

"It worked this time. I just know it," Zoe said as they left the clinic on a hot October afternoon. She threw her arm around Alison and steered her toward Shattuck. "C'mon, little mama. Let's celebrate. I'll buy you a shot of wheat grass juice."

Zoe had been running their fourth conception effort like a military campaign. She scoured the shelves of Berkeley's abundant bookstores, bringing home treatises on natural infertility treatments from Cody's, philosophical texts on the meaning of motherhood from Moe's, legal self-help workbooks for same-sex parents from Nolo Press, Chinese medicine guides from Revolution Books. She'd bought a wooden African fertility goddess at Gaia and glassine bags of herbs at Lhasa Karnak. She'd been force-feeding Alison nightly eyedroppers full of evening primrose oil, along with nauseating quantities of yams, spinach, and tofu, and herbs that she brewed into putrid-smelling teas.

Alison gazed longingly across the street at Berkeley's newest gelato shop, the Daily Scoop. "I could have a wheat grass gelato instead."

"Al . . . " Zoe tightened her grip on Alison's shoulder.

"Pretty please? With evening primrose sprinkles on top?"

"We'll never get pregnant if I let you have your way."

Zoe smiled at Alison teasingly. In the next instant her face became a mask of terror.

At the same instant Alison felt the sidewalk rippling beneath her feet. *How can the sidewalk move?* She heard, no, *felt* a thunderous boom, as if a plane had exploded in the sky. She looked up and saw the fifteen-story Wells Fargo building swaying like a conductor leading an orchestra, bowing to the left, then the right. *How can a building move?*

She heard glass breaking, car alarms shrieking, bricks shattering on impact with the street.

"Earthquake!" someone shouted. Time froze. People froze. Cars froze in place.

The ground kept shaking. People cried out, clutching at each other. Alison clutched at Zoe.

"We gotta get out of here," Zoe shouted. Her face was pale. Her eyes were wild with fear. "Al! Get me out of here *now.*"

Sirens wailed. Zoe's fingers dug into Alison's arms. The shaking stopped. The sudden stillness was shocking. Slowly, the scene came back to life. Cars inched through intersections. Sirens wailed. Alison pulled Zoe toward Reid's Home Appliances, where a crowd was gathering, watching the TVs behind the cracked plateglass window.

The same image appeared on each of the screens. The Bay Bridge, broken in half, its top span collapsed onto the bottom.

"Breaking News," the caption read. "Big Earthquake Hits Northern California."

"Oh, God," an elderly woman next to Alison shrieked.

The image switched to the scene at Candlestick Park. People with green and yellow Oakland A's hats and black and orange San Francisco Giants hats were scrambling, falling, stepping over each other, emptying the stands. For the first time ever, the Giants were playing the A's in the World Series. "My son's at the game. My son's at the game," a black man moaned.

Lines formed at phone booths on the corners. A fire truck sped south on Shattuck, horn blaring, cars creeping out of its path. A plume of smoke rose from a building just south of downtown. Alison turned and saw Zoe sitting on the curb, slumped over, her Doc Martens in the gutter, her head in her hands.

Alison crouched in front of her. She put her hands on Zoe's cheeks. Zoe's skin was pale and clammy, glossy with sweat. "I'm—" Zoe said. A helicopter clattered noisily over their heads.

"I'm scared." Zoe fell against Alison, her body quaking. "Everything's b-b-broken," she stammered.

Over Zoe's shoulder, Alison saw men in suits and women in dresses running out of the Wells Fargo building, horror on their faces. *How could the building still be there?* Alison wondered. Moments ago, she'd seen it lurching like a drunk.

A teenager walked by, the boom box on his shoulder blasting the news: "The Cypress overpass in Oakland has collapsed. As many as one hundred motorists are feared dead. The Marina District of San Francisco is in flames . . . " The voice faded as the boy walked on.

Zoe lifted her ruined face to Alison. Suddenly, the shaking started again. The window of the photo shop across the street shattered. Zoe cried out as if she'd been shot.

"Just an aftershock," a man standing above them said.

Alison looked up at him. *I miss you, Daddy.* It was more an ache than a thought.

"Better get used to it," the man added. "There's going to be a lot of those over the next weeks. Months."

Scenes from the past months flashed through Alison's head. Fighting with Zoe. Feeling unsure of Zoe. Feeling unsure of herself with Zoe.

Alison pulled Zoe close. "It's going to be okay," she murmured. "We're going to be okay."

I wanted everything to change, Alison thought. *And now everything will.*

11.

B erkeley's leafy streets were obstacle courses of fallen chimneys, crushed cars, uprooted sidewalks. Gingerbread bric-a-brac dangled from restored Victorians. Chicken wire poked through cracked stucco walls. Craftsman cottages leaned askew on brick foundations. The stately main branch of the Berkeley library, the banks, the shops, the restaurants were shuttered in plywood. Helicopters rat-tat-tatted overhead.

Their world shrank. The Bay Bridge was closed indefinitely. Getting to San Francisco—to Alison's job, to Zoe's gallery— meant taking BART through the tunnel beneath the bay. With fifty aftershocks up to magnitude 6.0 each day, no one wanted to be underneath anything. Alison and Zoe stayed home and read newspapers, listened to the radio, watched TV.

There was nothing on TV, on the radio, in the newspapers, in conversations at the grocery store, about anything else. On TV, disaster tape loops played again and again. A shuddering Candlestick Park shaking sixty-two thousand World Series fans out of their seats. Apartment buildings crushed and burning in San Francisco. Downtown Santa Cruz a pile of rubble. The upper span of the Bay Bridge snapping, tossing cars onto the shattered road below.

And the Cypress overpass. The Cypress overpass, crumpled and pancaked, crawling with engineers, construction workers, and neighborhood volunteers desperately combing through rubble while bodies decomposed in cars crushed like Matchbox toys in the simmering October heat. The Cypress overpass, which once filled the view from the windows of Zoe's West Oakland studio and now was a horror show.

Alison was shaken, of course. It was bad for everyone. But Zoe took the Loma Prieta earthquake personally. She lost her appetite. She couldn't sleep. Or laugh, or concentrate, or paint. She didn't even ask Alison about her pregnancy symptoms, real or imagined. All she did was read about the earthquake in the newspapers and watch earthquake coverage on TV. She sat on the couch with her legs folded under her, back rigid, knuckles white on her knees. She seemed to believe that the tension in her body was holding the world together, that if she moved or even breathed, it would come apart again.

Her only surviving hunger was for sex, and it was voracious. In bed at night, she grabbed at Alison with an aggressiveness that disturbed Alison more than it turned her on.

Zoe's mood improved briefly when a seismologist appeared on TV to support "the theory of small earthquakes," the popular belief that each earthquake released pressure on the fault line, reducing the chance of a bigger one. But then she plunged into despair again when the *San Francisco Chronicle* reported a 63 percent chance of a magnitude 8.0 earthquake in the Bay Area within the next thirty years.

Alison did what she could for Zoe, yielding to her hungry hands at bedtime, reading to her when she woke up thrashing in the night, cooking her favorite foods to tempt her to eat.

Painting would save her, Alison thought, but Zoe wasn't about to go back to her studio while rescue crews were still pulling bodies from the concrete graveyard across the street. So Alison snuck into Zoe's abandoned backyard studio and made it inviting again, propping a fresh canvas on the easel, tossing out dried-up tubes of paint, setting out new ones.

"Come with me, babe," she said, reaching out a hand to Zoe, who was lying on the couch. "I have a surprise for you." Zoe didn't seem to want any more surprises. She just curled herself into a tighter ball.

A few weeks and a lifetime before, Alison had been given her first assignment for *Mother Jones.*

When the contract came back to her in the mail, it included an invitation to an office warming party at *MJ*'s new digs on the edge of the Mission District, San Francisco's hottest up-and-coming neighborhood. The envelope was addressed to "Alison Rose and Guest." On the back her editor had scribbled, "Would be great to meet you. Best, Mark Miller."

Alison's first impulse was to run to Zoe, share her excitement, and start planning what they'd wear. But that was the old Zoe and Alison. Did she really want to show off her lesbian relationship in its current shaky state? Did she really want to take the chance that Zoe would embarrass her at the party, kissing her in front of everyone or hitting up the art director for an illustration gig?

No, she did not. Although Alison suspected that being gay might actually elevate her status at *MJ*, she hadn't yet turned in her first draft. She'd never met her editor. If she ever came out to Mark Miller, it certainly wouldn't be until their working relationship was established. So when Alison told Zoe about the invitation, she said it was for one.

Alison felt guilty for lying and for wanting to go to the party alone. She felt guiltier still about abandoning Zoe and edgy about taking BART just days after the quake. But she needed a night off from her own anxieties and from trying to soothe Zoe's. She needed to know that there was life beyond her struggles with Zoe and the nightmare she'd been living since well before October 17.

A lison walked into the living room to kiss Zoe goodbye. Zoe was lying on the couch, as usual.

"I'll be back in a few hours," Alison said.

Alison watched emotions blow across Zoe's face. She was sure Zoe was about to ask her not to go. Had she not done enough for Zoe since the earthquake? Didn't her own feelings count at *all*?

"Please don't make a big deal out of this," Alison said. "I'm a little nervous about it myself."

Zoe's face calmed. "Let me look at you." She got up, put her hands on Alison's shoulders, and turned her slowly, the way she used to do whenever Alison had somewhere special to go. She tucked an errant Banana Republic label into Alison's collar, smoothed Alison's khaki jumpsuit over her hips.

"There's mushroom barley soup in the fridge," Alison said.

Zoe nodded. "I'll be fine. But don't forget you might have a baby on board. No alcohol. No caffeine."

"Yes, boss." Once again, Alison was sure she wasn't pregnant. But she wasn't about to say that to Zoe now.

Zoe sank to her knees and pressed her ear to Alison's belly. "Hello? Anyone home?"

"The party starts at six, babe. I gotta go."

"I swear you're getting bigger." Zoe put Alison's hands on her own abdomen. "It worked this time. I know it did."

"We just inseminated five days ago," Alison said as gently as she could. "It's too soon to feel anything."

Zoe stood and pulled Alison close. She ran her hand between Alison's legs.

"Not now," Alison protested. But Zoe's fingers were moving, moving. She unbuttoned Alison's jumpsuit, slid her hand inside. Alison's body responded to Zoe the way it always did, her breasts tingling, her hips pressing against Zoe's hand, her legs shaking, her whole self wanting more, more, more.

"I can't do this now," Alison croaked. It seemed cruel to deny Zoe the one pleasure she still craved, the one pleasure they still shared. But Alison had a party to go to. And her career was more important to her than ever.

She buttoned her jumpsuit. Her underwear was wet. She didn't have time to change.

"Eat that soup," she said.

"Yes, Mom." Zoe closed the top two buttons of Alison's jumpsuit. "Have a good time," she said forlornly. For a moment, Alison considered staying home.

"I won't be late," she said.

"I love you, Al."

"I love you too."

* * *

The BART train was thundering toward the Nineteenth Street station when it bucked, then slammed to a stop. A gasp erupted from the passengers. The woman next to Alison grabbed her hand.

"Was that an earthquake?" The woman's face was pale beneath her makeup. The diamond ring on her finger bit into Alison's palm.

"I don't think so." The train lurched, then started moving again. "It's okay," Alison said, extricating her hand.

The woman looked embarrassed. "Sorry." She tucked strands of streaked blond hair behind her ear.

"It's okay. We're all a little nervous these days."

"You're so comforting. Thanks for being so nice."

Comforting? Alison thought. *Nice? That's not me. That's Zoe.*

And then she thought: *Not anymore.* Lately Zoe's love had been making Alison feel smothered, not safe. Possessed, not held.

If I were a good person, Alison thought, *I'd tell her how I feel. But I just can't do that to Zoe. Not now.*

Alison's hands fluttered to her flat, empty belly. *I'll get my period in a week or two,* she thought. *I shouldn't make any decisions till then. Maybe when the aftershocks stop and Zoe calms down, I'll fall in love with her again.*

Or not. Alison was flooded with sudden anger, remembering those last minutes before she left home. Why had Zoe grabbed her when it was time for her to go? Was she trying to keep Alison from going to the party?

Maybe I am *pregnant and that's why I'm in such a pissy mood.* Alison glanced down at her breasts. They didn't look a bit bigger.

Zoe was wrong. Again. The thought blew through Alison like a cold wind. Before they'd started inseminating, before the earthquake, Zoe had been right about everything—everything important, at least. Now, instead of grounding Alison, Zoe had become a wishful thinker. Now Zoe was afraid to leave the house, afraid to be in the house, afraid to go anywhere or do anything—and Alison was the brave one, taking BART beneath the bay.

Maybe the insemination isn't working, Alison thought, *because Zoe and I aren't good for each other anymore.*

The train emerged from the tunnel and screeched to a stop at the above-ground West Oakland station. The sun was setting, the platform lit by the day's last shards of light. A group of teenagers jostled each other onto the train, laughing and flirting, the girls giggling, the boys grinning, circling their arms around the girls' waists.

A tall white guy holding a pole above Alison's head stumbled. His backpack brushed her shoulder. "Sorry," he said, looking down at her.

"It's okay," Alison said. The guy was cute. He looked like a bike messenger, scruffy and young. He shrugged out of his backpack, dropped it at Alison's feet. "I'm Johnny," he said.

I'm not doing this, Alison thought. "I'm married," she said.

"Nice to meet you, Married," Johnny said. He picked up his backpack and moved away.

No good man would want you once he got to know you, she heard her mother's voice saying. *You're damaged goods now.*

She imagined telling her mother that she and Zoe were having a baby. And shuddered at the thought.

M arket Street reverberated with the booming sounds of demolition. Construction crews were everywhere. Cranes dangled over the Ferry Building. Wrecking balls tore holes in the Embarcadero Freeway. Excavators swallowed the debris in huge bites. Men in orange jumpsuits, construction helmets, and yellow earmuffs jackhammered the fractured sidewalks. The jaws of garbage trucks chomped chunks of cement.

A young man approached Alison as she waited for the light to change. "Weed, crack, H," he muttered. "Spare change," begged a woman who stank of urine.

Some things haven't changed, she thought, stepping over two people sleeping in the doorway of the nondescript five-story office building that matched the address on the invitation in her hand. She checked her reflection in the murky brass elevator doors, adjusted the shoulder pads of her brown linen blazer. She opened the top two buttons of her jumpsuit, the ones Zoe had buttoned up. She unbuttoned a third.

The elevator deposited Alison into a crowded office suite roaring with conversation. A young woman in a red and black *Mother Jones* T-shirt offered her a plastic tumbler of wine. Alison hadn't had a sip of alcohol since her first insemination. She took a cup off the tray.

Taking a long swallow, she looked around the room. She saw the shockingly handsome *Mother Jones* editor in chief, rumored to be a ladies' man, talking to his brother, a well-known filmmaker whose work appeared on PBS.

In the middle of the animated crowd she saw *MJ*'s founding editor, who kept the magazine afloat with the fortune he'd inherited. Was that dapper man in the white hat, white suit, and white shoes really the famous author she thought he was?

I don't belong here, Alison thought. Even the nobodies looked like somebodies. These people were the chosen few, San Francisco's literati: real writers, filmmakers, and editors, not imposters like her.

The wine-serving woman offered Alison another glass. She drank it quickly. And noticed that a man was watching her from across the room.

A handsome man. A tall, blond, sexy, Jewish-looking man with a strong jaw, an angular face, and a hooked nose. His lips were full and shiny, as if he'd been kissing someone all night.

His mouth curved into a smile. He walked toward her with an urgent tilt to his body. His eyes were almost as blue as Zoe's.

"Mark Miller." He extended his hand.

"You're Mark! I'm Alison Rose."

"I was hoping that was you." Mark let go of her hand, reluctantly it seemed.

They faced each other in awkward silence. "It's weird working with writers over the phone," Mark said finally. "I've done a dozen stories with one freelancer who lives in Seattle. We talk every week, but I've never seen his face." He ran a hand through his tangle of blond curls. "I'm glad to have the pleasure of seeing yours."

"I'm hoping you also had the pleasure of reading my first draft," she said.

"Ouch." Mark grinned at her. "I know I'm late with your revisions."

"So . . . we're talking about fixing the piece, not killing it?" Alison laughed nervously. "If I sound totally insecure, it's only because I am."

"No reason to be. Your draft is very good."

"Really?" Alison's body slumped with relief. Or was that the wine? Or was it a different feeling entirely?

"We're always swamped around here. But with the office moving this week and all . . . " Mark shrugged.

A man with a shaved head, trim moustache, and *Mother Jones* T-shirt squeezed past them. "Hey, Leo," Mark said. "Meet Alison, my newest writer. Alison, Leo's a senior editor here."

"You wrote the piece on the Menendez brothers," Leo said. "I read your draft. Very powerful."

"That's great to hear." Alison was starting to feel a bit less like a loser.

"Your writer's glass is empty. Why don't you buy her a drink?" Leo said to Mark. "Nice to meet you," he said to Alison, and he went off to talk to someone else.

"I've been remiss." Mark cupped Alison's elbow in his hand and walked her to the makeshift bar across the room.

Alison meant to say that she'd had enough. But then she was nodding and taking a gulp of the wine Mark had handed her. He stood close to her, his shoulder touching hers. Alison felt dizzy. And exhausted. She needed to lie down.

She felt a wave of nausea. *Oh God,* she thought, *what if I am pregnant?*

She leaned past Mark and put her wine glass down on the bar. Mark put his hand on her arm. His touch burned her skin.

"You okay?" he asked.

"I'm getting over the flu," she lied. "I'm a little out of it."

"Want to take a walk around the block? Get some air? It's a nice night for once."

Alison nodded woozily. Mark put his wine down. Alison noticed he wasn't wearing a wedding ring. They walked out of the office without saying goodbye to anyone. They rode the elevator to the lobby in tense, charged silence.

And then they were walking through the Mission in the warm darkness and they were talking. Talking and talking about the magazine business and whether the Menendez brothers would get life or be executed for killing their parents, and whether it was better to live in the East Bay or in San Francisco, where Mark lived, and why *Mother Jones* had moved, and how the Mission District was changing, and where the Latinos were going when their landlords raised their rent and yuppies moved in. Their conversation was a little vacation for Alison: they never even mentioned the earthquake.

"I could use an adult beverage," Mark said as they climbed Noe Street, bent against the steep hill. "I live two blocks from here. And I pour a mean chardonnay."

Alison reached for the thought of Zoe, almost grasped it. Did it slip beyond her reach? Or did she push it away?

"Sounds good," Alison said. *What are you doing?* she asked herself.

Mark put his arm around her.

Alison didn't say, *I'm a lesbian.*

She didn't say, *I have a girlfriend.*

She didn't say, *My girlfriend thinks I'm pregnant and she might be right.*

She said, "I can't spend the night."

12.

They stumbled onto the stoop of his Victorian and they kissed. *Not Zoe's lips.* She felt him hard against her thigh. *A man.* His tongue in her mouth, his hands on her back, on her ass. His face was sandpaper not velvet. *Don't think about Zoe.*

"Come inside with me." Mark's voice was as rough as his face. He wasn't gentle like Zoe. He didn't want. He needed. *Don't think about Zoe.*

He fumbled with the front door and pulled her to his bed. He didn't ask. He took her. He wasn't like Zoe. Her hands were everywhere on him, and nothing felt like anything she knew. His hard ass not Zoe's soft ass. His arms, the hair on his arms, his shoulders, the hair on his back. His hands were everywhere on her.

He was in her. It felt good, so good. It hurt. It hurt and she wanted more. "Oh God," she gasped. He asked if he was hurting her. She covered his mouth with hers. She didn't want to hear him. She didn't remember men.

Breathing hard, he moved his mouth down her body. "Let me make you come," he whispered. "No," she said. *That's for Zoe.* She pulled his head back to hers. His noise wasn't Zoe's rolling gentle moaning. It was hard, his thrusting, and she liked it. He huffed and he grunted and he came.

He rolled onto his back and pulled her to him. They were one big wet blob of sweat. He put his hand between her legs. She pushed it away. She glanced at the clock on the nightstand. The numbers were glowing red. 11:20. *I told Zoe I'd be home early.* She'd take a cab. Fifty bucks, but if she hurried she could be home by midnight. Midnight wasn't so bad.

Wait. The bridge was closed. BART was the only way home, and the trains stopped running at midnight.

"I've got to get to BART." Alison jumped up and started collecting her jacket, jumpsuit, bra, panties, socks, and shoes from around the room.

Mark rolled out of bed and pulled on his Levi's. "I'll drive you home."

Alison shook her head. "The bridge . . . "

"Oh, Jesus. Right." He tugged a T-shirt over his muscled shoulders. "Let me walk you to the station, at least."

Alison brushed her lips across his forehead. "I'll be fine," she said, and she left.

S tanding at the front door of the cottage in the dark, her guilty heart hammering, Alison prayed that she'd find Zoe asleep.

She crept down the hall to the bedroom. Zoe was splayed across their bed, snoring softly. Alison stifled a sigh of relief. She desperately wanted a shower, but she couldn't risk waking Zoe. So she scrubbed herself at the kitchen sink with a loofah in one hand and a mirror in the other, examining her body for evidence. Blessedly, she found none. She put on the pajamas she'd taken to wearing lately and slipped into bed.

"How was it?" Zoe murmured. She fell back to sleep before Alison had time to compose her first lie.

S omeone was making love to Alison. Not Zoe. A man. A man was making love to Alison and it was good. So good.

"Babe."

Not making love to her. Shaking her. "You're having a bad dream." Zoe's voice was furry with sleep. "You were moaning. Are you okay?"

"Fine," Alison said. *Did I say his name?* she wondered. She rolled to her side of the bed, where she'd been sleeping since she and Zoe had stopped spooning through the night. She lay there coiled with tension, waited for Zoe to fall asleep.

Alison was drenched in sweat and lust and remorse. She opened her eyes, then closed them again. *If I keep sleeping, maybe it won't have happened.* But there was no waking up from this nightmare. No undoing what she'd done.

"D id you have fun at the party?" Zoe asked again the next morning. They were out together for the first time since the earthquake, having brunch at their old hangout, the Brick Hut Café.

"Yup." Alison salted her tofu scramble, walking a tightrope, the thin line of truth.

Zoe looked at her, waiting for more. "How's your omelet?" Alison asked.

"Not as good as they were before."

During their first Berkeley years, the lesbian-collective-owned Brick Hut was the second-best part of Alison and Zoe's Saturday routine. They'd make love all morning, then drive across town, drunk on hunger and orgasms, and slide into a booth just before the closed sign was hung on the door. They'd sit staring starry-eyed at each other, sipping the Hut's muddy coffee, reeking of sex, surrounded by lesbian couples doing exactly the same thing.

Today they'd arrived at the Hut before nine. Today there were no smitten gazes. Alison fidgeted with the salsa jar, the jam pot, the cream pitcher, dreading Zoe's questions, avoiding Zoe's eyes.

"You got in so late," Zoe said. "You know how nervous I get these days." She laughed self-consciously. "I had a hard time falling asleep."

"Sorry. I couldn't find a pay phone." *Lie number one.*

Zoe shrugged. "You're my girlfriend, not my babysitter. It's not your fault I've been so insane."

How could I not be Zoe's girlfriend? That's who I am. "I don't like to worry you," Alison said.

Zoe spooned strawberry jam onto her croissant. "You didn't drink, did you?"

"Of course not." *Lie number two.*

Alison looked around at the lesbians snuggling at the tables for two, the groups of lesbians laughing in the booths. *I won't be welcome here anymore,* she thought. Bile bit the back of her throat.

"Be right back," she said, sliding out of the booth.

Zoe brightened. "You're peeing more than usual. That's a great sign."

Alison stared at herself in the soap-splattered bathroom mirror, seeing the person she'd been the day before, the person she'd been for the past six years. That person would have teased Zoe, or kissed Zoe, told her to get off her case. But today's Alison was filled with a strange and distant tenderness for Zoe—as if she'd already taken a few steps back and could see the wonderful things about Zoe that she'd miss.

Zoe had her Big Decision face on when Alison came back to the table. "I'm thinking I'll go back to my studio tomorrow," Zoe said, "and see if I can work."

"That's great, babe." *The sooner she gets better,* Alison thought, *the sooner I can go.* And then she remembered the pictures in the paper that morning, the view from Zoe's studio windows: the crumpled Cypress overpass, now a shrine of votive candles and plastic-wrapped photographs and supermarket bouquets. "You sure you're ready for that?"

"Sitting around counting aftershocks isn't helping. And believe it or not, I have an idea for a new series."

For Zoe's sake, for her own, not necessarily in that order, Alison was glad to see a glimmer of the old sparkle in Zoe's eyes. And imagining Zoe as she used to be made Alison's chest ache. Was she about to make the worst mistake of her life? Had she already made it?

Nothing's been decided, Alison told herself. All she'd done was fuck a guy for one night. If she still wanted her beautiful life with Zoe, she could have it. Zoe wouldn't ever need to know. "Promise me you'll go home if you don't feel good at your studio," Alison said. "And promise me you won't look out the windows on the Cypress side."

"I promise," Zoe said.

You're like any other sleazy, cheating, lying husband, Alison heard her mother saying. Or was that her own voice in her head?

On Monday morning, Alison was settling in at her desk at PMC when the phone rang. "How are you, Alison?" Mark asked in a low, intimate voice that made her insides roil. "I wanted to call you this weekend. Then I realized I only have your number at work."

Alison wished she could give Mark her home number. She wished it was a year earlier and that she and Zoe were still happy forever.

"Friday night . . . that was amazing," Mark said.

Alison felt Mark waiting for her to agree, but she couldn't speak.

"I guess we're going to do this backward," he said finally. "First we have wild, passionate sex. Then I call to ask you out on a date."

"Actually," Alison said, "first we had an editor–writer relationship. I don't think we can have both, do you?"

"You wouldn't be the first writer in history to date her editor."

Silence hummed between them.

"Is there something you're not telling me?"

Alison took a breath. "I'm at the end of a long relationship," she said slowly. "I should have told you."

This time Mark was silent. "Yeah," he said. "You should have."

"I'm really sorry."

"Sorry we slept together? Or sorry your relationship's ending?"

"Both," Alison said. "Neither. I'm not sure."

"Then there's hope."

"You're persistent."

"I'm turning thirty next year, Alison. I've dated a lot of women.

What happened between you and me the other night was . . . different. Big. It felt like something important could come of it. So I'm not giving up."

Suddenly Alison's desk shuddered. The picture of her and Zoe on Haight Street on their fifth anniversary toppled off the shelf. Someone yelled, "Everyone under your desks!"

Alison dove onto the floor, squeezing herself into the small space.

"It's just a little aftershock," Mark said. Alison was surprised to find the receiver still at her ear. "It's over," he said. "You okay?"

"Scared," Alison admitted. She realized she'd been so focused on Zoe's earthquake fears that she hadn't paid any attention to her own. She crawled out from under her desk and sank into her chair.

"I just assigned a piece on the politics of seismology," Mark said. "The odds of another big quake right now are actually lower than they were before Loma Prieta."

His voice, his certainty calmed her, made her eyelids heavy. But Alison had been in this movie before, and it didn't have a happy ending. "That's the difference between writers and editors," she said. "Writers know a lot about the few things we write about. Editors know everything about everything."

"Hardly," Mark protested, sounding pleased.

"I have a meeting in a minute," Alison lied.

"I'll let you go." Mark's voice was lighter now, more distant. "Oh, and I wanted you to know that we're really pleased with your Menendez piece. I'll be calling you with another assignment soon."

"That's so great, Mark. Thanks. And I'm sorry that—"

"Nothing to be sorry for, Alison."

If you only knew, Alison thought.

13.

Zoe went back to her studio. She hung velvet drapes from the windows that faced the demolition site.

Making art seemed to be good for Zoe. Her face was less drawn, her limbs hung more loosely, her need for reassurance was easing. That was the good news. The bad news was, she was back to obsessing about the pregnancy. Every night she X'ed out that day on their kitchen calendar. She'd drawn a red circle around November 17, the day Alison would be taking a pregnancy test if she hadn't yet gotten her period. "Are you nauseous?" she asked Alison every morning. "Are your breasts sore?"

Alison was doing a countdown of her own. Her period was due on Halloween. When it came, if it came, she'd be out of excuses to delay the inevitable. If her period *didn't* come, would she stay with Zoe, raise a child with Zoe? She didn't know.

In the living room, they'd hung a poster of Einstein and his quote, "You cannot simultaneously prepare for and prevent war." How could Alison simultaneously prepare to leave Zoe and prepare to raise a child with her? She couldn't. So the row of X's marched across their kitchen calendar as Zoe waited for good news, and Alison just waited.

With its employees' commutes and lives still disrupted, PMC was operating at half-speed. Luckily, Alison had a new *Mother Jones* assignment that kept her busy and kept her out of the bad neighborhood of her head.

The story was a series of profiles of Loma Prieta's unsung heroes, the West Oakland workers and residents who'd rushed to the fallen Cypress structure in the minutes and hours and days after it collapsed, risking their lives to save people trapped in their cars.

Alison was spending her after-work hours in the neighborhood around Zoe's studio interviewing young men who'd scaled cracked pillars and pulled survivors out through narrow spaces, and Pacific Pipe workers who'd driven heavy lift equipment from their factory to the Cypress to raise chunks of fallen freeway, and Oakland Public Works Agency employees who'd left the city yard where they worked to join the throngs of volunteers. The volunteers had started working around the clock on October 17 and hadn't stopped until they were forced to on October 21, when President Bush and Governor Deukmejian descended on the site to milk a media moment from the tragedy.

Their stories of sacrifice restored Alison's respect for the human race at a time when her self-respect was at an all-time low. She teared up when a factory worker told her, "Within a few minutes of the quake, a police officer came by, and we asked were they going to send help, and she said, 'There is no help to send now. You guys are on your own.'"

She tried not to compare her own moral fiber to that of the guy who said, "A company right across the street had some extension ladders. We went over there, climbed the fence, got some ladders, threw them back over the fence, and that's how we got up on top of the freeway."

When she called Mark to give him an update on the piece, his tone was professional and distant. Alison hung up wondering if he'd lost interest in her, telling herself it would be best for everyone if he had.

On Halloween morning, Alison awoke from restless dreams and found her thighs smeared with blood.

An ache began in the region of her heart and spread. It hurt to breathe. It hurt to think, *This is it. The end.* Instinctively, she turned to Zoe to tell her, to be held and comforted by her. But no. Not anymore. *This is the end of us.*

Alison lay on her side and watched Zoe sleeping, her hair nearly invisible against the white pillowcase, her lush mouth curved into a smile. Beautiful Zoe. Amazing Zoe. *If Zoe's dreaming about our baby,* Alison thought, *it's for the last time.*

Rosy morning light trickled through the swirls and curlicues of their lace curtains, shadows lighting the vase of pink tea roses from their front yard. Velvety, fragrant petals littered the butterscotch oak floor. Alison lay still, memorizing the moment.

Zoe opened her eyes. She saw the look on Alison's face and burst into tears.

Zoe pulled Alison into her arms and they wept together. How

many times had Zoe comforted Alison, loved her, taken care of her? How could Alison give up such good love?

Tell her. "Zoe, I—"

"I know things haven't been great between us lately," Zoe interrupted her. She pulled a wad of tissues from the box on her nightstand and blew her nose. "But I'm doing better. We're doing better. By the time the baby comes, we'll have our magic back. I know we will."

Zoe's desperation had once seemed pathetic. Now it broke Alison's heart. *Tell her.*

"Promise me we can try again next month," Zoe begged her.

I can't tell her now. I just can't. "I'm so sad," Alison wept.

A lison mailed her Cypress Heroes story to Mark with a note thanking him for the great assignment. A few days later, he called her at work. "The piece is really good," he said. "We've scheduled it for the March issue. But it needs work. Let's have a drink and go over my notes."

"Mark. I—"

"Hey, I'm your editor. Drinks with you is part of the deal. I'll see you here at six tomorrow."

S o much has changed so fast, Alison thought, riding the creaking elevator up to the *Mother Jones* office again, checking out her reflection again. The brass walls had been polished, providing an unobstructed view of a scattering of tiny pimples across Alison's forehead. As a teenager, she hadn't broken out. But everything was screwy now. Even her period had been a two-day dribble instead of her usual five-day flow.

"I'll tell Mark you're here," the receptionist said.

Alison perched on the edge of a stiff pleather couch, leafing through a back issue of the magazine she'd read a year before. Back when she was still hoping that someday she'd write for *Mother Jones*. Back when she was still pitching stories to local newspapers. Back when she was still Zoe's.

"There you are." Mark smiled down at Alison. She'd forgotten how handsome he was. He took her arm and led her to the elevator. She'd been hoping to be over her attraction to him, but she wanted to lean into him. She wanted to throw him down and fuck him. They descended to the lobby shoulder-to-shoulder in electric silence.

"Hungry?" Mark asked, as they walked into the misty night.

Alison remembered their hunger. The memory made her want to lie down. This time she couldn't blame the wine.

Slut, her mother's voice said. *Can't wait to get your hooks into someone new? Can't be bothered to tell the truth to the one you've got?*

"Not really," Alison said.

"The M&M Bar okay?" Mark asked. "It's kind of a dive. But it's got great atmosphere."

Hanging out at the M&M was high on Alison's career wish list. It was San Francisco's legendary newspaper bar, the last of its kind. It had been the watering hole of reporters, editors, pressmen, and delivery truck drivers since the 1934 General Strike. It was a place Alison had always wanted to go, and this was exactly the way she'd wanted to go there, as a journalist having a drink with her editor.

Alison's heart, so heavy for so long, skidded hopefully. *It's starting,* she thought, *my new life.*

But Mark wasn't just her editor. And she had to put an end to the life she had before she could start this part of her new one.

"Let's just have coffee," Alison said. "I've got to get home early."
Mark looked at her. "Are you and your boyfriend on again?"
"I'd rather not talk about that."

Mark frowned but didn't press her. They went to the coffee shop in the Pickwick Hotel, where Dashiell Hammett set *The Maltese Falcon*. They took care of their business, crisply, professionally. And then Alison went home to take care of hers.

A lison stood in the entryway of the cottage, gathering her courage, amazed by the seemingly endless excuses her mind was able to concoct. She knew it wouldn't be any easier to do this the next day, the next week, or the next year. Yet now felt like the worst possible time.

"Babe?" Zoe called from the bedroom.

Alison put her briefcase down and walked down the hall. She stopped in front of Zoe's Mammary Lane paintings, traced a whorl of red paint with her finger. *I missed you before I knew you,* she told Zoe silently. *I'll miss you for the rest of my life.*

She found Zoe in bed with a book propped open in her lap. Her oversized Dyke March sleep shirt was sprinkled with black cookie crumbs. A half-empty sleeve of Oreos topped the stack of fertility books on her nightstand.

"How did we not know that black cohosh improves mucous quality?" Zoe asked without looking up. "That explains so much. We'll try it this month."

"Zoe, I—"

"I know what you're going to say. But don't worry about the smell. It comes in pill form."

"Can we go sit in the living room? I need to talk to you."

Zoe closed the book. "What's wrong?"

"I can't do this in here." Alison walked to the living room. It seemed even more of a betrayal, somehow, to have this conversation on their funky, beloved couch. So she sank into the itchy orange wool armchair that Zoe had found at some outlet store. Alison had always hated the thing.

"Do what? You're scaring me." Zoe sat on the couch.

Alison had rehearsed this conversation. But now she felt sick to her stomach and completely unprepared.

"I slept with someone." Alison's voice sounded tinny to her, as if it were coming from far away.

Zoe's jaw dropped.

"I had sex with someone. I wish I hadn't. But I did."

"When?" The color drained from Zoe's face. "Who?"

"It doesn't matter."

"It matters to me."

"No one you know," Alison said. "A guy."

"A *man?*" Zoe's eyes widened. And then awareness washed across her face. "The night of the *Mother Jones* party. That's why you got home so late."

Alison nodded.

"That was two weeks ago. You're just telling me now?"

"I'm sorry."

Zoe stood up and started pacing the living room floor. "Okay. You fucked a guy. It happens," she said in a pinched voice. "We'll get through it."

"No," Alison said. "We won't."

Zoe ignored her. "I hope he used a condom at least."

Alison was shocked to realize that he hadn't. She hadn't even thought about it until that moment. Not having to use birth control was—had been—one of the benefits of being with Zoe. Not having to worry about AIDS was another.

"He didn't. I can see it on your face." A blue vein throbbed in Zoe's neck. "Now we're both going to have to get tested."

Alison shook her head.

"You're overtired," Zoe said. "We'll talk about this when you've had some rest." She forced a tremulous smile. "You know how you get when you're exhausted."

All this time I thought she was taking care of me, Alison thought. *And she's actually been taking care of herself.* "I love you, Zoe," Alison said. "I probably always will. But this isn't working."

She looked at Zoe pleadingly. "You must see it, too. I just told you I had sex with someone else, and you're telling me to get some *rest.* As if I'm your *child.*"

Zoe was crying. She wiped her face with the hem of her T-shirt. Alison winced at the glimpse of her perfect belly, smooth thighs, the thatch of incongruosly dark hair between her legs. The first body she'd ever loved. She'd never love it again.

"It's not your fault. I wanted to be mothered as much as you wanted to mother me," Alison said. "But I want to be a mother myself. I can't do that and be with you."

"What are you talking about? It's 1989, Alison. Of course you can."

Alison shook her head again.

"I know I pushed you too hard about the inseminations. You wanted to take a break. I didn't listen." Zoe was panting shallowly. "We can take three months off if you want to. Four months. A *year.*"

"It's not—"

"We bought a *house* together." The words were Zoe words, but her voice was quavering, unsure. "We're going to have a family together. We're going to spend our whole lives together." She looked at Alison through red, scared eyes. "Remember, Al? We said forever. That was the whole point of us."

"You can have the house. I'll sign my share over to you. It's yours anyway."

"I won't barge in on you anymore when you're writing. Or—" Zoe was gasping. "Or make you eat tofu."

Alison's eyes darted around the room, remembering. The dhurrie rug they'd bought at the Berkeley flea market. The wooden PG&E spool they'd found on the street and rolled the ten blocks home, congratulating themselves about what a great coffee table it would make. They'd built the base together, laughing about their first construction project at Oberlin, the Miss America auction block.

Now that she was leaving the things she and Zoe had found and bought and built and loved together—now that she was leaving Zoe, a thought that seemed to Alison, even in that moment of doing it, beyond belief—those treasures looked the same way their relationship felt. Sweet. Innocent. Outgrown.

"Look at me, Alison," Zoe begged through chattering teeth. "Every couple has down times. We can work this out."

Not for the first time in Alison's life she wished she could disappear in a puff of smoke, never to be seen again.

"You know how ambivalent I've been about the inseminations," Alison said. "You know I haven't been happy for a long time."

"It's because I freaked out about the earthquake, isn't it? Because you had to take care of *me*, for once," Zoe said, angry now. "And you say *I* treat *you* like a child. You *are* a child, Alison. You had a shitty childhood, and now you're almost thirty years old and you're taking your shitty childhood out on me."

"I'm sure you're right," Alison said.

Zoe looked panicked. "I didn't mean that the way it sounded. You know I love you." She started sobbing again. "You know we belong together."

Alison stared at a crack in the wall an inch above Zoe's head. They'd been talking about fixing that crack, painting that wall, since they'd moved in five years before. They'd never been able to agree on a color, so the repair had gone undone. Time, earthquakes, and aftershocks had widened the fissure. Alison felt a fresh surge of remorse, leaving Zoe to solve the problem alone.

Zoe stumbled into the bathroom. Alison heard her blowing her nose, running water in the sink. When she came back, she'd fluffed her matted hair and calmed her red, swollen face.

"You know you act impulsively," Zoe said. "Then you regret it later."

"You sound like my mother."

"If your mother had loved you the way I do, you wouldn't be doing this."

Tears sprang to Alison's eyes. Her throat was choked.

"Whatever's bothering you, we'll work on it together." Zoe was pleading again, her eyes latched onto Alison's. "Don't tell me you don't remember us, babe. Our magic . . . " Zoe started sobbing convulsively, her head in her hands, her tears splashing onto the couch.

The broken spell of Zoe's blue eyes gave Alison the strength to pull herself out of the chair. "I'm sorry," she said. "But I'm going now."

Zoe curled into a fetal ball on the couch, sobbing. She stayed there, sobbing, while Alison stuffed clothes, books, and a toothbrush into the suitcase she'd bought for that purpose and hidden in Zoe's backyard studio, knowing that Zoe never went in there anymore. Zoe kept sobbing while Alison emptied the file drawers from her desk into cardboard boxes she'd hidden in her office closet. She kept sobbing while Alison loaded the boxes, the suitcase, and her word processor into the Volvo. Zoe kept sobbing as Alison stood in front of her, as ready to go as she'd ever be.

"I'm taking the car," Alison said. "I'll bring it back tomorrow morning. I'll leave the keys under the mat."

"You *planned* this." Zoe lifted her ruined face, stared at Alison with her ruined ocean eyes. "You're moving in with him."

"I'm going to a hotel near PMC. So you can keep the car and I can walk to work."

"You're driving to San Francisco? How the hell do you plan to do that?"

"I'll go through Marin."

"That'll take you an hour. Why don't you—" Zoe seemed to realize the absurdity of what she was doing, telling Alison which route to take while leaving her. Her face collapsed again. "Am I having a nightmare? Please, baby, please. Tell me I'm having a bad dream. This can't be happening. Not to us."

"I'm sorry," Alison said again. She walked out the front door and closed it behind her. Zoe's wrenching cries ripped the night air.

14.

A lison pulled up to the Excelsior, a funky hotel that booked rooms by the day, week, or month. At one in the morning, she found a parking spot right out front.

Room 315 was the size of their bedroom—Zoe's bedroom. The carpet was stained, the dresser and nightstand chipped and ancient. The window, painted shut, looked out onto an alley littered with trash. Alison wondered whether the room had looked less depressing in the daytime, when she'd seen it on her lunch break and prepaid for a week. Or maybe her subconscious had decided that this squalor was what she deserved, a fitting place for the lying, cheating bitch she was.

It's temporary, Alison told herself, brushing her teeth at the dirty sink, and at 3:00 AM, lying sleepless in the swaybacked twin bed on pilled polyester sheets. At 4:00 AM she wondered what Zoe was doing. Was she sleeping, or crying into their goose-down pillows, thrashing in their crisp white cotton sheets, calling or cursing Alison's name?

At six Alison swore she felt Zoe's grief invading her body, an army of fire ants. Or was that hot, needling pain her own? She gave up on sleep and peace of mind, got dressed, and went to work. She stashed the photos of her and Zoe in her bottom desk drawer. She didn't expect anyone at PMC to notice or ask why. She wasn't close to any of her coworkers. She hadn't needed to be; she'd had Zoe.

Alison worked through the day, grateful to have work to do and a place to do it that wasn't Room 315. She wrote a direct mail fund-raising package for the Sierra Club, wrapping text around photos of adorable, endangered northern spotted owls. She wrote an ad for Planned Parenthood, protesting the Supreme Court's decision to give states more power to restrict abortion. When the office emptied for lunch, she finished the revisions Mark had given her on the Cypress Heroes story. She left a message on the *Mother Jones* answering machine telling him to watch the mail for her next draft.

At 8:00 PM, when Alison couldn't keep her exhaustion and grief and her sense of unreality at bay another minute, she left the office and walked to the Excelsior. She fell into a shallow, unsatisfying sleep.

A lison never stopped missing Zoe, but she got used to her new life. She arrived at PMC at seven or eight in the morning, worked through lunch, left by five, and walked the rainy streets to her room, where she stayed up late and wrote and wrote and wrote. It seemed she couldn't pound the keys of her word processor fast enough, emptying her head onto page after page after page.

She wrote pitches for investigative features. She wrote short stories and poems. She sent them to magazines and literary journals, using PMC as her return address. She had a big success almost immediately: her first assignment for *Ms.* magazine, about the hundreds of American preschool teachers who'd been accused of abusing the toddlers in their care.

Alison felt she'd been airlifted into someone else's city, someone else's life. She was eating in restaurants instead of cooking with Zoe, taking Muni to shop at unfamiliar stores, walking to work instead of taking BART. There was no car key on her keychain, no emergency contact name in her personnel file. She spent her days buried in work at her office. She spent her nights alone.

When she needed to talk, she had conversations with Zoe in her head. She wondered why she felt so numb if she'd done the right thing. "You're still in shock," she imagined Zoe answering. She wondered if she and Zoe could be in each other's lives again someday, and she heard Zoe telling her to take it one day at a time. The irony was not lost on Alison. When she cried, missing Zoe, the memory of Zoe comforting her was the only thing that helped.

Mark called to say the Cypress Heroes revision looked good. There might be some last-minute tweaks, but he was approving her $3,000 payment. He asked if she wanted to meet him at the M&M on Friday night to celebrate. He sounded pleased and surprised when this time she said yes.

As the evening wore on, she saw that he really did want to get to know her, and he really did want her to know him. When he asked about her parents, Alison answered briefly and turned the question back on him. He teased her about interviewing him, then ordered another round of Irish coffees and started talking. He told her that his parents still lived in the New Jersey suburb, a few miles from where Alison grew up, where they'd raised Mark and his younger brother. He talked about his brother, who'd married a South African woman and moved there to be with her. Alison asked if he missed his family. He said emphatically that he did not.

He told her about the two years he'd spent after college as a Peace Corps volunteer in Peru and about the Peruvian woman he'd fallen in love with and almost married. He reminisced about the newspapers he'd worked for in Dallas, Atlanta, and Sacramento before he'd landed at *Mother Jones*.

Alison liked the way Mark talked. He was articulate but plain-spoken. He seemed sincere. Unlike most men—and women, for that matter—he was neither self-aggrandizing nor self-deprecating. He kept circling back to Alison, asking her questions, probing her gently. His interest didn't make her feel invaded, the way Zoe's so often had.

"I don't want to pry," he said as they were finishing their second drinks. "But if there's anything you feel like telling me about your . . . relationship situation, I'd love to hear it."

"It's over," Alison said.

Mark looked ready to be sympathetic, or angry, on her behalf. He didn't fall all over himself telling Alison what he "knew" she must be feeling, the way Zoe used to do. He hung back, taking his signals from her. And that made her move toward him.

"It's hard," she said.

"It would have to be. Do you think it was the right thing to do?"

"I do." Alison grimaced. "Most of the time."

"For your sake, I'm sorry," Mark said. "But I'm not going to pretend this is bad news for me." He shoved their empty glasses aside and leaned across the cracked marble table. In the murky darkness of the wood-paneled, smoky bar, she saw the flash of his smile.

He took her face in his hands and kissed her. "Ready to go?"

He tossed a twenty onto the table. They walked outside and faced each other beneath the bar's awning, light rain pattering above their heads.

"Will you come home with me?" he asked.

"I thought you'd never ask."

Mark laughed. He put his arm around her and led her to his car.

They sped across the city on slick November streets, rain pelting the windshield, Mark's right hand stroking her left thigh. Alison's lust dissolved in a churning wave of nausea. She knew what the problem was. Having sex with someone who wasn't Zoe was one thing. Laughing with someone else—that was leaving Zoe behind.

A lison slept till nearly noon the next morning. Nausea hit her when she opened her eyes. *Too much happening too fast*, she thought. Ending it with Zoe. Living in a dump. Starting with someone else. No wonder she felt ill.

Hoping food would help, she woke Mark and told him she was starving. He seemed to hear the urgency in her voice. Twenty minutes later they were in a booth at a dim sum dive on Twenty-Fourth Street, a quick walk from his place.

Mark tapped a passing waiter on the shoulder. "Could you bring us some pot stickers right away?" he asked. "Then we'll order the rest."

The waiter nodded curtly and kept going.

"I'm not sure I can wait for pot stickers," Alison said.

"I'm afraid I've done all I can do for you, food-wise," Mark said lightly. *Zoe would have charged into the kitchen to get me something to eat right now,* Alison thought. *And I would have paid for her heroics, one way or another.*

It struck Alison that she hadn't just left Zoe. She'd left her old self, too. She got to be whoever she wanted to be with Mark. She got to make this thing with him whatever she wanted it to be.

The waiter brought glasses of water. Mark ordered the rest of their meal.

"You feel like telling me about your ex?" Mark asked.

Alison started composing a careful answer in her head. And then she realized that being a new person meant she could say whatever she wanted to say, however she wanted to say it. How unfair it was: Zoe's love had given Alison the confidence to be herself without Zoe.

"We met at Oberlin six years ago," Alison said. "We moved to Berkeley together."

"What's his name?" Mark asked.

If it's going to make him go away, Alison thought, *I'd rather he go now.* "*Her* name."

"Your ex is a *woman?*"

Alison tensed. "Is that a problem for you?"

"Are you hoping it is?"

"What do you mean?"

Mark took a sip of tea and put the cup down. "You put out some seriously mixed messages, Ms. Alison Rose. 'Come closer, go away.'"

The waiter set a platter of steaming dumplings between them. "Saved by the pot stickers," Mark said.

He forked two dumplings onto her plate. She devoured one, scalding her mouth. She took a long swallow of water and gulped down the other one.

"What's her name?" Mark asked.

"Zoe." It hurt to say her name. It was like conjuring Zoe, making her watch Alison eat brunch with a guy she'd been fucking all night.

"Have you been with men before?"

"Nothing serious."

"So Zoe's the only one you've really loved."

Alison nodded, disturbed by the sound of Zoe's name on Mark's sexy lips.

The waiter brought a platter heaped with noodles and bok choy. Alison was instantly queasy again.

"Are you okay?" Mark asked. "You look kind of green." He handed her a cup of tea. His hand, his wrist, his arm were covered with coarse blond hairs. *Man* registered in Alison's brain, a tiny electric shock.

"Not really," Alison answered, and she went to the ladies' room.

W hile she drank her first cup of coffee at her desk each morning—no Zoe to nag her about caffeine anymore—Alison pored over the *Chronicle* rental ads. Berkeley, Oakland, San Francisco. It exhausted her trying to pick a city, let alone a neighborhood, let alone a house, an apartment, or a room. Since she'd left Zoe, everything exhausted her. She chalked it up to spending sex-soaked nights with Mark.

Alison's lust astonished her. Her body seemed to be making up for all the years she'd gone without a man. She'd had great sex with Zoe right up to the end. But all those sweet kisses and caresses, all that merging and bonding, hadn't given Alison the forceful ferocity she couldn't seem to get enough of now.

Nothing felt better to Alison than Mark's cock inside her. And nothing seemed stranger to her than his cock when it wasn't.

Sometimes she'd reach between his legs and freeze, shocked by what she found. Lying next to him as he slept, she'd sneak peeks, trying to befriend the thing in repose. Soft, fat, and curled in its nest of dark blond hair, like a freshly dug-up worm. Stiff with piss first thing in the morning, ruthless, cavalier. Shrinking, sticky with semen in postcoital retreat—a criminal slinking off with the loot. Alison was working on cultivating unconditional affection for Mark's penis, one phase of her project to cultivate unconditional affection for him.

When they made love, Mark didn't wait for her to say what she wanted or how she wanted it. He didn't smother her or pull her back from where she went alone. He wasn't trying to prove how connected or present he was. He was in it for the pleasure of it—not just hers but his own.

Alison loved the raw honesty of Mark's desire. After they came, when she lay in his arms, she wasn't counting the minutes until he let her go. She found herself wanting more with him—more coming, more cuddling—which made her realize how wearing it had been, wishing Zoe would be satisfied with less.

Mark got her sarcastic sense of humor; he had one of his own. She felt like a slightly smarter, funnier version of herself when she was with him. He gave her abundant proof of his attraction to her, but he didn't talk about her looks all the time the way every other man—and Zoe—had.

She and Mark did the same kind of work, had the same politics, liked the same foods. They wanted the same amount of closeness and space. Mark's emotions didn't rise and fall with Alison's. When she was upset, he didn't come after her, probing and prying the way Zoe had.

"Is sex as good with me as it was with Zoe?" Mark asked Alison one night. They were tangled in postcoital collapse, their heads having landed, somehow, at the foot of the bed.

"I told you. I don't want to talk about her." Alison grabbed two pillows off the floor. She tucked one under her head, offered the other to Mark.

"You were with her for years. You're probably still in love with her. Don't you think that's relevant to me? To us?"

Alison wondered whether he was turned on by the idea of her and Zoe, if he'd use whatever she told him to juice up his sexual fantasies. The thought of it made her queasy. Again.

"Do you think about her a lot?" Mark persisted. "Do you miss her?"

If he really wants to know, Alison decided, *I'll tell him.* "I think about her all the time. I miss her all the time, the way I'd miss air if air went away." She squeezed her eyes shut, fighting tears. "She was the best friend I've ever had."

"Then why did you leave her?"

"That's all I'm going to say."

"It scares me, the way you feel about her."

Was this a new thing, Alison wondered: *a man admitting to being scared? Had men changed during the years she'd been with Zoe?* "You wouldn't want me to talk about you with someone else, would you?"

Mark propped himself up on one elbow and looked down at her. His eyes were luminous in the dark. "I don't want there to *be* anyone else. For either of us. I want to see where this goes. We can't do that if we're dating other people."

How did this happen, Alison asked herself. *I'm in a relationship again.*

"I'm not dating anyone else," she said.

"And you won't, as long as we're together?"

She waited for regret or claustrophobia to clobber her. Instead she felt soothed, settled, relieved. She liked this man. She liked the way he held her. Sweetly but not cloyingly. Close but not too tight.

"And I won't," she repeated, "as long as we're together."

Mark leaned over and they kissed a long, lingering kiss.

"Now that that's settled . . . " Alison traced Mark's ear with her fingertip. He shivered. She felt him getting hard again. "I need a favor. Can I stash a few boxes in your garage till I find a place to live?"

"Of course. Anything else I can do to help?"

Mark wasn't offering too much, more than he really wanted to give. He wasn't outthinking her, telling her what she needed, then needing to be rewarded for giving it to her. Alison was free to ask him for anything because he was free to say no.

"Can I borrow your car this weekend?" she asked.

"I need it on Sunday," he answered. "But Saturday's fine."

A lison dialed her old phone number at noon on Monday, when Zoe was likely to be at her studio. There was a new outgoing message on the answering machine. "Please leave a message for Zoe after the beep." She'd never known Zoe to make such a humorless message. She'd never heard Zoe's voice sound so flat.

"It's me," Alison told Zoe's machine. "I hope you're okay."

This had to be the weirdest phone call of Alison's life. "I need to come get my stuff. If you'll tell me when the best time would be, and where you'll leave a key, I'll be in and out as fast as I can. Call me at work, okay? Thanks."

The next morning Zoe left a message on Alison's PMC voice mail. Hearing Zoe's voice felt like hearing her own. Zoe had called at 2:00 AM and she sounded like she'd been crying. All she said was, "I'll be out of the cottage on Saturday from ten to four."

Alison made her first trip across the newly repaired Bay Bridge, white-knuckling the wheel of Mark's car, afraid of another earthquake and afraid of doing what she was crossing the bridge to do.

Her own restoration and the bridge's seemed to be keeping pace. The new section of the upper deck was not quite level with the old; the car bounced scarily as it crossed the seam between the two. Coming off the bridge, she saw a row of cranes like a flock of orange egrets looming over the Cypress demolition and construction site. *Just like me,* she thought. *Out with the old, in with the new.*

She drove east on University Avenue, a route she'd driven ten thousand times. Berkeley seemed to be returning to its pre-earthquake self, plywood windows replaced with glass, red-tagged houses with cars in their driveways again, bricks from fallen chimneys cleared from sidewalks, streets, and roofs. *Thanks to the sixties,* she thought, *Berkeley knows how to deal with chaos and rubble.*

Alison turned left onto Grant Street and parked in front of the cottage. Her greatest hope and fear had been that Zoe would ambush her, but the Volvo wasn't there.

Nor were the falling-down pickets, replaced, now, by a spiffy redwood fence. The top of each plank was sculpted into the shape of a tulip, a daisy, or a rose.

The new gate was firmly upright, perfectly plumb. Alison lifted its oiled black-steel latch and let herself in. The wild front yard that she and Zoe had loved, and watered, and cut roses from and otherwise ignored had been transformed. Gone were the curling vines of volunteer nasturtiums, the woody clumps of overgrown rosemary and lavender, the tea rose swallowing the tottering lath wall. Now a boxwood hedge marched around a geometric grid of manicured flowerbeds. A miniature wooden bridge arched over a curved, dry streambed—no river, just river rocks.

Alison couldn't imagine boundaryless Zoe living within that orderly, boring landscape. Had she hired a boring gardener? Taken a boring lover? This rebuke of a garden meant that Zoe was moving on.

For a moment Alison wished she'd taken Mark up on his offer to help her collect her stuff. But then she imagined him emptying the closet she'd shared with Zoe, in the bedroom she'd shared with Zoe, asking Alison which shirts, pants, and shoes were hers and which were Zoe's. Biting her lip, Alison followed the freshly raked gravel path to the door.

It felt wrong to fish Zoe's key out from under a glazed ceramic planter she'd never seen before, to be an intruder in the happiest home she'd ever known. Alison stood in the entryway, feeling the echoing emptiness of the house.

The living room was unchanged. A new series hung in the hallway where Mammary Lane had been—charcoal drawings of the crushed Cypress overpass, cars and bodies sandwiched between layers of concrete and steel.

Alison's office was Zoe's now, her desk replaced by a drawing table, a clamp-on lamp, and a rolling cart stacked with trays of art supplies. Alison's things had been shoved against the wall. She picked a paintbrush off the drawing table, ran her finger over the soft mink bristles, feeling Zoe's hair. *How did this happen*, she thought.

She saved the heart of the house for last. But yes, there was the kitchen, and there were the pots and pans scarred by the meals she and Zoe had cooked and eaten together. There was the boom box whose music they'd danced to, the Champagne flutes they'd clinked in celebration, the food-splattered cookbooks on the shelf above the stove. The 1989 Sierra Club calendar taped to the side of the fridge was still open to October, even though today was December first.

Alison read the notes scribbled on the days of her former life—some in Zoe's squiggly lettering, some in Alison's tidy hand. On October 17, the day of the last insemination, the day of the earthquake, Zoe had written "4 PM—Insem."

In the box for October 24, Alison had written "6 PM—MJ Party." She wouldn't have believed when she wrote it that she was going to have sex that night with a man.

October 31, the day Alison's period was due, was circled in red. She flipped the page to November and saw that she'd circled the twenty first. She counted the weeks again. And realized that November 21 had come and gone. Her period was ten days late.

It's stress, she told herself. She and Mark had always used condoms, except for that first time. And she'd had her period on Halloween—the period that ended her effort to have a baby with Zoe. The period that ended *them.*

That period had been lighter and briefer than any period she'd ever had.

Alison ran to the bathroom and vomited. And vomited again.

On her way to PMC, Alison stopped in front of Thrifty Drugs, gazing at the Christmas window display. Strings of red and green lights blinked. Green plastic wreaths hung from red plastic chimneys. Plastic Christmas trees sported shrink-wrapped candy canes. A tinny rendition of "Joy to the World" wafted out from inside.

Alison walked into the store, found what she was looking for, paid for it, and went to work. A few minutes later she sat in a stall in the PMC bathroom, unpacking the contents of the box, reading the instructions. "Please," she whispered, not knowing which outcome exactly she was pleading for.

She peed onto the pink plastic stick, wrapped it in paper towels, and carried it back to her office. She hid the bundle in her middle desk drawer and went to PMC's weekly marketing meeting.

Two hours and twenty-two minutes later, when the meeting broke for lunch, Alison went back to her office, closed the door, and sat down at her desk. Her eyes darted to the clock on the wall, to the blurry outline of the building across the street through the rain lashing her office window. She took the framed photo of Zoe out of her desk drawer and cradled it in her lap, tracing Zoe's face with her fingertip.

I'm sorry, she told Zoe silently. She put the picture facedown on her desk.

It's time.

She opened her middle desk drawer and stared at the cardboard box.

I need to know.

Alison pulled the box out of the drawer and rested it on her lap. It was almost weightless, but its verdict would shape the rest of her life.

She took the top off the box. Removed the plastic test stick from its swaddle of paper towels. And saw the results.

Tears sprang to her eyes. She felt she'd never been so happy. She felt she'd never been so sad. She felt the sun was shining inside her, bathing her in light.

· part two ·

15.

A lison couldn't quite believe it. After all that effort to have a child with Zoe, she'd drifted effortlessly into having a child with Mark.

There was a part of her, the "no" part of her, that didn't want to believe it. Her mother's miserable life and her father's early death had taught her the dangers of being a woman who counted on a man. So she didn't tell Mark when she made her first prenatal appointment at the Lyon-Martin Women's Clinic. She went to the appointment alone.

"You said your last period was in October?" the doctor asked, one hand inside Alison, the other hand pressing her belly.

"The thirty-first."

"How long did it last?"

"Two or three days."

"So it was short. Was the flow normal?"

"Pretty much," Alison lied. "Why do you ask?"

She knew why. But she needed to have had a period after her last insemination. She needed to know this baby could only be Mark's.

"Spotting in the first trimester is often mistaken for a period." The doctor pulled her hand out of Alison, snapped off her gloves, stepped on the trash can pedal, and threw them away.

She helped Alison sit up and looked her in the eye. "That's what's happened here. You're eight weeks pregnant, Alison. Not four."

Riding Muni from the clinic to Mark's house, Alison made a decision. She wouldn't upset Mark with information that was only relevant to her past with Zoe, utterly irrelevant to her future with him.

There was a *reason* she and Mark had made a baby so easily; a *reason* she and Zoe hadn't been able to, despite how hard they'd tried.

Alison knew that Mark would want this baby. She wanted this baby to be his. And so, she decided, that's how it would be.

No. That's how it *was*.

Mark and Alison, editor and writer, were no strangers to dead-lines. They had one now, and it was nonnegotiable. Ready or not, they'd be parents in July.

Mark was ready. As Alison had predicted, he was thrilled to hear her news. He was a river, pulling Alison from where she was to the next place, steadying her there, then pulling her to the next. They were having a baby, so of course they'd live together. They were having a baby, so of course Mark's one-bedroom flat was too small. It made no sense to waste money on rent, so of course they'd buy a house.

The Bay Area real estate boom had put San Francisco beyond their budget. Mark did some research and identified North Oakland as their ideal neighborhood, close to BART with easy access to their San Francisco jobs.

Alison's need for control was shrinking as her belly and her exhaustion grew. So when Mark drove her to see the North Oakland three-story, two-fireplace 1904 Victorian and proclaimed it their dream house, she was predisposed to agree.

"Wait till you see the view from the attic." The Realtor tugged on a rope dangling from the ceiling and unfurled a retractable ladder. Mark and Alison stood at the floor-to-ceiling windows, taking in the sweeping view of the Bay Bridge, the Golden Gate Bridge, the sailboats bobbing on the bay.

Of course they bought the house. And of course Mark hired and supervised the electrician, the plumber, the carpenter, and the gardener so they could move in a month before the baby was due.

Alison loved him for taking such good care of her and the baby. She loved him for his competence, his sunny disposition, and his quirky sense of humor. She loved him for adoring her, and she realized that these were many of the same qualities she'd loved in Zoe, and she found that a little bit scary and also very lucky. If only she could stop thinking of Zoe every time the baby kicked, it would feel less scary and luckier.

A lison escaped the noise and dust and chaos of their house one Saturday and took a walk to Telegraph Avenue.

She stopped at Scoop Du Jour for a child's-size cup of hazelnut gelato—no Zoe to tell her it wasn't good for the baby. Savoring each mouthful, she strolled past head shops, pizza places, and bookstores. She couldn't resist the samples of macadamia–chocolate chip cookies at Mrs. Fields, and she couldn't resist ducking into Wasteland to browse the used jeans, just in case she could ever wear an actual pair of pants again. As she was rifling through a rack of 501s, she looked up and spotted a colorfully dressed woman with a magenta crew cut striding out of the store.

Alison knew that walk. She ran outside and she saw the magenta-haired woman turn left toward Sproul Gate.

"Zoe!" Alison shouted. Cradling her enormous belly with both hands, she ran past the dreadlocked hippies, the black teen-agers smoking fat blunts, the uniformed cops on foot patrol. She caught up as Zoe was about to cross Bancroft. Alison put her hand on Zoe's shoulder. Zoe spun around. It wasn't Zoe. It was a punked-out teenager who glared at Alison and crossed the street. She stood on the corner of Bancroft and Telegraph, hands on her belly, sweat and tears coursing down her face.

A lison was at the kitchen table flipping through *The New Yorker*, fanning herself with a fistful of subscription cards. Mark's key turned in the front door.

"Hey, darlin'," he called.

"I swear it's a hundred fucking degrees in here," she greeted him.

"You're sweating for two." Mark poured a glass of ice water and stood behind her, pressing the cold glass against the nape of her neck. Like Zoe, Mark often knew what Alison needed before she did. Unlike Zoe, he didn't force his remedies down her throat.

Stop comparing, Alison told herself for the zillionth time in the past seven months. She took the glass out of Mark's hand, gulped the water down, and held it out for more.

"Just so you know," he said, refilling her glass. "This love slave routine ends the day the baby comes."

"Let's rediscuss the day the baby starts college," Alison said. "I'm kinda loving it."

Mark laughed and reached for the stack of mail on the table. "Nothing but bills," Alison said. "I swear this house eats money while we sleep."

"Now, honey," he said in the corny voice he used to mock what Alison called their Ma and Pa Kettle life. "Don't worry your pretty little head about that."

He bent over and kissed the low-slung dome of Alison's abdomen. "Heads, I mean."

Alison ran her fingers through his close-cropped blond curls. "I'm tired. And hot. And fat."

"Hot, yes. Fat, no. You're nine months' pregnant." He knelt before her. "And you're radiant."

"And you're delusional." Alison rested her cheek against Mark's chest. He wrapped his arms around her, rocking back on his heels.

"I should have taken a month off work. We'll never get this place ready in time," Alison said as she looked around despairingly at the tower of unpacked boxes in the corner. The half-assembled stroller, a gift from Alison's coworkers. The filmy water stains on the oak hardwood floor, a vestige of the earthquake that had toppled the water heater six months before they'd bought the house.

"If you'd taken a month off, we wouldn't *have* a house," Mark said. PMC offered its employees three months' maternity leave—half paid, half unpaid. *Mother Jones* gave fathers two weeks of paid leave.

Alison winced.

"Honey. What's wrong?"

"Ow!" Alison grabbed her belly. It was as rigid as a metal bowl.

She heaved herself up. Her legs wouldn't hold her. A paroxysm seized her body again. A rush of liquid splashed onto her feet.

"Alison! Your water broke." Mark's voice was barely recognizable. Alison was somewhere else, somewhere far away. There was no Mark throwing clothes into her overnight bag, there was no baby causing this cataclysm, there was no puddle on the floor. Alison and her writhing body were alone in a world of purpose and pain.

"Push, Alison!" Mark shouted. "Push!"

Alison clenched her fists and screwed up her face and bore down with every bit of strength she had.

"You can do this!" Mark urged her on.

Over her heaving belly and her splayed legs Alison saw the doctor whispering to the nurse beside him. "What's wrong?" Alison cried.

"Your baby's heart rate is falling," the doctor said through his white paper mask. "We need to get this baby out now."

Another contraction gathered Alison up and slammed her down. A nurse shoved Mark aside and leaned in close to her face. All Alison could see was her flapping guppy mouth. "Push, Alison. Push!" she shouted. "You're almost there."

"I can't," Alison grunted. She heard her own familiar voice. She recognized herself, and that brought her back to who she was. *I have to tell Mark the truth,* she thought, *or this baby will never get out of me.*

She clenched her teeth and pushed as hard as she could. Harder. Her body was swimming in sweat.

"That's good," the nurse said, but Alison knew she didn't mean it. The baby was still inside her. She knew why it wasn't coming out.

"Mark," Alison cried out. "I need to—"

"What do you need?" He put his ear to her lips. "Anything, honey. Just tell me."

But it was too late. The pain was building again.

"Now!" the nurse yelled. "Push, Alison. Push!"

But there was no Alison. There was only pain. The pain was hurling her around the room, tearing her insides out, setting her aflame. She heard a wolf howling, a cow bellowing, a woman screaming.

Alison roared, and she felt the pain pushing through her. Hope surged through her. She was in charge of the pain now. She could move it down and out if she just kept roaring. So she kept roaring and she kept pushing and she felt something slither out from between her legs in a wet, sticky rush.

From the other end of the table, the other end of the world, a baby mewled.

"Congratulations," the doctor said. "You have a son."

Mark's tears fell onto her neck. "We have a son, Alison," he wept.

Alison propped herself up on her elbows. The room looked like the OR on M*A*S*H. Blood was splattered everywhere: on the floor, on the walls, on the doctor's blue scrubs, on the nurse's white shoes.

"Is he—" And then she saw him in the doctor's bloody hands: purplish, reddish, crying.

"He's perfect," the doctor said. Alison fell back, limp with relief. The nurse took the baby, wiping blood and cottage-cheese blobs of vernix off his skin. "Ten fingers," she said, smiling. "Ten toes."

"You're my hero." Mark's tears mingled with the sweat on Alison's face.

The nurse wrapped the baby in a blue flannel blanket and laid him in Mark's arms.

"Look," Mark said hoarsely. "Look what you did, Alison. Look at our beautiful son."

Alison saw the baby's heart, the size of a kidney bean, beating inside his tiny pink chest.

My son. Alison's eyes stung with tears. Every bit of joy in the world poured into her chest and filled her heart until it hurt, the sweetest ache she'd ever known. *I have a son.*

"I want to hold him," she said.

The nurse put a pillow under Alison's head. Mark laid the baby across her chest. Alison cradled him, put him to her breast, guided her nipple to his lips. He latched on, gagged, let go, rooted frantically. He found her nipple again.

Alison closed her eyes, surrendering to the pleasure and the pain. She felt each tug of his mouth in both of her nipples, in her heart.

She touched her finger to her baby's tiny fist. He grabbed it and held on.

I've got you, Alison told her baby. *I'll never let you go.*

16.

oakland
August 1990

Corey was an exceptionally good-natured baby. He was rarely sick, cried only when he was hungry, hurt, or scared, nursed eagerly, slept deeply, and woke up beaming, eager to launch another day.

Alison had hoped that motherhood would warm her, soften her, give her an irrefutable purpose on this earth. Sure enough, being Corey's mom was turning her into the person she'd always wanted to be: a member in good standing of the human race, joined to the endless chain of mothers reaching back in time.

Corey wouldn't let Alison love him a little, love him *if,* love him *until.* He didn't care what she looked like or where her stories were published or what anyone else thought of her. She didn't have to try to love Corey fully, the way she'd struggled to love Zoe, the way she still struggled to love Mark. Every time she looked at her baby, smelled him, caressed his feathery head, her heart bloomed, a cactus flower unfurling in her chest. How could she have thought she knew what beauty was? What love was? She'd never known.

In the past, this abundance of goodness would have made Alison brace for the inevitable crash to come. But she was floating on a pink postpartum cloud of hormones and new-baby bliss. Feminism be damned. She was doing no writing, earning no money, thinking no great thoughts, not even having sex with her man. And for the first time in her life, she felt like a good person. She felt complete.

A healthy, loving family was what she'd always wanted, and now a healthy, loving family was what she had. She, Mark, and Corey were living a sweetly simple life, dancing to Corey's rhythm—no clocks, no schedules, no meetings, no calls.

The sun rose and set, food was cooked and eaten, diapers were dirtied and changed, cries were soothed, laughter was shared. Alison and Mark slept when Corey slept. When he was awake, Mark and Alison held him and stared at the wonder of him nursing, crying real tears, producing perfect green poops. Their big, rambling, unfinished house was a desert island. Alison, Mark, and Corey were blissfully marooned.

Out there somewhere, the world was turning. Demonstrators took to the streets of San Francisco, protesting the Gulf War. Mark and Alison and Corey stayed home. The Oakland A's lost the World Series, unleashing media memories of the aborted World Series game on the day of the Loma Prieta quake. Everyone was abuzz about two new TV shows, *The Simpsons* and *Seinfeld*. Black playwright August Wilson won the Pulitzer, Leonard Bernstein conducted the last concert of his career, Madonna pissed off the Catholics, having too much fun with a cross on her Blond Ambition Tour. All of it was background noise to Alison. Who had time to watch TV or wallow in memories?

The murkiness of Alison's normal life, the ambiguity of her normal emotions cleared like a glass of water long left on the sill. Moment to moment, hour to hour, she knew exactly what to do—whatever Corey's well-being required—and why—because he needed her. She gave Corey everything she had, and the well of her energy was endlessly, mysteriously refilled. She sailed through the incessant feedings, the up-and-down all-nighters, the confinement to the house, the bedroom, the bed.

It wasn't agonizing to care for a child, as her mother had always complained it was. It was a joy, not a contest, for a mother and a father to share a child. It was a joy, not a burden, to be a good mother to her son.

A lison was nursing Corey to sleep in the easy chair in their bedroom, half-asleep herself, when she heard a sound. She looked up and saw Mark in bed, looking at Alison and Corey and crying. "I love you both so much," he said.

If Corey wasn't his, Alison told herself, *I'd feel it by now.*

"We love you too," Alison whispered over Corey's head.

W hen Corey was four weeks old, Mark wrenched himself off their island and went back to work.

Alison was secretly glad to have Corey to herself. She loved the steadying weight of his body in her arms, the reassuring puffs of his breath on her neck, the private language that only their bodies spoke. Mark could comfort Corey when his diaper was wet, when he wanted to be held, when he needed to be walked to a nap. But only Alison could give Corey what he needed to stay alive.

He needs me, she thought happily when Mark handed inconsolable Corey over to her and she lifted her shirt and put him to her breast. *He needs me,* she thought happily when Corey paused to smile at her as he nursed.

He needs me, she thought wearily when Corey woke her for the fourth time in a night, and she felt utterly incapable of opening her eyes, let alone giving more of herself, even to him, and she would have traded a limb for a single night of sleep.

Exhaustion, tedium, and anxiety began to encroach on Alison's joy.

She stumbled through her days so groggy that she was nauseous, so sleepy that she was brain-dead. She'd walk into the kitchen, forget why she was there, then realize she hadn't eaten all day. She'd promise herself a nap when Corey went down for his and end up spending the whole two hours watching him sleep. What if he stopped breathing? What if there was another earthquake? How would Mark get home to them across the Bay Bridge?

And then there was the matter of Zoe. The more time stretched between them, the more things happened to Alison that Zoe didn't know about, the more she missed Zoe. While she washed the dishes, while she shoved the day's third load of laundry from the washer to the dryer, and especially when two-month-old Corey gurgled in her arms, Alison found herself wondering what Zoe was doing, who she was doing it with, what she'd say if Alison called her on the phone.

They hadn't seen each other in nearly a year. Zoe probably hated her guts. Zoe didn't even know that Corey existed. Still, Alison imagined calling her; imagined Zoe saying "I'll be right over," Zoe whirling around the house cleaning and cooking, telling Alison to rest while she gave Corey his bath.

And then Alison imagined what would *really* happen if she called Zoe. She'd think about facing Zoe's questions about Corey, facing Zoe's anger and pain. And Alison would put the thought of calling Zoe aside.

"I put the stroller together a week ago," Mark said over the dinner he'd come home early to cook. "Didn't you say you wanted to start taking Corey for walks?"

"You think I'm fat." Alison stopped pushing Mark's bland, mushy pasta around her plate and burst into tears. She'd come home from the hospital with an extra fifteen pounds. It felt like fifty. She was plump and flabby everywhere she'd been lean and muscular before—her hips, her thighs, her belly, her arms. She'd learned to avoid mirrors, but she *felt* the weight whether she saw it or not.

"You're not fat. You're bored," Mark said. "Except for doctor visits, you haven't left the house in weeks."

"You're right," Alison said. But every time she contemplated what it took to get herself and Corey out the door—taking off Mark's castoff sweats and putting on real clothes, packing Corey's diaper bag with pacifiers and diapers and burp cloths and breast pads and baby wipes and backup outfits—she curled up on the couch instead.

One morning when Corey was nine weeks old and the two of them were alone in the house, Alison braved a confrontation with her pre-pregnancy wardrobe. She managed to squeeze herself into her baggiest pair of pre-pregnancy jeans.

"Aren't you impressed?" she asked Corey, who was lying on his stomach on the bed like a blue velour turtle, trying to lift his wobbly head. Alison regarded her shape in the mirror. "You've never seen your mom wearing an actual waistband before."

Corey beamed at her. "You're right," Alison said. "This calls for a celebration." She dumped the contents of his changing table into the diaper bag, pulled the stroller out of the closet, and wheeled Corey out the door into the sunny August morning.

Alison shielded her eyes, taking in the sights and sounds of adult life. From the railroad tracks down by the bay, she heard a train's insistent whistle. A helicopter jackhammered the sky overhead. A rag-wrapped man pushed a rattling shopping cart down the middle of the street.

"Welcome to the world, Pickle," Alison said. She adjusted the stroller's canopy to keep the sun out of Corey's eyes and headed north on Shattuck.

At La Peña Cultural Center, a crew of painters was freshening the 3D mural that wrapped around the building's facade. Alison figured it was never too soon for a Bay Area kid to learn his revolutionary heroes. "Victor Jara," Alison pointed to the central figure, his papier-mâché hand strumming a guitar. "Pablo Neruda. He was a poet, honey." She squinted at the figures, straining her mommy brain. "Woody Guthrie. His son Arlo is closer to your age. Malvina Reynolds. She wrote a great song, 'Little Boxes.' I'll sing it to you someday."

Next door a Guinness truck was double-parked in front of the Starry Plough Irish bar. Alison stopped to read to Corey from the plaque beside its doors:

No revolutionary movement is complete without its poetic expression. Until the movement is marked by the joyous, defiant singing of revolutionary songs, it lacks one of the most distinctive marks of a popular revolutionary movement; it is the dogma of the few and not the faith of the multitude.

—James Connolly, 1907

* * *

As she pushed Corey past the Berkeley Bowl, the former bowling alley converted to an Asian produce market, she made a note to herself to do some shopping on the way home. "Daddy tries. But cooking isn't his forté," she told Corey. "You'll be much better at it. I'll make sure of that." She felt a stab, imagining Zoe teaching Corey to make her lentil soup.

The downtown Berkeley BART station was surrounded by the usual knot of demonstrators walking in the usual small circle, waving the usual handmade picket signs. The injustice du jour was the U.S. involvement in the Gulf War, but one rogue sign read, I'M ALREADY AGAINST THE NEXT WAR. Another read, STOP UNWANTED SEISMIC ACTIVITY. Another demanded LECH WALESA FOR PRESIDENT. Alison wondered briefly which country the guy wanted Walesa to be president of. *Berkeley being Berkeley,* she thought, *it's as likely to be the United States as Poland.*

Crossing University, Alison entered her old neighborhood, Zoe's neighborhood. "Mommy doesn't live here anymore," she told Corey, speed-walking him past the familiar corners: Delaware, Francisco, Virginia, Lincoln. Turning left on any of those corners would take her to Grant Street, to the cottage, to Zoe. "We're going straight," she informed her son. Never too soon to teach the kid to pun.

Inside Black Oak Books, Alison looked around hungrily, drinking it all in: the shelves overflowing with used paperbacks and first editions, the framed photos of Alice Walker, Sue Miller, Barbara Kingsolver, and a dozen others she didn't recognize. The tables piled with novels and journalistic exposés and spiritual tomes and cookbooks and art books and—

And at the art book table, her back to Alison, a woman who looked like Zoe.

Can't be, Alison told herself. It was too much of a coincidence to be true. First time out with Corey, first time walking through their old neighborhood, first time fitting into her jeans. But . . .

But. It wasn't just the bristle of turquoise hair, or the cherry red Indian cotton shirt, or the blindingly yellow parachute pants. Alison knew it was Zoe because her own chest seized and her own belly melted and because she thought, *Finally.*

Zoe put the book down. Her eyes met Alison's. The blood drained from her face. And then Zoe saw the stroller. She stared at Alison as if she'd been slapped.

Alison went to Zoe. Took Corey to Zoe. "There you are," Alison said.

"Here I am," Zoe said stiffly. She was pale and gaunt and slightly disheveled. Alison thought she'd never seen anyone so beautiful in her life.

"And who's this?" Zoe asked, looking down at Corey.

Alison swallowed hard. "This is my son."

Zoe's blue eyes darkened. "Your son."

"I wanted to tell you. I've thought of calling you a million times."

Zoe turned away. "I gotta go," she said.

"Please don't," Alison pleaded. "I know you're upset. Of course you're upset. But can we please, please go someplace and talk?"

"I'm not ready for this."

"But it's been so long." Alison hated the desperation in her own voice.

"That was your choice, not mine. You've got a lot of nerve. You know that, Alison?"

Zoe walked out of the store. Alison ran after her.

"Fifteen minutes," Alison begged breathlessly.

Zoe stopped walking. "Ten," she said.

17.

They went to Masse's, the French bakery next door. They both ordered chamomile tea. They took their little white teapots and their big black-and-white-striped mugs to a small round metal table in the window. They sat for a while without speaking, finding and avoiding each other's eyes.

Outside on Shattuck, people carried bulging pillowcases into the Laundromat and takeout bags out of Saul's Deli. A homeless man held a sign that read, WILL WORK FOR PASTRAMI. In his umbrella stroller, Corey slumped like a rag doll, sound asleep.

"Since when do you drink tea?" Zoe asked.

"I can't have caffeine. I'm breastfeeding." It was hard to say the word *breast* to Zoe. "You look great."

"I look like shit. Which is pretty much how I feel."

Same old Zoe, Alison thought. She'd never heard Zoe utter a disingenuous word about her own appearance. Zoe didn't crave compliments or deflect them the way most women did. She gained weight, lost it, did one crazy thing to her hair after another, went to parties in outfits Alison wouldn't sleep in, all cloaked in that irresistible, cocky confidence of hers.

"Are you still in the cottage?" Alison asked.

"Yup." Zoe blew on her tea.

"Are you painting?"

Zoe nodded.

"How's it going?"

"Oddly enough, it's going great." Zoe took a sip of tea. "What a cliché. Heartbreak, the great muse."

Alison's throat clenched. "I'm still at PMC," she said, as if she could turn this into a normal conversation by acting as if it were one. "They gave me three months' maternity leave. I wish I could take a year."

"You said you wanted to talk, Alison," Zoe said. "So talk."

Alison took a deep breath and let it out slowly. "Mostly I wanted to say . . . I'm sorry," she said.

"Sorry you hurt me? Or sorry we're apart?"

Tell the truth, Alison told herself. But what was the truth? "Sorry I hurt you."

Zoe winced. "Not the answer I wanted."

"I'm sorry," Alison said again.

"Are you with the baby's father?"

"Yes."

"Is he the guy you—?"

Alison nodded.

Zoe's jaw tightened.

"Zoe. You and I haven't seen each other in months. We don't need to have this conversation right now."

"Maybe *you* don't. But I do."

Nothing's changed, Alison thought. *I'm still disappointing her and feeling guilty about it. And she's still insisting that I tell her more than I want to say. Maybe the best thing I can do for both of us—for all of us—is to get up now and walk away.*

Alison sneaked a peek at Zoe and saw her watching Corey sleep. Zoe's face was a sky of changing weather: awe, anger, tenderness, grief. Alison knew that face—all those faces—better than she knew her own.

"What do you need to know?" Alison asked.

"What do you *think* I need to know? You left me eight months ago because you didn't want to have a baby with me. And now you show up with a baby you had with someone else." Zoe twisted her mug in her hands. "Did you *marry* the guy?"

"No." Alison knew her mind and Zoe's were traveling to the same place and time. On their fifth anniversary, Zoe had asked Alison to marry her. Alison had treated her proposal as a joke, saying she'd change her name to Alan, tape her breasts flat, and show up at City Hall in a tux. Zoe had never brought it up again. But even though there was no way for them to do it, not getting married became one more way Alison felt she'd let Zoe down.

Zoe glared at the man at the next table, who was blatantly eavesdropping. He picked up his *New York Times.*

"Do you love this guy?" Zoe asked.

"Yes."

"Are you in love with him?"

Alison hesitated.

"I didn't think so." Zoe leaned back in her chair. "What does he do?"

"He's a magazine editor."

"At *Mother Jones?*"

"How'd you know that?"

"You met him at a *Mother Jones* party. I've been reading the magazine. I saw your piece."

"I got that assignment before he and I—"

"I know when you got your first *Mother Jones* assignment, Alison," Zoe said icily. "I brought you flowers to celebrate, remember?"

"It surprised me, too, what happened," Alison said slowly. "I know you trusted me. And I—"

"Actually, I didn't trust you," Zoe said. "Because I knew you never really trusted me. But I did think that if I loved you well enough, for long enough, eventually you would."

"I wanted it to work with you, Zoe. You know I did."

"Until we started trying to have a baby."

She's right, Alison thought, *and she's wrong.* Since they'd broken up, Alison had realized that if she'd known Zoe was fallible— right sometimes, wrong sometimes, brave sometimes, scared sometimes, just like any other mortal human—things might have turned out differently for them. And that wasn't Zoe's fault.

"It wasn't just that," Alison said. "I felt too . . . " Alison swallowed the word *smothered.* She pulled a more neutral word out of the lesbian lexicon, a language she'd never spoken fluently, a language she'd been glad to forget. "Too *merged* with you."

"You were scared," Zoe corrected her. "Scared of being a lesbian mother. Scared of loving me the way I loved you. I thought we were working on that." She raked a hand through her magenta hair. Even her fingers were thinner. "I didn't know you had other plans."

"I didn't plan what happened."

"You wanted to get pregnant. You didn't want to raise a child with a woman. What else *could* have happened?"

"I tried to get pregnant with you."

"Is that the story you've been telling yourself? That you left me because we couldn't have a child?"

The man at the next table made a show of turning the pages of his newspaper. "Zoe," Alison whispered, "please lower your voice."

"I don't give a shit who hears me."

Part of the deal, Alison thought. *Take Zoe, take her as she is.*

"I always had to be the grown-up. The strong one. I freaked out about the earthquake. That made me worthless to you."

"You've never been worthless to me."

"Did you tell your boyfriend about us?" Zoe asked.

"Of course."

"Did you tell him we were inseminating when you met him?"

Alison's heart hammered. "There's no reason for him to know that."

"That's pretty major information you're withholding. The two of you must be very close," Zoe said sarcastically. She paused. "How old is the baby?"

I can get up and walk out of here right now and she'll never know the answer to that question, Alison thought. *But if I want her in my life, if I'm ever going to forgive myself, I have to tell her the truth.* "His birthday was July 18."

Watching Zoe doing the math in her head, Alison remembered watching Mark making the same calculation. "Which means he was conceived . . . " Zoe said.

"In October."

"We were still together in October. We *inseminated* in October."

"It didn't work."

"You don't know that."

"Listen to me, Zoe. This is important."

"You bet it is."

"I slept with Mark two days after we inseminated for the last time. And we . . . he didn't use protection."

"Wait a minute." Zoe looked confused. "You had your period in November."

"That was just spotting."

"Wow, Alison." Zoe shook her head in disbelief. "First you cheated on me. Then you left me when you were pregnant with a child we might have made together."

"I didn't know I was pregnant when I moved out, I swear. Corey is Mark's child. Mark's and mine."

"Get real, Al. That baby might be ours."

Alison felt a chill.

"How are you going to explain it to your *man* if Corey doesn't look like him?" Zoe asked.

"He already does. Everyone says that."

"What did you do, Alison? Pick a guy who looked like our donor?"

She hadn't done it deliberately, but in fact, that's exactly what Alison had done. Like the donor, Mark had fair skin, blue eyes, and curly hair. Still: how many men fit that description? Thousands. Millions, maybe.

A tiny yelp burst from the stroller. "The windup," Mark called it. Then, when Corey started wailing, "and the pitch." Sure enough, Corey began to wail.

Alison scooped him from the stroller, lifted her shirt, and held him to her breast. It wasn't until she was kissing the top of Corey's head, smoothing his sweaty baby hairs, that she saw Zoe's face.

The tightness and the anger were gone. Zoe's eyes were brimming with tears. "I wanted so much to see you like this," she choked out. "Can I hold him? When you're finished, I mean?"

"Of course." Alison was tearful herself. Who else could tell

Corey who his mother had been before she met his father? Only Zoe. Who else would teach him to draw, and cook lentil soup, and turn boring thrift store castoffs into fabulous clothes?

Alison had always believed that Zoe's confidence, her ground-edness, her fearlessness came from her mother's love. Alison wanted her son to have that kind of love. She hoped she could give it to him, even though she'd never had it herself. She knew Zoe could.

"This might really piss you off," Alison said. "But I miss you."

"It does piss me off," Zoe said. "And I miss you, too."

Alison's nipple popped out of Corey's mouth. "Sorry, Pickle," she murmured, and she helped him latch on again. Comically loud slurping sounds erupted from her breast. Despite them-selves, Zoe and Alison grinned at each other.

"I wish we could be friends," Alison said.

"How would your . . . how would *Mark* feel about that?"

"He knows how important you are to me. And I think the two of you would like each other."

The man at the next table stared at them openly.

"I want you to be in Corey's life. And I want you to be in mine."

"It should take me ten years to forgive you," Zoe said slowly. "But if I'm going to get to know this baby, I don't have that kind of time."

Corey stopped nursing. Alison lifted him from her breast, cupped his head carefully, and handed him to Zoe.

18.

berkeley
August 1990

Alison floated home, high on Zoe, high on hope that they had some kind of future waiting to be made.

As she pushed Corey's stroller south on Shattuck, Alison practiced telling Mark. Because of course she had to tell Mark, because she had to talk him into seeing Zoe with her next time, because whatever happened with Zoe from then on would have to include Mark and Corey, or at least the *idea* of Mark and Corey, and it would have to be honest and aboveboard and clean. Except for that one secret, of course. Zoe would have to promise that she'd never, ever tell Mark about the insemination; that she'd never, ever make Mark doubt that Corey was his son.

The thought stopped Alison cold. Zoe still wanted her, so why *wouldn't* she do whatever she could to get Alison and Corey away from Mark?

Zoe would never hurt me like that, Alison told herself. And then she thought, *That's what Zoe used to think about me.*

Alison didn't stop at Berkeley Bowl. She rushed home and sat at the kitchen table with Corey in her lap and the Yellow Pages in front of her. She opened the phone book to "Attorneys."

The National Lawyers Guild's listing advertised free fifteen-minute consultations. Alison dialed the number. She gave the receptionist a fake name and told the story of Corey's conception to the lawyer who took her call. What would happen, Alison asked, if "Sue," her ex-lover, insisted on a paternity test? Worse yet, could Sue claim Corey as her son?

The lawyer said that Sue had no parental rights, regardless of how Corey had been conceived. "According to the law, a child born to the wife during the marriage is presumed to be the husband's," she said.

"What if the father and I aren't legally married?" Alison asked.

"Do you live together?"

"Yes," Alison said. "Since before our son was born."

"Everyone will assume that you're married. Worst case scenario, it goes to court, the judge asks to see a marriage license, you run out and get one."

Alison hung up feeling relieved. Zoe couldn't force Alison to have Corey paternity tested. She couldn't take Corey away.

Now Alison had some convincing to do. Zoe had to agree to keep the secret of the insemination. Mark had to agree to let Alison's ex-lover into their lives.

"Corey and I went for a long walk today," Alison told Mark after they'd put Corey to bed and crawled into their own.

Mark didn't look up from the article he was editing. "That's great, honey," he said.

Alison noted that Mark no longer called her honey with the bite of irony that had made the corny endearment actually endearing.

"We went to Black Oak Books."

"Mmm," he said, crossing out a word, adding another.

Alison swallowed her annoyance. Since Mark had gone back to work, she'd been feeling more and more irritated by him, less and less close to him. Their most intimate moments these days were the smiles they traded over Corey's head.

Alison used to feel turned on just looking at Mark. Now she looked at him and saw an opportunity to hand off the baby or take a nap. If they'd made love in the past couple of months, she couldn't remember it—which either meant they hadn't or that she'd slept through it. Alison had been telling herself that they were going through classic new parent syndrome, that it would pass.

Her news, she was confident, would get his attention.

"I ran into Zoe," Alison said.

"*Your* Zoe?" Mark lowered the sheaf of paper in his hand. "How was *that?*"

"Good."

Mark raised his eyebrows, waiting.

"She was really sweet with Corey."

"That must have been weird," Mark said. "She never even knew we were pregnant, did she?"

"Nope."

"Does she have a new girlfriend? Boyfriend?"

"I didn't ask." Alison said a quick prayer and pushed on. "I figured I could ask her that next time."

Mark dropped the manuscript into his lap. "You're going to see her again?"

"I'm hoping we can all have dinner or something."

"All who?"

"You, me, Zoe, Corey." Alison plucked a speck of lint from Mark's T-shirt. "Can we just go to dinner with her? See how it goes?"

Mark scrutinized Alison's face. She felt herself reddening.

"She was really important to me for a long time," Alison said.

"Are you sure you're over her?"

"*I* left *her*, remember?"

"You're not answering my question."

"I'm over her."

"Not terribly convincing," Mark said. "But sure, let's have dinner. I'll check out the vibe for myself."

"That's going to be really weird for me, knowing you're sitting there analyzing my *vibe* with Zoe."

"Take it or leave it," Mark said and picked up his manuscript again.

A lison dialed her ex-girlfriend at her ex–phone number. "It's Alison," she said when Zoe answered. "How are you?"

"Surprised. I thought you'd change your mind. Or that your boyfriend would change it for you."

"Mark's looking forward to meeting you."

"I'm sure he is."

Had Zoe always been so sarcastic? Or had Alison's leaving done that to her? "When can you have dinner with us?" Alison asked.

After a long silence, Zoe answered, "I'm trying to figure out why I'd put myself through that. Meeting your *boyfriend*. Seeing the two of you together. Seeing the two of you with . . . "

"Corey," Alison said.

"Corey," Zoe said.

S itting in a booth at Szechwan Gardens on University Avenue with the man she'd chosen and the woman she'd left, her baby asleep in his infant seat on the table, Alison felt the tectonic plates of her past and future colliding.

Passing steaming platters of pot stickers and mu shu chicken, trying to make conversation, trying to show Mark that he had nothing to worry about, trying to make Mark and Zoe like each other, trying to make them both forgive her, Alison felt she was walking uphill, with one foot on each side of a fissure in the ground.

"Alison tells me you paint," Mark said to Zoe.

"Alison tells me you edit," Zoe replied.

Jaw clenched, Mark spooned vegetables onto Alison's plate.

Alison saw a tic working in Zoe's right eyelid. She braced herself. She knew that tic. "I don't believe in keeping secrets," Zoe said to Mark.

She wouldn't dare, Alison thought.

"So I'm gonna tell it like it is," Zoe continued. "I lost Alison. You have her. That hurts."

Zoe glanced at sleeping Corey, who took a few reflexive sucks on his pacifier. "But for all of our sakes, I'm going to put my jealousy aside. I hope you'll do the same."

"That should be easy," Mark snapped back. "Since I have nothing to be jealous of."

Alison wanted to reel Zoe in, tell Mark to play fair. But there

were so many ways for this fragile détente to detonate. Siding
with Zoe against Mark was one of them. Siding with Mark
against Zoe was another.

"If you want to make this work," Mark said to Zoe, "I need you
to respect my relationship with Alison. Do I have your word that
you'll do that?"

"Al made her decision," Zoe said. "I'll live with it."

"So. You'll support my family. And I'll support your friendship.
Deal?" Mark stuck his hand out.

"You really do go for the lay-it-on-the-line type, don't you," Zoe
said to Alison. Then she shook Mark's hand.

To seal the deal, Mark poured tea into Alison's cup, then Zoe's,
then his own.

Alison raised her teacup. "To Corey," she said. Mark and Zoe
clinked their cups against hers.

I t was surreal to hear Zoe's voice on Alison and Mark's answering
machine, to call Zoe back and make a date for brunch.

Second only to protesting, brunch was Berkeley's next-most
popular ritual. On weekend mornings, throngs of bleary-eyed,
caffeine-craving Berkeleyites clutching their Sunday *Chronicles*
and *New York Times* lined up outside Mama's on San Pablo, Café
Fanny on Cedar, Sam's Hideaway on Telegraph, the Homemade
Café on Sacramento. Leaning up against buildings and telephone
poles, they waited an hour or more for their lattes, silver dollar
pancakes, and applewood-smoked bacon; their huevos rancheros
and chorizo; their Alice Waters poached eggs on grilled Acme
levain toast. The *East Bay Express's* restaurant reviews were enter-
taining but superfluous. The size of the crowd milling around
each café was the most accurate guide to the best spots in town.

For Alison and Zoe, brunch was a minefield of memories. The Brick Hut was out, of course, and so were the other places they'd frequented. Alison suggested Bette's Ocean View Diner.

"You want to go to *Fourth Street?*" Zoe asked. As downwardly mobile, self-righteous lesbians, she and Alison had scorned the yuppie development.

"The food's great. And we can wander around while we wait."

"If you say so," Zoe said dubiously.

Alison left Corey at home with Mark and two bottles of breast milk and drove their Honda Civic across town. As usual on a weekend morning, Fourth Street was crawling with non-Berkeley rich folks in their Range Rovers and BMWs, vying for places to park. Alison beat out an Acura and walked toward the restaurant, zipping up her faded Oberlin sweatshirt. It was a cold, socked-in morning, the kind of August day that made Alison wonder why so many people were willing to live on a fault line and drive through eternal traffic jams with their car heaters on in the middle of summer. Of course, she was one of them. And the only thing she loved more than making fun of Berkeley was Berkeley itself.

Zoe was waiting at a sidewalk table in front of Bette's with a latte in front of her. Her hair was Day-Glo orange. Her expression was guarded. She and Alison hugged hello, a brief, measured embrace. "Where's Corey?" Zoe asked.

"Home. Nap time."

Zoe frowned.

"I like your hair," Alison said quickly. "What's that color called? Homey the Clown?"

"I was looking forward to hanging out with him."

"Next time. Did you put our name on the list?"

Zoe nodded, squinting at Alison appraisingly. "It's good to see you," she said.

"It's good to see you too."

They made small talk, watching the tube-and-tunnel couples ducking in and out of the fancy shops, the homeless men hawking copies of *Street Spirit*, the babies being pushed in seven hundred–dollar strollers. Alison felt she'd been breathing with one lung and she suddenly had two.

"Thanks for giving this friendship thing a try," Alison said.

"Considering the alternative, I don't have much choice."

"That's pretty harsh."

"It's a pretty harsh situation. For me, anyway. And for Mark, I'm guessing. It's pretty damn sweet for you."

"It's not sweet for anyone right now," Alison said. "But I'm hoping it'll be good for all of us in time."

Zoe looked surprised. *People change*, Alison wanted to say. *I'm a mom now. The job comes with a longer view.*

"Speaking of what's good for us," she said instead, "Mark and I talked, and we don't want Corey to know that you and I were lovers."

In fact, Alison had had to talk Mark into that decision. She had one secret to keep from Mark, two secrets to keep from her son. The secrets were knitted together. Yanking on one could unravel them both—which could unravel the life Alison was carefully constructing for herself, for Corey, for all of them.

"Kids' lives are confusing enough," she'd told Mark. "I want him to think of Zoe as an aunt or a godmother, not as my ex."

Mark had argued that withholding that information was homophobic as well as dishonest. Alison said that they could always tell Corey later, but they couldn't retract the information once it was revealed. Finally, he'd given in.

"Are you kidding?" Zoe asked. "You're ashamed to tell your son you're gay? *Were* gay, I mean. Or whatever." She paused. "I don't believe in secrets, Alison. That's *your* specialty."

Alison absorbed the blow. "Can I count on you to keep our past to yourself?"

"What's next?" Zoe sputtered. "You're gonna make me promise not to tell the kid you're Jewish? A writer? A woman?"

Alison leaned forward. Her elbows burned, digging into the metal mesh tabletop. "There is something else. I want you to promise you'll never tell Mark that you and I were trying to have a child."

"*What?*" Zoe sputtered.

"There's no reason for him to know."

"There's only one reason for him *not* to know," Zoe said. She paused. "I know why you're keeping that from him. You don't think the baby's his."

Manfred, the co-owner of Bette's, came to the doorway. "Alison for two," he called.

Zoe took her latte, and they followed Manfred to a table in the back, squeezing through the narrow aisle.

"Know what you want?" A young waitress with cotton-candy pink hair, black lipstick, and a yin-yang tattoo on her forearm flipped her pad open and cocked her hip.

"I'll have the apple soufflé," Alison said. "And a decaf chai, please."

"Whatever she's having," Zoe said. When the waitress left, she said, "I have a great idea."

I'm not going to like this, Alison thought.

"Let's give Corey a paternity test. If we find out that Mark is Corey's father, we'll never have to talk about this again."

And if we find out he isn't, Alison thought, *my whole life will fall apart.* "That's not going to happen," she said.

"I knew it! You think the baby's ours."

"Here's what I know. If you won't keep the insemination to yourself, I can't have you being around Corey and Mark."

"That's blackmail."

"That's me protecting my family."

"You're holding Corey hostage. You're taking away my rights to a baby who might be mine."

"If I wanted to keep you and Corey apart, I wouldn't be here. I'm not asking you to give anything up. I'm offering you the most important thing I have. I'm offering to share my family with you."

Zoe caught Alison's eyes in hers. For a moment, Alison felt that lying-down feeling, that fluttering belly, that swoon.

"Put yourself in my place, Al," Zoe said hoarsely. "I don't want to fall in love with Corey and lose him. I'm barely over losing you."

Zoe's gaze was a caress, a stranglehold. *How did I ever leave her?* Alison thought. "We're not going anywhere," she said.

"Until you and your *boyfriend* don't want me around anymore."

"We want what's good for Corey. Mark doesn't know yet how great you'd be with Corey. But I do. And he'll see."

The waitress delivered their food and strutted away.

"Okay," Zoe said. "I'll keep your goddamn secrets. We'll try it your way."

"That's a first," Alison joked.

"Not exactly. Us being apart is your way. It sure isn't mine."

Zoe picked up her fork and stared down at the dinner-plate-size soufflé in front of her. "How do you eat this thing?" she asked. "With syrup? Butter and jam?"

"I like mine straight," Alison said.

"Very funny," Zoe said humorlessly, twisting her mouth into something resembling a smile.

It's a start, Alison thought.

19.

O ne of many worries Alison had about opening the door
to Zoe was that she'd come charging through it in Zoe's
usual way: show up too often, stay too long, have too many opinions, make too many assumptions, take over as if she owned the
place.

But Zoe moved into their lives slowly, carefully. She was clearly
determined not to overstep her bounds. Who knew Zoe even *had*
bounds? She called before she came to visit, usually when Mark
was at work. Later, as she and Mark began to get to know each
other, she'd pop in after Corey's nap time on weekends, before his
bedtime at night. She never picked Corey up or changed his diaper
without asking Mark or Alison first. She offered advice only when
asked, and then lightly, not in her old "Zoe says so" way.

She cooked pots of food at her house and brought it to theirs,
and left it for Mark and Alison to eat. When they invited her to

join them for dinner, she demurred. Who knew Zoe could *demur?* *Who are you,* Alison wanted to ask, *and what have you done with my bossy, unboundaried, anything-but-demure ex-lover?*

"You're doing too much," Alison fretted.

"Too much for who?" Zoe said. "It's not too much for me."

It didn't seem to be too much for Mark either. Alison watched him watching her with Zoe. If he was worried, he was hiding it well. At first he'd fade into the background when Zoe came over, staying in bed, reading or working when she was there on weekend mornings; watching a football game while Zoe and Alison were doing the dinner dishes. Gradually he eased his way in—not between Zoe and Alison but with them. As he dropped his guard a bit, came to trust Zoe a bit, Alison dared to believe that a genuine, if wary, affection was growing between them.

Alison's cautiousness, making the limits of her relationship with Zoe clear to Mark, and to Zoe, was paying off. She suspected Zoe wanted more from her, but Alison wasn't being tossed around by Zoe's unspoken needs the way she used to be.

Alison told herself it was good for Zoe to learn not to process every little emotion when she didn't get everything she wanted. And it was definitely good for Alison to learn to resist Zoe's pull.

At eleven weeks old, Corey was pure delight: sleeping through the night, batting at the multicolored paper mobile that Zoe had made and hung over his crib, laughing as if he'd invented laughter.

"Now I know how you felt when you had to go back to work," Alison told Mark early one morning while she was nursing Corey. "I can't leave him next week. I just can't."

"Take another month off," Mark said.

"We can't afford it."

"We'll put stuff on credit cards. Spend less. Whatever it takes. It's worth it."

Alison switched Corey to her left breast, leaned over, and kissed Mark on the lips. "I can't tell you how happy that makes me," she said. She felt a surge of postpartum hormones. Or a resurgence of love for Mark. Or both. "How happy you make me."

"I'm staying home with Corey for another month," Alison told Zoe over tea at Alison's kitchen table that afternoon.

"That's so great," Zoe said authoritatively, in her old-Zoe way. "You're doing the right thing."

Alison poured tea into Zoe's mug, then filled hers.

"What's wrong?" Zoe asked. "You should be ecstatic."

"I am. But we can't really afford it. And it doesn't seem fair. Mark wants more time with the baby too."

"You're the mother. If only one of you can stay home, it should be you." She giggled. "Thank goddess Mariandaughter can't hear us now."

"Post-feminism is the new sexism."

"I'll be post-feminist in the post-patriarchy."

Alison smiled. Jousting with Zoe made her believe there might be life post-mommy brain.

"It's good to have you around," Alison said.

"It's good to be around." Zoe took a sip of tea. "Got any cookies?"

"I purged the pantry. I'm trying to lose this baby weight."

"Oh, Jesus, Al. Like you don't know how amazing you look."

Mortified to feel her face burning, Alison got up and rummaged through the cupboard. Zoe scowled at the Zwieback box in her hands. "What ever happened to Petit Écolier?"

"Teething biscuits are the new Petit Écolier." Alison handed Zoe a biscuit and took one for herself.

M ark suggested they invite Zoe over for dinner. "Let's cook for *her*, for once," he said. "She's doing so much for us."

Alison made her famous lemon roast chicken. Mark made salad and garlic mashed potatoes. Alison told Zoe not to bring anything, but she arrived bearing a chilled bottle of Möet & Chandon.

"Wow," Mark said. "Möet." Was that a tinge of resentment Alison heard in his voice? "We're supposed to be thanking *you*," he said.

Zoe handed the bottle to Mark, who handed Corey to her. "Hey, little boy," she crooned, feathering kisses up and down his neck. "We're celebrating," she said. "I sold a painting."

"Zoe! That's great," Alison said. "Who bought it?"

"I don't even know. The gallery handled the whole thing."

Alison frowned. Zoe always wanted to meet the people who bought her paintings. She often asked to see her work in their homes after it was hung. Why not this time?

Mark put the Champagne in the fridge, then held a chair out for Zoe. "Madame."

"I believe it's mademoiselle," Zoe said, but without rancor. "Or better yet—goddessmother."

Alison strapped Corey into his infant swing and cranked it up. Within seconds he was asleep. Mark scooped him up and carried him into his room.

"Be right back," Alison told Zoe, following Mark. "Thank you," she whispered.

"For what?" Mark whispered back.

"For being such a good, good man. For being you."

They held each other for a moment, and in that moment Alison thought, *I'm the luckiest person on the face of the earth.*

Zoe seemed subdued, not celebratory, over dinner. Alison felt guilty, imagining how hard it must be for her, seeing Alison with her man and her child in their home.

But then Zoe reached into her Israeli paratrooper's bag, pulled out a small white envelope, and handed it to Mark.

Mark looked puzzled. "Open it," Zoe said.

Mark's jaw dropped. He handed the envelope to Alison. In it was a check for a thousand dollars, made out to Mark.

Alison felt stirrings of her old ambivalence. *Is it just me,* she asked herself, *or is Zoe's gift controlling as well as kind?* Why had she made out the check to Mark? As a peace offering? Or to remind him that he couldn't take care of Alison without her help?

Mark seemed to have the same questions. "Why would you do this?" he asked her.

"Because I can. And because you guys are short on money." She looked at Alison. "Think of it as a gift for Corey. I want to support him having more time with his mom."

"This is really nice of you," Alison said. "But we're fine. We don't need your money."

"Actually," Mark said slowly, unhappily. "I wish we were in a position to refuse this. But we're not. In fact, it'll really help." He looked at Zoe. "This is incredibly generous of you."

"It's settled then," Zoe said. "Let's celebrate!"

She pulled a newspaper-wrapped bundle out of her bag and unwrapped two glasses: the flutes that had been hers and Alison's.

"I noticed you didn't have flutes. So I brought mine," Zoe said, avoiding Alison's eyes. "Someone'll have to use a wine glass. I only brought two."

Mark took the Möet out of the fridge and popped the cork. He filled Alison's flute, then Zoe's, then a wine glass for himself.

"Thank you so much," he said, raising a toast to Zoe. "You're such a good friend."

Zoe smiled and raised her glass. "To family," she said.

C orey got sick for the first time when he was three months old. Pacing the house with him, watching him pulling on his tiny pink earlobes screaming in pain, waiting for the antibiotics to kick in made Alison writhe inside her own skin.

His ear infection turned to croup. Alison's exhaustion turned to fevered flu. She moved Corey back to his bassinet so she could reach him from her bed. Every time she managed to doze off, he woke her, barking like a seal.

Mark couldn't take time off work. He was closing the winter issue of *Mother Jones*, cramming in breaking news of Nelson Mandela's release from prison. One afternoon he called to check on them. Alison could barely make herself heard over Corey's hacking. "I'm coming home," Mark said.

"No," Alison said. "Call Zoe."

Alison fell asleep. When she opened her eyes, Zoe was walking Corey around the bedroom, his limp limbs dangling from the Snugli on her chest.

"I called the pediatrician," Zoe said. "I'm taking him in. Go back to sleep."

The next time Alison woke up, the room was dark. Mark was leaning over her, stroking her hair. "Let's get you into some fresh pajamas. Your fever broke. You're soaking wet."

"Corey?" Alison croaked.

"He's better. Listen." She heard no baby coughing, no baby crying. All she heard was the clinking of pots and pans from the kitchen. The smell of food wafted up the stairs. She knew that smoky fragrance: Zoe's lentil soup. "The doctor said steam would help," Mark said, "so Zoe spent the afternoon with him in the bathroom, running the shower. His croup is just about gone."

He lifted Alison's nightgown over her head and helped her into her favorite flannel pajamas. He lowered her into the easy chair in the corner and stripped the bed. "She made soup while Corey was napping," he said. "The house is spotless. The dishes are done. She's *amazing*."

Zoe had rescued them. That didn't surprise Alison; that's what Zoe did. What shocked her was that Mark had *let* Zoe rescue them. Alison searched his face for signs of the suspicion she'd seen there when Zoe first came into their lives. All she saw was gratitude.

Mark tossed the damp sheets into the hamper. "You told me Zoe was a cool person. You never told me she was Wonder Woman."

By the time Corey and Alison were well again, Zoe wasn't just Alison's ex and Corey's goddessmother anymore. She wasn't Mark's nemesis anymore. Mark had experienced the Power of Zoe, and—how could he not be?—he was hooked.

Mark taught Zoe to play poker. She taught him to appreciate abstract art. Overhearing their raucous card games, their loud arguments about whether graffiti should be sandblasted off walls or hung in museums, Alison was stunned by her good luck.

Whatever it had taken to get them here; whatever compromises had been made, or were being made, or would be made in the future; even knowing that her mistakes and her demons might well be lying in wait, Alison was thrilled. She'd given her son a wonderful father and a wonderful goddessmother. She had Zoe in her life—her history, her mirror, her rock—and so did Corey. What Alison wanted, incredibly, was what she had. Corey's cheerful, even temperament seemed to prove his family's good intentions and their love.

"How's our Joy Boy?" Zoe would say when she called to ask Alison what to bring for dinner.

"What's Joy Boy up to?" Mark would ask when he called home from work.

"Same thing he was doing when you called an hour ago," Alison would say. "Making life better for us all."

The bulletin board that Alison hung on the kitchen wall became a multimedia collage illustrating the minutiae of their lives. Appointment cards for Corey's checkups. Receipts for questionable purchases. Doonesbury's latest, meanest snipe at Donald Trump. The latest, cutest snapshots of Corey. And a 1990 Great Women Authors calendar, on whose pages Alison had been counting down the waning days of her maternity leave.

Each night when she faced that calendar, black Sharpie in hand, Alison felt like a prisoner marking time. How could she leave Corey now?

A week before he'd held his head up and looked around. Yesterday he'd babbled all afternoon. This morning he'd discovered his feet. Curly blond hair was replacing the newborn fuzz on his head; his eyes were changing from blue to hazel; his weight had more than doubled. Soon he'd be eating rice cereal, and who would be feeding it to him? Soon his babbling would turn into words, and who would be there to hear what he had to say?

"We can't just hire some stranger to take care of him," Alison said. She and Mark were driving bundles of old *Chronicles* from their house to the recycling center on Dwight Way. Corey was behind them, slumped in his car seat.

The countdown was seventeen days. She'd been spending hours each day calling babysitters, nursery schools, and day care centers that accepted infants. All the calls had led to despair.

"The decent places charge two dollars an *hour,*" she said. "That's almost four hundred dollars a *month.*"

Mark pulled into the recycling center. They sat in the car, windows shut against the cold, watching a crew of young, muscular guys in Ecology Center T-shirts emptying dumpsters labeled GLASS, CANS, WHITE PAPER ONLY, NEWSPRINT into a huge, psychedelically decorated dump truck.

"What about Zoe?" Mark asked.

"What about her?"

"She could babysit Corey. I bet she'd love to do it."

"I bet she would." Alison's insides knotted at the thought. She saw Zoe rocking Corey. Zoe feeding Corey his first solid food. Zoe hearing Corey's first words.

"He'd be spending more time with her than he spends with us," she said.

"Get used to it," Mark said. "Kids spend more time with their babysitters than their parents. Then their teachers. Then their friends and girlfriends. Then their own kids."

"Mark!" Alison hated it when Mark went rational on her, especially when he was right. "Corey's three months *old.*"

"No matter how much time he spends with other people, he'll always know who his parents are." He got out of the car, piled his arms with bundles of newspapers, and headed for the dumpsters.

But his parents don't know who his parents are.

In her best moments as Corey's mother, Alison knew instinctively what he needed. In this moment, she couldn't distinguish between his needs and her own. Was she protecting Corey by keeping the secret of his conception from Mark? Or was she protecting herself at his expense?

Alison glanced at Corey, asleep in the backseat, saliva bubbling over the nursing blister on his rosy top lip. What would be best for him: for Alison to surrender to her fears of losing him to Zoe and send him to a day care center—or surrender to her love for Corey and leave him in the care of someone who loved him too?

Mark slid into the driver's seat. "I don't know why we have to spend our Saturdays doing this. The city should just pick up the recycling curbside along with the trash." He sighed. "It'll never happen."

"You're right about Zoe," Alison said. "There couldn't be anyone better to stay with Corey."

"Well, good." Mark started the car. "Hope she says yes."

"Zoe always says yes," Alison said.

"I thought you'd never ask," Zoe said. "Zoe Poppins. I like the sound of that."

Mark heaped mustard broccoli pasta onto her plate. "We'll pay you, of course. Market rate."

Zoe shook her head. "No way. I'm his *goddessmother*. And that's what goddessmothers do. We look out for our goddess-sons."

"It's too much, Zoe," Alison said.

"Too much of what?" Zoe asked.

Too much like you're his mother, Alison thought. "If you won't let us pay you," she said, "we'll find someone who will."

"Alison!" Mark said. "I want to pay her too. But could you be a little nicer about this?"

"That's one thing we love about Al," Zoe said, forking spinach salad onto Alison's plate. "She doesn't do nice. She does *real.*"

"How about fifty bucks a week?" Mark asked Zoe. "It's not nearly enough, but it'll make us feel a tiny bit less indebted to you."

"You owe me nothing. Make it twenty-five a week and you've got a deal."

Mark looked at Alison. She shrugged.

"Deal," Mark said to Zoe. "I don't know how we're ever going to thank you."

Zoe laughed. "Corey can support me in my old age."

Alison looked at Zoe, the first person she'd ever trusted. *Can I trust her now,* Alison wondered.

20.

A lison began the painful process of weaning Corey—yet another maternal act she was sure she'd feel guilty about until she died. She pumped her breasts, feeling like a factory cow, and filled the freezer with little pink and blue plastic bottles. She bought some new clothes. Got a $50 haircut. Bought a high-value BART ticket. And went back to work.

Within weeks her breasts stopped leaking, but she never stopped aching for Corey. The other moms at PMC kept telling her how lucky she was, having a babysitter who actually loved her child. But when Alison called home and heard Corey jabbering into Zoe's ear, she didn't feel lucky. She felt wrenched.

It wasn't that their arrangement wasn't working. Unlike her coworkers, who plucked their babies from strangers' arms each evening, Alison had dinner with her babysitter—and her baby's father—once or twice a week. The four of them would sit at the round oak kitchen table, Corey snuggled into one of their laps or asleep on the table in his infant seat like a plastic-and-flannel centerpiece. They'd eat Mark's lasagna or Zoe's lentil soup or Alison's lemon chicken while Zoe told them about Corey's day.

Despite the pain of being separated from Corey, sometimes Alison looked across the table at Mark and Zoe and Corey and felt so full of love that her teeth ached. This bounty, this family, was so much more than she'd ever thought she deserved. There was her perfect son, her miracle, surrounded by the people who cherished him. There was Zoe—*Zoe!*—loving Alison by loving Corey. And there was Mark, doing something few men would do, just to do what was best for his child.

Alison took Mark's openness to Zoe as one indication among many of his commitment to their family and to her. Except for Alison's lingering postpartum disinterest in sex, which he complained about sporadically, he was happy. For the most part, she was happy with him.

For the most part. As their relationship aged, Mark was to Alison as Alison had been to Zoe: an emotional hydroplane, hovering above love's turbulent chop and swill, two steps back from Alison's emotional life. But he was sweet to her without being dangerously self-sacrificing, as Zoe had been; attentive without being overbearing, as Zoe had been.

Mark told Alison often what a good mother she was, which eased her deepest doubts. It made her forgive the small indignities of heterosexual cohabitation: toothpaste cap missing, toilet seat up, whites washed with reds.

M ark burst into the house after work one night in early December and announced to Alison and Zoe, who were putting the finishing touches on Zoe's beef stew, that he was in the running for a promotion to senior editor.

"It's between me and Elaine, the other associate editor." Mark lowered his voice. "But Dave told me off the record: the job's mine."

"How long has Elaine worked there?" Zoe asked.

"Two years longer than I have. But she took a year off to have a kid."

"Uh-*huh*," Zoe said pointedly.

Mark's smile evaporated. Alison's stomach tightened. When tension flared between Mark and Zoe, Alison couldn't keep from feeling as if both of them were attacking her. Being the lowest point on an unhappy triangle was all too familiar. *They're not my parents,* she reminded herself. *Even if they don't quite love each other yet, they both love me.*

The good news was that Mark and Zoe were starting to treat each other like family. That was the bad news too.

"What a great reason for you to get a promotion," Zoe said. "Because a woman with more seniority had the nerve to get pregnant."

"Did it ever occur to you that I might be the better candidate?"

Alison agreed with Zoe. But this was Mark's big moment, and Zoe was ruining it. Also, if Mark got a promotion, they might be able to actually afford their life.

"I've always wondered how it would feel to *personally benefit* from sexism," Zoe said, pulling a bag of carrots from the fridge. "But of course, I'll never know." She squeezed past Alison, pulled a knife out of the drawer, and started chunking carrots into the stew.

"That's why God made affirmative action, right?" Alison asked, trying to derail their argument. They both frowned at her and went on arguing.

You wanted this, Alison reminded herself. *And it works so well most of the time.* The problem was that when it didn't, she felt ripped in two.

A few nights later, Mark went out after dinner on a secret mission and came home with a six-foot-tall Christmas tree. Zoe shook her head, fringed with jet-black, two-inch-long spikes. "Excuse me, but last I heard, you guys were Jewish. We should be teaching Corey about Hanukkah."

Déjà vu all over again, Alison thought. Zoe had been just as indignant years before, when Alison told her she hadn't celebrated a Jewish holiday since her father died. "If you were an Average White Girl like me," Zoe went on, "you'd realize how lucky you are to have any culture at all."

Each year Zoe had given Alison eight nights of Hanukkah gifts, made a ritual of lighting the menorah, dragged Alison to liberation Shabbat services and feminist Seders. Now she glared at the tree in Mark and Alison's living room as if it were a stealth missile poised to take out the house.

"We always had a Christmas tree growing up," Mark said. "I like them. They smell good. And look—" He held up a small silver peace sign. "Corey's first politically correct ornament."

Breathe, Alison instructed herself. *You're not their referee.*

Zoe went out to her car and came back with a box of Hanukkah candles and a wax-splattered brass menorah—the one she and Alison used to light together every year. Zoe put the menorah on the mantel as if it were *her* house, *her* Jewish holiday, *her* decision about Corey's first Christmas. Mark stared at the menorah as if it were about to explode.

"Either the kid's gonna grow up thinking of his Jewishness as an ethnicity to be proud of," Zoe said without turning around, "or he's going to experience it as an *affliction,* the way you guys do."

"Corey's five months old." Mark's voice rose. "What do you want me to do? Sign him up for Daddy-and-me Yiddish lessons?"

Alison felt the usual tug-of-war tension in her gut. She didn't want a fight, especially now. Her parents had had their worst fights around the holidays, often about the same thing. She could still see her mother brandishing the menorah, her father shaking his head.

"We could keep the tree and get a Hanukkah bush too," Alison said.

"I just want Corey to feel good about who he is," Zoe said. "Are you guys really going to raise another self-loathing Jew?"

"We're not going to raise a religious Jew at all," said Mark. *Bad timing,* Alison thought. Mark had spent the past week editing a piece about a riot in Williamsburg, Brooklyn, between rival members of the same Orthodox Hasidic sect. The more he learned about the riot, the more anti-Zionist he became.

Zoe shot Alison a look that meant "Jump in here and take my side," a look that made Alison feel she was holding the four of them together with her two bare hands. Alison depended on Zoe now—for different reasons and in different ways than she had when they were lovers, but no less profoundly. Every time she told herself to let Mark and Zoe hash their arguments out themselves, she worried that *this* would be the fight that finally undid them; *that* would be the accusation that would damage their bond beyond repair.

Alison knew some things about Zoe that she hadn't known before. She understood that Zoe drew her strength from being other people's strength, from slaying other people's dragons, making them feel safe and known and loved. Zoe needed to be needed. Alison and her family needed her. The meshing gears of their needs and neuroses were their equilibrium.

Although he complained about Zoe's stubbornness and self-righteousness and her radical politics, even if he felt threatened by Zoe, as Alison suspected he did, Mark had the home court advantage. He was Alison's man. He was the father of her child.

"You guys work it out," Alison said and went to check on Corey. She expected the shouting to follow her up the stairs. But when she came back down with a wrinkle-faced, freshly diapered baby in her arms, Mark and Zoe were chatting companionably, threading paper clips through the blue and silver Star of David and dreidel ornaments Mark had bought, hanging them among the tinsel and candy canes. The candles in the menorah were burning, their reflections dancing in the shiny red and green balls.

"We came up with the perfect compromise," Zoe announced. "From now on, we're going to celebrate *Hanuchris*. The best of both worlds."

"Ba ba ba ba," Corey gurgled, batting his hands at the twinkling lights.

Alison kissed Corey's head. Everything she needed to be happy, red and green and blue and silver, was right there in that room.

At seven months Corey started teething, and he went back to waking them several times a night. When she heard him crying at two in the morning, Alison stumbled into his room and brought him back to bed with her. Without thinking about what she was doing, she nursed him back to sleep. Four hours later, she woke up with leaking breasts, a crying baby, and the sinking realization that she'd have to wean him all over again.

"Maybe I'll call in sick," she groaned, rocking Corey in her arms.

Mark rolled away from her, muttering.

"What?" Alison asked.

"Nothing."

"I'm getting tired of you ignoring me whenever I ask what's going on with you," Alison said over Corey's cries.

Mark sat up, glaring at her. "And I'm getting tired of you complaining about having to work. You got to stay home with him a lot longer than I did."

"We made that decision together. If you didn't want me to take the extra month off, you shouldn't have agreed."

Alison slid out of bed, holding Corey against her shoulder, walking him around the room. Corey wailed, wanting her breast. Alison felt like wailing, too, wanting to give it to him. "It's okay, baby. It's okay," she hummed into his ear. Finally he slumped against her, asleep.

"You know how bad I feel about not making enough money for you to stay home," Mark said in a stage whisper. "You don't have to keep rubbing it in."

"So when I say how I feel, I'm rubbing it in?" Alison hissed.

Mark got up, scooped Corey out of her arms, and laid him in the middle of the bed. Then he walked over to Alison and put his hands on her shoulders.

"We're both exhausted and stressed out," he said. "But let's not take it out on each other, okay?" He lifted her chin with his fingers, looked her in the eye.

Alison's anger didn't dissipate that fast. "I guess."

"If I get that promotion," Mark said, "maybe you can go part-time."

Side with me against Zoe, Alison heard him say. "Fingers crossed.

Eyes crossed. Wires crossed. Every fucking thing crossed." She dragged her weary bones into the bathroom, where she made the mistake of looking in the mirror. She looked like she was fifty years old. She looked like her mother.

B eing away from Corey was getting harder, not easier. Week after week, Alison sat at her desk missing deadlines, missing Corey, thinking, *this is so wrong.* She didn't care if this happened to every working mother. She couldn't stand it happening to her.

Her job seemed meaningless now. In the middle of writing an ad for Berkeley's new curbside recycling program, Alison found herself wondering, *If people still don't know how to separate a bottle from a newspaper, is an ad really going to teach them?* Assigned to write a "triumphant" fund-raising letter about the FDA's approval of a long-acting contraceptive implant for Planned Parenthood's newsletter, she could barely restrain herself from mentioning that this "triumph" was already in use in sixteen "less developed" countries.

What am I doing here, she asked herself again and again. Nearby, her son was sitting up and gumming a Zwieback and doing things he'd only do once for the very first time.

Oh, Mariandaughter, Alison thought, *how I have failed you.* The exciting, self-realized, self-fulfilling existence that feminism had promised her had morphed into a replica of every working mother's treadmill life. Her son was growing up without her, spending most of his waking hours with someone else. Her sex life was non-existent. She never had time to enjoy the house she worked her ass off to pay for; it was just a pit stop between races around the track.

One February morning, Alison pulled herself out of bed in her usual state of weekday panic and then realized it was Lincoln's birthday. Mark had already left for the office, hoping for a quiet catch-up day while no one was around. Miraculously, Corey was still asleep.

A whole day, just Corey and me, Alison thought, diving back into the big warm bed. She was planning the fun day they'd have when she heard the front door open. She jumped up and struggled into her robe.

Zoe stood in the hallway. "You're running late," she said.

Alison racked her sleepy brain for a reasonable way to get Zoe to go home. "Today's a holiday, remember?"

"Shit." Zoe shook her head. "I totally forgot."

Corey's morning babbling wafted from his room. Alison went to get him, Zoe right behind her. Corey was sitting up in his crib, gumming a red plastic bagel.

"Hey, Pickle," Alison greeted him from the doorway.

"Morning, sunshine," Zoe trilled.

Corey beamed as Alison walked toward him.

"Mama," Corey said, reaching for Zoe.

Whom could Alison tell about the heartbreak of that moment? Not Zoe. Not Mark. Whom could she blame for the heartbreak of that moment? Not Zoe. Not Mark.

Clinging to a cold metal pole on a packed BART car the next morning, Alison realized whom—what—she *could* blame. *Fucking feminism.*

Like her fellow feminist devotees, Alison had come of age determined to have a bigger life, a better life than her mother's. She'd swallowed the sisterhood Kool-Aid, believing that being *just a mother* was personally degrading and politically incorrect. In her desperation to avoid her mother's empty dependency,

Alison had become a caricature of the postfeminist superwoman, turning herself inside out to be the world's best copywriter and the world's best girlfriend and friend and mother. Now she knew it in her bones. Nothing was more important than mothering her son.

The train squealed to a stop. Alison pushed through the crowded car and across the swarming subway platform and rode the densely packed escalator up to Market Street. It was drizzling on this side of the bay. That morning, more wrenched than usual to leave Corey, she'd stolen a few extra minutes with him, then rushed out without her umbrella. And her lunch, she realized. And the folder she needed for today's marketing meeting.

On the corner of Columbus and Montgomery, Alison closed herself into a phone booth and called Mark at work. "He's not answering," the receptionist said.

"Page him," Alison said.

"Is Corey okay?" Mark picked up the phone, sounding terrified.

"He's fine."

Mark exhaled loudly. "You scared the shit out of me."

"I needed to talk to you before I got to work. I'm going to quit my job today."

"What the *hell*—"

"I'll freelance. I'll waitress if I have to." Alison started to cry. "I can't be away from Corey for fifty hours a week anymore. I just can't."

She heard Mark close his office door and then pick up the phone again. "We've gone over and over this. Which part of 'we can't afford it' do you not understand?"

"He's going to take his first steps any day now. I want to be there when he does."

"Guess what, Alison. So do I. So why don't you keep your job and I'll quit mine? You make more money than I do anyway."

"You don't need to be with him as much as I do."

"Why? Because you're his *mother?*"

"Yes. Because I'm his mother."

"What the *hell* kind of 1950s bullshit are you spouting?"

If I don't quit my job today, Alison thought, *I'll resent you for the rest of my life.* "If I don't quit my job today," she said, "I'll regret it for the rest of my life."

Mark sighed. Alison's heart soared. He was going to say yes. She could feel it. "Can you at least take a leave of absence instead of quitting?" he asked.

"I'll try. Thank you, honey. So much."

"I'm not a total asshole, you know. I do want you to be happy."

"I know you do."

When Alison got home that night, Zoe was in the kitchen washing dishes. "How was your day, dear?" Zoe said, filling the kettle, setting it on the Wedgewood stove, a bigger and slightly newer version of the stove in her cottage.

Corey was on the floor, chewing on his rubber alphabet rug. Alison dropped her briefcase and scooped him up. *Soon I'll be home with you every day,* she told him silently, nuzzling his velvet neck.

"Actually, I need to talk to you about my day."

Corey wiggled in her arms. He reached for the blue Nerf football on the floor and clearly said "ball."

"Oh, my God!" Alison and Zoe exclaimed at the same moment. They stood stock still, staring at Corey, who was now trying to eat his football.

"Do you think if we stand here long enough," Zoe asked into the silence, "he'll recite the Gettysburg Address?"

"I would hope for nothing less than 'I Have a Dream.'"

Zoe laughed. "You gotta love our boy. He saved his first word for his mom."

The kettle whistled. "Chamomile?" Zoe asked. Alison shook her head and took a bottle of Chardonnay out of the fridge. "Much better idea," Zoe said.

They took their glasses to the kitchen table. "So," Zoe prompted Alison. "Your day."

Alison took a sip of wine. "Things have been working out so well with you and Corey," she began. "It means so much to me, Zoe."

"Me too." Zoe smiled down at Corey. "Him too. Right, sunshine?"

On cue, Corey grinned at Zoe.

"But you know I've been unhappy since I went back to work," Alison said. "So Mark and I are going to make some changes."

Zoe's smile faded. "Like what?"

"I'm taking a one-year leave of absence from PMC."

"I thought you had to work."

"I do. I'm going to try and make money with my freelance writing."

"You think you can write and watch Corey at the same time?"

"God, no," Alison said. "I'm hoping you can still be with Corey two or three days a week."

"So you're downsizing the nanny."

It's a good thing I'm doing this now, Alison thought. Another year and Zoe would have forgotten whose baby Corey was. And Corey might have forgotten who his mother was.

"If two days a week doesn't work for you . . . " Alison said.

"You said two or *three*," Zoe said.

* * *

M ark offered to turn their unused attic guest room into an office for Alison. While he was painting and earthquake-proofing the bookshelves, Alison went to Pier 1 and bought curtains made of tangerine gauze, dense enough to keep the glare off her computer screen, filmy enough to let in the light.

As she hung them, Alison realized that they were exactly the orange of Zoe's hair the day they'd had brunch at Bette's—the day she'd promised Zoe she'd never take Corey away from her.

A lison woke up on her first day of freedom with her heart singing and her nipples on fire. When Mark left for work, he put Corey in bed with her. She held him close. His lips nuzzled at her breast.

Alison hadn't nursed him in monhts. Weaning him had been hell. She told herself she shouldn't put them through that again. She told herself it wouldn't work anyway. And then she lifted her T-shirt and cradled Corey to her breast. *He's my baby,* she thought. *If I want to start nursing him again, that's up to me.*

Corey began to suck. Alison closed her eyes, suffused with pleasure.

And then he stopped. Her nipple fell out of his mouth and lay against his puffy cheek, red and swollen and glistening wet.

Alison shifted him to her other breast. He smiled at her, giggled, swatted at her nose. She took her breast in her hand, guided her nipple into his mouth. He sucked on it once and spat it out.

Corey tugged on her earlobe, laughing.

Alison kissed his tiny fist and wept.

* * *

A lison sold a story to *Ms.* about feminists who want both
motherhood and careers.

She sat at her new desk in her new attic office, struggling to
stay focused on her writing as Corey's voice drifted up the stairs,
crying, then quieting as Zoe soothed him, then cooing along as
Zoe sang to him. They both sounded so happy. Alison felt great
joy and only a bit of envy.

Mark edited her first draft and brought her a bouquet of irises
when her editor accepted it. Zoe brought a bottle of Möet to
dinner to celebrate. Corey gummed Cheerios and banged his
spoon against his high-chair tray as the three of them toasted her
success.

"To Alison Rose, star journalist," Zoe said.

Mark clinked his glass against hers. "And to Zoe Poppins, who
makes it all possible."

"Ball!" Corey burst out, holding a Cheerio aloft. The three of them
laughed. After studying their faces, Corey starting laughing too.

"Either he's a ten-month-old genius and he gets that Cheerios are
round," Mark said, "or he has absolutely no idea what *ball* means."

"I'm going with genius," Zoe said, plucking a Cheerio off the
wall.

Alison looked across the table at the three people she loved.
Less than a year before, she'd been sure Zoe would never forgive
her. But here she was, and they were learning to be friends. She'd
doubted that Mark would find room in his life or his heart for
Zoe. But here they were, enjoying the baby together, enjoying
each other.

And here was Corey, the center of their constellation,
changing, as they all were, but at warp speed. Alison understood
now why parents everywhere longed to stop time.

Sipping her Champagne, Alison imagined what each of them

would look like a decade later. Would she still find Mark handsome when the lines around his blue eyes deepened, when his little potbelly thickened, when his lush blond curls thinned and turned gray? Would Mark still love her the way he did now when her own body slipped and slid into middle age? Would she and Mark find their way back to the passion that had brought them together? Or would they sacrifice it—willingly or resentfully—to raising the child who kept them together?

And Zoe. Alison smiled, imagining her stomping up their front steps as a fifty-year-old, with a magenta crew cut, turquoise paint under her fingernails, rainbow laces in her Doc Marten boots. It was easier to imagine Zoe stooped and wrinkled than it was to imagine her all grown-up.

Alison squinted at Corey's eager face, trying to envision his velvety armpits, his Buddha belly, the pink soles of his feet becoming coarse and calloused, unavailable to her touch. She saw him waving good bye to her on his first day of kindergarten, riding away from her on his first two-wheeler, lying to her as a teenager with a girlfriend and zits and a piercing or two.

How could she predict what kind of person he'd turn out to be, or what he'd be good at, or what he'd look like? The thought broke Alison's pleasant reverie. Would Corey look like Mark as he grew up? Or would he be a ringer for Number 1893?

She told herself it didn't matter. Corey had the parents he needed, the parents who had brought him into being, in one way or another. What difference did the details make? How could biology compete with the miracle, the triumph of that?

"Enough with the Cheerio art, little man." Mark took the spoon out of Corey's hand. Corey opened his mouth to wail a protest. Zoe slipped him one of the brightly colored plastic bangles that jangled on her wrist.

Alison pushed her chair back from the table and lifted Corey out of his high chair. He squirmed in her arms, kicking his feet in the air. She kissed the top of his head, held him out at arm's length, looking into his eyes.

"Hey, Pickle," she said. Her throat was tight; her voice was hoarse. "You still going to let me smooch you when you're a big boy?"

Corey whimpered, reaching for the smeared Cheerios and the sticky purple plastic bangle on his high-chair tray. He swiveled his head and looked at Alison beseechingly.

"Mama," he said.

· part three ·

21.

A lison and Zoe were navigating a rickety shopping
cart through the labyrinthine bulk food aisle at the
Berkeley Bowl, talking about Corey. Zoe had picked him up
at Berkeley High after basketball practice as she often did
when Alison was on deadline.

"How'd he do at practice?" Alison asked.

"He didn't play." Zoe scooped organic pink lentils into a plastic
bag. "He said the coach benched him. He wouldn't say why."

Alison's heart sank. "Something's up with him."

"He's thirteen years old." Zoe twisted a green tie around the
bulging bag. "That's what's up with him."

Alison rolled her eyes. Since Zoe had started volunteering as
an art teacher at Alameda County Juvenile Hall, she'd become,
in her own unassailable opinion, the world's leading expert on
adolescents.

"Hey!" Alison yelped as a gray-haired, bushy-bearded man in a Food Not Bombs T-shirt ran over her foot with his cart.

"My bad," he said, giving Alison a "we're all in this together" smile, the standard apology for shopping injuries inflicted in the well-stocked sardine can of a store. The man reached over Alison's head to grab a bunch of organic arugula, assaulting her this time with his undeodorized underarm.

Alison glared at the back of his head, a bald spot topping his stringy ponytail, and pushed her cart down the aisle. She stood next to Zoe, surveying the bins of white, yellow, purple, and red French, Russian, and local potatoes.

"Fingerlings?" Zoe asked. "Creamer? Yukon Gold?"

"I'm going to call his coach tonight," Alison said. "His teachers too."

"Chill, Al." Zoe hefted a bag of organic French fingerlings, the most expensive potatoes in the store. "Corey's doing what boys his age do."

"He's in trouble. I can feel it."

Zoe gave her an empathetic look. "You're really worried," she said.

Alison hated it when Zoe used her Juvenile Hall counseling techniques on her. It made her feel like Zoe's client, not her best friend. "Thanks for the *mirroring*, doc," Alison said.

A woman in a motorized wheelchair sped through the narrow, congested aisle. Alison and Zoe flattened themselves against the mushroom bins to let her by.

"I'm sure Corey's been picking up on the tension between you and Mark," Zoe said. "He's probably worried. So many of his friends' parents are divorced—"

"Mark and I are *not* splitting up." Alison had had the same thought herself. It made her feel worse, hearing it from Zoe. She tossed a bag of portobellos into the cart's kiddie seat, remembering when Corey used to sit there gnawing on whole wheat bagels, kicking his fat little legs.

"Of course you aren't." Zoe checked her Minnie Mouse watch. "If we're going to get out of here before Corey graduates college, you'd better go get the chicken. I'll stake out a place in line."

Alison elbowed her way through the knot of shoppers clustered around the poultry case. The ticket she ripped from the dispenser was number seventy-two. "Forty-eight," the butcher called.

Mark and Zoe insisted on free-range, organic chicken. Alison decided that once it was smothered in Marsala sauce, they wouldn't know the difference. She grabbed a package of frozen thighs from the Foster Farms case, stopped at the freezer for a pint of Corey's favorite ice cream, Ben & Jerry's Chocolate Fudge Brownie, and slid into place beside Zoe, ignoring the glares and mutterings of the people in line behind them.

Zoe raised her eyebrows at the frozen chicken. Alison shrugged. "What he doesn't know won't hurt him."

Zoe winked at her. "I'll never tell," she said.

You never did, Alison thought. "I'm counting on that," she said.

The bed shook Alison awake. Her eyes flew open. The windows rattled in their panes. *Is this the big one?* she thought.

She bolted upright. *Please,* she prayed, her earthquake prayer. It felt like a 747 was roaring through the room. The bed lurched again. *Please.*

"Mark?" she whispered into the dark. Her hand swept the · empty bed. *I'm in my office. He's downstairs.* The pull chain of her bedside lamp tapped the shade frantically. *Gotta get Corey before the house falls down.* She leapt out of bed.

The shaking stopped. A car alarm shrieked. Alison stood still, waiting. Was it really over?

She listened for sounds from the bedrooms below. Nothing. Mark was her in-house seismograph; he slept through any quake smaller than 6.0. Corey slept through everything.

It was over. For now. Alison glanced at the clock on her nightstand. 5:45 AM. In an hour she'd begin her daily morning tussle with Corey, attempting to separate him from his bed. She decided to get some work done. She went to her computer to work on her *Redbook* piece, a roundup of women who'd had breast implants, then breastfed their babies. Alison nicknamed all of her stories; this one was "Tits for Tots."

She was too rattled to work. She went downstairs to the second floor, the boys' floor as she thought of it, and drifted toward the front bedroom: hers and Mark's, now Mark's. The door was closed, of course. *How did this happen to us,* she asked Mark silently. *Why are you in our room, and I'm out here alone?*

Alison touched her hand to the door. She imagined sliding into bed with Mark, kissing him, making love to him, finding him again. She slid to the floor, hugging her knees to her chest, unpacking her hope chest, summoning memories of their better times.

The sex that had brought them together. The wonder of Corey's birth. The weeks at the Tahoe cabin they'd rented each winter, snuggled up with their beautiful boy, drinking hot chocolate in front of the fire. The hikes with Zoe through Yosemite's wildflower meadows, the four of them dipping their toes into icy snowmelt streams, screaming. The hours and the paychecks they'd spent stripping woodwork and planting gardens and painting walls, the sweet satisfaction of turning Casa Money Pit into a home.

Alison knew exactly when she'd last felt good with Mark: on the last vacation they'd taken together, two years before, in mid-October 2001. Along with the rest of the world, they'd still been reeling from 9/11.

Remembering that Tuesday morning made Alison shiver in her fuzzy robe. Corey had been asleep, as usual. Mark had turned on the TV news as he was getting ready for work, as usual. But then Alison heard Mark calling her name, and there was nothing usual about his voice.

She got to him just in time to watch the second tower collapsing, the white cloud swallowing lower Manhattan, the ghostly figures barely outrunning the tsunami of debris. The newscasters said a third hijacked plane was headed for San Francisco. CNN said the target might be UC Berkeley, a mile from Mark and Alison's house. While Mark frantically dialed his parents in New Jersey, Alison frantically tracked the progress of the third, missing plane.

Corey woke up, finally, and Zoe arrived. The four of them sat on the couch for hours, unable to wrench their eyes from the screen. At eleven years old, Corey had questions the adults couldn't answer. "Who's flying those planes?" "Why are they mad at America?" "Is it going to happen again?" "Is it going to happen to *us?*" Alison had never felt so impotent as a mom.

Over the next few months, the four of them went to demonstrations in Oakland, Berkeley, and San Francisco, protesting anti-Muslim profiling and hate crimes and Bush's threats of war. The attacks made their way into each of their work and school lives. Alison put aside her *Ladies' Home Journal* piece about the benefits of early morning exercise and started writing an unassigned essay on fear. Mark assigned an investigative piece on the threats to civil liberties in the name of homeland security. Zoe started a series of paintings called Collateral Damage, images of children fleeing through Manhattan streets. Corey helped organize a walkout at Claremont Middle School behind a banner that read OUR SCHOOL IS A HATE-FREE ZONE.

One month later, Mark and Alison decided to escape their CNN addiction and celebrate their twelve years together—their "sexiversary"—since they had no legal marriage to celebrate. They left Corey with Zoe and spent three blissful days at a Wine Country inn outside Sonoma, marooned on an enormous feather bed, reading no newspapers, watching no TV.

They drank good coffee in the morning and good wine at night. In between they read voraciously, slept voraciously, and made love voraciously, none of which they'd had the time, privacy, or inclination to do for years. Alison privately declared the weekend a no-self-hatred zone. She took a much-needed break from obsessing about the ten pounds she'd been carrying since Corey's birth, the southward migration of her breasts and butt, the ever-deepening grid of wrinkles on her face. She and Mark left Sonoma brimming with fresh hope and promises to keep that spark alive.

It was a dreamy drive home through a canopy of mossy oaks, soft green slopes of espaliered grapes, turrets of stone wineries towering above groves of manzanita and madrone. Mark was steering with his left hand, caressing Alison's thigh with his right. And then he cleared his throat in that *something's coming* way of his that always made Alison tense up.

"I know this sounds cheesy," he said, "but 9/11 is making me think about what really matters. We've been talking about having another baby for years. I want us to do it now, while we still can."

Alison swallowed her rising panic. She'd always imagined having two kids, maybe three. She didn't want Corey to be the lonely only child she'd been. She wanted another child.

But having a second baby could upset the delicate balance that Zoe had called Alison's "house of cards." A new baby could expose the lie that Alison had been living since Corey's conception. A new baby could shatter the family she'd built around that lie.

As much as Alison wanted a sibling for Corey, an infant to glue her and Mark back together, another chance to feel as full and as purposeful as only pregnancy had made her feel, she couldn't take the chance.

"I'm only thirty-nine," Alison told Mark. "Annie Leibovitz is pregnant, and she's fifty-one."

Mark took his hand off Alison's leg. He hit the gas, passing an old pickup truck loaded with bales of hay. "Every time I bring this up, you say the same thing."

"Impossible. This is Leibovitz's first kid."

Mark scowled. "You know what I mean, Alison."

She did. The first time they'd talked about having a second child, they were cleaning up after Corey's third birthday party. "We already have the perfect kid," Alison said. "How could we ever get that lucky again?"

Mark brought it up again when Corey was five. They'd taken him to see the herd of buffalo in Golden Gate Park. Impervious to the winds whipping off the ocean, bundled into a wool hat and his Tahoe snow jacket, Corey had hooted and hollered at the hulking, anachronistic creatures as if they were a party put on just for him.

When they finally managed to drag him back to the car, Corey started begging for a treat he'd had on their last visit to "San Farisco," a Ben & Jerry's Fossil Fuel ice cream cone that had apparently been the gastronomic high point of his five years.

How could his parents deny him a repeat experience with a mouthful of tiny chocolate dinosaurs? They could not. So they strapped their excited son into his car seat and headed for Haight Street. As they walked past Wasteland, Zoe's favorite used clothing store, Mark stopped to read a T-shirt in the window. The shirt featured a horrified-looking woman clutching her heart, saying, OH, NO! I FORGOT TO HAVE A CHILD.

As soon as Corey fell asleep in the car on the way home, Mark cleared his throat and said, "If we started trying now, and we got pregnant right away, Corey would be six when the baby was born."

"That's a lot of ifs," Alison stalled.

"You said you wanted more than one."

"I do. But our finances are so shaky. Can we really afford another kid?"

Mark looked at Alison. She felt him weighing the pros and cons of pushing her.

"Maybe it *would* be smarter to save some money first," he said. Then Corey woke up and started pleading with them to stop at Adventure Park in the Berkeley Marina. They hadn't discussed it since.

"Everyone's saying 9/11 is going to put magazines out of business," Alison said. "It's a bad time to jeopardize my career."

After a decade of writing predictable pap for women's magazines, Alison had just gotten her first big break. *The New York Times Magazine* had published one of her essays in its "Hers" column. Since then assignments had been coming more often, from more prestigious magazines, for better pay.

"*Mother Jones* isn't going out of business," Mark said. "You'll still get assignments from us. And I can always support us if I have to."

"You think we can pay for the house and the car and Corey's guitar lessons and Corey's Air Jordans and Corey's CDs on *your* salary?" Alison asked.

Mark had been promoted to senior editor years before, but the magazine was always on the verge of going under. He still made less than $75,000 a year.

"Given 9/11," Mark said slowly, "don't you think having a baby is more important than Corey's sneakers and your career?"

Alison was stung. "You know nothing's as important to me as Corey." Her words hung in the silence. "And you," she added, too late.

Mark pulled the car off the road, unbuckled his seat belt, and turned to Alison.

"I want us to be happy again," he said.

"No one's happy these days."

Alison stared out at the madrone trees lining the road, their branches naked dancers, mango trunks shedding chocolate bark.

"You are—when you're with Corey," Mark said. "Or Zoe. But when it's just you and me, it's like you can't wait to go on to the next thing."

He's right, Alison thought. After all these years, she still felt safe and loved by Mark. And increasingly, she was bored by Mark. Her trips to gather material for her articles, her nights out with Zoe, her mini writing retreats had become her escape from domesticity—and from him.

"We used to make love every day," Mark said.

"You think having a baby will fix our sex life? That's what wrecked it in the first place."

"I'm starting to wonder if you even *want* another kid." Mark raked his fingers through his thinning hair. "It's a good thing Corey was an accident. If we'd had to plan him, you'd still be making up your mind."

"That's not fair!"

"I'll tell you what's not fair," Mark said, his voice rising. "It's not fair that you've been bullshitting me for ten years."

Alison froze.

"You've been leading me on, telling me you wanted another kid," Mark said. "And I've been stupid enough to believe you. I'm done with that now."

Alison's heart slowed.

Mark yanked the car back onto the main road, tires spinning, wheels spitting gravel.

"*You* tell *me* if you ever want another baby. I'm not asking you again."

Mark was as angry as Alison had ever seen him. But all she felt was relief.

Two years and one deep-freeze later, Alison rose from her post outside Mark's bedroom, knees creaking. MAYBE WE'D BE HAPPY NOW, she thought, IF I'D AGREED TO HAVE A CHILD THEN.

She went to the kitchen to make herself a cup of Peet's. Zoe's blue Le Creuset pot was sitting on the counter, washed and waiting for Zoe to take it home and refill it with lentil soup or pasta sauce or chicken stew.

Alison turned the kitchen radio on to *Morning Edition*. "An earthquake of magnitude 6.5 shook California's central coast moments ago," Steve Inskeep was saying. "It was felt as far south as Los Angeles and as far north as San Francisco."

"In Paso Robles," Inskeep went on, "two women died when the quake destroyed the city's 1892 clock tower and the adjacent building. Their bodies were found in the rubble."

Why do I live here, Alison asked herself for the second time in an hour. She glanced at the clock on the wall. 6:05 AM. Too early to call Zoe. Anyway, Alison knew what Zoe would say; she'd said it all before. "Your ambivalence made you leave me, and it made you check out on Mark. If you ever make up your mind to be closer to him, he'll be right there, waiting for you."

Alison had never told Zoe that Mark wanted another baby, or that Alison was afraid to say yes for reasons only Zoe could understand.

Zoe was a great friend to Alison, a great friend to Corey, and a great friend to their family. It had taken Alison twenty years to realize what Zoe *wasn't*: put on earth to take care of Alison. Much as both of them might wish she did, Zoe didn't have the power to fix what ailed Alison's character or her circumstances. So Alison had grown pickier about the damaged parts of herself that she brought to Zoe to repair.

Also, Zoe had been distant lately, a sure sign she was dating someone. She didn't talk to Alison about the women she slept with, but Alison could always tell. She'd show up with bluish shadows beneath her eyes, a new scarf wrapped in a new way around her neck, an unfamiliar name tossed into the conversation once, twice, then never mentioned again.

The first few times it happened, Alison panicked, thinking, *This is how we'll lose her.* Eventually she learned to wait out Zoe's affairs. Zoe always came back, drenching them in her lavish attention, posting flyers on the fridge as if it were a café bulletin board, dragging the three of them to gallery openings, poetry slams, and always, always demonstrations: for gay rights, against the cover-up of the Enron scandal, against the pending war in Iraq.

Alison applied the theory of small earthquakes to Zoe's affairs. She chose to see them as tiny tremors that might prevent a bigger quake. As long as Zoe was having regular releases of her indefatigable sexual energy, Alison figured, Zoe was less likely to fall in love, to start her own family, to disappear from their lives.

Alison set the kettle on the stove, gazing at her reflection in the shiny stainless steel. Even in the pale dawn light she could see the creases that puckered her mouth, the coarse white curlicues erupting from her mane of auburn hair.

Suddenly the kettle rocked on the burner. The pots and pans on the hanging rack clanged. *Just an aftershock,* Alison prayed. *Please.*

The shaking stopped. Alison took a deep breath, turned the kettle off, and went upstairs to wake Corey for school. She knocked on his door, called his name. She knocked again, heard nothing, and took the opportunity to penetrate the forbidden fortress of his room.

Her eyes landed on the splatter of socks and underwear on the floor. "If you can make a basket from the three-point line," she'd asked him the night before from her permitted position in his doorway, "why can't you land a T-shirt in a hamper?" Corey had pulled the shirt off his back, rolled it into a ball, and tossed it into the hamper. "Nothing but net," he'd bragged, stepping toward her, lifting his palm for a high five. Alison had slapped his palm, barely able to contain her pathetic gratitude.

As usual, his desk was buried under the detritus of his life: manga magazines, empty CD cases, baseball caps, outdated notes brought home for his parents' signatures, scribbled notes for the songs he loved to write—sweet, soft tunes until recently; now harsh, pounding raps with lyrics Alison tried not to understand. His bookshelves were loaded with trophies for soccer and softball games from his grade school days, basketball since he'd changed sports in middle school.

The daffodil yellow walls were grayish now, spider-webbed by a decade's worth of earthquakes large and small. Whenever she and Mark threatened to repaint them, Corey begged them not to "ruin his life" by taking down the keepsakes he'd spent years putting up. The black and orange Giants pennant Zoe had bought him at Candlestick Park. The blue and gold Warriors pennant Mark had bought him at the Oakland Coliseum. Posters of his current heroes, Allen Iverson, Rosa Parks, Bob Marley, Tupac Shakur. Photos of desert sunsets, snowcapped mountains, and bare-breasted tribeswomen ripped from Mark's old *National Geographics*. Photos of rappers draped in fur coats and big-bottomed women ripped from *Vibe*.

The wall Corey saw from his pillow was reserved for his most treasured collection: an ever-changing, multilayered, push-pinned collage of snapshots, the storyboards of his life to date. There was tousle-haired, two-year-old Corey, making macaroni art with Zoe at their kitchen table. Corey bundled in wool and fleece, shoveling sand into a green plastic pail on socked-in Stinson Beach. Corey on Mark's shoulders, laughing ecstatically at something off camera at the annual How Berkeley Can You Be? Parade. Corey at ten, shooting baskets in their driveway with Zoe. Corey at twelve, building a snowman outside their Tahoe cabin with Alison and Mark.

The quality of the collection had suffered from the advent of digital photography. The latest additions were dull computer printouts; there would be no more glossy prints. There was Corey a few months before, playing his first game for the Berkeley High freshman basketball team, sprinting down center court, managing to keep both his macho posturing and his baggy shorts up while he ran. Corey a few weeks before, mugging for Alison's camera, ironing his size five thousand jeans before school. Corey and Mark at the dinner table a few nights before, caught by Alison in a rare, precious moment of actual conversation.

Sighing, Alison traced Mark's profile with her finger. *He's such a good dad*, she thought. *He doesn't deserve this trouble with Corey, and he doesn't deserve the trouble with me.* He'd changed diapers, gone to more parent–teacher meetings than she had, spent long nights discussing every Corey-related decision with her. He'd taught Corey how to shoot a basketball, make hot chocolate, build a fire in the woodstove. Like Corey's relationship with Alison, the connection between Mark and Corey had been effortless and joyous—until now.

Alison turned and gazed at her sleeping son. Even at rest, his face was dimmed by adolescence, like the fog that brought the curtain down early on Bay Area summer days. Until he'd started at Berkeley High, Corey had been a straight-A student. Now that they mattered, his grades had plummeted to Cs and Ds, barely good enough to keep him eligible for the team. Most worrisome of all, he'd dropped his friends from elementary and middle school, and he'd started hanging out with a bunch of boys who seemed even more basketball obsessed and less interested in schoolwork than he was.

Alison laid her hand lightly on Corey's chest, feeling its certain beat. *Just be okay,* she willed him. *Everything else in my life, every building, every government, every religion on earth can collapse, as long as you're okay.*

22.

A lison stepped out of Corey's room, closed the door
behind her, and knocked on it again, louder this time.
When she heard him mumble, "I'm up," she went downstairs to
"make his breakfast." Most days, this consisted of either handing
him a granola bar or fighting with him about the importance
of eating a real breakfast and *then* handing him a granola bar.
Keeping hope alive, she put out a box of whole-grain Oatios, a
quart of organic milk, and the Peter Rabbit bowl he'd insisted on
eating every meal out of when he was two.

Ten minutes later, Corey's size twelve Air Jordans came
clomping down the stairs. "Hi, Mom," he greeted her.

"Morning, Pickle," Alison said, surprised by his sweetness.
She noticed he was wearing a Phat Farm shirt she'd never seen
before. She wondered where he'd gotten the money to buy it.

"Mo-o-m," he complained. "Don't *call* me that."

Second surprise of the morning: Corey poured himself a bowl of cereal and started shoveling dripping spoonfuls into his mouth. "Where's Dad?" he asked.

"Work, I guess."

Corey paused mid-slurp. "What's up with you guys?" he asked.

Alison's heart sank. Zoe must be right. Corey was acting out because of the distance between his parents. "What do you mean?" she hedged.

"Come on, Mom. You and Dad never hang out. You don't even *yell* at me together anymore."

"We don't yell at you."

Corey shot her an annoyed look. "Mom. I'm thirteen. I'm not stupid."

"Dad and I have both been working really late," she said. "If we slept in the same room, we'd wake each other up."

And they say teenagers lie to their parents, Alison thought. "Also," she added, "Dad and I haven't been . . . close lately."

Corey stopped eating and stared into his cereal bowl. "Honey." Alison wanted to pull him into her lap and hold him. "Every relationship has its ups and downs. We'll be fine."

"I guess you guys are going through a major down." Corey swallowed another spoonful of cereal. "Same as you and me."

"Dad and I love each other. Same as you and me."

Alison glanced at the clock. If Corey didn't leave the house in thirty seconds, he was going to be late for school. If he was late for school, he'd be kicked off the basketball team. If he was kicked off the team, he'd lose the only thing he seemed to care about.

"You gotta go," she said, as she did every morning.

Corey stood and shrugged into his backpack, a back-to-school gift from Zoe. On his third day, he'd brought it home covered with strange symbols—gang symbols, Alison feared. She'd sneaked into his room when he was sleeping, snatched it, then emptied and washed it. The markings hadn't come out.

"I'll pick you up after practice," she said.

"Can't Zoe do it?"

Alison wondered whether Corey was trying to keep her from talking to his coach or if Zoe were a more desirable chauffeur. She suspected both were true. Neither made her happy.

"Sor-ree. You'll just have to handle ten whole minutes in the car with your old mom." Alison was trying to keep it light. These days, she was always trying *something* with Corey. Trying to be stricter than she naturally was or wanted to be. Trying to lift him out of his sullen, surly moods. Trying to sneak in a bonding moment when he wasn't paying enough attention to push her away.

Mothering Corey used to be the most natural thing she'd ever done. Why did she have to *try* to be close to him just because he was bigger and older?

Shoulders hunched, backpack flopping, Corey shuffled toward the front door. "Peace out," he called, and slammed the door behind him.

At four o'clock that afternoon, an hour before practice ended, Alison drove to the Berkeley High gym. She needed to see Corey happy and animated. She needed to see that he was still good at something, that he still cared about something— even if it was just a stupid ball game.

She heaved the heavy gym door open, stepped onto the court, and surveyed the boys shooting and dribbling at the other end. Corey was usually easy to pick out; he was the second-tallest boy on the team and the only white kid. She didn't see him.

Alison raked her eyes over the players again. Corey wasn't there.

Coach Davis barked, "Give me ten laps" and walked toward Alison. There was no good news in his step.

"I sent him home," Davis said, his voice barely audible above the thundering slap and squeal of sneakers on varnished wood. "He skipped practice yesterday. So he doesn't get to work out today."

"But he's not home." Alison felt ill. "And he told his . . . godmother that you benched him yesterday."

"Would have if I could have. But he never showed."

The coach blew a whistle that hung from a plastic lanyard around his neck. It looked like something a grandchild might have made for him. Alison wondered if Coach Davis had a family, if a child of his had ever made him sick with worry.

"Pick up the pace," Davis yelled at the players. Alison stared at the boys jogging around the perimeter of the gym, as if Corey would materialize if she looked hard enough.

"He missed two days last week too," Davis said. "Kid's on shaky ground. Bad grades, bad attitude. Been like that for a while."

Alison's stomach roiled. Where had Corey *been?* "I know about his grades," she said. "I didn't know he's been missing practice."

Davis blew his whistle, two shrieking blasts. The boys stopped and turned to him like show dogs at attention, awaiting his next command.

"Let me see some layups," Davis shouted. The boys divided themselves into two wriggling lines. The first boy on each line in turn ran up to the basket, dropped the ball in, retrieved it, bounced it to the next shooter, ran to the back of the line, and did it again. Their movements were so smooth, so choreographed. They looked more like a dance troupe than a gangly group of thirteen-year-olds.

"Boy's been mouthing off to me," Davis added. "Ignoring what I tell him, hotdogging on the court. So I benched him a couple times. He wasn't happy about it. They never are."

"He didn't tell me." Alison twisted her car keys in her hands.

Davis glanced at her, then back at the court. "I been coaching kids a long time," he said. "I can tell which ones got real problems and which ones are just trying it on for size. Corey's a good kid. He'll settle down. But the time to get on him is now. So it don't get more serious than it is."

Alison was hot with worry and shame. She wanted to ask Coach Davis how to stay on Corey exactly. How to keep it from getting more serious than it was.

"Would you call me the next time he misses practice?" she asked.

"I wish I could," Davis said. "But I got three teams. Fifty kids to keep track of. Half of 'em got something going wrong in their lives most of the time. Serious stuff, I mean. Not like your boy."

Coach Davis watched his team, his hand on his whistle. "Tell you what. I'll give you my cell number. You can call me to check up on him."

"Thanks. His dad and I will talk to him tonight. Maybe I won't have to bother you again."

"Can't hurt to hope," Coach Davis said dubiously. He turned back to his team.

A lison got in her car and drove slowly past Martin Luther King Park, where Berkeley High kids were always playing hacky sack and smoking pot before, during, and after class.

The lawn was littered with nests of homeless people. A woman in rags, her face creased and crumpled, sat talking to herself on a bench. The swings in the little playground hung empty. Her heart leapt at the sight of a boy sitting on the Peace Wall, a red Berkeley High sweatshirt hood shadowing his face, his long legs dangling over the mosaic of hand-painted tiles. Alison pulled over. He was Corey's size and build, but he wasn't Corey.

Corey had painted one of those peace tiles a couple years before, at the Berkeley Y's summer camp. Alison had sent him there for the same reason she'd sent him to Oakland public schools, the same reason they'd used Zoe's Berkeley address to enroll him in Berkeley High—so he'd get to know all kinds of kids. So he wouldn't grow up to be a racist or a snob. So he'd grow up to be a good person. Not the kind of person who cuts practice, lies to his coach, lies to his parents.

Sighing, Alison turned the Saab toward Shattuck. She drove past the kids clustered in the doorways of Starbucks, Taco Bell, Mel's Diner. She scoured the crowds lining up for the 5:30 movies outside the UA multiplex. No Corey.

Her cell phone rang. "Did you talk to the coach?" Zoe asked.

"He cut practice yesterday. The coach sent him home today. I'm driving around looking for him right now." Suddenly Alison was fighting tears. "I don't know where he is."

"That can't be right. I picked him up at the gym yesterday."

"Inside or outside?"

After a moment, Zoe said, "Outside."

"He's been lying. A *lot*." Alison was crying now. She pulled into a space in front of Jamba Juice. "He even lied to *you*."

"Teenagers lie," Zoe said. "That's the only control they have over their lives. Try and keep some perspective. He's not shooting heroin. Or his classmates."

How does she do it? Alison wondered. *She's actually making me feel good about the fact that my son hasn't killed anyone.*

"Go home," Zoe said. "He'll show up as soon as he gets hungry. Want me to come over?"

Of course she did. But now that she knew how much her troubles with Mark were affecting Corey, she needed to fix that even more than she needed Zoe's comfort. If she and Mark were going to get closer, she'd have to start counting on him instead of running to Zoe first.

"Thanks," Alison said. "But I'm going to call Mark so we can figure out what to do."

"You and Mark," Zoe repeated.

I can't take care of you right now, Alison wanted to say. "I think you were right about Corey acting out because of Mark and me," she said. "So I've got to make things better with Mark."

"Too bad that means leaving me out."

"Zoe—"

"Call me when you find Corey." Zoe hung up.

A lison met Mark at the door, cell phone in one hand, cordless phone in the other.

"I can't believe he's been lying to us," Mark said. He dropped his briefcase on Corey's chair. "I can't believe he lied to Zoe."

"I know." The distraught look on Mark's face was oddly comforting to Alison. He was Corey's dad. He cared about Corey as much as she did. He would be her partner, if only she'd let him be.

"Teenagers lie," Alison said. "It's their way of having some control over their lives." She stood behind Mark's chair and put her arms around him. His shoulders tensed. Then he let his head fall back against her.

"What's happening to our baby?" Mark choked out. "He was such a sweet, innocent boy. I feel like we're losing him."

Alison led Mark into the living room. They settled onto the couch, inches apart. "I don't understand it either," Alison said. "But I don't think the situation between you and me is helping."

Mark looked sad. He looked scared. He looked like he loved her.

"The distance between us . . . " Alison said. "Sleeping separately. Not talking. Not making love. That's not the way I want us to be."

"I don't want that either," Mark said. "I don't know how we got here. I swear I don't. But I want us to try and love each other again."

Footsteps pounded up the front steps. "That's him." Alison squeezed Mark's hands. "Oh thank God, that's him."

The front door opened. "Mom?" Corey called. Relief whooshed through her, then left her limp. Corey alive was all she wanted. And here he was.

"We're in here," Alison answered. Another set of footsteps came up the steps. Zoe's.

"She found him," Mark said quietly.

"She found him," Alison repeated.

Corey swaggered into the living room, reeking of pot. Zoe was just behind him. Corey leaned against the wall. Zoe perched on the edge of the couch between Alison and Mark.

"What are *you* doing home?" Corey asked Mark.

"Sit your butt down," Mark said.

Corey didn't move.

"Now," Mark roared.

Corey's hooded eyes widened. He folded his tall, skinny body into the easy chair, his long legs sticking straight out in front of him. Alison saw that his eyes were bloodshot. His face was a closed fist. Fresh tears sprang to her eyes. *Who is this hostile, shut-down kid?*

"Where *were* you?" Corey asked Alison. "I waited for you for *hella* long. I had to catch the *bus*."

"Where did you wait?" Mark asked.

"At the gym," Corey answered.

Alison stared at him, horrified by the proficiency of his deception.

Zoe stood up and beckoned to Corey. "Come with me," she said and walked into the kitchen. Corey followed her like a lamb.

"You're being a jerk," Alison heard Zoe say, quietly enough to pretend she and Corey were having a private conversation, loudly enough for Alison and Mark to hear.

"They're jerks," Corey said. "Did you hear Dad yell at me?"

"Do you remember anything we talked about in the car? About what it does to your soul to lie?"

After a long silence, Zoe said, "You ready for a little attitude adjustment, dude?"

And then she led him back into the living room. He plopped onto the chair. Zoe didn't sit down.

"I'll let you guys talk," she said. She turned to Corey. "I love you," she said.

"I love you too," Corey mumbled.

Zoe shot Alison a sympathetic glance and left.

"I went to the gym at five," Alison said, watching Corey's face. She saw her words registering slowly, as if on a seven-second delay. "I know the coach sent you home. I know you've been missing practice. I know you've been lying to him. And to Zoe. And to us." She swallowed around the lump in her throat. "I know you're high right now."

Corey picked at a loose thread on his jeans. "So what if I smoked a little weed?" he said. "You guys did it. I bet you still do."

"Where were you after school today?" Mark asked.

"Hanging out."

"That's not an answer."

"You guys are trippin'. I don't have to tell you every little thing I do."

"When Zoe picked you up yesterday, you told her you'd been to practice," Mark said. "That's called lying."

"That's called my right to privacy," Corey said. "You guys don't tell *me* everything. Does that make *you* liars too?"

Corey glared at Alison. "You told me you sleep in your office so you and Dad won't wake each other up. Talk about *lying*."

Mark shot Alison a startled look. "What goes on between Dad and me is our business," Alison said. "Not yours."

"So . . . " Corey said slowly. "Your privacy is your business. But when I want some privacy, I'm a liar."

"Exactly," Mark said.

Corey snorted.

"You're in trouble, Corey," Mark said. "Your grades are down. You're jeopardizing your place on the team. You're in a crappy mood all the time. We're worried about you."

"I'm only in a bad mood when I'm with you guys." Corey slouched deeper into the chair. "Maybe I should go live with Zoe."

Alison felt the blow in her belly, Corey's first home. His being was either a success of technology or a failure of human will, but he was her miracle boy, her most beloved on this earth. Wherever he'd come from, he'd gotten here through the portal of her body. However many parents she'd given him, she was his mom. She could blame her mother for her own suffering, but she had only herself to blame for his.

Alison felt every mistake she'd made with Corey, a pile of bricks on her chest. His first year, when she'd left him with Zoe for ten hours a day. Her business trips. Letting her relationship with Mark fall apart.

Mark was right. Even now, when he was being the *difficult child* he'd never been before, Corey opened her, softened her, changed her. And now he was demanding even more of her, acting like an utterly unlovable kid, needing her to love him anyway.

It wasn't easy for Alison to be that selfless. Since the day of Corey's birth, being his mom had made her feel loved and loving, grown-up and competent, exactly what she'd always longed to feel. It was hard to give that up. But lately being Corey's mom made her feel like a needy, suspicious failure, begging hugs from a six-foot, angry teenager, surreptitiously sniffing him like a drug dog, hoping not to detect a whiff of pot or booze.

Instead of showering him with art supplies and guitar lessons to feed his creativity, she'd become his jailer. And the deepest cut of all: instead of basking in the reflected glory of her son's sunny disposition—proof positive of good mothering, of a good mother, of a mother who is a good person—Alison had to face her own shadow side in Corey's adolescent darkness.

She looked at her son, stoned and sullen, and she thought about the secrets she was keeping. She wondered if those secrets were poisoning him somehow. She wondered if she were any better than her own mother.

"We love you, Pickle," she said. "Whatever's wrong, we want to help."

"Then stop fucking calling me that. And just fucking leave me alone." Corey's voice cracked, skittering from one octave to another.

Alison felt an instinct take hold. She followed it. She walked over to her son and kneeled in front of him. She took his face in her hands.

Corey tried to shrug out of her grip. She didn't let him. She turned his head and made him look at her. She saw pot and panic in his eyes.

"I'll *never* leave you alone," Alison told him. "I love you. I'll always love you. No matter what happens, I promise you. I'll never leave you alone."

Corey stiffened, the way he used to arch his back as an inconsolable infant. And then he fell against Alison, his narrow shoulders shaking with sobs. The weight of him almost knocked Alison down, but she steadied herself and she held onto her son.

23.

A fter Corey went to bed, Mark and Alison sat on the couch, sharing a bottle of wine.

"I'm sorry I let things get so bad between us," Alison said.

"We both had a part in that." Mark cracked his knuckles, a habit that made Alison cringe. She noticed that the blond hairs on the backs of his fingers were going gray.

"I love you, Alison," Mark said. "How can I say this without sounding like a bad rock 'n' roll song? You're it for me. But I want to know all of you. Not just the parts you want me to see."

"I don't think it's me you love," Alison said. "I think it's the person you wish I was."

Mark considered this. "It's both," he said.

Alison stared at him, taken aback by his honesty.

"I wouldn't have put up with your ambivalence all these years if I didn't think you could change." He cupped the bowl of his wine glass in his hands. "You *have* changed. With Corey. You're so soft and open with him. I just wish you could be that way with me."

"I am. I mean, I was, until—"

"Let's not bullshit each other, okay?" Mark said. "I see how you look at me. I see you listing all my faults in your head." He licked a drop of red wine off his upper lip. Alison remembered the first time she'd met him, how badly she'd wanted to taste those luscious lips.

"Even loving Corey terrifies you," Mark added. "No wonder you don't want another child."

"That again," Alison sighed.

"That *still*," Mark said.

Alison heard Zoe twenty years earlier, complaining about her intimacy issues. She heard Mark now, complaining about the same thing. Alison had convinced herself that she'd left Zoe because she felt smothered, because she didn't want to inflict lesbian mother-hood on her kids, because she'd fallen in love with Mark.

Ten years later, she'd convinced herself that she'd lost interest in Mark because he bored her, because he didn't know her, because he didn't turn her on anymore. *Maybe I do need to do something about myself,* she thought. *But can I let him in more than I have without telling what he can't ever know?*

"It *is* hard for me to trust people," Alison said slowly. "I guess it's because—"

"Your childhood sucked," Mark interrupted her. "I'd give you a better one if I could. But I can't. No one can. Not even Zoe."

Mark understood her so much better than she'd thought he did. "I'm asking you not to let your past ruin what we have," Mark said. "Or what we could have."

Alison's throat ached. "I wanted to give Corey everything," she said. "And I screwed it up. I screwed *him* up."

"Don't give yourself too much credit, Alison. Corey's on his own path. And he's a great kid. He'll be fine."

Alison sniffled. "An hour ago, you were totally freaked out about him."

"I am freaked out about him. And I also know he'll be fine."

Mark put his arms out. Alison leaned back against his chest. He smoothed her hair back from her forehead. He stroked her arms. His hands moved to her breasts. Alison felt a tingling between her legs.

"Let's go to bed," she said.

Mark didn't hesitate. He took Alison's hand and led her upstairs. He kissed her all the way to the bed. He pulled her down, still kissing her, and wriggled them both out of their clothes. He pulled her naked body onto his. Alison had forgotten his penis, hard now and urgent against her thigh. Mark's lips burned a path across her body. She lifted herself up, lowered herself down onto him.

"Alison," he gasped. He flipped her over, got on top of her, and crouched there. Alison closed her eyes.

"Please," she moaned.

"Look at me," Mark said hoarsely.

I can't.

"I love you, Alison," Mark said. "Open your eyes."

She tried. Her eyes were hummingbirds flitting around the room. She turned her head to the side on the pillow and lifted her hips. Mark guided himself back into her.

"Don't stop," she groaned.

Mark thrust into her and then he let loose. She felt it happen. She felt him fly off into her. He took her with him, and then they were grunting and gasping, wet flesh slapping wet flesh, hands grabbing hair, skin, sheets.

Thoughts flipped through Alison's head: *Can Corey hear us?*

Should we stop? Her body blew them away. And then there were no thoughts, only her body, only Mark's body, only Mark, Mark, Mark taking her back.

"Wow," Mark said. They lay tangled up together in the fragrant swamp they'd made, their nest a twist of soft yellow sheets. Pale pink light seeped through old wooden windows that faced the Oakland hills.

Mark wrapped his arm around Alison's shoulders. She nestled her head into her favorite place, the hollow below his neck. She closed her eyes. He let her.

It was too late to sleep, too early to get up. They started talking again, making plans to save their son. Mark said he'd try to get home by dinnertime on weeknights. Alison said she'd do more of the after-school chauffeuring herself. They'd divide up the list of Corey's teachers and call each one of them every week.

"We need to pay more attention to each other too," Mark said.

They agreed to take a yoga class together at the Funky Door, a studio they could walk to from their house. They'd start a vacation fund for romantic getaways. Alison would move back into their bedroom. They wouldn't forget to make love.

Alison dozed off. Mark woke her, saying her name. The bedroom was bathed in light. "There's something else I need to talk to you about," Mark said.

Fear yanked Alison up from sleep.

"I don't want to fight about this again. But I really, really want us to have another kid," Mark said. "We're forty-two years old. This is it, Alison. Our last chance.

"I really think it would make us all happy," he said. "Even Corey."

Alison imagined Corey softening up to a brand-new baby, just as Alison had softened up to him.

She looked at Mark, reflexively scouring his face for resemblance to Corey, and she found it. His eyes were hooded. His jaw was girded for her refusal.

Alison reached up and stroked his cheek. "Let's do it," she said.

Mark's jaw went slack. "You mean it?"

"I do," Alison said.

Two years after 9/11 had disposed of so many people's disposable income, the serious magazines that used to run Alison's investigative pieces had folded. The magazines she still wrote for had been steadily losing ad pages. Which meant they were losing editorial pages. Which meant they had less room for the kind of serious stories Alison wrote. Which made her queries harder and harder to sell.

She knew that the story she was working on would be a hard sell. Parenting magazines were only interested in kids up to age twelve. Fashion magazines only cared about raising hemlines and heels, not children. Housewives' magazines wanted "inspiring" parenting stories, not "depressing" ones.

She reread her query, hoping to uncover an uplifting hook.

"TEENS IN TROUBLE"

query for a feature story

In the past six months alone, high school shootings in big cities and small towns across America have taken a dozen lives. The number of teenagers who live in chronic conflict with their parents, run away, drop out of school, and/or are incarcerated in juvenile halls is on the rise.

The crisis among American adolescents of both genders and all races and classes has been escalating since the 1960s, when teenagers' rebellion was a movement with its own politics, music, and drugs. Today's teens smoke pot and groove to reggae, hip-hop, and rap, but they're also drinking, smoking, shooting, and swallowing harsher substances: methamphetamines, heroin, cocaine, Ritalin, Prozac. They seem driven not by idealism, but despair.

If our children are the canaries in America's mine, what is the warning they're sounding? What can parents, teachers, communities, and social and political institutions do to make teenagers' lives worth living?

To answer these questions I'll interview kids and their caretakers in juvenile halls, suburban families, foster homes, therapy offices, and high school halls. I'll also bring a personal touch to the piece, interviewing and writing about my almost-fourteen-year-old son.

U plifting? Not so much, Alison sighed.

She heard Zoe's Volvo squeal to a stop outside. *Today's the day*, Alison told herself. She couldn't put it off any longer.

"Mom?" Corey yelled.

On her way downstairs, she met Corey coming up. The size of him stunned her, and his handsomeness. His backpack hung off one broad shoulder. His basketball was tucked under his long, lean arm. Alison's heart swelled in her chest, as it did each time she laid eyes on this boy.

"Corey Iverson," she greeted him. Corey's full lips—*Mark's* lips, Alison always told herself—twitched into a pleased smile. Allen Iverson, the superstar point guard of the Philadelphia 76ers, was Corey's idol. Alison indulged Corey his hero worship, hoping it was inspired by Iverson's basketball skills and not his proclivity for landing in jail.

"Wassup, Mamacita." Corey smiled. Encouraged, Alison went to hug him, an old habit dying hard. He leaned into her embrace for an instant, then ducked away. "I have homework." He headed for his room.

Zoe was standing on the porch, scuffing at flakes of paint with her foot. "These steps need repainting," she said.

"Those steps needed repainting a week after they were painted," Alison agreed. She ducked her head at the '72 Volvo in the driveway. "Speaking of repainting   "

"I love that color," Zoe said.

"It isn't a color."

"It's wabi-sabi. That's better than a color."

"That heap is thirty years old, Zoe. Keep the paint job and change the car."

"I'm attached to it." Zoe gave Alison a meaningful look. "You know how I get when I'm attached."

She crossed the threshold and draped her chartreuse corduroy jacket over the tipsy wooden coatrack that guarded the entryway. "Nice jacket," Alison said. "Is it new?"

Zoe nodded. "Buffalo Exchange. The clearance rack. Not too many white people will wear this color."

"Except for crazy you."

"Except for crazy me."

"Want some tea?"

Zoe followed Alison into the kitchen. Alison filled the kettle and set out black and red *Mother Jones* mugs. Zoe stood in front of the fridge, reading the scraps taped to its door. A Doonesbury strip mocking the recall of California governor Gray Davis and his replacement by Arnold Schwarzenegger. The Berkeley High parent newsletter's review of *Finding Nemo*, which Corey wanted to see. Flyers for MoveOn antiwar candlelight vigils. Coupons for Crest Whitestrips and Tom's of Maine deodorant.

"That stuff doesn't work," Zoe said.

"The Whitestrips? Or MoveOn?" Alison asked.

"The deodorant," Zoe answered. "It covers up the stink with a smell that's even worse."

The kettle whistled. Alison dropped two chamomile tea bags into a cow-shaped teapot, her birthday gift from Zoe the year before. The two of them sat in ladder-back chairs at the round oak table in the window, sprays of winter sunshine splashing over their hands.

"New place mats," Zoe said, fingering the one in front of her.

"Crate & Barrel," Alison admitted, resisting a vestigial tug of guilt. Zoe could live the rest of her life on the interest from her inheritance, but she still gave Alison grief about buying anything new.

"Great colors," Zoe conceded, fluffing her asymmetrical purple bangs.

Alison put out a plate of Zoe's favorite cookies, the new bittersweet version of Petit Écolier. Before the plate had quite landed on the table, Zoe had pried a chocolate tablet off a cookie and popped it into her mouth. Her hands were stained with blue, green, and yellow paint.

"What are you working on these days?" Alison asked.

"I'm doing a poster for the Human Rights Campaign's gay marriage campaign. San Francisco's going to start letting gay people get married. Maybe next month!"

"I bet every gay artist in the country wanted to do that poster. And they picked you." She lifted her *Mother Jones* mug and clinked it against Zoe's. "Major mazel tov," Alison said.

Zoe's face was radiant. "Thanks."

"I need to talk to you about something," Alison said, lowering her voice. "I don't know how to tell you this . . . "

"You're scaring me. Spit it out."

"Mark and I are trying to have a baby. Another baby, I mean."

Twin crimson spots bloomed on Zoe's cheeks. She leaned back in her chair. "When did you decide?"

"Last month. After—" Alison paused. She'd told Zoe that she and Mark had been getting along better. But, in keeping with their unspoken agreement—Zoe didn't share the details of her flings, and Alison didn't share the details of her relationship with Mark—Alison hadn't told her how their reconciliation had come about. "After that trouble with Corey."

Zoe raised her eyebrows. "Does Corey know?"

"We'll tell him when there's something to tell. At our ages, who knows how long this might take."

"Right," Zoe said flatly. "Who knows how long getting pregnant might take." She pushed her chair back and put her mug in the sink. "Gotta go," she said. She took off down the hall.

"Zoe, wait."

"Bye, Corey," Zoe yelled up the stairs. "See you tomorrow at four." The next thing Alison heard was the slamming of the door.

24.

Alison felt her abdomen cramping, felt familiar stickiness in her underwear. "Dammit!" she cursed. She had her period. Again.

She tried telling herself that she'd spotted when she was pregnant with Corey—the same bit of denial that had failed her four weeks before, eight weeks before, and twelve weeks before, when each of her periods came right on time.

Fifteen years earlier, when she couldn't get pregnant with Zoe, Alison had a choice of factors to blame. The unnatural artificial insemination process. Zoe's stressful obsessiveness. Her own ambivalence. Alison had nothing and no one to blame now. She and Mark were using the oldest, most natural insemination method on earth. And they'd been trying for three months. And she was fifteen years older now, and their time was running out.

Alison called Mark at work. "Oh, honey," he said.

Alison started to cry. "I feel like I failed you again."

"When have you ever failed me, my love?"

Every day I haven't told you I've been through this before.

"I was thinking," Mark said. "Maybe we should see a specialist. There's a place near my office. Redwood Fertility Center. It's one of the top-rated clinics in the world."

Alison drew in a sharp breath. "You keep telling me it'll happen. But you've been researching fertility clinics. You knew it wouldn't work."

"You know me, Alison. Always with a Plan B. So what do you think?"

What Alison thought was, *I should have told you the whole truth from the start. I wish I could tell you the whole truth now.*

"I bet those doctors cost a fortune," she said instead.

"Our insurance will cover most of it." Mark paused. "But if you don't want to do this—"

"I want to try," Alison said, stuffing the lie inside the truth. Or was it the truth she was stuffing inside a lie?

Alison heard the pneumatic rattle of a streetcar outside Mark's window; the clatter of phones ringing, printers printing in the rabbit warren of *Mother Jones*'s new offices on Market Street.

"It's weird," Mark said. "I thought this would just *happen*, didn't you? We sure didn't have any trouble getting pregnant the first time."

Alison imagined telling him the whole story. She imagined him hurt and furious. She imagined him leaving her. Leaving her and Corey. "We were twenty-seven the first time, remember?" she asked. "Give me the number of that clinic. I'll make an appointment."

Alison's cramps were worse, and her headache had blossomed. It was the middle of a workday and she had two stories due on

Monday, but she decided to break her own stringent work rules and lie down for a while.

She made herself a cup of the Women's Wisdom Fertility Tea Zoe had given her and carried it to bed. She got under the covers and flicked on the ABC midday news.

"Gay Marriage Debate Heats Up," the headline read. A film clip rolled, dated the day before, February 13, 2004. In the rotunda of San Francisco City Hall, two women in white bridal gowns stood holding hands with a little girl between them, facing a beaming city clerk. "I now pronounce you wife and wife," the clerk proclaimed. "Congratulations. You may now kiss the brides."

The women lifted their daughter off her feet and wrapped their arms around her and each other, their faces streaming with tears. The crowd in the rotunda applauded. Rose petals drifted through the air.

Lucky them, Alison thought. *They picked the right place at the right time. Fifteen years ago, no one would have given Zoe and me a marriage license, let alone a wedding on TV.* She remembered the way she'd laughed off Zoe's marriage proposal: a joke in 1988, no laughing matter now.

"Was it me you stopped wanting?" Zoe had asked Alison ten years before, the only time they'd talked about their breakup. "Or did you just want to be a normal mother more than you wanted what we had?"

Alison couldn't answer that question then, and she couldn't answer it now. *I wish I'd been with Zoe when being gay wasn't such a big deal,* Alison thought. *Maybe then I'd know why I really left Zoe—because I was afraid to trust her, or because I couldn't trust the world not to break our child's heart.*

* * *

"When did your last period start?" Mark whispered.

"Two weeks ago," Alison whispered back.

They were sitting in matching mauve chairs in the window-less, mauve and gray waiting room of Redwood Fertility Center. Mark was bent over the clipboard in his lap, filling out forms. Alison was trying not to see herself in the waiting room of the East Bay Sperm Bank with Zoe in 1989.

This time she had more to worry about than the humiliating questions and the tedious temperature taking, and the high-tech tests and painful procedures. What if these new fertility doctors could tell, somehow, that she'd been inseminated in the past? What if someone who'd worked at the East Bay Sperm Bank in 1989 worked at Redwood Fertility now? What if the tests proved Mark was sterile and couldn't be Corey's father? What if trying to make her family bigger and better tore her family apart?

Attempting to distract herself from the train wreck happening in her head, she checked out the other people in the room. A heavily made-up, suburban-looking single woman. Two young women, obviously a couple, but when did lesbians get so stylish and so hot? A tense-looking straight couple with salt-and-pepper hair and deep parentheses around their eyes and mouths. It did not improve Alison's mood to realize that they were probably her age.

Mark returned the clipboard to the woman behind the front desk and picked a copy of the *San Francisco Chronicle* off the coffee table. "Shit. Look at this," he said, pointing to the head-line. "Bush Lead Widens in New Poll."

"Bush probably paid for that poll himself," Alison said. The straight couple glared at her. One of the lesbians gave her a two-fisted thumbs-up.

Alison went back to studying the author bios on the *Vanity Fair* contributor's page. For once her chronic professional jealousy was coming in handy, helping her forget how she felt about being where she was.

"Alison Rose and Mark Miller." The nurse summoned them from the doorway, holding a manila folder. "I'm Nancy. Welcome."

Nancy led them down a long corridor decorated with blurry watercolors in mauve plastic frames and into a luxurious office. Floor-to-ceiling windows framed views of the city's boxy skyline and, beyond it, the choppy gray bay. Photos of beaming parents holding newborn babies covered the bulletin board behind a glass-and-chrome desk.

Nancy waved Mark and Alison into leather-and-chrome chairs. "Dr. Schrier will be right with you. Can I get you anything while you're waiting? Water? Coffee? Herb tea?"

"Shot of Stoli?" Alison asked.

Nancy smiled. "Second choice?"

"Herbal tea."

Nancy nodded and left the room.

"You sure you're all right?" Mark asked.

"Uh-huh. Why?"

"You usually don't make Stoli jokes when you're fine."

"I guess I'm little nervous," Alison admitted.

"About what?"

Alison shrugged, wishing she could tell him.

Mark took her hand, looked around the office. "Nice digs, huh?"

"If you like Roche-Bobois." Alison had been threatening to toss every stick of make-do furniture that had accumulated in their house and start over with a $4,000 Roche-Bobois couch. That plan was on hold now that she and their funky furniture might be facing another eighteen years of spit-up, grape juice, and sweaty teenagers.

Mark tugged on a hank of Alison's hair. "Die, yuppie scum."

"Let them eat Ikea." Alison let her head fall back into the cup of his hand. She closed her eyes, wishing she were anywhere else.

"Careful. This is hot." Nancy handed Alison a steaming mauve mug imprinted with the Redwood Fertility Center logo, which seemed to depict sperm chasing one another around an endless circle. On her way out, Nancy nearly collided with a tall, balding man in a white lab coat, knife-pleated gray trousers, and gleaming leather loafers.

"Don Schrier." He shook Mark's hand, then Alison's, leaving behind a faint medicinal smell. "Good to meet you both."

Schrier settled into the chair behind the desk, perched a pair of glasses on his nose, and flipped their chart open. "Let's start with why you're here."

"The Transamerica Tower was closed," Alison said, "and we heard you had great views."

Mark shot Alison an annoyed look, then turned to Schrier. "She makes jokes when she's anxious."

"Guilty as charged," Alison said. "Sorry."

Mark cleared his throat. "We've been trying to get pregnant since December," he said. "Alison's forty-two. I'm forty-three. We don't want to miss our chance."

"Understood." Schrier peered at them over his glasses. "Most of our patients are in your age range. And the fact that you've already conceived a child together bodes well for your chance of doing it again."

If we actually conceived a child together, Alison thought.

"You have one son, age thirteen?"

"We got pregnant by accident." Mark grinned. "The first time we were together, actually. But we were in our twenties then."

Alison felt queasy. "I've heard the miscarriage rate is high for women my age," she said.

"True. But less so in a second pregnancy than in a first." Schrier pulled out a lab slip, checked a few boxes, and handed it to Alison. "Give this to Nancy on your way out. We'll get started with some noninvasive tests. In a few days, when the results are in, we'll have you come in again."

Schrier stood up. "Much as I wish I could, I can't promise you an outcome. But I can guarantee that we'll give you the best fertility treatment available."

He looked at Alison. "You're in good hands. Really, Alison, you have nothing to be nervous about."

You have no idea, she thought.

A lison knocked on Corey's bedroom door. As was his habit lately, he actually opened it. Alison pointed to his ears and he removed his iPod buds.

"The meeting starts in ten minutes." Alison peeked around him, scanning his room the way she checked her breasts in the shower, hoping not to find what she was looking for. It had been months since Corey had given them reason to worry, but Alison's plan was to keep a close eye on him for a while. Until he was thirty-five or forty.

Like lots of kids at Berkeley High, Corey skipped school for anti–Iraq War demonstrations, wore a BUCK FUSH button on his backpack, and lay down in the school courtyard at lunchtime, dressed in black, for "die-ins." But despite the resurgence of his good nature since the night he'd broken down in Alison's arms, Corey still refused to appear in public with his parents.

Always on the lookout for things they could do as a family,

Alison had invited him to the MoveOn meeting and *Fahren-heit 9/11* screening that she and Mark were hosting that night. Anything happening on a video screen, she figured, gave her an advantage. Also bribe-worthy: the food.

"What meeting?" Corey's voice cracked. He cleared his throat, reminding Alison of one of Mark's annoying habits.

"MoveOn," Alison said. "I told you two days ago, remember? You said you'd come."

"Oh, yeah."

"We're having Zachary's Pizza."

"Cool," Corey said noncommittally.

"See you downstairs," Alison said optimistically.

At seven, Mark arrived with a stack of steaming Zachary's boxes in his arms, followed by a stream of people. Alison found the twenty-three of them a predictable bunch. They were white, mostly, mostly her age or older, most of them wearing T-shirts pledging allegiance to the San Francisco Mime Troupe, KQED, Sierra Club, Kerry for a Stronger America.

They came bearing predictable platters loaded with predict-able foods—wilting green salads and browning fruit salads, lumpy homemade hummus and whole-wheat pita bread, carrot sticks and bowls of French bread filled with veggie dip. They pulled bot-tles of Sierra Nevada and Calistoga from coolers, piled their plates with Zachary's four-pound slices of spinach and mushroom pizza, and settled onto the couch, the chairs, the floor. They talked and argued predictably about the prediction that Bush would win by a landslide in the election, only eight months away.

Alison fought her chronic cynicism, reminding herself why she'd invited these people into her home. As Corey got older, and Zoe got busier with her Juvenile Hall job, and Alison started anticipating the isolation a new baby would bring, she'd been forcing herself to connect with new people. Since their reconciliation, she and Mark had been making efforts to do things together. And then there was the little matter of George W. Bush.

"We're going to start," Alison said. Mark turned on the computer and sat down beside her. The Internet broadcast began with Joan Blades, cofounder of MoveOn, announcing that thousands of people across the country were doing what Alison and her houseful of predictable people were doing. She introduced Michael Moore, who introduced his movie.

"Corey would love this," Alison whispered to Mark.

"Or so his mom would like to believe."

"I'm going to go get him."

"Don't." Since Corey's troubles ended, Mark had been advocating giving him more space. Alison had intensified her campaign to reel him in.

As the movie was starting, Corey came thumping down the stairs. Alison patted the patch of floor beside her. Corey ducked his chin at her and headed into the kitchen. Moments later he reappeared with a plate full of pizza. He made his way through the crowd and plopped himself into the space between Alison and Mark. It took every bit of discipline Alison had and Mark's warning glance to keep from throwing her arms around him.

The movie came to its dramatic, distressing conclusion. Corey beat a hasty retreat before the lights came on. The people in the living room hooted and applauded, gathering themselves to go. As she closed the door behind the last of them, Alison realized that Zoe hadn't shown up. She'd been around less than usual lately. *She must be seeing someone,* Alison thought with the usual twinge of worry.

Mark and Alison cleaned the kitchen in proficient, practiced harmony, filling their recycling bin with cans and bottles, spooning leftover hummus and browning fruit salad into empty yogurt containers, washing serving bowls and spoons.

On her way to bed, Alison stopped in front of Corey's room. "Goodnight, Iverson," she said through the door.

"Goodnight, coach," Corey called back.

Alison's heart swelled. "I love you," she couldn't help saying.

She waited. Silence. She waited some more, then went to bed elated. Corey had watched the movie. And said goodnight to her nicely. For a mom of a nearly-fourteen-year-old, two out of three wasn't bad.

25.

"The news is good," Dr. Schrier said. "I see nothing unusual in the test results."

Alison released the breath that she felt she'd been holding since their last visit. She'd been more worried about finding out that Mark was sterile, and what that would mean about their past and their future, than she'd been about her own fertility.

"Your hormone levels are excellent, Alison, especially for a woman your age. And Mark, your sperm count is seventy-five million, which we consider to be in the high-normal range."

"That's great." Mark took Alison's hand and squeezed it.

"We did find a little polyp on your uterine lining, Alison," Dr. Schrier said.

Mark's smile faded. "Is it dangerous?"

"Not at all. But an embryo needs a smooth surface to attach itself to. So a polyp *can* contribute to infertility. I can take it out here in the office, under light anesthesia. There might be a bit of cramping. Otherwise, there should be no side effects."

"If you take it out," Alison asked, "is there a chance we could get pregnant on our own?"

"It's possible. We already know you two don't have the problem some couples have: their eggs and sperm just don't mesh. On the other hand, your age is definitely a factor."

Mark looked at Alison. "It's your call. I really want to give this our best shot. But I hate the idea of you going under the knife."

"Let's do it as soon as possible," Alison said. *If you could please remove my secrets while you're in there*, she told Dr. Schrier silently, *I won't miss them.*

C orey wasn't quite his old self—Alison's favorite person on earth, a person she knew she was unlikely to see again. But since their confrontation, his grades and attitude were holding steady. He wasn't confiding in his parents as much as they wished he would, but as far as they knew, what he was saying was true.

Unlike what they were telling him. Alison told Corey about her upcoming surgery, but she didn't tell him why she was having it.

"It's a tiny little growth," she said. "Nothing serious."

"Where is it?"

"In my uterine lining."

Corey winced. "Do you have cancer?" he asked.

"Absolutely not."

Corey looked at her suspiciously. "Would you tell me if you had cancer?"

God, I love this kid, Alison thought. "Probably," she said.

On the day of her surgery, Corey insisted on skipping practice to come right home after school. Alison awoke from a nap with a Vicodin hangover to find him sitting at her bedside, holding a steaming bowl of soup. "It's Campbell's Chicken Noodle," he said proudly. "I bought it at EZ Stop on my way home."

He watched as Alison ate as much as she could stand of the salty broth and mushy noodles, his mouth mirroring each motion of hers. Alison remembered her own mouth doing the same thing as she spooned baby food into his.

"Have some more, Mom," he urged her when she put the half empty bowl on her nightstand. "It's good for you."

"Who's the Jewish mother now?" Alison teased him.

"You. But I'm the Jewish son." He climbed onto the bed, turned on the TV, worked the remote until he found a *Law & Order* rerun.

"Look, Mom! I found your favorite show!"

Alison didn't tell him that there was *always* a *Law & Order* rerun playing on one channel or another, and she didn't tell him that *Law & Order* was too violent for him to watch, as she'd said when he asked to watch it with her in the past. Milking this rare moment, when the episode ended, Alison asked Corey to play her some Beatles songs.

He went to his room to find his long-abandoned guitar. When he came back with it, he didn't ask which song she wanted to hear first. He knew it was "Blackbird," and he played it for her. And he didn't stop singing, even when hearing her son sing about a bird learning to fly with broken wings made her cry, as it always had.

A lison's cramping lasted only a couple of days. Her next appointment was two weeks away. Corey was doing fine. Alison was too. She was finally free to work.

She started outlining a query called "Gray Area" about the baby boom among middle-aged, middle-class Americans:

- Is feminism to blame, or to be credited, for the increasing number of career women having babies at forty-five?

- Are claims of higher intelligence among children of middle-aged parents a form of eugenics in modern-day disguise?

- Is having a baby at forty-five intrinsically a selfish act?

Waiting for a killer opener to present itself, Alison doodled on her notepad, doing the math. If she got pregnant within the next six months, she'd be fifty-seven when she was driving around Berkeley, looking for her next surly fourteen-year-old. At sixty she'd be planting her sagging butt on a brutal stone bench in Berkeley's Greek Theater, watching that kid graduate Berkeley High. When she was seventy-five or eighty, they'd be wheeling her into that next baby's wedding—if she even lived that long. "Is midlife parenting a good thing or a bad thing," Alison typed. "And for whom, and why?"

It was blue sky springtime when Alison boarded BART in Oakland, gray sky winter in San Francisco when she got off the train. Mark met her at Schrier's office, eight blocks from *Mother Jones*.

"Now that we know you're both fertile, and we've taken care of that polyp, we have two choices." Schrier ticked them off on his fingers. "One, intrauterine insemination using Mark's sperm. Two, IVF. That's in-vitro fertilization, which is more invasive and more expensive. But it's also the most effective."

"How much does each method cost?" Alison asked.

"Intrauterine insemination is about three thousand dollars per cycle."

Three hundred the last time I did it, Alison did not say. She saw herself with her feet in the stirrups at the East Bay Sperm Bank in 1989, Zoe at her side; Naomi with a fat syringe of milky semen in her rubber-gloved hand.

"IVF is about ten thousand dollars per cycle," Schrier said. "And it often takes several cycles."

"What would you do if you and your wife were in our situation?" Mark asked.

"But with our income," Alison added.

"If you were in your thirties, I'd probably advocate insemination," Schrier said. "But given your ages, I'd go straight to IVF."

Mark's eyes were on Alison. She knew what he wanted to do, and she knew he'd put their house in hock, if he had to, to do it.

She remembered the feeling she'd had just before Naomi inseminated her the first time: in the front seat of the front car at the top of a giant roller coaster, heart in throat, hands in the air. She had that feeling now.

"Let's do the IVF," she said.

Zoe reappeared. She took Corey to a Saturday movie matinee. "Al?" she called when she dropped him off.

"Up here." Alison was in her bedroom, editing her wardrobe. Zoe plopped herself onto the bed.

"What did you guys see?" Alison asked.

Zoe rolled her eyes. "*Anchorman,*" she answered.

"You must really love that kid," Alison said.

"I do." Zoe lowered her voice. "And that kid loved the stupid-ass movie."

"Where have we gone wrong?"

Alison had missed Zoe, as she always did. Falling back into their friendship was like stepping into a hot bath on a cold day. But Zoe's latest hiatus had been well timed; it had given Alison a good excuse not to tell her about the IVF. If it worked, she'd decided, she'd deal with Zoe's reaction then.

Alison held up a men's linen shirt. Zoe stuck her fists out, thumbs down. Alison tossed it into Zoe's lap. "Here. You can paint in it."

Zoe slipped the shirt on, rolled up the sleeves, stiffened the collar, and tied the tails into a knot above her flat belly. Alison was mesmerized as always, watching Zoe play with clothes. Only Zoe could make the most boring shirt look hip.

Alison showed Zoe a clingy scoop-necked top. Zoe had convinced her to buy it years before.

"Are you nuts? You look great in that. Next."

Alison went on pulling T-shirts and sweaters off hangers and out of drawers, offering them up for Zoe's appraisal. Zoe went on giving a nod to the keepers, thumbs-down to the things that had to go. They weren't saying what Alison knew they both were thinking. The last time they'd purged Alison's closet was twenty years ago, and it had ended with hot sex on a soft mountain of velvet and velour. They weren't saying that Alison was purging her closet in case she got pregnant with Mark's child.

"What about this?" Alison frowned at a faded black Planned Parenthood T-shirt with white lettering that read, PRO-CHOICE, PRO-WOMAN.

Zoe didn't answer. Alison saw that she was half-buried in a pile of keepers, staring into space. Her face looked burnished, as if she'd had a chemical peel.

"Earth to Zoe."

"I'm seeing someone," Zoe said.

"Oh." Alison held a royal blue jumpsuit in front of her, taking a moment to compose her face. "What's she like?"

"Young. Cute. In a kind of exotic way." She paused. "Hot. Funny."

"What's her name?"

"Trudy Fleischer. Her mom's a writer, and she named Trudy after Gertrude Stein. She and her mother are really tight. Like Mom and me."

Zoe had never mentioned a lover's last name before. "How young is she?" Alison asked.

"Very." Zoe giggled.

"What does she do?"

"She's in theater."

"Which theater?"

"You're acting weird, Al."

"What's weird about wanting to know about this hot young thing?"

"Are you jealous?" Zoe threw her head back and laughed, as if Alison was making her almost as happy as her new girlfriend did. And if she was so happy, it didn't matter what Alison said.

"I'm just surprised," Alison said. "I've never heard you talk about anyone the way you're talking about . . . her."

Zoe nodded. "I've never met anyone like Trudy before."

Alison decided not to solicit Zoe's vote on her lavender 1988 Michigan Womyn's Music Festival T-shirt. She balled it up and stuffed it back into her bottom drawer. "I'm happy for you," she lied. "When do we get to meet her?"

"Zoe has a girlfriend," Alison told Mark later that night. They were undressing with their backs to each other, preparing for what now constituted foreplay.

Every night for a week, Mark had been injecting Alison in the stomach with follicle stimulating hormone. Every morning she'd been injecting herself in the thigh with Lupron to control her ovulation. Three sets of shots and two ultrasounds from now, if her eggs were plentiful and big enough, she'd be scheduled for her first egg extraction. Then Dr. Schrier would fertilize her eggs with Mark's sperm in a petri dish and implant the embryos into Alison's womb.

"Zoe *never* has a girlfriend." Mark opened the closet door, reached up to the top shelf, and pulled down a brown cardboard file box labeled "Tax Returns." Since they'd reactivated their sex life, he and Alison had been stashing their carefully curated porn collection in that box. Recently they'd added a new, distinctly unsexy collection: the syringes, alcohol swabs, vials of drugs, and hazardous medical waste container they called their weapons of mass conception.

"She does now," Alison said.

Mark raised his eyebrows and went back to readying her injection, flicking the syringe with his forefinger like a seasoned junkie or a nurse.

Alison was starting to feel like a junkie herself. Her belly was swollen and covered with black and blue marks from the shots. Her ovaries were so engorged that she could feel them through her jeans. Her emotions were swollen too. The hormone highs gave Alison a taste of how the other half—lighter, more carefree people—lived. The lows plunged her into deeper darkness.

"Ready?" Mark asked, holding the dripping syringe aloft.

Alison stepped in front of him, offering her naked body. With the tenderness of a lover and the sanguine efficiency of a lab tech, Mark swabbed her skin with an alcohol rub, then emptied the syringe slowly into Alison's belly.

"Owwwwww," Alison moaned.

"All done."

"Till tomorrow."

In one smooth gesture, Mark gave Alison a kiss and deposited the used syringe in the red plastic medical waste container. He replaced the box in its hiding place in the closet.

"That's what I call safe sex." Alison dug through her bottom drawer for her one remaining flannel nightgown. When she'd moved back into the bedroom with Mark, she'd replaced most of her tattered sleepwear with a trousseau of uncomfortable, impractical, sexy negligees. This was not a negligee night.

"Doesn't it seem weird that we're going through all this to make a baby," Mark asked, "when we did it by accident the first time we made love?"

Alison noted that Mark had now made this observation twice. "Totally weird," she said.

Zoe called Alison and said she wanted to bring Trudy over for dinner. "Make sure the boys are home," Zoe said. "We'll bring food. Trudy's an amazing cook."

Alison was nervous, washing the day's dishes while Mark and Corey set the table for five. By the time Zoe used her key to open the front door and called out, "Honeys! We're home!" Alison wasn't sure she'd be able to eat, no matter how *amazing* Trudy's cooking was.

Alison had spent fifteen years wondering what it would be like to meet the next person Zoe loved. Looking at Trudy now, her long, straight blond hair; her smooth, pale skin; her curvaceous, muscular body; her bright, friendly, pretty face, Alison had one clear thought: *she's just right.*

And then, a tangle of murkier emotions.

"It's great to meet you." Alison glanced at Mark and saw that he was staring at Trudy too.

"Welcome," Mark said. "Any friend of Zoe's is a friend of ours." *Mark can be such a dork*, Alison thought.

"I am so very glad to meet you too," Trudy said. Her accent was thick and guttural. "Zoe speaks of you often." She pronounced it *So-e*. "You mean so much to her, you three." It sounded like *zree*.

Alison realized Zoe hadn't made eye contact with her since they'd arrived. Zoe grabbed Trudy's hand. "We left the food in the car. We'll be right back."

"She's pretty," Corey said as soon as they were gone.

"*Corey*," Alison scolded him.

"What? Am I supposed to say she's *ugly?*"

"You're supposed to notice something about her besides how she looks."

Mark was grinning at Corey as if he were about to give him a high five. "Hey! You too," Alison barked.

Zoe and Trudy bustled back into the kitchen, emptying Berkeley Bowl bags, arranging platters and bowls on the table. Mark lit the candles. "Let's eat," Zoe said.

Trudy took Alison's chair. Zoe shot Alison a questioning look. Alison gave her a small smile: *it's fine*. Zoe asked the next question with her eyebrows, and Alison nodded: *she's great*.

"Where are you from in Germany?" Alison asked.

"Freiburg. A very pretty town in the south." *Zouth*, she said. Trudy reached for one of the bottles of wine they'd brought. "We make wine in Freiburg. Like here in California."

"What's that?" Corey pointed to a steaming bowl of something that looked like squiggles of pasta.

"Spaetzle," Trudy answered. "It's a favorite dish in Germany."

"Are there still Nazis there?" Corey asked her.

"Not all Germans are Nazis, Corey," Alison reproached him. Her mother had died years before Corey was born. How had Alison managed to transmit her mother's stupid stereotypes to her son?

"I *know*," Corey said. "But that's where the Nazis *came* from."

"I'm sorry," Alison said to Trudy. "I swear, we're not the kind of Jews who blame every German for the Holocaust." She forced a little laugh. "God knows we don't want the world to blame *us* for George W. Bush. That's why we're trying to get rid of him in November."

Trudy smiled at Corey. "My grandparents were in Berlin during the war. They joined the resistance against the Nazi Party. Do you know about the resistance, Corey?" Alison liked the way Trudy kept her eyes on Corey as she spoke to him.

"Sort of," Corey hedged.

"If you like, after supper I can tell you some of the stories of the resistance that my parents told me. It was an exciting time. Bad guys chasing good guys and good guys running away. Like your American films . . . " Trudy turned to Zoe. "How are they called?"

"Action movies," Zoe said, smiling at her affectionately. Zoe turned her smile on Alison, sharing her delight.

As usual, Zoe's childlike pleasure was irresistible. Alison smiled back.

26.

t felt strange to take BART into San Francisco on a Saturday morning instead of a workday. But Alison's ovaries were setting the schedule now.

Mark held Alison's hand as Dr. Schrier guided the ultrasound probe inside her. Her ovaries appeared on the monitor above her head, gray sacs filled with tiny white balloons.

"Wow," Mark said "Am I seeing things, or—"

"You're seeing follicles." Dr. Schrier looked up at the screen. "Sixteen of them, each about twenty millimeters. That's a good number, considering your age, Alison, and the low dose of hormones you've been on."

"Low dose?" Alison asked. "If I were any more hormonal, Mark would sell my body to science."

Schrier withdrew the probe and snapped the gloves off his hands. Alison sat up, clutching the blue paper gown to her chest.

"I'm going to give you a shot now, to release the eggs from the follicles."

"How nice for all of us," Alison said. "More hormones."

Dr. Schrier smiled. "I'm imagining we'll end up with seven or eight eggs. You'll come back thirty-six hours from now. We'll harvest and fertilize them and watch them grow for two days. Then I'll implant as many of the highest-ranked embryos as you want me to."

"We want one baby," Mark said. "Can't we just implant one embryo?"

"The fewer we implant, the lower your chances of pregnancy," Schrier said. "But the more we implant, the greater the chances of multiples."

"Twins?" Mark asked.

"Or triplets," Schrier said. "Or more."

"More than *three*?" Mark asked.

"If more than two fetuses take, I'd strongly recommend a fetal reduction."

Alison's head spun, imagining having to abort one or more of the babies she was working so hard to conceive.

"You mentioned ranking. What's that?" Mark asked.

"Based on how fast the cells divide, and whether they're dividing symmetrically, we rank each embryo grade A, B, or C."

"And then you decide which ones live or die," Mark said.

Schrier frowned. "We're not doing Hitler's work here, Mark. Some people oppose a woman's right to abortion. Some people oppose stem cell research for the same reason. It's all a matter of what your priorities are."

And what you can live with, Alison thought. *And what you can't live without.*

Mark's health insurance paid 80 percent of their infertility treatments. Even so, "baby" was a significant line item in their monthly budget.

Mark's salary wasn't about to change unless a miracle was visited upon *Mother Jones* in the form of a well-endowed donor. It was up to Alison to fill the gap. So she sat at her computer cranking out queries and sending them to multiple magazines, feeling like an ATM that spit out follicles and articles instead of cash.

As usual, the ideas she came up with didn't stray far from her current obsession.

"WHY BABY?"

Query for a feature story

The majority of humans on the planet do it. The survival of the species depends on it. Sometimes it happens by accident, sometimes by design. Increasingly, it happens for middle-class, middle-aged Americans only as a result of many thousands of dollars spent, dozens of difficult decisions made, and buckets of tears shed. *How* babies are conceived has become a topic of dinner-party conversation. But regardless of the process by which they participate in this miracle, few people even those who spend months or years of their lives undergoing fertility treatment—ask *why* they, or anyone else, choose to have children.

"Why Baby" will explore that question with women and men who are parents, those who are considering becoming parents, and those who are grieving their inability to become parents. My own experience with infertility will provide the story's narrative thread; experts will provide professional opinions.

* * *

A lison reread the last sentence, reconsidered, and
rewrote it: "I'll find a couple whose experience with infertility will provide the story's narrative thread and experts who
will provide professional opinions."

She hit "save," went downstairs, and flopped onto the couch.
She slipped into a daydream about having Mark's baby. About
having *another* baby with Mark.

Alison had a new secret, a sweet one. She was hoping for a girl.
She saw herself pushing a little girl on the swings at the toddler
park near Alta Bates Hospital, where she swung Corey when he
was small. "This is my daughter," she was telling another mother.
"This is my daughter, Emma."

Alison had always loved that name. As she imagined Emma,
her mouth quivered into an uncertain, hopeful smile. She
closed her eyes and dozed into a dream. Emma was playing with
a noisy toy. A toy that was getting noisier. Alison opened her
eyes. By the time she got to the phone in the kitchen, it had
stopped ringing.

The mechanical voice on the answering machine announced,
"One new message." Alison hit the "play" button.

"Hi, you two. It's Nancy at the clinic."

Alison's mouth went dry.

"Dr. Schrier wants to see you as soon as possible. I've penciled
you in for this afternoon at four. No need to call unless that time
doesn't work for you. See you then."

Alison played Nancy's message again to make sure she hadn't
dreamed it. For no reason she could explain, she went to the
bathroom and looked at herself in the mirror. Then she went to
call Mark.

* * *

N ancy greeted them in the waiting room.

"She looks happy," Mark whispered to Alison as they followed her to Schrier's office.

"He'll be right in." Instead of offering them tea or water or vodka, Nancy sat in the extra chair beside Dr. Schrier's desk. *A good sign*, Alison thought. She and Mark sat clutching each other's hands.

Dr. Schrier walked in and leaned against his desk instead of sitting behind it. He had a smile on his face. "Hello, Alison, Mark. Nancy and I wanted to tell you the good news in person." He beamed at them. "Congratulations," he said. "You're going to have a baby."

Alison burst into tears.

"Oh, my God." Mark jumped up and lifted Alison out of her leather chair and swung her around.

Alison leaned into the circle of Mark's arm, light-headed, faint.

"You said *baby*," Mark said. "Does that mean there's only one?"

"It's too soon to be absolutely sure. But based on Alison's hormone levels, I think so, yes." Schrier glanced at his Rolex.

"How can we thank you?" Mark asked giddily.

"Just take good care of your beautiful wife."

Alison started to correct him and stopped. She and Mark were having a baby. How much more married could they be?

T hey took Corey to Szechwan Gardens to tell him the news. Clearly, he sensed his parents' mood of largesse. "Can I have broccoli beef?" he asked.

Alison and Mark didn't eat beef, didn't buy beef, and didn't want Corey to eat beef. Alison had found enough Double Whopper wrappers in his trash can to know that Corey had exempted himself from the ban. She and Mark had adopted a "don't ask" burger policy. Corey wasn't about to tell.

"Have whatever you want," Mark said.

"Pot stickers?" Corey asked.

"Sure."

"I get to have *pot stickers?* What's up with you guys?"

Mark gave their order to Sam, who'd been waiting on them since Corey sat on a booster seat at that table, eating rice with his hands.

"We have good news," Mark said.

Corey raised his eyebrows.

"Honey," Alison said, "we're going to have a baby."

"What?" Corey sputtered.

"We knew you'd be surprised," Mark said. "We're pretty surprised ourselves."

"You're too old," Corey said.

"We had a little help from a doctor," Mark said. "He—"

"No!" Corey waved his hands frantically in front of his face. "Don't say anything gross."

Sam brought a tray loaded with steaming platters. He winked at Corey as he set the broccoli beef in front of him.

"Why didn't you tell me you were planning this?" Corey asked.

"We didn't know if it would work," Mark said.

"You make me show you my report card the day I get it, whether it's good or bad."

Alison wondered whether all teenagers thought families were democracies or if that delusion was particular to Berkeley teenagers.

"Can I have a Coke?" Corey asked.

"Don't push your luck," she answered.

Corey spooned a small mountain of beef onto his plate. He glanced at Mark and added a single spear of broccoli to the pile.

"This is your fault, you know," Alison said to Corey. "If we didn't love you so much . . . " Tears caught the words in her throat.

"I know what you mean," Corey said. He handed Alison his dirty napkin. "Don't cry, Mom," he said. "Maybe you'll get another one as good as me."

That night Alison was pulled out of a deep sleep by a strange presence in the room. A large, dark form was bent over her. She opened her mouth to scream.

"It's me," Corey whispered.

"Oh, honey. You scared me." Without thinking, she pulled back the covers. He crawled in beside her. Alison put her arms around him.

"What's wrong?" she whispered back.

"I'm sorry I didn't say congratulations," Corey said quietly. "I wasn't that happy about the baby when you first told me. But I'm happier about it now."

"Oh, babe." Alison stroked Corey's stiffly gelled hair, his soft wide forehead. "You'll probably feel happy about it sometimes and not so happy other times."

"Duh, Mom. That's what I just said."

Alison smiled in the dark.

Corey was getting fidgety, awake enough to realize where he was. Alison scratched his shoulders, hoping to keep him with her for another moment or two.

"You're so good at that," she whispered.

"At what?"

"Being honest about how you feel."

"I know," Corey said and went back to his own bed.

Alison called Zoe and invited her out to dinner. "I'll buy," Alison said. "You pick the place."

After a brief, charged silence, Zoe said, "You're pregnant, aren't you?"

"Yes." Telling Zoe made the truth of it, the joy of it, swell inside her.

"Wow," Zoe said. "That was quick."

"We got really lucky." *Please share this happiness with me,* Alison begged silently.

"Did you tell Corey?"

"Last night."

"How did he react?"

"He was shocked. But he's coming around."

"Poor kid. He's dealing with a lot these days."

"We're giving him a sibling, Zoe," Alison said, "not a disease."

After another pause, Zoe said, "I'm happy for you. I know how much you've wanted this. The problem is . . . " Zoe sucked in a breath and exhaled noisily. "The problem is what I want for myself."

Alison felt a quickening in the region of her heart. Most of the time, she managed to ignore what the deepest part of her knew: that in spite of Mark, in spite of Trudy, in spite of the friendship and the family they'd made, Zoe wanted more from Alison. As long as they never spoke of it, they could go on as if it weren't true.

"You being pregnant . . . " Zoe said, "it brings up a lot of stuff for me."

"I understand," Alison said gently.

"I'm not sure you do. I've been thinking about having another—having a baby, too."

"You *have?*"

"With Trudy."

Alison's mind raced. For fourteen years Alison had thanked Zoe, and thanked the goddesses for Zoe, perhaps a million times. But until this moment, as Alison contemplated how she might ever repay it, she'd never grasped the enormity of Zoe's gift.

"That's great." Alison coughed, clearing a lump from her throat. "Oh, and hey. Guess when the baby's due." She didn't wait for Zoe to do the math. "April 8. Your birthday."

"Really?" Zoe's voice was thick with emotion.

"Really. And I'm hoping she'll be a beautiful, crazy, talented, generous, loving Aries," Alison said. "Just like you."

Every Tuesday at 9:00 AM, Alison went to Redwood Fertility for her weekly ultrasound. Mark went with her the first few times, but as Election Day approached, he was too crunched to take time off work. Like every media outlet, *Mother Jones* was projecting an easy Bush win. Unlike most media outlets, *Mother Jones* was on a mission to keep that from happening.

Alison looked forward to her appointments now. The news was always good, and her visits doubled as research for her article. She interviewed Nancy, Dr. Schrier, and Lowell, the sweet, shy Filipino ultrasound technician. Nancy was helping Alison find patients willing to be interviewed.

Those initial, painful visits to the clinic seemed to have happened to someone else. Alison was pregnant, and everyone knew exactly how that had happened: no secrets, no lies. She was a Redwood Fertility Center success story. One of the lucky ones.

* * *

A lison was standing naked in the bathroom, looking at her body in the mirror.

She was looking for signs. Signs of what? She wasn't even three weeks pregnant. She turned and examined her profile. Maybe her breasts were a little fuller. She turned again. Maybe not.

All that technology. They knew everything so soon now. She'd already had an ultrasound. They knew that there was only one baby. They knew how big the baby was, down to the centimeter. In four weeks she'd hear its whooshing heartbeat. If she asked, they'd tell her whether her baby was a boy or a girl.

Alison wanted her baby to be a girl. She wanted Emma to be just like Corey, but with everyone knowing everything this time, right from the start.

She spread her fingers across her flat belly. "Who are you in there?" she asked her new baby.

Tears blurred her eyes. This was Alison's first time talking to her daughter. To Emma.

27.

A lison was belly-up on the table in the exam room at
Redwood Fertility, draped in a stiff blue paper gown, her
barely bulging abdomen glistening with conductive jelly. The
flimsy white paper on the table was sticking to the backs of her
thighs, as usual. She was elated, as usual. As usual, Lowell was
gliding the ultrasound wand over her belly, watching the monitor
to the right of her head.

The digitized date stamp on the ultrasound read October 17,
2004—the fifteenth anniversary of the Loma Prieta earthquake,
Alison realized. She saw herself and Zoe after their final insemination, standing outside the juice bar on Shattuck, arguing. What
were they fighting about? Alison couldn't remember. They were
always fighting back then. But she'd never forget the sidewalk
rippling beneath her feet, the Wells Fargo building swaying, the
sirens screaming. And Zoe, her hero, terrified.

"How's my little clump of cells doing?" Alison asked Lowell gaily. Each of her eleven weekly exams had been a shared moment of triumph, a walk around the winner's circle with the team that had brought the long shot in.

Lowell didn't answer.

"Lowell?" Alison's heart banged once, hard, against her chest. She propped herself up on her elbows. "Is everything okay?"

Lowell replaced the wand in its holster. He didn't meet Alison's eyes. "I'll be right back," he said. He closed the door behind him.

Alison sat up. She stared at the back of the door. Her clothing was hanging in perfect order on the shiny metal hook. Pale blue Indian cotton tunic. Black drawstring yoga pants, the only ones that still fit. To keep from embarrassing Lowell, Alison always hung up her bra and panties first, even though she took them off last.

Alison didn't believe in God, but she started praying. *Please don't let Schrier be the next person to come through that door. Please let Lowell come back and say, I'm sorry I scared you. Everything's fine.*

She cupped her hands over her belly. "You're fine, Emma," she told her baby. "Don't worry. You're okay."

The door opened. Schrier came in first. "I don't want you to worry," he said.

"I am worried," Alison said.

Lowell followed. "Lie back, please, Alison," he said in the softest, saddest voice she'd ever heard. He squirted jelly onto his small gloved hands, spread a fresh coat over Alison's belly—over *Emma*—and inched the sensor over her skin in slow, overlapping circles. Schrier stared at the monitor, his lips a thin flat line across his face.

Lowell turned off the monitor and left the room without speaking or looking at Alison. Dr. Schrier offered a hand to help her sit up.

"It's possible that everything's fine," he said. Strange sounds were seeping out of Alison's mouth, small whimpers.

"Should I call Mark?" she asked.

"No need for that."

He didn't say *yet*, but Alison heard it. "Tell me what's wrong."

"The measurements haven't changed since your last ultrasound. At eleven weeks, that's somewhat concerning. But it isn't entirely uncommon."

When Schrier handed her a small, square box of tissues, Alison realized she was crying.

"I'm going to have you come in for another ultrasound on Friday." Dr. Schrier stood up, met her eyes briefly, then busied himself washing his hands.

"Is it possible that—"

"I know you have questions, Alison. But it's too soon for me to give you any answers. The best thing you can do is think positive."

Was he kidding? *Think positive?*

"I'll see you in a few days," Schrier said, and he was gone.

Alison got dressed and trance-walked out of the office, out of the elevator, and onto Sutter Street. On her way to BART, she passed a Stanley's Steamers hot dog stand. The stench of boiling beef made her gag.

At a red light at Montgomery and Market, Alison laid her hand on her belly. And then she realized that for the first time in eleven weeks no one at the clinic had said the word *baby*.

Alison followed her feet to *Mother Jones*. She let herself into Mark's office. He wasn't there. She closed the door behind her and sat in his desk chair, staring out the window at men in suits with briefcases, young women swinging Anthropologie shopping bags, homeless people squatting on blankets on Market Street.

"Honey!" Mark said. "What are you—"

Alison spun around in his chair. Mark's face fell. He crouched in front of her. "Tell me," he said, and she did.

"I should have been with you," he said. "From now on, I'm going with you."

From now on? Alison knew why Mark didn't want to admit what was happening. Mark was thinking positive. Mark was telling himself a lie.

That night Mark fell asleep over the story he was editing. Alison lay beside him, envying his oblivion, trying to quiet the clanging in her head. At eleven she gave up and turned on the late-night news.

Al Sharpton and Jesse Jackson were touring black churches throughout the South, trying to convince lifelong Democrat parishioners not to vote for Bush. Alison thought, *Now we have to work to get black people not to vote for Bush?*

"Ninety percent of African Americans voted against George W. Bush in the 2000 election," the newscaster said. "But abortion and gay rights have become such powerful wedge issues that even the constituents the Democrats have taken for granted are threatening to abandon the fold."

The shot shifted to an African American pastor delivering election advice from the pulpit. "I cannot tell you who to vote for. But I can tell you what my mama always told me: 'Stay out of the bushes!'"

Back to the anchor: "While many African Americans hold a

strong animus toward the current administration, Kerry does not appear to be a desirable alternative."

Bush is going to fucking win again, Alison thought. She heard Schrier telling her to think positive. She couldn't imagine any amount of *positive thinking* making a president go down, or making her baby live. She didn't even know how she was going to make it to Friday morning.

Alison turned off the TV, pulled the covers up over Mark's shoulders, closed her eyes, and pitched a deal to God: *I swear I'll never complain about the war or even George W. Bush again if you'll just let my baby live.*

M oveOn was sponsoring a nationwide bake sale, "Bake Back the White House," on a Saturday in September in one thousand locations coast to coast. On the MoveOn website, Alison had typed in her zip code and found seven bake sales within a five-mile radius of her house. She'd also downloaded recipes for Bush Is Nuts Brownies and Condoleezza Rice Crispy Treats.

Mark stumbled into the kitchen the morning before their appointment at Redwood. He found Alison sifting unbleached cake flour, melting unsalted butter, ripping open packages of chocolate chips. Pans of brownies were cooling on the counter. Plates of Condoleezza Rice Crispy Treats covered the table.

"What are you *doing,* Alison?" Mark looked haggard and unhappy. "The bake sale isn't till Saturday. What time did you get *up?*"

"Early." Alison stood in front of the open freezer, shuffling packages of Trader Joe's vegetable pot stickers and Peet's French roast. "I'm going to freeze it. I won't have time to bake tomorrow."

"Oh, honey." Mark came up behind her, wrapped his arms around her waist. "Maybe we should talk about what we'll do if—"

"Wow, Mom," Corey shuffled into the kitchen. "Opening a bakery? Going for a second career in case that writing career doesn't work out?" He grabbed a rice crispy treat. "No extra charge for being your taste tester." Trailing crumbs, he headed out the door.

Alison wriggled out of Mark's grasp. She handed him a jar of extra-crunchy peanut butter and told him to open it. And then she went on cracking cage-free brown eggs on the rim of her favorite big blue ceramic bowl.

F riday morning. Redwood Fertility. *Please,* Alison prayed silently. She was on the table. Mark was sitting next to her in an orange molded plastic chair. "Please," she said out loud.

Mark got up, stood beside her, and stroked her forehead. Since Tuesday, Alison realized, he hadn't touched her belly once.

Dr. Schrier walked into the room with Lowell in his wake. "Good morning," Schrier said. Lowell twisted the cap off a fresh tube of conductive jelly. Alison wanted to thank him for doing his very best to find her baby's heartbeat, but she thought she might vomit if she opened her mouth. Mark took Alison's hand. His was ice cold.

Dr. Schrier turned on the monitor. Lowell rolled the sensor over Alison's belly. Every creak and gurgle of her churning intestines was broadcast into the stillness of the room.

"You're checking for a heartbeat, aren't you?" Alison asked.

Dr. Schrier was silent, listening. Mark gripped Alison's hand so tightly it hurt.

No one said a word except for Alison's mother.

That's what you get, liar.

A lison went to bed and bled. For the first few days after the miscarriage—that's what they called it, although what ended the pregnancy was actually a D&C, technically an abortion—Mark stayed in bed with her. They didn't talk. They held each other and cried.

Zoe took Corey to school in the mornings. After practice, she brought him to the cottage for homework and dinner. After dinner, she brought him home. One night Trudy sent over a caraway-scented chicken stew and a dozen yellow tulips in a tall, slim glass vase. Zoe put the bouquet on Alison's dresser. Each day their yellow heads drooped lower, their petals wilting in surrender, as if the sadness in the room were wearing them down too.

On Sunday morning, Corey appeared at Alison's bedside. "Here, Mom," he said. He handed her a lavender Hallmark card. Under the printed "get well soon" message, he'd written his own, in the same loopy handwriting he'd used since he was ten.

Dear Mom, I'm sorry about the baby. I really want a little brother or sister and I hope you and Dad will try again and I hope it works next time. I love you. Your son, Corey (Pickle).

Alison looked up at him and opened her arms. Corey bent to hug her. Their bodies collided in an awkward embrace. Alison started crying again.

"I'll get Dad," Corey said, and he backed out of the room.

Alison pulled the covers over her head and wept, and wept, and wept.

A lison was looking for a rope to grab onto, a story to tell herself, something strong to pull on. There was no silver lining to losing her baby, but the miscarriage did make everything crystal clear. The petty things that normally bugged her fell away. What mattered to her—Mark, Corey, Zoe, even Trudy—mattered more than they ever had. More than she'd ever let them.

A lison woke in the night and heard the sound of crying and realized it wasn't her own.

She reached for Mark.

"I can't stand it," he sobbed. "I wanted that baby so much."

"I know," Alison murmured.

"I was happy when we were pregnant with Corey. But this was different," Mark choked out. "We worked so hard to get that baby. Not just the fertility stuff. But everything that happened between us."

"I know." Alison stroked his hair. "At least we still have us," she said. "We're still here."

Mark went on crying and Alison went on holding him. They fell asleep sharing a pillow soaked in the one river of their tears.

A few hours later Alison bolted upright in bed. This time it wasn't her own crying or Mark's that woke her. It was a promise she'd made in her sleep.

Now that she'd seen Mark suffering the loss of their second child, she knew she could never tell him that he might not be the father of their first.

* * *

Zoe called at eight each morning and asked if Alison was hungry, if she wanted company, if there was anything she could do. Sometimes Alison said no, thank you, nothing. Sometimes she cried and Zoe listened, really listened, as only Zoe could.

Zoe's attention cosseted Alison's heart. In the damp darkness of her grief, a seed of gratitude grew. She'd lost so much when she lost Emma. But there was still so much she had.

Alison lived by deadlines and she gave herself one. By Election Day, she'd start acting as if she were okay, no matter how she actually was.

On Election Night she granted herself an extension, since she was so *not* okay, and neither was anyone else with a brain, which, based on early election results, was well under half of the U.S. population.

Mark and Alison fell asleep at 1:00 AM with the TV on and Kerry's lead evaporating. When they woke at five, the newscasters were still talking about votes yet to be counted. By the time Mark took Corey to school at eight, the only question was when Kerry would concede.

Alison went back to bed, flicking from one channel to the next, as if finding the right one would give her the right results. At noon Mark called from work to commiserate. His voice was low and sad. Alison couldn't even remember what Mark's happy voice sounded like. She wondered if she'd ever hear it again.

Zoe called in tears. "I keep thinking we should have done more. Gone to Cleveland to register voters. Given money to Michael Moore. Hung banners from freeway overpasses. Something." Alison heard Trudy talking in the background. "Trudy says we should all move to Brazil. Or the moon."

Corey came home from school in a foul mood. "At lunch everyone was throwing their Kerry buttons on the ground and stomping on them. My English teacher was *crying*."

He sat on the floor, leaning against Alison's bed, and together they watched the news. "In the end, this wasn't an election about the war, or the economy, or health care," Dan Rather said. "It was an election about gay rights and abortion and God."

Check, check, and check, Alison thought. I'VE BEEN GAY, I JUST HAD A D&C, AND GOD JUST BLEW HIS FIRST AND LAST CHANCE WITH ME. She saw her mother's waggling finger. *See? The whole country agrees with me, not you.*

Shut up, Mom, Alison told her. "Enough," she said out loud. She clicked off the TV, got out of bed, went to her closet, and started rifling through her clothes. Sensing imminent maternal nudity, Corey skittered out of the room. *No more wallowing,* she told herself. *If I have to fake it till I make it, faking it will have to do.*

A few days later Alison, Mark, and Zoe were in the Berkeley High bleachers, watching Corey warming up with his teammates before their big game against their fiercest rival, De LaSalle.

"Is that the cutest thing you've ever seen?" Zoe pointed down at Corey, who'd stopped mid-dribble and was staring intently into the crowd. Alison followed his gaze to a tall, mocha-skinned, dreadlocked, voluptuous girl in a skintight Berkeley High tank top, baggy red Berkeley High sweatpants, and red patent leather Air Jordan basketball shoes.

The girl blew Corey a kiss. Corey spun around and sent a three-pointer whooshing through the net. The kids in the bleachers hooted and screamed.

"That's his new girlfriend," Zoe said. "He was gonna talk to you guys about her. I guess he hasn't gotten around to it yet."

"Stop gloating," Alison said. "Just tell us everything you know."

"Her name's Justina," Zoe shouted over the eardrum-popping noise in the gym. "She's in his African American history class. She's a starter on the girl's basketball team. He told me they're in love."

"She looks . . . formidable," Mark said.

"She looks like she's twenty-five years old," Alison said.

The next night Corey called home at 6:05 PM, five minutes past his legal limit, to say he was having dinner at a friend's. "Which friend?" Alison asked.

"Justina." Corey paused. "My girlfriend," he explained, as if they'd already had the conversation Alison had been waiting for him to begin.

"Are her parents home?"

"Yup." Corey lowered his voice to a whisper. "Please, Mom. Don't make them talk to you."

Alison tried to keep her smile out of her "strict voice." "I won't. Just this once. But it's a school night. Be home by nine."

She and Mark were cleaning up after dinner when the doorbell rang. Alison checked the clock before she went to answer it. 8:55.

She opened the door and there they were—her baby and his *girlfriend*. And a tall, handsome black man in a suit.

"Mr. Hamilton drove me home," Corey said. His eyes were a neon sign flashing, "Don't embarrass me."

Alison ushered them into the entryway. Mark made his entrance from the kitchen, wearing a tie-dyed Ben & Jerry's apron over his *Mother Jones* T-shirt. Corey looked mortified.

"Mom. Dad. This is Justina." Corey blushed to the roots of his bleached-out, stiffly spiked hair. Mr. Hamilton cleared his throat theatrically. "And her dad," Corey added, turning redder than Mark's shirt.

"Nice to meet you," Alison said.

Justina was stunning, her skin smooth and glowing, her eyes bright and alert. Silver studs and hoops marched up her earlobes, flashing through the plaits of her shoulder-length hair. She bounced in place on platform shoes that brought her to Alison's height. "I'm so psyched to finally meet you," she bubbled. "Corey talks about you all the time."

"Really," Mark said drily. Alison elbowed him in the ribs.

"I need to get this young lady home," Mr. Hamilton said. "School night. Homework. All that good stuff."

"Bye, Mr. and Mrs. Miller," Justina said to Mark and Alison. "See you soon, I hope." Justina and Corey tumbled out the door. Corey pulled it closed behind them.

"Corey's a great kid," Mr. Hamilton said. "And such a talented musician."

"How do you—?" Mark stammered.

"Corey and Justina play guitar together at our house. Mostly Bob Marley songs. They're quite the duet, those two."

Mark and Alison exchanged a shocked look. They hadn't heard Corey playing anything other than rap in months.

Mr. Hamilton opened the door, startling an entwined Corey and Justina, who quickly jumped apart.

Justina pecked Corey chastely on the cheek, followed her father to his late-model Mercedes, and folded her long body into the front seat.

Corey galloped up to his room. As Mark and Alison headed for the kitchen, the soft strains of a reggae tune wafted down the stairs.

"Good-bye 50 Cent," Mark said. "Hello Bob Marley."

Alison stopped drying silverware and turned to Mark. Her eyes filled with tears. "He's never brought a girl home before. Let alone a girl's *dad*."

"That was no girl. That was a *woman*. Our little boy is growing up." He smiled at Alison. "Justina reminds me of you."

"What about her, exactly?" Alison asked sarcastically. "The perky boobs? The dreadlocks? The perfect sixteen-year-old skin?"

Mark shook his head. "Her energy. She's curious. She glows, like you." He hung up his apron and looked Alison in the eye. "You're always worrying about how Corey's going to turn out. Well, if his first girlfriend is any indication—which it is—he's doing great. Can you let yourself feel good about what a wonderful mom you are? Just for a minute?"

Alison considered the possibility that despite every mistake she'd made, every secret she'd kept, every lie she'd told; despite the flawed character she was and the *selfish bitch* her mother had sworn she'd always be—she had somehow done a decent job of raising her son.

"Why don't we make sure he graduates high school," she said dryly, "before we congratulate ourselves too much."

Mark shook his head at her. "What am I going to do with you?"

"Love me," Alison said.

S ix weeks after the miscarriage, one month after the election, Alison told Mark she wanted to try again.

"I don't want to give up," she said. "We have to act like we have more hope than we actually have."

"I don't want to give up either," Mark said.

And so, six months after their first visit to Redwood Fertility,

Mark and Alison returned, downgraded from happy pregnancy checkups to grim consultation in Schrier's office; downgraded from views of sun and fog to windows blurred by driving December rain.

"We ran some tissue tests after your D&C." Schrier peered at them over the glasses on his nose. "I have to be honest with you. The results do not bode well."

"What—" Mark stammered.

"Alison's uterine lining is too thin to sustain fetal development. Eight millimeters is optimal. Six is feasible. Alison's is four."

"But I had Corey," Alison said.

"The uterine lining changes with age," Schrier said.

"Are you saying I can't—" Alison's voice caught. She swallowed hard. "Are you saying I can't get pregnant again?"

"You could," Schrier said. "But it's unlikely that your body will sustain a pregnancy."

Reflexively, Alison's hands drifted to her belly.

"We have to fix this," Mark said. His voice broke, like Corey's. "There has to be something you can do."

Schrier took his glasses off and rubbed the bridge of his nose. "We could do a few trial cycles with estrogen to try and make the lining grow. But that could take months. And the odds of success aren't good." He ticked their choices off on his fingers. "You could adopt . . . "

"No." Mark shook his head. "We want a child who's biologically ours."

"You could consider yourselves lucky that you've had one biological child and come to terms with not having another."

"And?" Mark prompted.

"And then there is one other choice. Surrogacy."

"You mean hire another woman to have our child?" Mark blurted.

How crazy will we get? Alison wondered. *How much money will we spend? How far will we go?*

Hadn't she asked herself and Zoe the same questions fifteen years before?

"Biologically," Schrier was saying, "the baby would be both of yours. Exactly as if Alison carried it herself."

If you'd lived your life right, her mother's voice was saying, *you'd have a real husband and two children by now. But no, not you.*

"You're good candidates for surrogacy," Schrier added, "because we know the two of you can create a viable embryo. A lot of our couples don't have that going for them."

Mark took Alison's hand. "I'm not saying we want to do this. But how would it work?"

"You'd go through the same regimen you did to prepare for the IVF. At the same time, the surrogate—we call them gestational carriers—would take hormone shots to prepare her uterus for the implantation."

You never could do anything the way everyone else does.

"When your eggs, and her uterus, are ready," Dr. Schrier continued, "we'd harvest your eggs, fertilize them in a petri dish with Mark's sperm, and transfer them to the surrogate. Forty weeks later, you'd have your baby."

"How would we find the woman?" Mark asked.

"We work with a number of gestational carriers. They're stable women, married, mothers of their own children. You'd look through their profiles and pick one. We'd arrange a meeting. Assuming all goes well, we'd take it from there."

"Do the women ever change their minds? Decide to keep the babies?" Mark asked.

"The terms of the arrangement are clear. The baby would be biologically and legally yours."

Mark squeezed Alison's hand. She shook her head.

"Surrogacy isn't anyone's first choice," Schrier said. "And it's not for everyone. Among other considerations, there's the cost. The payment to the gestational carrier alone is twenty thousand dollars."

"That's the end of it, then. We don't have that kind of money." Mark's hand slipped out of Alison's. He pulled a tissue out of the box on Schrier's desk and used it to wipe his eyes.

I can't give this up, Alison thought. *I won't.*

"What about our insurance?" she asked.

Dr. Schrier shook his head. "Even the best insurance doesn't cover surrogacy. But there *is* an option that can make it less expensive."

Alison and Mark looked at him, waiting. "Some of our patients ask women they know to be their gestational carriers," he said.

"Women they know?" Mark asked.

"Typically a sister or a sister-in-law."

"Neither of us has a sister," Mark said.

"The carrier doesn't have to be a blood relative," Schrier said. "She can be a sister-in-law, a friend . . . "

I have a friend, Alison thought.

"It's best if she's younger than forty," Dr. Schrier said.

Zoe, Alison thought.

28.

berkeley
December 2004

Over the years, Zoe had given Mark and Alison gifts too
big and too many to count or even remember. But Mark
and Alison sat in stunned silence, driving through the misty
December night to meet Zoe for dinner, contemplating the enormity of what they were about to ask of her.

Downtown Berkeley rolled by Alison's fogged-in passenger
window. The Shattuck strip was dressed for the winter holidays in its usual festive, nondenominational style. Sodden
banners dangled limply from faux antique lampposts, offering
equal-opportunity tidings to celebrants of Christmas, Kwanzaa,
Hanukkah, and winter solstice. Strings of twinkling white lights
draped the spindly, malnourished trees that never quite greened
the median divide. Plaques affixed to parking meters—typeset
in the City of Berkeley's own custom font—promised two free
hours to those thinking global but shopping local. Homeless

people huddled in doorways holding signs festooned with scribbled trees and wreaths, soliciting funding for their own holiday cheer.

Under the neon awning of the multiplex, formerly Hink's, where Alison and Zoe had bought curtains for the cottage a lifetime before, throngs of moviegoers bought tickets to see *Ocean's Twelve* and *The Incredibles*. At the UA Theater one block north, there was no line for *The Passion of the Christ*.

A taxi veered toward the Saab. Mark blasted the horn, rousing the knot of antiwar protesters at the corner of Center Street, who took his honking as a gesture of solidarity.

The demonstrators cheered and waved, pumping their umbrellas and picket signs:

SOMEWHERE IN TEXAS, A VILLAGE IS MISSING ITS IDIOT

NO BLOOD FOR OIL!

IF YOU CAN READ THIS, YOU'RE NOT OUR PRESIDENT

JAIL TO THE CHIEF

WHO WOULD JESUS BOMB?

HOW DID OUR OIL GET UNDER THEIR SAND?

"At least he's good for making fun of, that fucking Bush," Alison said.

"Hardly justifies the damage he's done," Mark said, turning left on University.

They parked in the twenty-four-hour lot behind Szechwan Gardens and zipped up their matching REI anoraks. Alison reached for the door handle. Mark reached for her.

"Whatever happens," he said, holding her face in his hands, "we'll be okay."

Alison nodded. They made a run for it, dodging raindrops, slipping and sliding through the restaurant's open doors, wet dogs shaking off the rain.

Zoe waved at them from their usual booth. Her tight white T shirt and her face were pink beneath the red lanterns strung along the wall. As Mark and Alison slid into the booth, Sam appeared, greeted them by name, and guessed their order with flawless accuracy.

Zoe poured tea. "Did you ever notice that Sam walks like the people in those weird, rolling-along-the-pavement scenes in Spike Lee movies? Maybe Sam was Spike's role model." She paused. "His *egg roll* model."

Alison barely summoned a smile. Mark didn't respond.

"Okay, I'm officially worried," Zoe said. "What's up with you two?"

Alison took a breath and released it. "I can't have a baby," she said.

Zoe's hand shot across the table, landed on Alison's. "Oh, Al. I'm so sorry. Are you sure?"

"We're sure," Mark answered quickly, before Zoe could launch one of her alternative medicine monologues. "Alison's uterine lining is too thin to sustain a fetus. And there's nothing they can do to fix it."

"Then how did Corey get here?" Zoe asked.

Liar, Alison's mother said. "My uterus was younger then," Alison said. *You remember my uterus then,* she thought.

Sam arrived with a dish of mu shu vegetables and a plate of pancakes. "Chow fun coming," he said, and he went back to the kitchen.

"What are you going to do?" Zoe asked.

"We have three choices," Mark said. "We can adopt, which we don't want to do. We can give up, which we *really* don't want to do." He took a sip of tea.

"Or?" Zoe prompted him.

Mark put his teacup down on the sticky Formica table. "Or we can find a surrogate to carry our baby."

"You mean . . . *pay* someone to be pregnant for you?"

Mark nodded.

Zoe looked at Alison. "You'd do that?" she asked, incredulous. Alison heard the rest of her question: *Fifteen years ago, artificial insemination was too unnatural for you. And now you're going to hire a surrogate?*

"It's our last chance," Alison said.

Sam arrived with the chow fun. "No pork, the way you like it." He noticed the untouched platters. "Something wrong with food?"

They all shook their heads. Sam shrugged and disappeared.

"How can I help?" Zoe looked at Mark. "Do you need money?"

Mark gave Alison a pointed look. They'd agreed that she'd be the one to ask.

"Anything," Zoe said. "Just tell me."

"We're wondering if you'd consider being our surrogate," Alison said.

Zoe's jaw dropped. "You want me to be the mother of your child?"

Mark shook his head. "The baby would be mine and Alison's. My sperm, her egg. You'd be the gestational carrier."

"So . . . " Zoe frowned. "I'd give birth to the baby. And then I'd give the baby to you?"

Again, Alison heard Zoe thinking.

"Essentially," Mark said.

"Have you talked to Corcy about this?" Zoe asked.

"We wanted to talk to you first," Alison answered.

"I think he'll be okay with it," Mark added. "Ever since the miscarriage, he's been saying he wants a baby sister."

"Yeah," Zoe said. "He told me that too." She poured a pool of soy sauce onto her plate, dipped the tip of her chopstick into it, drew a dark face against white.

"Trudy and I have been talking about having a baby," she said.

Alison's throat tightened. *Things are going to change,* she realized. *Things are already changing.*

"Are you two that serious?" Mark asked.

Zoe nodded. "I've haven't felt this way about anyone since—" She flushed. "In a really long time."

In the awkward silence, Mark filled a pancake with shredded vegetables. Alison passed the red lacquer rice bowl to Zoe.

"I know the miscarriage broke your heart," Zoe said to Alison. She glanced at Mark. "Your hearts."

She pushed rice around her plate. "I want to help you guys. You know I do. But I need some time to think."

"Of course you do," Mark said.

"Trudy and I are going to Point Reyes for Christmas. I'll talk to her about it while we're there."

Alison fought a memory of being with Zoe in Point Reyes on their third anniversary, making love on a hot fall day in the cool dunes of Heart's Desire Beach.

"We'll be back for New Year's," Zoe said. "Maybe we could all get together then."

"Zoe," Mark said, "I'm sure you know that surrogacy isn't my first choice, or Alison's." He swirled his tea, big hands eclipsing tiny white cup. "But if we *are* going to use a surrogate, you're our first choice."

Zoe looked at Alison and quickly looked away. "Whatever happens," she said, "I'm honored that you asked me."

Mark stabbed a serving fork into the platter of noodles and held a forkful aloft. "Who's ready for chow fun?" he said, a little too loudly.

"I'll take any kind of fun you're dishing up," Zoe said.

A lison was going crazy, waiting for Zoe to decide. She tried to lose herself in planning Hanuchris. But all roads led back to Zoe, including that one. They'd never celebrated it without her before.

Alison wasn't a writer who spent hours plugged in and nursing a latte in a Wi-Fi café. She found the ambient activity distracting, not convivial. But right now distraction was what she needed. So she packed up her iBook and left the house and started walking.

It was one of those warm, blue sky winter days that made her feel smug about having left the East Coast for the West. Narcissus unfurled and hyacinths poked up from gardens soaked with rain. Princess trees nodded, cartoonish purple blossoms bobbing. Pink camellia heads crowned from tight green buds.

A decent cappuccino, a three-pronged outlet, and a Wi-Fi signal used to be a mile or more away. But now Alison had her pick of cafés within a few blocks of home. There was a price to pay, and the neighborhood was paying it. The Thai One On import shop had replaced the office of Vernon W. Jackson, real estate agent and notary public, where Alison used to get her documents notarized. Stepping into Mr. Jackson's dim, smoky office, she always felt she was stepping back in time.

There was always a group of elderly black men sitting on folding chairs in the corner, wearing ironed white shirts and suspenders clipped to their cuffed, creased trousers, playing dominos, smoking cigars, watching the TV that was mounted overhead. The men kept up a running commentary on the news of the day, reserving their most scathing remarks for the foibles of George W. Bush. "The lights are on, but nobody's home," one man would say. "If his lips are moving, that's how you know he's lying." On the rare occasion when Bush did something that won their approval—increasing funding to fight AIDS in Africa, doubling trade with African nations—they'd dismiss it as a fluke. "Even a blind hog finds an acorn now and then."

Mr. Jackson would not be rushed. When Alison brought him a pink slip or a passport application to be notarized, he'd open the notary book on his big oak desk and thumb through to the proper page. Then he'd ask for Alison's driver's license and peer at it carefully, comparing her photo to her face. Slowly, deliberately, he'd take out his notary stamp, open the stamp pad, and affix stamp to document with a surgeon's precision. The deed done, Mr. Jackson would look Alison in the eye, take her $10, give her a handwritten receipt, and say, "I thank you very much for your business, Miss Rose, and I surely do hope that you have a blessed day."

Alison wondered where Mr. Jackson was now, and where his friends were smoking their cigars and having their conversations. Sixteen years after she and Mark had chosen it for its funky affordability and ethnic diversity, their neighborhood was yuppifying at warp speed, becoming a buffed and polished, manicured version of its former ragged self.

Hipster cafés and drought-resistant plant nurseries were replacing barbershops and barbecue joints. Ersatz "industrial live–work lofts" were appearing where lots littered with crack vials and used condoms had been. Dilapidated backyard cottages were being stripped down to the lath, earthquake-reinforced, skylighted, and landscaped, interiors by feng shui, kitchens by Sub-Zero and Wolf. The peeling Victorians that once housed sixties communes and food conspiracies were being sandblasted to the bone, intricate gingerbread curlicues and dentil details custom replicated, period authenticity provided by Urban Ore. The stucco sea-foam-green and pale pink Mediterraneans, bought for $12,000 in the forties by black folks who migrated to California for shipyard jobs, were being bought up by young white families with thousand-dollar baby strollers and achingly astute design sensibilities, who restuccoed and painted them celadon with terra-cotta trim, or periwinkle with chocolate brown, or gradated shades of elegantly titrated blues. The dueling mainstays of the neighborhood, corner liquor stores and Baptist churches, were the only sentries standing guard against the firestorm of gentrification.

Although she scorned it, Alison couldn't entirely deny her own part in the defunkification or its benefits to her own bottom line. In 2004 their house was worth three times the $200,000 they'd paid for it in 1990—great on paper, as she often reminded Mark, but only useful in real life if they cashed out of the Bay Area and moved to Des Moines or Detroit.

As Alison approached one of those ramshackle churches, she saw an old black man in baggy coveralls, plaid flannel shirt, and porkpie hat sweeping Doritos wrappers, forty-ounce Old English malt liquor bottles, and wet leaves off the steps. "Good morning, young lady," he greeted her, squinting into the bright morning glare.

"Beautiful day," she answered, and he nodded. The neighborly exchange and the sun warmed her as she walked on.

Just past Alcatraz Avenue was the Nomad, the spiffiest of the new Wi-Fi cafés. Alison ordered a decaf low-fat latte with extra foam, grabbed a handful of recycled brown paper napkins, went outside, and wiped yesterday's rain off a polished aluminum chair. She opened her laptop and logged onto the Nomad's Wi-Fi network, sipping her coffee, taking in the view.

The café was aptly named; its customers carried their lives in the Macs on their backs. Around her, twentysomethings surfed the Net on their iBooks and PowerBooks, adjusting their iPod buds, talking on glowing cell phones that flashed like pinball machines and played loud, tinny hip-hop song fragments when they rang. Alison figured she had twenty years on most of the people there.

Whatever it was they were typing about, talking about, worrying about, she was fairly certain it wasn't what she was there to distract herself from: her age-related infertility and the hope that her best friend would agree to be the "gestational carrier" of her second child.

On New Year's Eve afternoon the Christmas tree was shedding its needles; Alison, Mark, and Corey were enjoying a late afternoon of family togetherness, playing a raucously competitive game of Scrabble, munching on Alison's homemade caramel corn before a roaring fire.

The kitchen phone rang. Alison waited for Corey to race to answer it. Then she realized that thanks to the cell phone they'd given him for Hanuchris, the landline wasn't his umbilicus to his social life anymore. She jumped up, wincing at the protest from her knees.

"Corey's house," she answered it.

She heard Zoe's belly laugh. "Honey, we're home."

Alison's mouth went dry. She took the cordless phone into the bathroom and closed the door. *What did you decide, what did you decide, what did you decide,* she thought. "How was Point Reyes?" she asked.

"Gorgeous. Perfect. Except I missed you guys."

"We missed you too."

"So, Al. I want to talk to you about the baby thing in person. Do you have time to go for a walk? Inspiration Point? It'll be too muddy everyplace else."

Alison was listening for the answer in Zoe's voice. She didn't hear a yes, but she didn't hear a no. "I'll meet you there in half an hour," she said.

After days of relentless rain, Tilden Park was a chartreuse chiaroscuro. The new-growth redwood needles were the color of lime Popsicles; the old-growth branches, Crayola Forest Green. The eucalyptuses were dripping and glistening, backlit by breakthrough beams of sun.

A wagon train of cars circled the trailhead parking lot, kids' and dogs' noses pressed against windows, mud-caked mountain bikes strapped to roofs. And there was Zoe, leaning against her beat-up Volvo, a standout in her kelly green sweater, violet velvet pants, and olive-green leather aviator hat. Alison greeted her by adjusting an earflap.

"Great hat," Alison said. "Is it new?"

"New-old. I got it at that great thrift shop in Point Reyes."

The two of them fell into step, their waltz familiar, bent against the incline and the sharp wind whipping up from the bay. Runoff rivulets streamed down the steep hillside, carving crevices into the soaked earth. A pair of lesbians walked by them. The women cruised Zoe and ignored Alison. *Same old, same old,* Alison thought.

They paused at a vista point, looking down at the boxy cross-hatch of Berkeley's city streets, the maze of cars and houses converging at the shoreline, the tiny rainbow-striped sails of wind-surfers skipping across the bay.

"Beats Ohio, don't it?" Zoe asked.

"Good thing you got us out of there," Alison said, waiting and trying not to wait.

They entered a tunnel of trees, fragrant blue eucalyptus buttons crunching beneath their feet.

"About the baby," Zoe said.

Alison caught her breath.

"You know I always want to say yes to you."

Alison wanted to scream to keep from hearing the *but* she was sure was coming.

"But some old stuff came up when Trudy and I were talking about it." Zoe snapped a branch off a French broom bush, swatting its yellow flowers against her leg as she walked.

"Old stuff," Alison repeated.

"My trust fund paid for the inseminations. If that's where Corey came from, what happened is that you and I made a baby, and you and Mark got to be his parents. Now you're asking me to do pretty much the same thing."

"But that's not what happened." *Don't piss her off,* Alison told herself. Not now. "I mean, that's not how I see it."

"Let's sit for a minute," Zoe said, nodding at a wooden bench that faced east, overlooking the San Pablo Dam. Unlike the wet playground of the bay on the west side of the trail, the human-made reservoir showed no sign of human life.

"Trudy's open to it," Zoe said. "But she doesn't want me to hurt myself to give you what you want."

Alison was stung. "Is that what she thinks you do?"

"That *is* what I've done. Our relationship—our family—has been really good for me, Al. You know how happy it's made me to be Corey's goddessmom. But I don't want to do what's good for you at my own expense anymore."

"Trudy thinks our friendship is bad for you?" Alison heard herself whining, but she was too hurt, too worried to stop.

"Case in point." Zoe smiled, not unkindly. "Be a big girl, Al. Don't make me take care of you. Tell me what you really want to know."

Alison took a deep breath and let it out. "This is the first time you've ever been closer to someone else than you are to me. To *us*. I'm scared we'll lose you."

The whole truth, she scolded herself. "I'm scared I'll lose you," she said.

Zoe took Alison's hands and gazed into her eyes. "You're never going to lose me, Al. I've been telling you that for twenty-one years. When are you going to believe me?"

"July 4, 2008," Alison said, pulling her hands out of Zoe's grip. "That's my target date."

"I'll mark my calendar." Zoe leaned back. She draped her arm along the back of the bench, her fingertips grazing Alison's shoulder. "You and I have unfinished business," she said quietly. "I can't carry a baby for you until we clean it up."

Zoe's fingers moved to Alison's neck. Alison felt a jolt, their old electricity.

Lightly, Zoe's fingernails massaged Alison's scalp.

Alison had often wondered where their hunger had gone, where lust like theirs went to die. Now she knew. It wasn't dead. It was right there, smoldering, ready to be ignited by a breeze or a breath, by the briefest of glances, the tiniest of moves. Ready to ruin all of their lives.

Zoe's fingers teased at Alison's ear.

Alison wanted to lie down.

Alison wanted to lie down on that hard wooden bench and she wanted Zoe to kiss her and she wanted to kiss Zoe back and she wanted them to catch on fire, she wanted to feel the flame of them again.

Alison's brain said "Don't." Alison's body leaned back, ever so slightly, into Zoe's.

"Al," Zoe murmured.

There it was, right there, the heat, the fire, hers, Zoe's, theirs. Alison's breathing scraped her chest.

Zoe wrapped her hand in Alison's hair and tugged, the tiniest of tugs. *Come to me*, her hand said, hot against Alison's head. *Come back to us. Right here. Right now.*

Alison's body was smoldering. Alison's mind cried, "Don't, don't, don't burn it all."

Alison bent over, away from Zoe, head between her knees. She took a deep breath, another. She untied her bootlaces and tied them again, tighter this time. And then she sat up and rested her elbows on her knees, holding her body to herself, as far from Zoe's fingers as she could.

"Al," Zoe said.

"I know."

A moment passed. Another.

Zoe took her arm off the back of the bench, gripped her knees with both hands. "I want us to get Corey's DNA tested," she said.

Payback, Alison thought. "I'll think about it," she said.

Alison stood up, zipping her jacket. Silently, the width of a body between them, they walked back down the hill.

When they got to the trailhead, Zoe leaned against her car and Alison leaned against hers.

"What about the baby?" Alison asked.

"I'll think about it," Zoe said.

For the next three days, Alison and Zoe didn't speak or email or see each other. On the fourth day, the phone rang while Mark and Alison were doing the dinner dishes. "It's me," Zoe said.

"Hey, you." Alison sank into Corey's chair.

"I'll do it," Zoe said.

Alison had wanted so badly to hear these words. Now she could barely wrap her mind around what they meant.

Mark touched Alison's arm. "Yes or no?" he whispered.

Alison nodded yes. Mark's eyes widened.

"I don't know what to say." Alison was croaking, not talking. "I don't know how to thank you."

"You're welcome," Zoe said. Her voice sounded strangely flat.

"Let me talk to her," Mark said. Alison handed him the phone.

"You're really going to do this for us?" Mark asked. As he listened, his smile faded. An alarm sounded in Alison's head. He heard it too. Zoe sounded strange.

Mark handed the phone back to Alison with a puzzled look.

"Are you sure about this?" Alison asked Zoe.

"Uh-huh."

"Is Trudy okay with it?"

"Yup."

"What's wrong?" Alison asked.

"I'm just tired."

"You're never tired."

"Well." Zoe sounded annoyed. "I'm tired now."

Alison had spent forty-two years duking it out with ambivalence, her closest companion, her nemesis. For the first time ever, she felt it in Zoe. She thought, *This must be what it's like for her, trying to get the truth out of me.*

"Trudy and I thought we'd come over for dinner tomorrow. So we can all tell Corey together."

"Perfect," Alison said. "Zoe—I can't tell you how happy this makes me."

"You're the best!" Mark shouted into the phone.

Alison waited for Zoe to say how happy it made *her.*

"Good," Zoe said.

"I love you," Alison said. She heard the plea in her own voice.

"See you tomorrow," Zoe said.

29.

M ark stood at Zoe's left side, holding her left hand. Alison stood at Zoe's right. Lowell turned the monitor on.

"I'm inserting the catheter now," Dr. Schrier told Zoe. "You'll feel a pinch."

They all watched the screen as Schrier threaded the catheter, loaded with three microscopic embryos, into Zoe's uterus, a thin white line in a sea of grainy gray. Zoe gasped.

Alison remembered that pain. "Squeeze my hand," she said. She couldn't believe Zoe was going through this for her. Zoe, who refused mammograms and dental X-rays, and ate only organic food, and cured her headaches with milk thistle, her mood dips with Saint John's wort. Zoe, who had as much respect for Western medicine as she did for George W. Bush. Zoe, who'd been taking blood tests and gynecological exams, meeting with experienced surrogates, undergoing sessions with the asinine psychologist who'd grilled her, and then Mark and Alison, about how they'd deal with every possible worst-case scenario: fetal reduction, ectopic pregnancy, miscarriage, stillbirth, birth defects.

Never having used a contraceptive in her life, Zoe had taken a month's worth of birth control pills to synchronize her cycle with Alison's. Trudy had been giving her hormone shots every morning and night. And she hadn't complained once—not to Alison, anyway.

Alison was incredulous and worried. Zoe was still as flat as she'd been since she said yes. Alison felt she was racing Zoe's ambivalence to the finish line, hoping that yes would hold— exactly as Zoe must have felt, doing battle with Alison's ambivalent yeses for the past twenty years.

Three days before, Dr. Schrier had harvested twelve eggs from Alison's ovaries then mixed them with a fresh batch of Mark's sperm. Three grade-A embryos had been selected, and Zoe's uterus was primed to receive them.

"Here we go," Dr. Schrier said.

Zoe's lips were white. Her hand in Alison's shook.

Alison had never loved Zoe as much as she did in that moment. She squeezed Zoe's hand. "I'm here," Alison said.

On the monitor, three white specks erupted like tiny cannonballs from the catheter's tip. Slowly, Schrier withdrew the catheter.

Alison's chest ached. *Mark's sperm, my eggs in Zoe's body,* she thought. *How could I deserve this?*

In that moment, all the complications and permutations of her love for Zoe—the pulls and tugs of lies and truth; of past, present, future; of man, woman, child; the questions of possession: sexual, biological, emotional—evaporated. All that was left was the love, the love, the love.

Dr. Schrier set the catheter and speculum on the instrument tray. "You can sit up," he told Zoe.

Alison saw that Zoe's face was green.

"I'll give you an injection to help those embryos along," Schrier said. "And then we'll see you in two weeks for a pregnancy test." As he aimed the syringe at Zoe's belly, Alison turned her head, unable to watch.

When she heard Dr. Schrier snap his gloves off, Alison turned back to Zoe. Zoe's face was closed into itself, contorted with pain. Alison had seen her like that only once before: the day Alison left her.

As Mark drove them across the bridge, Zoe said, her voice faint from the backseat, "That really hurt. I don't feel well."

Alison swiveled to look at her. Zoe's hands were resting on her abdomen. Beads of sweat were pooled on her face.

"You didn't tell me it was going to hurt this much," Zoe said.

"I'm so sorry," Alison said. She felt utterly helpless. "I'd go through it for you if I could."

Zoe's eyes lit with anger. "How generous of you." She unlatched her seat belt, curled up in a ball, and closed her eyes.

Mark shot Alison a worried look. Alison's own worry burrowed into her chest.

A lison called Zoe the next morning and asked how she was.

"Worse," Zoe said.

Alison's heart sank. "What hurts?"

"I don't know how to describe it." Zoe sounded small and young. "Maybe I have the flu." She paused. "I have a rash too."

"Have you taken your temperature?" Alison asked. "Corey used to get hives after he had a fever, remember?"

"Corey used to get that rash all over his body. Mine's only in one place."

"Where?"

"On my right breast."

"Your *breast?*"

"Trudy called a doctor friend. He said artificial hormones can cause all kinds of weird side effects."

"My breasts hurt the whole time I was pregnant with Corey," Alison said desperately.

Zoe yawned. "I'm going to try and sleep it off."

"Sleep well," Alison said. "I'll check in on you later."

How could I have done this to her, she thought.

Alison awoke the next morning with a plan. As soon as Mark and Corey left, she went to the kitchen and started mincing garlic and chopping onions. She sautéed them until their fragrance filled the house. She added the carcass of chicken they'd eaten the night before, filled the pot with water, and set it simmering on the stove.

While the soup cooked, Alison went upstairs to check her email. There was a message from an editor at *The New York Times Magazine*. She wanted to buy the midlife motherhood story.

The good news registered in the small sector of Alison's brain that was still interested in anything besides Zoe's symptoms and what they might mean.

I got an assignment from The New York Times, Alison told herself, waiting for the thrill of it to kick in. She didn't feel a thing.

Alison emailed a quick reply to the editor, now *her* editor, agreeing to the terms of the assignment. Then she went downstairs and chopped carrots, sliced mushrooms, and shelled fresh green peas. She cooled the broth, shredded the meat, picked out the bones. Then she put the pot in the Saab and drove it to the cottage.

Trudy's worried face at the front door answered Alison's question. It wasn't the answer she wanted.

"I brought soup." Alison hefted the pot in her hands. "Can I come in?"

Trudy hesitated and then stepped aside. "Of course. Zoe sleeps."

Alison went to the kitchen and set the pot on the stove.

"Thank you," Trudy said. *Sank you.* "Would you like to have a coffee? A tea?"

"No, thanks."

They sat at the table together. It was covered with a hand-embroidered linen tablecloth Alison had never seen. Alison imagined Trudy's grandmother in an easy chair in some German town fifty years earlier, tiny skeins of red, blue, and yellow silk thread in her aproned lap.

"Sorry I came over without calling," Alison said. "Whenever I call, Zoe just says she wants to sleep."

"She is very tired," Trudy said.

"I'm worried about her. Are you?"

Trudy got up and filled the kettle at the sink. She put the kettle on the stove. The right front burner lit with a huge blue whoosh, just as it always had.

Trudy busied herself shaking tea leaves into the strawberry-shaped teapot that Alison had bought with her first paycheck from PMC. Its spout was chipped, Alison noticed, white clay showing through red glaze.

Trudy sat down. She didn't look at Alison. "She gets a tiny bit better each day."

She blames me, Alison thought. *She thinks the hormones are making Zoe sick. And she might be right.*

"Trudy. Please. At least tell me why she won't talk to me."

"It is for Zoe, not for me to tell you about that."

They sat in strained silence. Then Trudy looked over Alison's shoulder, and her tense face collapsed into a smile.

"I just need a little space to think," Zoe said from the doorway. Alison was shocked by her appearance. Her skin was flushed. Her face was haggard. A rumpled pair of white cotton pajamas hung on her thin frame.

Trudy waved Zoe into a chair. "Alison brought soup," she said. "Would you like some, darling?"

Darling? Alison wondered if the word had a different meaning to a German. Who said *darling?*

"No thanks, babe."

"I go to work in the garden," Trudy said, and she left.

"You sure you don't want some soup?" Alison asked.

"Positive." Zoe fidgeted with a loose thread on the tablecloth. Finally, her eyes met Alison's. "I want to help you and Mark. I really do. But I'm not sure this is good for me." Her lips quivered. "I think the hormones are making me sick."

Good Alison wanted to say, *Stop, then. Thanks for trying.* Bad Alison wanted to say, *I need you to do this for me.*

"I'm so sorry," Alison said. "I had no idea this would be so hard on you."

Zoe's eyes filled with tears. "I don't want to let you down."

"Let's not make any decisions till the pregnancy test next week."

Zoe's face relaxed. "Thank you for understanding," she said, a flicker of light in her blue eyes. "Thank you for not pressuring me."

"Let's get you back to bed," Alison said, hoping she could make it to her car before she cried.

The four of them met at Mark and Alison's house the afternoon of the pregnancy test. Mark looked shocked by the sight of Zoe.

"Are you okay?" he blurted.

"Pretty much," Zoe said.

Trudy's Rabbit was even older than Zoe's Volvo, so they took Mark and Alison's Saab. As they passed the exit for Treasure Island, Alison watched in the rearview mirror as Trudy loosened Zoe's seat belt to slacken it across her chest.

"Fifteen years since the earthquake," Mark said, navigating the orange cones and barriers and narrowed lanes, "and this damn bridge is still a mess."

Fifteen years since the earthquake, and Zoe's still taking care of me, Alison thought. *Fifteen years since the earthquake, and I'm still counting on her for what I need. And what's she getting out of it? Sick.*

You're a user, Alison's mother said. *Always have been, always will be.*

Mark pulled into the Sutter-Stockton Garage. Alison caught Zoe wincing, unlatching her seat belt. Trudy helped her out of the car.

Nancy greeted them in the waiting room.

"This is Trudy," Mark introduced them. "Zoe's girlfriend." If Nancy was taken aback by this latest addition to their entourage, she didn't show it. *A San Francisco fertility nurse,* Alison thought. *I bet she has some stories to tell.*

Nancy beckoned to Zoe. "I'm going to borrow you for the blood test. As soon as the results are confirmed, Dr. Schrier will meet you guys in his office."

"I come with you," Trudy said, helping Zoe out of her chair.

Mark and Alison sat in their usual chairs in Schrier's office. "How you doing?" Mark asked.

"Okay." Alison squeezed Mark's hand, then got up and walked to the wall of glass. She looked up at the sky, remembering the weather she'd seen through that window during the past eleven months: moody spring, foggy summer, sweltering autumn, rainy winter, and now again the shifting sky of spring.

She thought about the stupid jokes she'd made and the secrets she'd kept in that room, and the feelings she'd had, and the feelings she'd tried not to have. And she wondered now, as she did each time, whether all the money and effort and heartache would ever give them the baby they wanted. Or the redemption Alison wanted.

Zoe and Trudy walked back into the room. "How was it?" Alison scrutinized Zoe's face. *She's keeping something from me,* Alison thought.

"Fine." Zoe avoided Alison's eyes. Her lips were pursed, her shoulders hunched.

She's not going to go through this again, Alison realized. *This is the only chance we get.*

"Zoe," Alison said suddenly, "what are you hoping for?"

Zoe looked startled. "You mean a boy or a girl? That's *your* call."

"I mean, what's the best thing that could happen here today? Not for Mark and me. For *you.*"

Alison watched Zoe's face stiffen, then relax. "For your sake, I hope I'm pregnant." Zoe glanced at Trudy, then back at Alison. "For my sake, I'm not sure."

Exactly what I would have said if you'd asked me that question fifteen years ago, Alison thought. She wondered if Zoe had felt then the way Alison felt now: torn between wanting a baby and wanting what was best for the person who could give that to her.

Dr. Schrier came in and sat behind his desk, a grim look on his face. Alison knew that look. *It's over,* she thought.

"I'm sorry," Dr. Schrier said.

Zoe gasped, a small, sharp, animal cry.

"We can try again," Dr. Schrier said.

Zoe looked at Alison. Her eyes were dark with pain.

"It's over," Alison said. "We're done."

"Alison!" Mark said. "That's not a decision you can make alone."

"I didn't make it alone."

Alison got up and stood behind Zoe. "Zoe hasn't been feeling well," she said. "And she has a rash on her breast. Would you take a look at it, please?"

"I'm not a gynecologist," Schrier said. "I can't—"

"Now, please," Alison interrupted him.

Mark and Alison sat side by side, quiet and still. For once, they had the waiting room to themselves.

"I'm sorry I called it off without talking to you first," Alison said. "I didn't know what I was going to say until I said it."

"You did the right thing." Mark ran his hand through his hair. "I knew Zoe wasn't really into it." He frowned. "Do you think Trudy told her not to do it?"

"I think Trudy told Zoe to do what's best for her, not what's best for us."

"It *could* have been good for Zoe. And for Trudy. We could have shared the baby with them, same as we share Corey."

"Maybe they want a baby of their own."

A single tear rolled down Mark's face.

"I'm so sorry," Alison said. "I hope you can forgive me somehow."

"Forgive you for what?" Mark stared at her, uncomprehending. "Mark—"

"Al," Zoe said, her voice small and shaky. She stood in the doorway, leaning against Trudy. Zoe's eyes were red and swollen. Her face was tight and shiny with fear.

Alison didn't see Trudy and she didn't see Mark. She only saw her Zoe, her hero, her rock, her true love.

"Al," Zoe said again. Alison went to her and took Zoe in her arms.

30.

They drove back to Oakland in silence, Zoe and Trudy in the backseat, Mark and Alison in the front. Mark parked in front of their house and turned the engine off. No one spoke or moved.

Alison unlatched her seat belt and turned to look at Zoe. "I'll take you to your appointment tomorrow," she said.

"Thank you," Trudy said. "But I bring her. And we call you as soon as we know."

Alison imagined herself home alone, waiting. "I can just drive you there and back. I don't have to come in."

Zoe leaned forward, touched Alison's cheek, tucked a few strands of hair behind her ear. "I need you to listen to me, Al," she said in the tender voice she'd only used in the past when the two of them were alone. "Whatever happens with me, you're going to have big feelings about it. And big needs."

"I won't—"

Mark took his hand off the steering wheel and laid it on Alison's thigh. Alison quieted.

"If you want to help me," Zoe said, "the best thing you can do is take care of yourself."

"I want to take care of *you*," Alison said.

"I know you love me, Al," Zoe said. "And you know I love you. But I need you to understand the difference between things you do for me and things you do for you."

What's she talking about, Alison thought. "I'll try," she said.

"I know you will," Zoe said. "You always do."

And then Zoe and Trudy got out of Mark and Alison's car and climbed into Trudy's and drove away.

At eleven the next morning, Zoe called Alison from Trudy's car.

"It's probably just an infection," she said. "The doctor put me on antibiotics. We'll know more in a few days."

"What else might it be?"

"Inflammatory breast cancer. Which wouldn't be good."

Alison swallowed hard. *Do what's good for Zoe*, she reminded herself. "How can I help?"

"Please don't ask me that kind of question, Al. It takes energy to think about it. Right now I need all my energy for me."

"I'll call Trudy later. I love you," Alison said.

She went to her desk, googled "inflammatory breast cancer," and scanned the listings. "Flu-like symptoms may be mistaken for breast infection." "Difficult to treat successfully." "One of the most lethal forms of the disease."

I can't lose her, Alison thought. *I won't.*

Alison called Trudy's cell phone. Trudy didn't answer. Alison desperately wanted to call Zoe. But that would be to ease her own suffering, not Zoe's.

She had to do *something* for *someone*. She Googled "best florist in Berkeley" and browsed its $200 bouquets. She went to Epicurious.com, searched for "anticancer foods," and found a disgusting-sounding recipe for citrus tilapia. She went to the Warm Things website and priced goose-down duvets. She knew that Zoe didn't want any of those things.

The next morning Alison called Trudy again and got her voice mail again. An hour later, Trudy called back. She sounded as if she'd been crying.

"I need your help," she choked out. "Zoe is so sick. Her breast is red and swollen and so painful. She feels too ill to get out of bed."

Trudy's voice broke. "The appointment with the doctor is not until the day after tomorrow. I don't know what to do. I am so afraid."

Alison's hands were shaking, but her mind was clear. "What does she need?"

"She needs you," Trudy said.

The cottage garden was a sodden mess, the river rocks buried beneath drifts of dead leaves, hyacinth buds poking through a thick carpet of weeds. Alison stepped around clumps of mud, through shin-high weeds, and took a breath and knocked on the door. Trudy opened it. Wordlessly, she nodded toward the bedroom.

Zoe was asleep. Alison drew a chair up to the bed and looked around the room. The gauzy lace curtains that she and Zoe had hung twenty years earlier looked freshly washed and ironed, opened to the gossamer winter light. A bunch of yellow tulips on the dresser bowed from Zoe's favorite glass-brick vase. The nightstand was cluttered with a dozen amber bottles with rubber droppers. In a wicker basket beside the bed, a hot water bottle dressed in a gray cashmere cozy lay at the ready, like a small dog waiting for his person to wake up and take him for a walk.

"What are you doing here?" Zoe glared at Alison, her eyes blue ingots in her pale face. Her platinum hair was askew, brown roots creeping. "I told you I'd call if I needed you."

"I heard you had a Meg Ryan hair thing going on," Alison said. "I wanted to see it for myself."

Zoe's pale lips curved into a small grin. As she reached for the glass of water on the nightstand, the covers slid off her shoulders. Her left breast was its normal small, pink self. Her right breast looked like a bright red rubber ball.

Alison resisted the urge to pull the duvet up over Zoe's chest. She resisted the urge to throw herself into Zoe's arms and weep.

"How are you?" Alison asked.

"Pretty shitty," Zoe said.

That's a good sign, Alison told herself. *Cancer doesn't make people feel sick.* She reached over and stroked Zoe's soft, warm forehead. How long had it been since she'd touched that delicious velvet skin?

Alison imagined how hard this must be for Zoe: being helpless when she'd always been strong. Being scared when she'd always been brave. Suffering when she'd given herself meaning by healing other people's pain.

Alison took Zoe's hand and massaged her fingers, up and down one finger, up and down the next. Oh, those fingers of Zoe's, those fingers that made beautiful, disturbing art; beautiful, disturbing love. Alison had never seen Zoe's hands before without paint beneath her nails.

Zoe's breathing slowed. Her limbs went limp. Alison remembered Zoe's body tense and straining against hers, and then the sighing, and then the repose. That was one kind of beautiful Zoe. This was another.

"I'm so sorry you're hurting," Alison murmured.

"It's not your fault."

"I hope not."

Normally Zoe would have reassured her. But this was not a normal time.

"Thanks for coming," Zoe said.

"Thanks for letting me."

Zoe seemed to fall asleep. Then she opened her eyes. "I don't think the medicine's working," she said.

Alison knew what Zoe needed because Zoe had given it to Alison so many times. "It'll work," Alison said. "Just give it a few days."

Alison wondered whether Zoe had felt this helpless, wanting to rescue Alison from every bad feeling, every bad thing.

"I brought you some treats," Alison said.

"I'm not hungry."

"It's not food. Can I help you sit up?"

Zoe nodded. Alison put her hand on Zoe's back. Her spine felt like a row of marbles. Alison leaned Zoe forward with one hand and fluffed the feather pillows with the other. She leaned Zoe back into the down cloud.

"Want me to get you some matzo ball soup from Saul's?" Alison asked.

Zoe gestured at a half-eaten bowl of muesli on the tray beside the bed. Next to the bowl, an orange gerbera daisy leaned out of a glass bud vase. "I'm ready for my treats."

Alison reached into the messenger bag at her feet and pulled out the current issue of *The New York Times Magazine*.

"Your story!" Zoe stared at Alison's name on the cover, her eyes big and wide. "You did it, Al. I always said you could. Remember?"

"I remember." Suddenly, strangely, Alison was suffused with joy. Right there, right then, she had Zoe to share this moment with her. Only Zoe knew what it meant to her. And here they were, together.

"I'm so proud of you." Zoe brought Alison's hand to her mouth and kissed each finger—first one, and then the next, and the next.

Alison let Zoe do it. She didn't rush her. She didn't stop her. Alison was a light show flashing every sensation Zoe had ever given her. The lust. The desperate dependence. The fear. The delight.

The love. The love. The love.

Zoe had been Alison's touchstone for the better half of her life. She'd been Alison's mother and her child. Her lover and her son's other mother. Her best friend. Until she met Zoe, Alison had spent a lifetime longing for someone to crawl inside her, never leave her, turn her into the better person she'd always wanted to be. Zoe had done that for her. Zoe was doing that for her now.

Alison looked at Zoe, who might wake up healthy tomorrow, who might be dying. Alison thought, *Zoe couldn't fix me then and I can't fix her now. But no one will ever love me the way she does. And no one will ever be what she is to me.*

Alison felt certain, in that moment, that Zoe would be okay.

And in that moment, she found the strength to silence her own self-protectiveness, her pessimism and fear.

"Ready for your next treat?" Alison asked. She pulled Corey's boom box out of her bag, plugged it in, and popped in a CD. Corey's deepening voice, accompanied by his acoustic guitar, wafted into the room. "Blackbird singing in the dead of night, take these broken wings and learn to fly . . . "

Zoe closed her eyes, her lips mouthing the words of the song. Silently, she began to cry.

Alison handed her a wad of tissues.

"Corey's back to playing guitar?" Zoe choked out.

"It's the Justina effect," Alison said. "Behind every vastly improved teenage boy is a teenage girl."

"I can't wait to meet her," Zoe said.

"You'll love her. And she'll love you." Alison tossed Zoe's soggy Kleenex into the wastebasket in the corner.

"Two points," Zoe said.

"Three." Alison held her finger to her lips. "Shhh. Listen. There's more."

"Hey, Zoe," Corey's voice filled the room. "I'm really sorry you're sick. I wish I could be there, but Mom says you need privacy. I didn't even know you *liked* privacy. But anyway, I hope these songs help you get better soon. I love you. Oh, yeah. This is Corey."

"Play that again," Zoe said.

As they listened together, slants of sunshine moved across the room like a slow-motion camera, lighting the loosening tulips, lighting the 1987 Michigan Womyn's Music Festival poster on the wall, lighting Zoe, naked in a white nest of feathers and crisp white cotton.

"That kid of yours is really something," Zoe said hoarsely.

"That kid of *ours* is really something. And he wouldn't be who he is without you." Alison touched Zoe's cheek. "Neither would I. That's why I brought you this." She reached into her bag and handed Zoe a sealed white envelope.

Zoe turned it over in her hands. "Since when do you have a post office box?" she asked Alison. "And what's DNA Discovery?"

Alison sat silently, waiting. And then Zoe looked at Alison disbelievingly. "Did you get Corey's DNA tested?"

Alison nodded.

"How?"

"You always said it would be easy," Alison answered. "You were right. I ordered the kit online. Swabbed the inside of Corey's cheek while he was sleeping. And sent the kit back."

"Why did you do that?" Zoe asked. She looked at Alison, terrified. "You think I'm going to die."

"I know you're not going to die."

"Then why this? Why now?"

"You've wanted this from me for fifteen years," Alison said.

"I've wanted a lot of things from you for fifteen years, Al. You haven't given them to me."

Alison gazed into Zoe's ocean blue eyes. She saw the sailboats sailing. She sailed with them and she held on, held on, held on. "I know," Alison said.

Watching Zoe's face was like writing a poem or a story, only knowing how it would begin, never knowing how it would end.

Zoe looked down at the envelope in her hand. "You didn't open it."

"It's yours to open, or not. It's my gift to you. A tiny thank-you for all you've done for Corey. And for me."

Alison pushed her chair back and stood up.

"No!" Zoe blurted. "Don't go, Al. Don't leave me with this. Please!"

"I'm just going to the bathroom, babe," Alison said. "I'll be right back."

Alison paused in the bedroom doorway, gazing at Zoe in the sick bed that once was their love nest, in the sick room that once was their sanctuary, now cluttered with medicine bottles and heating pads and Blockbuster videos and fear.

"You don't have to decide this minute." Alison said what Zoe would have said to her.

"I feel like I do," Zoe said. "I feel like I have to do everything right now."

"But you don't," Alison said, smiling at Zoe. "You have time."

Alison wondered if she was lying to Zoe or if this was what it meant to be kind.

Alison walked down the hall and closed the bathroom door behind her. Whether Zoe knew it or not, she needed time alone to make her decision. Alison needed a moment too.

She gazed at her murky reflection in the antique mirror she and Zoe had hung on that wall together, so many years before. She saw their delight, discovering it at the flea market, lugging it to their car, no man required.

Fogged by years of usefulness, the mirror blurred the creases that crisscrossed Alison's face, the salting of gray hairs on her head, the sadness that lived in her eyes. In its hazy reflection, she could be Alison now or Alison fifteen years before, when she lived in this cottage with Zoe, when she looked at herself in this mirror each morning, deciding how much of herself to hide and how much of herself to show.

I still hide, Alison thought, *but not as much as I did.*

She remembered playing hide-and-seek with Corey when he

was a baby, and then a toddler, and then a little kid. Each time he reached a new threshold, it had taken her a while to catch up. "You *let* me find you," he'd complain, Alison's cue to make the game more challenging the next time. Soon she wouldn't need to *let* Corey find her. He'd find what he needed, all by himself— including, if she was very, very lucky, his mom.

Alison washed her hands with Zoe's gritty black soap, dried them on the purple towel that hung from the crooked white ceramic middle finger screwed to the back of the bathroom door. Zoe's bumper sticker collection was still plastered there, a short history of American activism, a short history of Alison and Zoe's life together from 1983 to 2005.

Each slogan delivered a memory of a demonstration, a meeting, a political act—come out, come out, wherever you are—made personal. Zoe starred in every scene.

SISTERHOOD IS POWERFUL. Their ridiculous, romantic Mari-andaughter year.

U.S. OUT OF GRENADA. Signing petitions in Tappan Square, Zoe's body pressed up against Alison's for the first time.

U.S. OUT OF MY BODY. Saying yes to their new life in Berkeley, where Zoe's mom had always wanted her daughter to be.

MONDALE FOR PRESIDENT: AMERICA NEEDS A CHANGE. A losing campaign for president, starting to lose their love.

STOP UNWANTED SEISMIC ACTIVITY. When everything shook and changed and rattled and fell apart.

WELCOME HOME, NELSON MANDELA. Finding each other again. Making a friendship. Making a family.

Alison wondered if any of it had done any good: the wimmin's studies projects, the petitions, the marches, the boring electoral campaigns? The coming out? The going in?

Of course it has, she thought. She could draw a straight line, so to speak, between Mariandaughter's over-the-top dogma and Justina's calm self-assurance; between two women marrying each other on TV in San Francisco City Hall and gay marriage spreading to New Paltz, New York; between protestors and bad wars ending and bad laws being overturned and bad ideas slowly, slowly, slowly changing to good.

All of it had made Alison who she was and all of it had given her what she had, a good and getting-better career, a good and getting-better man, a great and getting-even-greater kid, who wore a BUCK FUSH button to Berkeley High School, which Alison had lied to get him into because she knew they'd let him wear a button like that to school.

And Zoe. Alison had Zoe. Her everything, who kept everything. The mirror. The bumper stickers. The Volvo. Her.

Alison had made a life on a fault line crisscrossed with fissures, walking on unsolid ground. Nature, and her nature, kept that time bomb ticking. Any minute the whole thing could come crashing down. But Alison's life felt different now. She felt different now.

Maybe there was an upside to aging, which also brought wrinkles and pounds and gray hairs. Maybe there was an upside to living in an earthquake zone, where unwanted seismic activity produced stunningly beautiful scenery and imminent disaster in the same place at the same time.

Right there, right then, with Zoe in the next room sick and scared, Alison could say this with certainty. The four of them—the five of them now—had built something solid and true, right on top of a shuddering lie.

Mark would never be the love of her life. Zoe sat in that chair. She always had, and if Alison's optimism was warranted, she always would.

But Mark was the partner Alison needed: steady, uncomplicated, unfailingly kind. Unlike Zoe, unlike Alison's mother, he kept himself at just the right distance. He didn't scare her or come after her or know her better than she knew herself. He didn't make her fight to protect herself, claws outstretched, back against the wall.

Alison needed both of them. And finally, *finally*, what she wanted was what she had. She would go on having it because Zoe would be okay.

Her eyes drifted to the bumper sticker she and Zoe had brought home from Gay Pride in 1989, the summer they were trying to conceive. LOVE MAKES A FAMILY, it said, NOTHING ELSE, NOTHING LESS.

We did that, Alison thought. *We made a family out of love. Not the way we meant to do it. Not the way most people do it. But we did the best thing any family can do. We raised a healthy, happy child. And who knows? One way or another, we might get to raise another one.*

"Al?" Zoe called.

Normally, Zoe's voice told Alison whatever she needed to know. But Zoe's tone wasn't saying whether she'd opened the envelope or if she had, what she now knew.

Alison was surprised to realize that it didn't much matter. She knew who Corey's father was. Corey knew who his family was. No DNA test could challenge that or change it.

"Al?" Zoe called again, her voice edged with impatience. Alison smiled. Zoe was bossing her around. That had to be a good sign.

Alison paused, her hand on the doorknob. Once she faced the truth in that envelope, the truth on Zoe's face, there would be no more denying it. No more not knowing it. No more pretending not to feel whatever it made her feel.

"Al!" Zoe's voice was more insistent now.

That's my girl, Alison thought, and she opened the door.

acknowledgments

Words fail, except these two: *Thank you.*

Alfred Corn, Andy Ross, Anne Connolly, Anne Lamott, Avril Gau, Ayelet Waldman, Barb Burg, Caroline Leavitt, Christina Baker Kline, Cornelia Durrant, Dani Shapiro, Dawn Raffel, Drew Maran, Elisa Tanaka, Elizabeth Rosner, Ellen Sussman, Ilsa Brink, Jane Juska, John McMurtrie, Joyce Maynard, Julie Whitten, Kate Christensen, Kathleen Caldwell, Katie Crouch, Kayne Doumani, Kim Hubbard, Lalita Tademy, Leslie Berkler, Lolly Winston, Lorraine Glennon, Meg Wolitzer, Michael, Abe, Rosie, Sophie, and Zeke Chabon, Michelle Richmond, Nancy Johnson, Nicole Lamy, Pamela Redmond Satran, Patricia Chao, Peter Barnes, Philippe Bompard, Rita Maran, Roxana Robinson, Sabrina Sayre, Sandra Slater, Sheri Holman, Sid and Anny Maran, Siobhan Cassidy, Susan and Tony DiStefano, Susanna Sonnenberg, Suzy Parker, Terry Gamble, Terry McMillan, Word of Mouth New York, and Word of Mouth Bay Area.

Mabel Dodge Luhan House, Mesa Refuge, Ragdale, Virginia Center for the Creative Arts, Yaddo. Precious. Priceless. And they all need money. If you can, please send them some.

Independent bookstores, independent booksellers, independent readers: unsung heroes, keeping writers and writing alive. Buy local!

My agile, able, and adored independent publisher, Soft Skull Press. Charlie Winton, Jack Shoemaker, Laura Mazer, Maren Fox, Jodi Hammerwold, Julie Pinkerton, Liz Parker, and Sarah Cantor.

Dan Smetanka, My editor, my better literary half, my prince.

Linda Loewenthal, agent, friend, and human being extraordinaire. I can't imagine doing this without you.

Katrine, l'amour de ma vie, maintenant et pour toujours.

about the author

M eredith Maran is an award-winning journalist and the author of several nonfiction books, including *My Lie, Class Dismissed,* and *What It's Like to Live Now.* She's a book critic for *People, Salon,* the *San Francisco Chronicle,* and *The Boston Globe,* and she writes for many national magazines. The mother of two grown sons and one growing grandson, she lives in Oakland with her wife. Since she published a poem at age six in *Highlights for Kids,* she's dreamed of publishing a novel. This is her first.

You can reach her at www.meredithmaran.com, on Facebook, and on Twitter.

reading group guide

1. When we meet Alison, she's full of judgments and fears. Did these characteristics make you dislike her, identify with her, want to know more about her? All of the above?

2. When Alison was mocking Oberlin's feminists, trust fund kids, lesbians, guilty white liberals, and pretty much every other group on campus, did you laugh at her or with her? How did her prejudices resemble or challenge or differ from your own?

3. If you've never been attracted to someone of the same gender, did Alison's lust for Zoe help you understand same-sex attraction? If you've experienced same-sex attraction, did Alison's feelings ring true?

4. How did Alison's relationship with her mother impact her attraction to Zoe?

5. What were Alison's real reasons for wanting a child so badly? How did her true motivations play out in the kind of mother she was to Corey?

6. Did you find it credible that Mark accepted Alison's ex-lover as a member of his family? If so, why? If not, why not?

7. What were the healthy and unhealthy aspects of Alison and Zoe's romantic relationship? Of their friendship? What did each of them contribute?

8. What did you think of Alison's decision not to tell Mark that Corey might not be his biological child? What did you think of Mark and Alison's decision not to tell Corey that Zoe was his mother's ex-lover?

9. How do you see the distinctions between privacy and secrecy? Between withholding and deception? Are you keeping any big secrets? If so, why and to what effects? Have you ever regretted disclosing a truth?

10. The novel parallels twenty-two years of American history and twenty-two years in the characters' lives. What did you learn about how the external world impacts the inner world and vice versa?

11. As this novel goes to press, Don't Ask Don't Tell has recently been overturned, Jane Lynch recently became the first out lesbian to host the Emmy Awards, and gay marriage is legal in six U.S. states and Washington D.C. Do you think Alison would have stayed with Zoe if being gay had been as acceptable in 1989 as it is in 2012? Was Alison being a coward or a good mother by choosing to raise her son with a man instead of staying with Zoe?

12. Did reading this novel change your thoughts or feelings about what makes a healthy family and/or what makes a family healthy?